JUDAS GENE

Gary Moreau

DEDICATION

For my wife,
Gloria Osdoba Moreau

ACKNOWLEDGEMENT

There is no greater gift that can be given to a writer than help in making the story and the telling of the story better. To this end, I am deeply grateful to my editors, Selina and Lynn Rosen. In addition, I wish to thank Jane Fancher who took the time to make specific recommendations as well as general comments. Thank you so very much.

CHAPTER 1

Jack Nichols was late. He hurried down the center aisle; some of the academicians turned to stare. *To hell with them.* He'd done his best to arrive on time. He slid into one of the few available seats, near the front of the auditorium. When he leaned back, the seat squeaked.

The speaker glanced in his direction. Her gaze slid past, dismissing him. She gestured toward a projection and commented on the nucleotide sequences.

He tried to listen to what she was saying. It wasn't that it was beyond his understanding. His mind wandered and he rubbed his chest in a futile attempt to massage away the burning and swallowed against the bitterness.

The speaker's husky voice drew his attention back to her. Her eyes glinted when she focused on the audience, but it was not her eyes that distracted him; it was her mouth, upturned at the corners. And her lips, they were nearly obscene. The burning in his chest faded.

"As you can now appreciate," she said, "this gene cluster is found in every genome searched to date, from Paramecium aurelia to Canis lupus familiaris to Homo sapiens. Although that finding alone is remarkable, what we discovered next can be categorized as nothing short of extraordinary."

Does she toss her hair like that on purpose? Jack wondered.

She gestured toward the screen and arched her back, causing her silky blouse to cling.

Jack nodded in appreciation. This was a woman to be reckoned with.

"The next organism we evaluated was that of Zea mays, variety indentata, which we have a lot of around here." She smiled and raked her fingers through her coppery hair.

The man next to Jack snickered. Jack turned to him with open hands.

The man raised his nose perceptibly and said, "Field corn."

"Hilarious," Jack murmured.

After the modest laughter subsided, the speaker continued.

"And then an organism with much older lineage, cyanobacterium Synechocystis, species PCC6803. The gene cluster was found in both. Here is the evidence." Numbers and DNA sequencing graphs scrolled across the screen behind her. Disdaining the laser pointer, she stretched to make a point and her short skirt road up, revealing an indecent length of shapely leg.

Jack's eyes remained fixed on her while he listened to the rich timbre of her voice. She was an unusual woman. One minute she flaunted her sexuality and in the next was intensely involved with the interpretation of mathematical probabilities. His mind began to wander. There was something missing...and then he had it. He hadn't thought about his ex-wife since he'd entered the auditorium. He studied the speaker with new interest and his face flushed with an uncomfortable realization; he was going to award her the grant simply because she made the pain go away.

"This is the only gene cluster which is identical in all respects among such diverse species in the Phylogenic tree. Is it the primordial genome?" She raised her hand in a fist. "The first life on Earth, living within all of us to this day?" She opened her hand and then lowered it to run it down her hip and onto her thigh. The smile was back, the one that aroused appetites. "I welcome comments."

An elderly woman in the front row raised her hand.

"Doctor Clark."

"Doctor Wiley, I must commend you on your meticulous research. However, I do have both a comment and a question. Although you've discovered a gene cluster that is present in a number of diverse organisms, it would be a stretch to make any generalization at this point. Have you identified a function?"

The speaker shook her head. When she looked up her red hair framed her face. Her eyes were green.

Jack sat straighter. She seemed to be looking at him. This was ridiculous. It was jet lag, that and the memories awakened by his return to the university. That was it. He exhaled with a grunt of self-rebuke.

The slight man who sat to Jack's right heard him and leaned close. "Doctor Wiley's work is exquisite, don't you agree?"

Jack nodded. "Exquisite. One might even call it seductive."

The man responded with a stare.

"The potential implications of her research," Jack added.

"Oh…yes…the implications."

Jack's attention was drawn back to the front of the auditorium.

The man who had been sitting next to Doctor Clark stood. He sported a trimmed mustache and turned a few calculated degrees to reveal gray steaks in his black hair. "Doctor Wiley, your work, the actual research, appears well documented, but to claim that this is the primordial genome, the wellspring of all life—" He shrugged. "—is a premature conclusion at best." He turned his back to her and faced the audience. His well-practiced smile revealed stark-white teeth.

"It was a question, not a conclusion." Doctor Wiley wasn't smiling. "What is your point, Dean Rathburn?"

Rathburn looked over his shoulder. "My point is that your work represents an interesting finding, possibly an interesting coincidence, but at this juncture, all a prudent researcher would conclude is that it is an area for future study." He nodded to Doctor Clark and again looked over his shoulder to address the red-haired speaker. "Don't you agree?"

"I do agree. More research is needed. Is this an offer for funding?"

Rathburn chuckled, aware that the gathered academicians listened with amused interest. He pivoted to face her.

"You know this isn't the proper forum to discuss funding," Rathburn said. "You *naughty, naughty* girl," he added in a soft voice, meant for her but heard by many.

Her eyes opened wider. "What did you call me?"

Rathburn turned away. His smile had become a grin. There were numerous raised hands, well-behaved intellectuals, patiently waiting their turn. He addressed the hands. "It's been a long day. Let's adjourn so we can freshen up and enjoy ourselves this evening. Who knows, after a glass or two of wine, perhaps even Doctor Wiley's conclusions will make sense." He waited a beat for laughter.

"Rathburn!" Wiley yelled.

The titter of nervous laughter was cut short.

Jack leaned forward. He knew what was going to happen next. She was going to dive off the podium and go for his throat.

Rathburn ignored her. He motioned for them to rise. When he saw obedience, he began walking up the center aisle.

Jack frowned, but didn't relax. His instincts were rarely wrong. As Rathburn walked past, Jack spoke. "You're a lucky son of a bitch."

Rathburn stopped and stared down at him. "What did you say?"

"I said you're lucky. If I were her, I would've broken your neck."

Rathburn glared down at the seated man in the blue suit. "What audacity! Are you a student here? Look at me when I speak to you!"

Jack didn't try to intimidate people; it came naturally. Beneath black hair, his cool blue eyes stared back at Rathburn. There was darkness, the thick stubble of a day's growth of beard, and within the darkness, undisguised contempt.

Rathburn took a step back. "I'll.... I'll remember you," he sputtered, and then briskly retreated up the aisle.

The beginning of silence spread out from where Jack sat. Others stood; the silence of the room filled with the "slapping" of seats as they flipped upright and then the white noise of many voices in conversation. As they exited, more than one person peered down at the man in the blue suit. Jack's neighbor had chosen the long way, preferring the narrow passage along the row of seats rather than be seen walking out of the auditorium with him.

Jack stood to leave, but then saw Doctor Wiley marching toward him. It was hardly appropriate to discuss her grant in the aisle, but to escape and then meet in her office seemed childish.

She stopped with her hands planted on her hips. "What did you say to him?"

A scar marred the skin of her forehead and she wasn't as tall as he'd imagined. He let his offered hand fall to his side.

"I told him that his management style could use some work."

"Damn it! If you've screwed this up for me..."

Her green eyes had not lost their sparkle.

"Who are you?" she demanded. "I've never seen you before. Were you even supposed to be in this lecture hall? You come in late and now this."

"So, you did notice me."

"Notice you?" she managed through compressed lips. "How could I miss you? You come in late, in the middle of my presentation, and then begin playing with your seat, squeaking back and forth like...like—"

"Hold it." He raised his hands in surrender. "Give me a minute and I'll explain. I—"

"Forget it. I've got an appointment."

As she made to walk past, he grabbed hold of her arm.

She whirled around. "Take your hand off me, or I'll break your fingers. I know how."

He released his hold and smiled. "I bet you do."

"Up yours."

She nearly ran up the aisle, leaving the few who remained, frozen in place as they watched.

Jack turned toward a man and two women. They immediately tucked their monitors under their arms and hurried past.

"A real friendly place," he muttered. "Not quite like I remember it."

He walked out of the auditorium and down the hallway until he found the lobby and the information desk.

"Could you tell me how to get to Doctor Wiley's office?" he asked.

The woman nodded toward the opposite hallway. "You just missed her. She seemed to be in a real hurry."

"I know. Could you direct me to her office?"

She pointed. "Go down to the second set of elevators and up to the third floor. It's in the older part of the building. Room—" She looked at her screen. "—312."

"Thank you."

On his way, he passed a men's room. He stopped. *Don't,* he told himself. But, before he had another thought, he pushed the door open and walked in. His coarse, black hair was defying him again, sticking up with a cowlick. He brushed it down with water and watched it spring back up. He tucked in his shirt and brushed his hand across imagined wrinkles. When he had finished, there was no obvious change in his appearance. He considered returning to his hotel room and rescheduling, but then shook his head. "To hell with it."

He exited the elevator on the third floor. His shoes clicked against the terrazzo floor. The plaster walls were spotted where chips of institutional-green paint had flaked off to reveal a darker green. The overhead florescent lights hummed and one of them flickered off and on. The only other person in the hallway didn't even glance in his direction. It looked like the research wing of the damned.

He stopped in front of room 312. "Roxanne Wiley, MD, PhD" was stenciled in gold on the frosted glass of the door. He opened it without knocking.

"And then this creepy guy—" Wiley stopped. Both she and her research assistant turned toward him.

Jack kept his grip on the doorknob.

"You! What are *you* doing here?" Wiley demanded.

He could hear "get the hell out" just beneath her words. "I have an appointment with you," he said with a smile and winked.

"I'm flattered," she replied flatly. "Perhaps some other time."

He laughed. "No, you see I have an appoint—"

"Hey, I know who you are," the young woman in the lab coat gushed. "You're that astronaut, aren't you? The one who...I mean...."

"Yes, I'm the one. But I'm currently on leave of absence, assigned to NIH."

"NIH?" Wiley's cheeks blanched.

"That's right. I have an appointment with you to discuss your grant proposal."

She shook her head while her eyes surveyed the floor. She raised her gaze to his and her lids narrowed.

Jack knew he looked like a boxer down on his luck. "Honest," he declared. "I have an appointment with you. I dropped off my bags and hurried over to catch your lecture. Didn't even stop to get cleaned up." His hand patted at the cowlick. He forced his hand back to his side.

She sighed and looked up at the ceiling before refocusing on his face. "I really blew it, didn't I?" He was about to speak when she waved him off. "Never mind. It wouldn't be the first time."

"Could we speak in your office for a minute?" Jack asked.

She smiled and tossed her hair. "Of course. Follow me."

She led him through stacks of printouts and books.

He looked around and wondered how she could get any results when her office was in such disarray.

"Is this the way to the lab?" he asked.

"No, it's down the hall." She squeezed through a partially jammed door and sat down at her desk, motioning him toward a chair that was piled with printouts. "Put them on the floor."

He stood next to the chair and stared down at the stack of papers.

"Would you like me to do it for you?" she asked.

"You don't play the game very well," Jack said as he set the papers on the floor.

"That's what Rathburn says. Don't you find it peculiar that he's so critical of a researcher in his own department?"

"Yes, I do." He settled into the chair.

"I'm being punished. He's been trying to get into my pants for the last year. Dream on Rathburn. Do I shock you?"

He smiled. "Not really." He extended his hand. "My name is Jack Nichols."

She leaned forward and shook his hand with a firm grip. "Of course, Jack Nichols."

It was on all the newscasts. He could see the story coming back to her as she stared at him, while those lips taunted him with a smile.

"Have a little trouble with authority, huh?" She picked up a pen and flipped it, catching it in a well-practiced maneuver.

"Some saw it that way."

"What did you think of my presentation?" Her eyes were on him.

"Interesting stuff."

"Interesting stuff?" She arched her eyebrows, highlighting the scar on her forehead. "What kind of sophomoric comment is that? As I recall, you were supposed to have commanded the second Mars mission."

"Yes." The burning in his chest returned.

"Then you must know at least a little about macromolecular biology, or did you skip those classes?" She took a deep breath and shook her head with a wry smile. "Sorry. It's been a really bad week."

"Is that an apology?"

"I suppose."

"Apology accepted. Would you like to discuss your project over dinner?"

"Hell no." She massaged her hands. "I don't mean to take it out on you, but you didn't have to make it worse. What exactly did you say to Rathburn?"

"Exactly?" He cleared his throat. "I told him he was lucky you hadn't killed him. Or something like that."

She nodded. "You're right, that's exactly what I was

thinking. I was going to poke his eyes out and—is it hot in here?" She unbuttoned the first button of her blouse and then the second. The lacy fringe of her bra bordered the cleavage of her breasts. She began toying with the third. "Of course we can have dinner," she said, all sweetness. "What harm could there be in that?"

He forced his attention back to her eyes. "It will mean missing Rathburn's banquet."

"Yes, it will."

"Very well, Doctor Wiley, should I message you, or—"

"I'll make arrangements and message you. Would that be satisfactory?"

"I'm staying at the Gardston. You can contact the front desk."

"I hope you have a better suit and plan to shave. You look like a bum. It's no wonder I responded like I did."

There was no boyish charm in the gaze that met hers.

"Did I hurt your feelings? Because if I did, get over it."

He rubbed the black stubble of his beard. That was something his friend Pie might have said. He smiled. "No, you didn't say anything wrong."

"Good. See you this evening."

CHAPTER 2

Jack closed the lid and turned away from his packing trunk. It was inconvenient, but he was glad he had continued to travel with his military uniforms. He stood straight. He was military, regardless of his current circumstances. He surveyed the room. It was neat; all was in its place. He walked over to the dresser drawer he had assigned to his socks. They were tightly rolled and lined up, blue on the left, black on the right and white in the middle, just the way his uncle had taught him. He fixed an imagined irregularity and shut it. Next, he stood in front of the full-length mirror. His dinner dress whites had traveled well; all creases were perfect and his shirt was immaculate against the gold cummerbund. He turned toward the door, but then stopped and returned to the mirror for a final inspection. He straightened his black bowtie. He was ready. He tucked his hat under his arm and marched out the door.

He exited the elevator into the hotel lobby. Doctor Wiley was already there. Her tailored suit hugged the curves of her body and stopped at mid-thigh. In ways, it was more revealing than the blouse and skirt she had worn earlier. She wasn't alone; a man in an expensive suit laughed at something she said and stood unnecessarily close.

Wiley looked past the man and saw Jack. She deserted the man in mid-sentence. Her hips had a natural sway as she walked toward him, transforming a mundane act into a sexual statement. Every male in the lobby watched, but Jack was the chosen one.

"Hello, Admiral. Dressed for a parade?" she asked with a smirk.

The glow of adoration faded. "Good evening, Doctor Wiley."

"Aren't we formal? Call me Roxanne. I didn't know the government was that strapped. Still wearing your old clothes, huh?"

"Although reassigned, I'm still active duty. And I'm not an admiral. I'm a captain."

"Fine. Whatever. *You* are paying. Let there be no doubt of that. I made a reservation at Bijon's." She looked him up and down. Pointing, she said, "That's a pretty medal. Was it for perfect attendance?"

"It's called the Navy Cross and has nothing to do with attendance."

"You don't have to get all huffy. I said it was pretty." She nodded. "You look good in your cute uniform with all those shiny gold buttons, very nice."

"Thank you, ma'am," he said and snapped to attention.

"The Captain has a sense of humor. Who'd have guessed?"

A young couple walked passed. The father was holding a toddler and both mother and father were singing. "...X, Y and Z and now we've sung our alphabet."

Jack followed them with his gaze.

"Got something against kids?" Roxanne asked.

"Why do you ask?"

"You look like you want to kick all three of them in the butt."

He shook his head. "That's not it. It's just that I thought this was a hotel for adults. Kids are okay, just not something I want in my space."

"Yeah, whatever. Let's get out of here."

He cupped his hand over his ear. "Yes, I've arrived." He paused. "No, I'm managing." Another pause. "Very good. I'll call you in the morning." He lowered his hand and looked to Roxanne with an apologetic shrug. "My office."

She held out her hand. "Give it to me."

"What?"

"I'm not going to spend the evening listening to you talk to whoever decides to call." She wiggled her fingers. "Give it to me."

He hesitated, but then pried the earphone out and put it in his pocket. "Satisfied?"

"Rarely."

She started across the lobby without waiting to see if he was following. He had to hurry to catch up.

She stepped off the curb and glanced over her shoulder. "We'll take my car."

"You have a car?" Jack looked around. There was only one car under the hotel portico.

"It's not against the law you know."

Jack looked for another car, but she walked toward the red sports car. By the time he arrived, she had already gotten into the driver's seat. He opened the passenger door and had to duck his head to slide into the bucket seat.

She turned the key and the engine rumbled with power. When she shifted into gear and pressed on the accelerator, the car shot ahead. Jack instinctively reached out to steady himself.

"Don't touch the dash. It's real leather."

Jack removed his hand and she shifted into the next gear. The power of the engine rumbled through him. It felt good. He relaxed as they cruised down the boulevard and turned to study her. She was blessed with features that were a pleasure to look at, even in profile.

"What kind of a car is this?" Jack asked.

"It's a 2011 Aston Martin DB9 Volante. I've had it completely restored. Are you interested in classic sports cars?"

"Not really."

"Then why did you ask?"

"Because I like it."

She smiled and nodded. "A sign of good taste. It has a 48 valve V12 with a top speed of 300 kilometers per hour. It's a beauty. My husband paid for it."

"Your husband? You're married?"

"Was. He's dead."

"I'm..." He was going to say "not surprised", but swallowed his words.

"You're what?"

"I'm...sorry."

"Why? You didn't do it. Did it himself, crazy bastard. Always pushing the limits. Fell off a damn mountain. God I miss him. What about you?"

"Do you mean am I married?"

"No, I want to know if you fell off a mountain. What do you think I meant?"

He turned away to stare out the side window while the last of the university's Greek inspired architecture passed by.

"Are you married?" she persisted.

"Was. She decided to move up the chain of command."

"So, you bashed him in the nose and got kicked out of the space program. Was it worth it?"

"No."

"Too bad."

"I appreciate your sympathy."

She laughed. "You're all right...in ways."

She pulled into the driveway and screeched to a stop. Jack managed to get out of the low-slung car in time to see her hand the keys to the valet.

"If you even leave a smudge on it, I'll have your ass." She gave the valet a look. "Do we understand one another?"

The valet nodded and glanced toward Jack. Jack knew what the valet was thinking; he was wondering what kind of a man would tolerate such a bitch, even a beautiful one. Jack was wondering the same thing while memories of his ex-wife wafted through his mind, but could find no hold. He followed Roxanne through the doorway.

They were escorted to a table in a quite corner. It was an upscale restaurant, the kind where service would never be in question, the kind where a little stool was placed next to Roxanne so she would have somewhere to put her purse.

Jack pulled out the chair for her.

"Do you think I can't do it for myself because I'm a woman?" she asked.

"I'm sure you can. It was meant as a courtesy not as a comment on your gender."

She looked him in the face and decided he wasn't making a joke. She sat and allowed him to push the chair in.

"Kind of old fashioned, aren't you," she stated.

He took his own seat. "Good manners are never old fashioned."

"Yours are."

He scowled down at the linen tablecloth and then looked up. His anger melted away. It was a pleasure to spend time with a woman again, even if this particular woman used her beauty like a club.

The sommelier approached their table. "Welcome to Bijon's. Would you like to study the wine list?" Without waiting for an answer, he handed the leather bound book to Jack and stood by.

"Why don't you give us a few minutes?" Jack suggested.

"Very good." He took a few steps back and paused.

"What kind of wine would you like?" Jack asked her.

"I wouldn't presume to choose. I'm only a woman."

He began paging through the wine list. The first time

through he didn't read a single word. She was such a piece of work. So twisted. Well, he had wanted to be distracted. He began chuckling.

"What are you laughing about?"

"Not a thing." He refused her the satisfaction of a look and continued to study the wine list.

"You know, when you smile, you don't look half bad."

He looked up. "Thank you. The green you're wearing brings out the color of your eyes. You look quite stunning."

"Yes."

"Is this some kind of act?"

"What do you mean?"

"Haven't you ever heard of humility?"

"My husband taught me the importance of speaking one's mind."

"I'm not your husband."

"You certainly are not. How old are you anyway? I find it disgusting when older men pursue younger women."

"I'm only thirty-two." He brushed non-existent lint off his sleeve and considered escaping to the men's room to confirm his grooming.

"You look older."

My first date in years and it's the date from hell.

"Your lips are moving," she said. "Did you put the earphone back in?"

"No, I did not." He hesitated, but then said it, "Would you like to leave?"

"Hell no."

"You don't seem to be having a good time."

"On the contrary, I'm having an excellent time." She smiled and her lips tweaked upward at the corners. Her eyes flashed and she laughed. "Captain Jack," she shook her head, "you are too easy."

"Easy? Not a single person who was ever under my command would agree with that assessment."

"I'm not under your command."

He closed his eyes for a moment and then opened them to study the wine list. He waved the sommelier over and selected an expensive California Chardonnay.

"Very good choice, sir," the sommelier declared and hurried away.

Jack leaned forward. "Why don't you tell me about your

research?"

"I knew you weren't listening today."

"I was listening." The lie caused him to flush. "I just arrived late, through no fault of my own."

"Kind of defensive, aren't you?"

"I *am not* defensive." He slammed his hand down on the table and flipped the salad fork onto the floor. "The plane was late, the airport van was late and public transportation here is no better than when I was a student."

"And, you have anger management issues, but I guess we've already established that, haven't we?"

While he glared at her, the sommelier returned and made a show of uncorking the wine and offering the cork to Jack for inspection. He poured a small amount in Jack's wine glass. Jack took the obligatory sniff and sip and nodded.

The sommelier poured for them, set the bottle in an iced bucket on a stand next to the table, and then turned to face Jack.

"Do you think you'll be ordering a red wine to go with the meal? If so, I could open it now to allow it to breath."

"Leave us," Jack growled.

The sommelier stiffened and then pivoted to march away.

"You weren't very nice to him," Roxanne said. "He's only trying to do his job."

"Look who's talking."

Roxanne raised her glass and waited for Jack to do the same.

"A toast," she said, "to Captain Jack and to this evening, which promises to be more amusing than I ever thought possible." She took a sip. "Good choice."

He felt ridiculously gratified and shifted in his seat. "So, tell me about this primordial genome and your plans."

She set her wine down and met his eyes. "I've discovered a gene cluster that I believe will be found in every living thing, microbes to plants to mammals. The exact same sequence, which means that it must have been present at the beginning of the diversification of life, the beginning of life itself."

He refused to be infected by her enthusiasm and took another sip of wine before responding. "How do RNA based viruses work into this scenario?"

"My, my, you do know a little. When I say primordial, I'm referring to the primary genomic line of inheritance, DNA based life."

"I guess I don't grasp the significance, other than metaphysical. What is the significance?" He had the premonition that she was going to throw her wine in his face.

Her response was unexpectedly soft. "Don't know. That's why I need the grant."

"As I understand it, from *listening* to your presentation today, you don't know what the function of this gene cluster is."

"Not really. I've tried to activate it, but...well...."

"Well what? Tell me."

"I know more than I said today, but it's preliminary work. There is an active molecule associated with the cluster, but I haven't identified it yet."

"What does it do?"

"I'm not sure."

"Care to hazard a guess?"

"The only result I've seen is that it seems to cause an organism to go dormant."

"Asleep? You've discovered a sleep aid?"

She laughed. "Having a little trouble with insomnia, huh?"

He closed his lips and refused to respond.

She smiled. "Not a sleep aid. Sorry. I have only used it on bacteria so far. They stop dividing."

"I see, a new anti-infective. Now we're getting somewhere."

"Would you like to order, sir?" The waiter had been patiently standing next to the table.

They had not read the menu.

Jack looked to Roxanne.

"You've done well so far, why don't you order for me," she said.

"Do you eat meat?"

She smiled.

"Of course." He switched his attention to the server. "Two fillet mignon, medium rare, with vegetable of your choice and Cesar salads, no soup."

"Would you like to have wine with your meal?"

Jack glanced back to Roxanne, who shook her head.

"We'll have water."

"Would you like sparkling, still or tap?"

"Just bring us some water, okay?"

"Whatever you say, sir." The waiter walked away.

"I hope someone doesn't spit in it," Roxanne said.

"What do you mean?"

"You haven't exactly been making friends here."

Jack frowned, but then decided they wouldn't dare.

"What are your plans?" he asked.

"I need to identify the molecule involved and I'd like to review older genetic material. I should be able to obtain some mammoth DNA and perhaps some DNA fragments from insects trapped in amber, for an even earlier sampling."

He nodded.

"Does that mean I get the grant?"

He stopped nodding.

"Why *are* you here anyway? This isn't the way the NIH usually reviews grant proposals."

"I'm a source of potential embarrassment for an important person in the Washington power structure."

"The person higher up the chain of command?"

"Correct. Mitchell Mason. And, if you ever see him, run like hell in the opposite direction. He's a conniving bastard. Anyway, we negotiated a settlement. He gets to keep my wife and I'm out of the space program, but I maintain my rank and have special privileges."

"That sounds like a crappy deal. Who negotiated it?"

"I did."

"I see. Well, what's done is done."

"I also avoided an extended stay in the brig."

"Good for you. So, why did you come here?"

"I thought it would be nice to come back for a visit." He looked down. "I met my wife here."

"You mean your ex-wife."

He looked up with genuine hurt in his eyes. He couldn't hide it.

She reached across the table and patted his hand. "I'm sorry. I always push. I didn't mean to...you know."

He forced a smile. "Coming back was a mistake. Nothing is the same."

"Some truisms are true."

Their salads arrived and Jack asked the waiter to replace his salad fork.

"Use the other one," Roxanne suggested as she began to eat.

"The salad fork is for salads."

"You know, Jack, you really do need to learn how to break rules."

"I tried that once. They were right to kick me out of the space program. Rules are important."

"Bullshit," she said with her mouth full.

"Rules maintain our society. Without them there would be chaos."

She shrugged. "I have nothing against chaos."

"That makes sense. I was wondering what system you used in your office."

"To each his own."

The fork arrived and Jack began eating.

"Why do you use paper?" he asked. "Digital has been around for ages."

"I like paper, and books." She put her fork down and stared at him.

"What?" he asked, stopping with his fork half way to his mouth.

"I was thinking about what you said."

"About rules?"

"No. I was thinking about why you're here. As I understand it, you came here without a clue about my research. Not even interested. Just a whim. Are you the one who decides if I get my grant?"

"Yes."

"This is really crap. I can't believe it. Damn it! You saw where Rathburn has me. I've told him I want to transfer to another institution, but he swears he'll undermine any attempt I make. That asshole! He's going to hold onto me until I submit, in everyway. Noble Prize shit head. This is God's truth. One of his research assistants stumbled across the fix for type one diabetes mellitus while looking for an acne treatment and Rathburn took the credit. No joke. Damn it. Damn it to hell!"

Diners at nearby tables stopped eating. Jack smiled apologetically at them and then focused on his partially eaten salad.

"I guess that means you'll do anything to get the money you need," he said in a whisper.

"Haven't you heard anything I've said? If you're implying what I think you are, you can go to hell and take Rathburn with you! Why would you even think such a thing?"

"Well...when you were presenting your paper today

you...the way you move. To say nothing of your clothing."

"Are you accusing me of using my sexuality to get what I want?"

He must have had expectations because he now felt their loss. Her green eyes glared at him.

"Yes, that's exactly what I believed."

"You know, Jack, you are such a dork. Of course I do. I use every tool at my disposal, but if you're talking about submitting, sexually or otherwise, forget it. Now what do you have to say, Captain Jack? Feeling cheated? Going to take your grant and run back to Maryland because little 'ol Roxanne wouldn't put out for you?"

Jack's face felt hot. He wiped beads of sweat from his brow with his napkin.

"Would you speak a little softer?" he asked.

The waiter stood near the next table and stared at Jack and Roxanne while nodding to whatever the well-dressed man and woman were saying to him.

"Am I embarrassing you?" Roxanne asked.

"Yes."

"You should be embarrassed. I've worked hard to get to where I am and now the good old boys' club wants to take it all away from me and claim my work for themselves. You may think it's about sex, but it's really about power. Sex is an incidental. No one has helped me, even a little. I've done it all on my own."

"I'm sorry. Really I am. I do understand."

"How could you possibly understand, mister big shot Captain?"

"I've had my own difficulties to overcome."

"Don't tell me. You grew up in an orphanage."

"Not exactly. After my parents died, I was shuttled from one foster family to another. I'm told I was a difficult child. If my uncle hadn't taken me in, I'd probably be in prison by now. He taught me the importance of rules and order, and the Navy provided me with a home and a family, of sorts."

Her cheeks flushed. The color looked good. It seemed her beauty was immune to circumstances.

"Sorry about that," she said.

"Why are you sorry? You didn't do it."

Her smile returned.

During the silence that followed, the waiter served their

entrees and then stood by. When Jack glanced up, the waiter spoke. "Some of the patrons have been complaining. Please keep your voices down."

Roxanne's glare could've vaporized him.

The waiter's lips puckered with distaste, but he wisely walked away without saying more.

"Just when I was making friends with him," Jack declared with a grin.

"What do you mean?"

"Believe me when I tell you that your looks can speak, and what you just said to that man cannot be repeated in public."

"If you say so."

While they ate, Jack considered his position. Her research was worthy of support and he did like her, despite her sharp edges, perhaps because of them. He felt more alive and engaged than he had in two years, since Jane had left him, but he sensed that the moment he revealed his decision she would abandon him and he would be alone. He didn't like being alone. He had spent too much of his life alone.

"Did you see the news today, about that plane crash?" Roxanne asked. "An astronaut was killed. Did you know him?"

"A little. He was to have been the commander of the next mission. The Mars base is ready for habitation."

"Can we talk about the Mars program?"

"It's up to you."

"I don't want to open old wounds."

He felt an urge to laugh. All she had done is dig around in his wounds. He looked into those eyes. Was it his imagination, or was she not as tough as she put on?

"Go ahead," he said. "What do you want to know?"

"Months ago, there was a hint in the news that they had discovered something totally unexpected." She waited, but he said nothing. "Is it true? Did they discover life on Mars?"

"Want a specimen so you can look for your primordial gene?"

"Could you?" She leaned forward.

He regretted his flippant remark. "No. I don't know anymore than you do."

"Cut you out, did they?"

"You could say that."

"They left Mars almost a year ago. Aren't they supposed to arrive within the week?"

"So I understand."

"Is that why you escaped back here to Iowa? Couldn't take it?"

"Once you start opening wounds, you dig right in, don't you?"

She sat back in her chair. "You'd do better if you said what you meant, rather than agreeing when you don't want to. My husband could've helped you."

"I don't need a husband. I've already had a wife."

"Amusing," she said with no hint of amusement. "Do you listen to their transmissions?"

"Hard not to. They're broadcast everywhere."

"Notice anything odd about them?"

He shook his head. "What do you mean?"

"They seem too generic to me. 'Hi, Earth. We're fine. See you soon.'"

"What do you expect them to say?"

"I don't know. It just strikes me as odd."

It did seem odd. He must have been blocking it out.

"What are you thinking about?" Roxanne asked.

He glanced up at her with new respect.

"Are you busy tomorrow?" he asked

"Yes."

"I see, okay."

"Have you made a decision about the grant?"

He took a deep breath and released it before he finally committed. "I'll see to it that you get whatever you need."

She nodded. "Good decision."

She pushed her chair back and stood, her meal half eaten. He stared up at her. It was just like he imagined it would be.

"Come on. Let's go." She picked up her purse.

He was still hungry. He glanced down at the meat on his plate and then up at her. Not that hungry. He waived the waiter over. It was as if the man had been waiting for this moment and hurried over with the check. Jack was a little shocked by the amount but added a tip. By the time he had concluded the exchange, Roxanne was nowhere to be seen. He walked toward the front door, half expecting to discover that she had deserted him after all.

Her car was out front. The valet must have been on the lookout for her. Roxanne took an extra moment and walked around the car again, inspecting it.

"Give him a good tip," she said before sliding into the driver's seat.

Jack dug into his wallet and handed the valet a bill.

"She said a good tip," the valet said with a sneer.

"Would you excuse me for a minute?" Jack asked Roxanne.

"Sure."

Jack put his arm across the valet's shoulders and walked him around the corner of the restaurant. A few moments later Jack reappeared, but the valet did not. He walked over to the Aston Martin and swung into his seat.

"What did you do to that man?" she asked.

"I just gave him the rest of his tip. Advice on how to show respect." He glanced over at her, expecting to see that smile, but it was a stern face that confronted him.

"Did you hurt him?"

"Not much."

"What do you care? It's just government money."

"Is that what you think?" She didn't respond so he continued. "The government isn't paying for this. I am." He pointedly glanced at the car around him. "And, in case you're wondering, I'm not rich, like some people."

"I'm not rich either. My husband always said that when he died he'd make sure somebody would pay. And, as always, he was true to his word. The life insurance company complained, but they paid." She put the Aston Martin in gear and pressed the accelerator, leaving a cloud of burned rubber behind as the car roared onto the street.

He wondered where they were going, but wasn't about to ask. She put the top down. It was a balmy summer evening and there was a harvest moon in the night sky. The engine rumbled with power and they flew down the road with not another car in sight; cars were again a plaything of the wealthy.

She glanced toward him. "Want to see what this baby can do?"

He nodded and her smile grew. She punched the accelerator and shifted into fourth, fifth and then sixth. The rumble turned into a high-pitched whine. If the car hadn't been designed properly, they would have taken to the air.

Jack felt the skin of his face stretch into a broad smile of exhilaration.

Too soon for his liking, she began downshifting. She exited the interstate at high speed. The car clung to the roadway and the tires screeched as she swung onto an asphalt road.

After a few miles, she turned onto the gravel driveway of what appeared to be an abandoned farmhouse. She drove the car into a garage that had been a machine shed and that smelled of dirt and oil. She shut the Aston Martin off. The silence that followed seemed almost deafening.

She turned in her seat to face him. "Did you like it?"

"Like it? It was fantastic! Can I drive it sometime?"

"I don't know, Jack. We've only known each other for a day...but, I'll think about it."

"Where are we?" he asked.

"Home. I told you I wasn't rich. Everything I earn goes into feeding this beauty." She patted the steering wheel and got out of the car.

Jack pulled down the garage door and followed her toward the old house. In the light of a full moon, it looked like a condemned building; some of the windows were boarded up and the screen door hung askew on its hinges. The door was unlocked. It "creaked" when she pushed against it, as if this was the very last time it would open. She flipped on a light switch. The sofa had exposed stuffing, at least as much of it as could be seen beneath heaps of clothing, and the floor was piled with cardboard boxes.

"Did you just move in?" he asked.

"No. Why would think that?" She wove her way among the boxes and then paused to look back at him. "Aren't you coming?"

He stepped forward, watching where he put his feet, concerned that he might step in something. She disappeared up an enclosed flight of stairs and he hurried after her, pausing a moment to glance into the kitchen. The sink was piled with dishes. In his imagination he visualized mold and ants.

"Roxanne," he called.

"Up here."

This was simply disgusting. He shook his head as he climbed the last few steps, prepared to thank her for her hospitality and ask for a ride back to his hotel. He rounded the corner and stopped. Her skin was alabaster white. His eyes traveled from her face to her breasts, to her waist and then lower still. She held out her arms and he walked forward, no longer seeing the towels in the corner, or the unmade bed. He wrapped his arms around her and met those delicious lips, full and warm, so soft, just as he imagined, and then her lips parted. He felt her hands working at his belt. He reluctantly broke the embrace and dropped his clothes in a pile to join the assorted clumps of clothing around it. Touching her was so exciting that he didn't give the room another thought, until they lay side by side, each in their own private thoughts.

Jack's eyes wandered across the peeling, flowered wallpaper until he spotted a picture. It was of a burly, bearded man with his arm draped possessively across Roxanne's shoulders. It looked like it had been taken in an alpine forest. It was probably that dead husband she talked about so much. His thoughts turned to his ex-wife. *How could Jane have deserted me?* It was such a recurrent thought, it was nearly a mantra, but on this night it was powerless. He shifted his position and snuggled close to kiss Roxanne's cheek.

She combed her fingers through his thick hair.

"How are you, Captain Jack?" she asked in that husky voice.

"Peachy fine."

"Having sex with me is like fuzzy fruit?"

"A fine fuzzy fruit, very fine." He drew her hand to his mouth, kissed her palm, and wrapped his arm across her to hold her securely against him.

She traced her fingertips along the scars on his arm. "How did you get these?"

"I was attacked by an angry pack of Chihuahuas." He chuckled.

"And this one?" She brushed her fingers across a jagged scar on his flank. "More Chihuahuas?"

"You guessed it."

"Yeah, sure." She rolled over and pressed her body against his. Her tracing fingers began to caress.

The second time was even sweeter, slower, but fulfilling. While they rested, he cuddled against her and savored her warmth. He nuzzled her hair and inhaled her fragrance. He couldn't quite place it. Sweet and spicy and something else. It was intoxicating. He reached across her, cupped a soft breast in his hand and fell asleep. He slept peacefully, for the first time in two years, if he were honest with himself.

"Jack." She shook his shoulder. "Jack, wake up! There's someone pounding on my door."

Jack's eyes flew open and he heard the thudding. "Your husband?"

"Yeah, right. It's my husband, back from the grave. Maybe it's your ex-wife."

"Real funny."

Jack swung his legs over the edge of the bed and rubbed his face. If they were burglars, they were well-mannered burglars. The door was unlocked, yet they continued to pound on it.

He put on his pants and tried to brush out the wrinkles before putting on his shirt, carefully tucking it in.

"Jack."

"Yes," he said as he pulled on his socks.

"If we were the three little pigs, our house would be blown away by now."

"I'm hurrying." He slipped on his shoes and tied the laces before putting on his coat.

"Don't you want your cute little hat? It might be raining down there."

He gave her a look before he walked to the stairwell and descended. He peeked around the corner. There were two men standing next to the open door, studying the doorknob they had just broken as if wondering how they'd repair it. He might not know who they were, but he knew all about military police. He stepped around the corner and both men saluted. Jack automatically returned the salute as he walked toward them.

"What the hell do you think you're doing?" Jack demanded in a commanding-officer tone.

"Captain, we've been sent to bring you back with us. We're under orders from—" The man's eyes strayed.

Jack glanced behind. Roxanne stood there with a towel wrapped around her, wearing his hat.

"What are you doing?" Jack demanded of her, still in military mode. "Get dressed!"

"This is my house. I'll wear whatever I want, whenever I want to." She allowed the towel to drop to the floor.

Jack immediately returned his attention to the two men, who stared with amazement. He held out his arms and herded them outside, standing between them and a view of the interior of the house.

"What the hell do you want?" Jack asked.

"Sorry, sir. I can see we're interrupt—"

"What do you want?"

"Sir, we've been trying to find you for hours. There must be something wrong with your earphone."

"You found me. Is that it?"

"No, sir."

He handed an envelope to Jack marked "CONFIDENTIAL" in red letters.

Jack broke the seal and used the headlights of the military vehicle to read the official looking document. It was an order to return to the space center at Copper Mountain, without delay. There was no sense in questioning the Lieutenant; he was only a deliveryman.

"Sir, there is air transport waiting for you."

Jack folded the orders and slipped them into his pocket. "All right, Lieutenant. I'll need to stop by the hotel and pick up my stuff."

"It'll be picked up for you, sir. I have been instructed to take you directly to the airport."

There was nothing more to be said. An order was an order.

"I need to say good-bye to the young lady," Jack said.

"Understood, sir."

Roxanne had scooped a handful of clothes off the sofa so she could sit and was wearing a silky robe.

Jack moved another pile of clothes aside and sat down next to her. "I've got to go. They've been trying to reach me all evening but, guess what? I wasn't wearing my phone."

"Don't tell me. You're being arrested and taken directly to cell phone prison."

"I shouldn't have taken it off. I have to go. Orders."

"Then go."

"You don't understand. I really have to."

"So, why are you still here?"

"I'm here because I don't want to go. I want to stay with you."

"Then stay."

"Roxanne." He shook his head and then held her with his eyes. "I'd like to see you again. Would that be something you'd be interested in?"

"Try me and find out."

"You said I could drive your car."

"I said I would think about it. I have a question for you."

"What?"

"Why did you decide to support my grant proposal?"

He thought about the evening and then looked up to meet her eyes. "I did it because I think you're a very bright woman and I believe you've discovered something that should be investigated further."

She smiled. "You can drive my car anytime you want."

"Now I have a question for you."

"Go for it."

"Did you have sex with me because you wanted to make sure of the grant?"

She swung her fist and landed a solid blow to his mouth.

He rocked back, more from surprise than pain.

"There," she declared, "that should cancel out the sex. Does that answer your question?"

He nodded and when he smiled he could feel that his lower lip was already beginning to swell.

"Thanks," he said.

"Anytime. Would you like another?"

"Not really. That's quite a punch you have."

"At least I got something out of growing up in Detroit."

"I'll make sure the grant approval goes through. You should be hearing in a week or two."

He leaned toward her and she met him half way. He tried to memorize the feel of those lips.

"I have to go," he said and stood.

She handed him his hat. He waited, but she remained seated. He couldn't recall a more awkward moment and knew she was doing it on purpose. He walked toward the door and paused to turn back to her.

She smiled.

"You are such a little devil. Later," he said with a grin.

"Later, Captain Jack."

He was still grinning while he walked across the yard and climbed into the military vehicle.

CHAPTER 3

It had been a direct flight aboard a government plane. Questions concerning his recall to Copper Mountain remained unanswered. He peered out of the car at the approaching facility. Above ground the space center was deceptively simple: a landing strip, a row of barracks and a few warehouses, all of concrete. He remembered watching his ex-wife through the back window of a car while he was being driven away, in the custody of military police.

"Damn her," Jack said.

"Excuse me, sir?"

"Nothing, Lieutenant Wahlberg." At least that's what he said his name was. One never knew when it came to security personnel.

The Lieutenant continued to study him.

These were not stupid men. His behavior would go into the man's report. He shook his head. What the hell difference could it make? Mason would never allow him back in. He was that kind of man. The bastard.

His attention fixed on the launch rail as soon as it was visible. In the early morning sun, it was a gleaming ribbon of metal rising up the mountainside. He could picture it as it climbed above the snowline. He leaned back and closed his eyes, not to rest, but to relive the crushing pressure of acceleration and the final punch of power, followed by the weightlessness of space. He had ridden the rail eight times, had spent time aboard the space station and the Mars Explorer, but he'd been denied the culmination of his training, the chance to step onto the iron-red soil of Mars. His teeth ground against one another.

"Captain Nichols?"

He felt a touch on his arm. The grinding stopped.

"Are you all right?"

"Just peachy fine." He forced his tense muscles to stand down. The car passed behind a building and he tried to push the thought of riding the rail from his mind. He had missed his chance. And for what? He raised his hand to his face and rubbed the bristly stubble as he thought, accidentally brushing his sore lip. *Roxanne.* He smiled. For most of the flight out he had been on the comm-link calling in favors, imagined or real, and had succeeded. Fastest approval in the history of the NIH. He could take some satisfaction in that.

The car stopped in front of a one-story building, concrete-gray and functional. The long, low building was little more than a doorway to the real space center, which was underground, better insulated from the weather they said. Right. Secrecy and control ruled the WSA.

The only color was the agency symbol, a "Flash Gordon" rocket within a red-rimmed circle, surrounded by the words "World Space Agency". It was a world agency, when it came to accepting money, but there was little doubt about who ran the agency; it was headquartered in Colorado.

Two uniformed men approached. This was for show; they would never have gotten this far if they hadn't been authorized.

Jack wasn't impressed; he wasn't a first year congressman. He opened the car door and stepped into the morning sunlight. The air was crisp and fresh. It brought a renewed sense of life and energy to him, and memories, some bad, some good.

The guard was dressed in a darling red uniform with green lapels. To Jack, he looked more like an overgrown elf than a military man, but he returned the man's salute.

"Captain Nichols, will you follow me?"

Jack looked down and brushed his hands over his dress whites.

"Sir, will you follow me?"

Jack read the man's name badge. "Sergeant Tiaatila, is it?"

"Yes, sir."

"Lead on."

The sergeant approached the doors, which opened by remote. Passing from the raw concrete outside to the finished interior was like passing from a prison yard into a wonderland. Hidden within the polished granite and indirect lighting were sensors, all of them busy in a quiet way, estimating if anything was amiss.

The hall that stretched along the elevator-lined wall opposite them was surprisingly empty. He joined the sergeant to wait in front of an elevator. There was only one way to go from here, down.

The elevator opened and two men and a woman stepped out. The woman stared at Jack and squeezed to the side as she passed to avoid any possibility of contact.

Jack entered and saw his reflection in the mirrored wall. He concluded that he couldn't possibly look that rough and angry. It must be the lightening. He tried to smile, with little success.

The sergeant inserted his card into the priority slot; there would be no stops for them.

The elevator dropped, accelerating enough to tease Jack with the memory of weightlessness, just a hint. Unexpected nausea arose and he leaned against the wall, not enough sleep, not enough food and way too much anxiety. The sergeant acted as if he hadn't noticed, but Jack was irritated with himself. It was only an elevator; even it was dropping like a bucket down a well. He straightened and watched the numbers flicker on the screen above the door. It looked like they were going all the way. The pressure of deceleration pushed against his feet. They were a mile beneath the surface when the elevator came to a stop. The doors slid open and unpleasant memories arose.

"Sir?" The sergeant stepped out and gestured for Jack to follow.

With a churning in his gut, Jack walked in the direction of Mason's office. It was to be Mason then. Why? Had something happened to Jane? He stopped before the door. It had been over two years, but it seemed like no time had passed.

The sergeant stepped forward to open the door, but didn't follow him in.

The secretary looked up from his monitor and then stood, extending his hand. "Hi, Jack. Good to see you again."

Sam's hand felt warm in his own.

"Good to see you too, Sam."

Colonel Sam "Smoking" Cohen smiled; his weathered face displayed a full set of creases, around his mouth and eyes, and across his forehead.

"Know anything about what's going on?" Jack asked and nodded toward the inner office.

Of course Sam did and of course he would say nothing.

"Just thought I'd ask. Don't want to go in there swinging."

The smile fell from Colonel Cohen's face.

"Just a joke." Jack forced a grin, but could feel the real anger that remained. Maybe it wasn't a joke.

Sam saw it as well; he was the sort of man that could see into a man's soul. No need for surveillance equipment when good old Sam was around.

"This is important," Sam said in his gravely voice. "Don't blow it."

Jack nodded. "Thanks for the tip." He turned toward Mason's office.

"No," Sam said from behind, "in the conference room. They're waiting for you."

"They?" He paused, but it was obvious Sam was done talking. Jack wanted to know if he meant Jane was there, but forced the question to remain unasked. He would know soon enough. He paused in front of the door before opening it; his heart pounded as if he were about to go into battle. He walked in.

Mitchell Mason sat at the head of the oblong table. There were three other people in the room, two men and a woman; the woman was not Jane.

It had been an absurd expectation. They would never have brought him back for a personal reason. He focused on Mason and animosity sparked across the room.

It was Mason who relented. "Thank you for coming, Captain, but you needn't have gotten all dressed up."

"I thought it was an order. If not, I've got things to do."

Mason addressed the others. "Would you excuse us for a moment?" He approached Jack, but stopped short of handshaking distance. "Come with me."

Jack followed Mason out of the conference room and down the hallway. He managed a glance toward Sam, who frowned and shook his head.

Mason entered his office and immediately walked over to sit behind his desk, establishing a neutral territory between them.

Jack waited in the doorway. Even though he saw the delicate features and slight frame of Mitchell Mason, Director of the WSA, all he could think about was Jane. *Damn her!* Damn them both.

"Close the door," Mason ordered.

Jack took another step into the room and allowed the door to shut. He was disappointed that he could detect no lasting damage from the beating he'd given the man. But, now that they were alone again....

Mason pointed his finger at him. "Before your primitive urges overcome you, I suggest you listen to me."

"How's my wife? Did she send her greetings?"

"She's not your wife. You're divorced. She's my wife. For God's sake, grow up and get on with your life. She doesn't even know you're here."

"Afraid to tell her?"

Mason exhaled audibly and leaned back in his chair. His lips tightened with disgust. "No, I thought it was best. You see, she's eight months pregnant and I didn't want to upset her. I'm sure you can understand—stay back." Mason tensed and then relaxed. His fingertip rested on a panic button hidden beneath the edge of his desk. He was prepared this time. "Or don't. It's up to you." He smiled to reveal his teeth, the kind of smile any carnivore would recognize as a challenge.

"Why did you bring me here?"

Mason raised his bushy eyebrows, the only thing about him that wasn't patrician. "Not bad. I would've expected more from you. Perhaps you are the right man for the mission."

"Mission?" Jack felt his way forward with his feet and sank into the only other chair in the room.

"I see I have your attention." When Jack said nothing, he continued. "Pie Traynor insisted you were the best choice."

Jack shook his head. *Pie.* It was simply an act of charity after all.

"Are you telling me you don't want to hear more? Would you rather return to your paper pushing at NIH? It can be arranged."

Jack looked down. "I don't want to go back to NIH."

"I didn't hear you."

"The hell you didn't!"

"Now, now. If you can't control these emotional outbursts, I'll be forced to recruit another mission specialist. We need a man with complete control of his emotions. Do you have that?" He tapped his index finger on his chin. "I wonder."

Jack's clenched jaw was beginning to ache.

"Well, do you?"

"If I say I'll do a job, I'll do it."

"Umm, in a way, I'm disappointed. I won't deny it. I think you're an immature man. It's no wonder—well, that's neither here nor there, is it?"

"I know what you're trying to do and it won't work. If Jane has the taste of a gutter rat, I can't do anything about that."

"I'm sure Jane will be interested to know what you think of her," Mason said with a rapacious smile.

Jack clasped his hands, using one to control the other. "Don't do that."

"Are you threatening me?"

"No," he answered quietly, "I'm asking. I'd like you to give her my best wishes on her—your—upcoming child."

"I'll consider it. Now that we have this little housekeeping task out of the way, are you ready to rejoin the others? I'm sure they're wondering what we're doing."

Mason stood but Jack remained seated.

"What is the mission?" Jack asked.

"You'll find out at the same time as the others." He waited for Jack to enter the hallway before following.

On his way back to the conference room, Jack glanced toward Sam, who nodded and smiled. It helped, a little.

Jack took a seat across from the other three while Mason resumed his place at the head of the table.

"This is Captain Jack Nichols," Mason said with a dismissive wave of his hand, "a former Mars mission specialist."

The two men stared at him from across the table. The woman cocked her head as she studied him.

Mason gestured toward the first man to his left, who wore a checkered sweater and squinted despite corrective surgery. "Captain Nichols, you already know Doctor Zerke, chief of landing site selection and base development."

Zerke nodded to Jack.

"Next, we have Colonel James Patterson of Army Special Forces and Doctor Katherine Smith-Jones, pathologist."

It was an odd group to Jack's way of thinking, especially this Doctor Smith-Jones. He studied her. She had ruddy cheeks and blue eyes with a too small mouth. Her blond hair was chopped short. She had the bones of a rugby player and sat slouched in her chair, as if schooled in bad posture and proud of it. But, a pathologist?

Jack winked and she answered with a smile.

Mason continued. "I'm sure you've all been speculating, but what I'm about to reveal will go beyond your wildest imaginings."

Jack opened his mouth to speak, but Mason halted him with a raised hand and then brought his finger to his lips before continuing.

"The moment of truth," Mason declared. "From this moment on, you're either part of the mission, or staying down under. If anyone wants to change—"

"Get on with it," Jack demanded. He hated the condescending bastard, would've hated him even if he hadn't stolen his wife.

Mason glared at Jack but didn't rise to the bait; instead, he turned to Doctor Zerke and nodded for him to begin.

A holographic projection of Mars appeared above the end of the table. A blue dot flashed near the South Pole.

"The dot represents the Mars base." Zerke cleared his squeaky voice, but couldn't suppress his excitement. "Aside from the completion of the final phase of base development, the team's other mission was to explore the edge of the permafrost, looking for evidence of life."

Jack couldn't remain still. He began tapping his foot. This had been his mission. He knew everything about it: how they would collect the samples, where they would collect them, what they would do with them. He felt ill with missed opportunity; they must have discovered evidence of extraterrestrial life.

Zerke continued. "Prior to the lander being deployed, the Mars Explorer completed a series of transits around the planet, surveying for changes. Standard operating procedure. A storm had just scoured the base site and extra care was taken in viewing that area. The base had survived beautifully. And that was when the anomaly was discovered. The storm had uncovered something north of the base site that was reflecting sunlight. Deployment of the lander was delayed until the images could be studied at Goddard."

Jack leaned toward the projection, as if a closer look would reveal something. The squeak of Doctor Zerke's voice was no longer important, only what he said was important and for Jack he couldn't possibly speak fast enough.

"The image analysis revealed that the anomaly was approximately two-kilometers long and was in three parts, each separated by about fifty meters. It didn't appear to be a geological formation. No further conclusions could be drawn. It was decided that the original mission would be altered."

Zerke looked to Mason.

Mason answered the look. "Exploration involves risk taking."

Jack stared at him. It was a peculiar statement, true or not.

"Get on with it, Doctor Zerke," Mason ordered.

"Samples were still to be obtained, but aside from the final base preparation, the primary mission became the investigation of the anomaly."

"Get to the point. Tell them what happened," Mason urged.

Zerke frowned. "As you wish. Here are the initial images sent back from the site of the anomaly."

A distorted mirror replaced the image of Mars. It was partially buried in sand. Jack tipped his head to the side as if seeing it on end would give it a recognizable shape.

A figure in a canary-yellow suit loped toward the convex mirror in a slow motion gait. It was Dodd, the one who had replaced Jack as mission commander.

Jack rubbed his stomach beneath the table. He could hardly stand to watch the figure as it approached the brightness, becoming smaller and smaller until the true size of the object was apparent.

Zerke spoke again. "This is the smallest section of the artifact. It's about one hundred meters long and thirty meters high and that's only the portion of it that's exposed."

The next image was at night with bright lights shining on the reflective object, too close to see any shape. There were two figures now; both were using shovels. It had to be Dodd and Slater.

"There were no gouges or dents in the surface. It appeared pristine. They couldn't find an entry point and when they tried to slice into it with the laser cutter, it seemed to absorb and disperse the energy. They couldn't find a way to get inside until Dodd had the bright idea to dig at one end. At first it appeared that the end was solid as well. The hull of the spaceship—yes, there can be no doubt that it's a ship—looked like it had melted downward, but when they dug beneath it, they found that there was a breach were the hull met the sand. Here's a sample of video from inside."

Sand had drifted in and begun to fill the hulk. The reflective bulkhead curved upward without markings or instrumentation. Slater dug until his shovel hit something. He bent down and brushed away sand with gloved hands. Out of the sand, he lifted a golden sphere, the size of a softball.

The video jumped ahead, days ahead. The two men were outside the hull of the derelict ship, but now there were hundreds of the golden spheres, stacked like cannon balls. The video zoomed in and Zerke froze the image; a pyramid of the golden balls appeared to be suspended above the end of the table.

Mason allowed the silence to stretch on before speaking. "What you have just seen is the first evidence of life beyond Earth and, without doubt, from beyond the solar system. We are not alone."

Doctor Smith-Jones was first to find her voice. "Did they find any...any of them?"

Mason shook his head. "The mission time table required them to leave before the ship could be excavated to any extent, and remember, the wreck is huge. There is far more that we don't know than what we do know. For one, the propulsion system. Neither the tail nor the nose of the ship was explored. Who knows what amazing technology is buried in the sand?"

"God be with us," Colonel Patterson declared. "Any idea how long it's been there?"

"Not really. We don't know enough about the geology and weather of Mars, but most estimates put it at between fifty and a hundred years."

"Do we know why it crashed?" the Colonel asked.

"Not a clue."

Jack found the question that had been snaking its way through his mind. "Are we to be on the next launch, the next to visit the site?" It was a moment of joy.

Mason shook his head.

"Then what do you want?" Jack snapped.

"There's more," Mason said quietly.

"Are we supposed to guess?" Smith-Jones asked with a dry lilt to her voice.

Jack smiled. He could like that woman.

Mason continued. "A fragment of the ship's hull was found away from the crash site. That and a dozen of the golden spheres were taken aboard the Explorer. The artifacts were kept in strict isolation to prevent any possibility of contamination. The problem is...the crew got sick during the return trip to Earth. The illness was analyzed here at Copper

Mountain and at the CDC, but nothing seemed to help."

"What are you saying?" Even though Jack asked the question, he didn't want to hear the answer.

"You know what I'm saying. They're dead."

If Jack had eaten anything, he would have up-chucked right there and then. Fatigue, constant reminders of his failed marriage, and now this. It could've been him, should've been him. He lowered his head to the table; it was cool against his forehead.

"Captain Nichols, are you all right?" Smith-Jones asked.

He didn't raise his head until he heard her chair legs scrape against the floor. His scowl did not invite compassion. She retook her seat.

Jack finally understood. He looked to Mason. "We're to be the autopsy team. Do their families know? They must. Those last transmissions were particularly banal. Pieced together from earlier communications. You can't fool their families." He thought about Roxanne. "Hell, even people not associated with the program suspect there's a problem."

"Who?" Mason shot back.

"None of your business. What're you going to do? Arrest Iowa?"

"Don't underestimate us, Nichols. We told the families that the crew had made important discoveries and that we needed their cooperation until the ship returned to Earth. They knew the transmissions were faked for the media and general public's consumption."

"You're not fooling anyone."

"To the contrary. We've brought the families to Copper Mountain. Down under. And that's where they'll stay until we decide to release them."

"I see," Jack replied. "And to hell with their civil rights."

"Don't give me that look, Nichols. This is damn important!" Mason paused as he defiantly glared around the room and then returned his attention to Nichols. "We've been controlling the ship for the last eight months. You heard me right. They've been dead for eight months. I think we've done pretty damn well keeping this undercover. The Explorer will be arriving in one week. We're going to dock it at the International Space Station, but no one will enter the ship until you arrive. You'll be our investigation team. Doctor Smith-Jones will be our pathologist. You, Captain Nichols, will serve as the technical expert on the Mars Explorer. Colonel Patterson will be commander of this mission. He'll also pilot the scramjet and assist as needed."

"Assist as needed?" Jack nodded. "I can imagine."

Patterson returned Jack's gaze with a cool estimation of his own.

Dr. Smith-Jones looked up from studying her short fingernails. "Why did you wait so long to tell us? I've been here for over a month. I could've been working on this. Instead, I've been in this pseudo-training you've been putting me through. Wasted time."

"Not wasted," Mason replied. "You needed to be trained to go to space."

"Why didn't you tell me?" she asked.

"That was my decision. The fewer who knew the better. It won't take you more than a day or two to review the data. The answer isn't there. If it were, we wouldn't need you, would we? No, the answer lies aboard the Explorer."

"But, what about planning? Determining the best approach to the problem?" Smith-Jones asked.

"I'm sure you'll have adequate time. Whatever you need will be provided."

"But, there are going to be special equipment—"

"Enough, Doctor. We've anticipated your needs."

"I hope you're right. I'll need access to all data about their deaths, immediately."

"You can start today, if you'd like."

"Are there any theories?" she asked.

"Of course, but I don't want to muddle your thinking. You've a deserved reputation for solving difficult cases. We're depending on you."

"Will we be allowed to return if we fail to determine the cause of their deaths?" Jack asked.

Mason smiled. "Of course you will."

"I bet," Jack muttered.

"Captain Nichols," Patterson growled, "enough! I will *not* tolerate insubordination in those under my command."

"Shut up, Patterson. You don't out rank me."

Patterson's face was ruddy with anger. "I expect even a *former* Seal is aware of the chain of command and, in this case, I've been designated as your superior officer."

Mason addressed the Colonel. "Captain Nichols has had a

difficult day, but he will respect the chain of command." He switched his attention to Jack. "Won't you, Captain Nichols?"

Jack met Mason's stare without responding.

Mason continued, emphasizing each word. "You will respect the chain of command, won't you."

Jack relented. "Yes."

"Yes, what?"

Jack took a deep breath. "I will respect the chain of command."

"Very good."

Smith-Jones spoke. "I'll need to meet with all of you so that we can discuss containment issues. If it's an infectious disease, no one will be exposed if we follow a well thought out plan and stick to protocol." She focused on Jack. "I'm an expert in the pathology of infectious disease and poisoning. I've been in similar circumstances before."

"I see," Jack said dryly. "So you're the one who investigated the other alien ships that killed everyone who came in contact with them. Very impressive."

"I said 'similar', not identical. Learn a little English, will you?" She was also an expert at shaping her face into a sneer.

Jack wanted to apologize but couldn't manage the words, not here, not now.

Mason continued. "You'll have complete access to all data, including the video record of the crew, from the beginning to their deaths aboard the Explorer. You'll each be assigned an assistant until you ride the rail. That will conclude our meeting for today. We'll meet again at fifteen hundred tomorrow. Captain Nichols, I'd like you to stay. The rest of you are dismissed."

No one moved for a moment, held in place by the weight of the information they had just learned. Doctor Zerke was the first to stand, followed by Smith-Jones and Colonel Patterson.

When only Jack and Mason remained in the room, Mason spoke. "Nichols," he held his thumb and index finger until they were almost touching, "you're this close to being dismissed from the mission. If it wasn't so God-damned important, you'd be gone right now."

"Stop threatening. You need me."

Mason nodded. "We do. If Nguyen hadn't killed himself in that unfortunate plane crash, we wouldn't even be having this conversation. But, if you don't toe the line, I will replace you, even if it's with someone less knowledgeable about the Explorer. I continue to question the wisdom of including you."

"What do you mean?"

"You aren't exactly acting like a team player."

"You just told me three of my friends are dead. How should I respond?"

"I wouldn't call them friends. You hardly knew Dodd."

Jack stood. "I knew him. I helped train him. It was part of our deal, remember? You're such an asshole."

"Sit!" Mason ordered.

Jack reluctantly obeyed.

Mason continued. "This isn't about you or me. I don't care what you think of me. I need to know if you can do the job."

"I'll do the job. You don't have to worry about that."

"That's all I ask." Mason said. "One more thing. Since you have so much empathy, when the time comes, I want you to be the one to tell the families."

"Hell no! It's your mess. You deal with it."

"We'll see. You can leave now."

Jack immediately stood. He slammed his hand against the door and strode out of the conference room. His face felt like it was on fire when he walked past Sam's desk. Sam was gone, but the sergeant remained, waiting in the outside hallway.

"Don't tell me," Jack said. "You're to be my assistant, correct?"

"Yes, sir, part of the time."

"Then show me to my quarters. I could use some rest."

"Yes, sir, you could."

Jack eyed the sergeant.

"Sorry, sir. Follow me."

The sergeant led Jack back to the elevators and then to the surface. They walked across the parade grounds toward one of a handful of above ground structures.

What the hell? Jack thought, but said nothing. All he wanted was a warm shower and a bed. The rest could wait.

CHAPTER 4

Jack awakened and reached across the bed to touch Jane. The sheet was cold and the bed was empty. He was alone. He opened his eyes and looked at the wall. His favorite picture, a reproduction of "Nighthawks", had been replaced by a picture of an F-35 Lightning above cumulus clouds. He lay back in his bed and stared at the ceiling. Housing him in the apartment he had shared with Jane hadn't been accidental. There were two possibilities: either it was an effort to make him feel at home, or another jab at his underbelly. Probably a jab. He rolled out of bed and staggered into the bathroom to get cleaned up.

Someone had put his traveling trunk just inside the door. He took out a carefully folded uniform and applied the captain's eagles to the collars. He was on his way to the door when he stopped in the living room to stand in front of a large window. The rail was a line of reflected sunlight that stretched up the mountain slope. In the distance were snow covered peaks. Jane had sat with him in front of that window, sharing a view that rich folks paid plenty for. He turned away; it didn't seem so special without her.

On his way out, he noticed a comm-unit on the table next to the door. He picked it up and pushed the button.

A young man answered. "Communications. How may I assist you, Captain?"

"I'd like to be connected with Dr. Roxanne Wiley at the Genomics Research Laboratory, Carver College of Medicine."

There was a pause and then, "Captain, I regret to inform you that outgoing calls are restricted."

"For everyone or just me?"

"All outgoing calls require approval. Would you like to speak with my supervisor?"

"Forget it."

Jack cut the connection and tossed the comm-unit onto the table. He opened the door and turned into the hallway, barely avoiding the man who stood there. It wasn't Sergeant

Tiaatila, but it could've been his brother.

The sergeant stepped back and saluted. "Good morning, sir."

"Good morning," Jack said, managing to make "good" sound bad. He returned the smart salute with a causal wave of his hand and walked past with the sergeant dutifully trailing after him.

Jack walked across the empty parade grounds. All the windows in the row of three story barracks were dark. There was no movement. Was he the only one living in the above ground apartments?

When he exited the elevator in the down under of the spaceport, he had to wait for a crowd to pass. He didn't recognize a single face. He glanced at his watch; breakfast was nearly over. He had chosen the Arboretum Cafeteria. It was Jane's favorite. Just inside the door, he paused. The air was filled with voices speaking in various languages of the world, but he wasn't listening. He had nearly forgotten what it was like. His eyes were drawn upward. There were fully grown trees whose upper most branches did not touch the high ceilings. The hidden lights reminded him of a summer morning. Such extravagance.

He walked over to the buffet and chose a glass of orange juice and a bagel, while the sergeant began filling his tray, seemingly with one of everything.

Jack wandered down the sidewalk, taking care not to step on the grass. He rounded an oak tree and spotted a man who could only be described as a giant. He walked over and, as he pulled out a chair, the giant looked up. He was just like Jack remembered him, biggest damn nose you ever saw.

"Jack! Great to see you back."

Jack smiled as he sat down.

"I've been meaning to look you up," the giant continued in his rumbling voice, "but I've been absolutely buried with work."

Jack nodded. "Thanks, Pie."

"For what?"

"For the chance."

"No thanks needed. You're the best man for the job."

"I won't let you down."

"Never crossed my mind. Pretty horrible situation, isn't it?"

"It's unbelievable, but I'd rather be here then back at NIH, come what may. Have you seen Jane lately?"

Pie studied his friend's face, while Jack focused on his bagel, rolling it like a wheel, back and forth.

"Yes," Pie finally replied, "of course I've seen her."

Jack stopped. "How does she look?"

"Good."

"Mason told me she was pregnant."

Pie nodded. "I'm glad that hurdle's been passed. I was a little worried about how you'd take it. She looks great, for a woman carrying a basketball under her shirt." He chuckled. "I'd almost forgotten how good you are at giving dirty looks."

Jack's face relaxed.

"Jack."

"Yes?"

"Your lip looks a little swollen. You didn't get into a fight with Mason, did you? Tell me you didn't."

Jack smiled and touched his lip. "No, of course not. It was a woman I met recently."

"A woman?" Pie grinned. "A love pat?"

"I guess you could call it that."

"God damn! It's about time. What's her name?"

"Roxanne Wiley."

"Damn. I wish I had time to hear all about it, but I have to go. Got a lot to do. I'm having a hard time convincing the station crew that they need to come home. Too many governments involved. It'll be a miracle if we can arrange for their evacuation before the Explorer docks, but I'm certain we can at least keep them out of the ship. Who's your buddy?" Pie asked with a nod toward the sergeant who stood nearby, balancing his plate in one hand while he shoveled food into his mouth with the other.

Jack shrugged. "Just my little helper, according to Mason."

Pie stood. "I've got to hear more about this woman. I'll find some time so we can get caught up."

Jack nodded. "I'd like that."

Jack turned in his seat to watch the big man walk away. No one would ever guess that within that world-class wrestler's body was a world-class mind. He drank his orange juice and stood.

The sergeant gazed longingly at his eggs and sausage, but duty called. He set his plate down on an empty table and followed Jack to the elevators where they descended to the launch room.

Jack wondered how free his access was, like before, or was he forever tarnished? He touched the door pad and waited while it read his hand. The door opened and he walked toward the lifting body, less aerodynamic than any fighter plane, but able to glide back to Earth with directional jets alone, all the way to Copper Mountain.

The shadowy motion of people could be seen behind the dark glass of the elevated control room. It was a busy time prior to a launch. Across the cavernous room was the big board. The launch was set to occur at twenty-two hundred. Soon, it would be his turn.

He led the sergeant back to the elevator. He had to give the man credit; he never asked a question, just followed him around like a well-trained dog.

He exited the elevator on the medical floor. He passed by windows and looked at the technicians within; there was more instrumentation than evidence of biology. He walked down the central hallway, all the way to the end. He knew this was the right direction because there was an armed guard standing before the door. The guard wore the black of WSA security and did not move when Nichols approached him.

"Sir," the sergeant said from behind, "we should probably go back."

Jack stood in front of the expressionless man in black. "Get out of my way." He'd been planning on using his charm. "Don't make me ask twice." That was as much charm as he could muster.

The man's eyes took on a vacant look. Jack knew that look. The guard had been fitted with a full implant, so much more invasive than a simple transponder. The implant did something to them; they weren't known for their stability. The guard blinked and then stepped aside.

Mason did intend for him to be part of the team. It was the closest he could ever recall to thinking a good thought about the man. The sergeant remained in the hall while he walked through the door. A tingle made the hairs on his arms go erect; without proper clearance, a bolt of electricity would have shocked him unconscious.

He froze. Beyond a row of seats, viewing screens filled a wall. Three of the large screens revealed a real-time view of the crew aboard the Mars Explorer. It didn't take a doctor to tell they were dead. Renshaw was in a sleeping web with his arm floating above the deck. Dodd hung above the deck, half in and half out of the commode room, naked from the waist down. Slater was strapped into one of the command chairs with his arms suspended in front of him as if he were about to play a piano. They were dead and by all rights he should be alongside them.

"Captain Nichols," Smith-Jones said from where she sat. "Come on over," she added with a welcoming wave. "I want your take on this."

Jack forced himself toward the images of the dead men. He broke away from the macabre sight and looked down at her. "Good morning, Doctor Smith-Jones."

"Call me Kate."

She stood and gave his hand a manly pump.

"You can call me Jack."

"Jack, I've been going over this. I want to show you the video record of their actual deaths."

"No."

Kate looked at him with surprise and then nodded.

"You look a little pale," she said. "Is it the first time you've seen a dead person?"

"I've seen many dead people, but not many dead friends."

"Oh…yes…of course. I understand."

Jack ignored her. He couldn't keep his eyes away from the screens. There was a dark stain on the deck and bulkhead around Dodd's body.

"What's that black stuff?"

She turned to look. "It appears to be dried blood. Their red and white cells as well as platelets plummeted over the weeks preceding their death. It must be whatever blood he had left. That's Michael Dodd, right?"

Dodd's skin was shades darker than he remembered it. His spine was a row of knobs down his back and was flanked by shoulder blades that looked like small wings. He appeared to have starved to death.

"Yes, that's Michael. Did he get cut?"

"Not at all. I'll replay the recording of the time leading up to his death, you—"

"No."

"Captain, we're being sent to find out why they died and I intend to find out. He was starving and then bled to death, vomited and defecated blood until there was nothing left. If you look closely," she pressed a key on her remote and the screen zoomed in on Dodd's body, "despite his pigmentation you can see black patches on his skin. He probably bled into his skin and who knows where else? Possibly into his brain."

"They had plenty of food and an emergency supply of blood substitute. Why didn't they use it?"

"They couldn't digest the food and they ran out of blood."

"Radiation poisoning?"

"First thing the medical team thought of, but the ship's sensors didn't record any unusual exposure. During the one significant solar flare, they were within the protection cylinder. No, that's not it."

"Why are they all bald? Did they shave their heads?" Jack asked.

"No, it's part of the pattern. All cells, characterized by rapid turnover, failed. It reminds me of something,...I know it has to do with historical medical practice. I just can't quite place it. Well, it'll come to me."

On a screen to the far left, an earlier video was playing. Although the figure was wearing a containment suit, Jack could see Michael Dobb's face through the clear faceplate of the hood he wore. Dobb held a laser in one of his gloved hands, having just completed a slice through a plate-sized piece of the alien ship's hull. In his other hand, he held the cut edges of hull fragment toward the camera. The edges shimmered in a rainbow of colors. He put the two pieces into a drawer in the worktable.

"What did they find out about the ship's hull?" Jack asked.

"Nothing, except what you just saw and there is no record that they cut into one of the golden spheres. Shortly after that video was recorded, they became too sick to work anymore."

"You are right about one thing," Jack said.

Kate turned to him.

"We're going to find out what happened. We better, or we'll never come back."

"What do you mean?" She frowned. "If we follow proper procedure, we won't be at risk."

"Once we enter the Explorer, they won't take the chance of us returning to Earth without an explanation and a solution."

"That's not what Director Mason said."

"Yes, well, Mason is sending the good colonel along for one reason and one reason only."

"What reason?"

"Come on, Doctor, I know you're smarter than that. He's going along to make sure we don't return unless Mason gives the okay."

Her complexion took on a blotchy redness. "I'm going to ask Mason about that."

"Changing your mind about going?"

She shook her head. "Not at all. This is the chance of a lifetime."

"Excellent choice of words. I'll see you later." Jack walked away from the frowning Smith-Jones.

The images of his dead friends remained in his mind as he entered the hallway. He needed to go topside, into the open. He hurried to the elevator and the sergeant hustled after him. The elevator opened. Jack and the woman within stared at one another until the door began to close. Jack stuck out his hand to stop it.

"Hello, Jane, how are you?"

She giggled, not at all typical for her, and her normally dark complexion flushed.

"I'm doing well," she said. "Really surprised to see you. I didn't know you were back."

Jack dropped his gaze to her abdomen. The bulge of advanced pregnancy couldn't be ignored. The door tried to close, but he kept it open with his hand pressed against the sensor strip.

"Would you step out so we can talk for a few minutes?" he asked.

"I don't know if I should."

Her deep brown eyes were just as he remembered them. Her face had filled out, more round and softer appearing, but pregnancy couldn't hide her beauty.

"There's an alcove down the hall. I just want a few minutes, that's all. Please."

"All right, Jack, but just for a few minutes."

She stepped out with her hand resting protectively on the fullness of her abdomen.

Jack turned to the sergeant. "Why don't you go get something to eat?"

"I don't know, sir. I—"

"Get lost."

"Sir, I've been ordered to remain with you."

"Then stay right here. I'll be right down the hall."

"Yes, sir."

Jack escorted his ex-wife away from the sergeant. She walked with that waddling gait of advanced pregnancy and plopped onto the bench; little of her usual grace was evident.

Jack sat next to her. "So, how are you feeling?"

"Good, and you?"

"Fine."

"Not peachy fine?"

He shook his head. "Not exactly."

"What are you doing here, Jack?"

"I've been invited back into the program."

"That's really wonderful! I'm happy for you." She put her hands on the edge of the bench in preparation for standing. "I shouldn't be here like this. Mitch is expecting me and he'll be worried."

"Please, Mitchel Mason can wait a minute."

"Only a minute."

"So, how are you doing?" he asked again.

"Good," she repeated and leaned forward to look up and down the hallway.

"You look great." Jack was rewarded with a smile that made his heart ache. "We didn't get much of a chance to talk there, you know, at the end."

Her smile disappeared and she reached over to rest her hand on his. When she realized she was holding his hand she withdrew from the touch and laced her fingers across the fullness of her pregnancy.

"I didn't know you wanted to have a child," he said.

"You should have. I tried to talk with you about it often enough, but you weren't interested. There was a lot you didn't know, because you didn't listen, not really."

He sat straight. "What do you mean?"

"I should go."

She was about to rise when he placed his hand on her arm.

"What do you mean?" he asked more softly.

She relaxed back onto the bench. "Jack," she paused, choosing her words, "you weren't ready for what I needed, a devoted husband—wait let me finish—I'm not criticizing you.

We just weren't at the same place in our lives. Didn't want the same things."

"No, I—"

"Jack, I got lonely. Every time the Navy wanted somebody, you were there. Off to Sri Lanka, off to Pakistan, and then, when you came back from Mexico, you were so terribly injured. Every time you left I was scared to death you'd never come home alive. When you got involved in the space program, you promised me it'd get better, but it got even worse. The danger, and your mind was always elsewhere, on the ship, on the mission."

"That was Mason's doing. He told me I needed to fully commit if I expected to be chosen for the Mars mission. He was the one who sent me to the Cape, to Houston, out to Vandenberg. How do you think I got to ride the rail so many times? He wanted me out of the picture."

"Can you sit there and tell me that I was more important to you than getting to Mars? Can you?"

"You had your own career."

"I wanted more."

"But, in the end I threw it all away. You were more important, are more important."

"Stop it, or I'll leave right now. True, you did get angry and did lose your position in the program, but I know you, Jack. You regretted that beating you gave Mitch because it took away the one thing you wanted most, to go to Mars." When he didn't deny it, she continued. "This is the best thing for both of us and I really am happy for you, that you're back in the program. I know how important it is to you. More important than our relationship ever was."

"That's not true!"

"I have to go."

"I'm, sorry, I didn't mean—"

"I know. You never did. I really believe that."

"You never let me finish what I'm going to say! That damned—" His voice caught in his throat.

"If you're referring to Mitch, he's good to me, considerate and attentive. Constant."

"All the things I wasn't."

"If you must, yes, the things you weren't. I'm going now and I think it's best we not meet again."

She stood and he didn't attempt to stop her.

"You'll always be important to me," she said in a soft voice.

He stared at his highly polished boots and failed to see the tears in her eyes. He listened to her footsteps while she walked away. There were things he'd wanted to say, about how he was happy for her, and— *Damn it to hell!* He wasn't happy for her; he wanted her back. He stood and rushed to the elevators, but she was gone.

The sergeant stood by, but Jack ignored him and began punching the elevator button, repeatedly, when a simple touch would've sufficed. They took the elevator all the way to the top and left the building to walk across the concrete of the grounds.

When Jack turned the corner around the apartment complex, he could see the mountain slope and the magnetic track that would launch him into space. He walked toward the mountain with the sergeant behind him.

Jack stopped and turned. "What's your name?"

"Faaula"

"What do your friends call you?"

"Faaula."

"All right, Faaula. If you insist on following me everywhere, at least have the courtesy to walk at my side."

The sergeant stepped forward and began matching Jack step for step, never a step behind or ahead. It tickled Jack's sense of the absurd and he chuckled.

"Good to hear your mood improving, sir."

"Yes, I'm in a great mood. Have you ever been up the hill?"

"No."

"Well, it's about time."

"I don't know, sir."

"It's okay. Just stay by me. I'll protect you."

"I'm supposed to protect you."

"It was a joke."

"Oh, I see. A joke. I get it."

Jack shook his head, but didn't express his doubts as he led them to a paved road that ran next to the rail, up the hillside. Razor wire topped the electrified fence that bordered the road and rail. There were metal posts set at intervals, topped with silvery globes. The globes were filled with enough sensors to be able to detect not only who they were, but even what they had eaten for breakfast.

The path led upward and the exertion felt good. Finally, Jack stopped and sat down on a boulder at the edge of the road and faced the rail. They all called it a rail, but it was shaped like a trough, a perfect match to the belly of the scramjet, the lifting body used for space flight. The boulder was sun warmed. Jack closed his eyes to listen to the soothing whisper of the wind and inhaled the pine scent. The sergeant stood at his side.

There was the beep of a comm-unit. The sergeant put the device to his ear and listened for a moment. "Yes, sir. Right away, sir." He slid the comm-unit back in its holster. "They want us to return to base."

"Can I see that?" Jack pointed at the comm-unit and Faaula handed it to him. Jack stood and threw it over the fence, as far into the woods as he could.

Faaula's mouth dropped open. "Why did you do that?" He started walking in the direction of the electrified fence.

"Stop, Sergeant. That's an order."

Faaula looked back to him. "But...how am I—"

"I'll take full responsibility. Sit down."

Faaula remained standing, staring at him.

"Sit!"

The sergeant sat, directly onto the paved surface of the road.

Jack sat back down on his boulder. "Do you know how this works?" he asked, nodding toward the rail.

"Yes, sir. It's magnetics."

"I guess that about sums it up. The ship is pulled along, just above the rail. Frictionless acceleration. Did you know that the rail can be heated or cooled? It doesn't vary by more than a millimeter despite the fact that the temperature down here is pleasantly warm and near the top it's freezing. It's as straight as the laser beams that monitor it. A marvelous construction feat."

The sergeant looked down the road toward the spaceport and then to Jack. "Are we supposed to be talking about this?"

"Don't worry. I won't compromise you. Anyone with a subscription to Scientific American knows more than I could possibly tell you."

"I don't have a subscription to Scientific American."

"No, I don't suppose you do. You are rock-solid perfect for your job."

The sergeant smiled. "Thank you, sir. That was real kind of you."

"Where are you from, Faaula?"

"L.A."

"I mean, where are your ancestors from, your heritage?"

"My parents live in Long Beach."

"Okay." Jack nodded. "It's good to know your roots."

The sun arose overhead and passed into the afternoon sky, but Jack continued to sit in the dappled shade of the trees and listen to the wind. Sargent Faaula was again standing. He paced back and forth; his stomach grumbled.

"Hungry, Faaula?"

Faaula pointed to the late afternoon sun, as if that was answer enough.

Caring for a body the size of his was not a responsibility to be taken lightly. Jack smiled at the thought. "Why don't we go back down."

Faaula waited for Jack to lead the way.

They were walking downhill when there was a "rustling" in the brush, followed by the beat of flapping wings. It was rare to see a dove in this part of the country. The automated lasers that protected the rail fixed on their target. The bird exploded and its remains blew downwind, reduced in a second to ash.

Faaula was grinning. "Did you see that! Man, that was really something! I mean, sir. I'm glad you decided to bring me up here." It was the most he had spoken all day.

Jack turned away. There was an odor of charred flesh and burnt feathers in the air.

When they cleared the trees, the landing strip was visible, and farther in the distance, the nuclear reactors, three large domes. They produced enough power to meet the demands of a city, yet, when the power hungry rail was active, every light in the spaceport dimmed.

By the time they were walking across the concrete of the base, the apartment buildings cast long blue shadows across the parade grounds. It was too late to make it to the afternoon meeting.

Mason hadn't sent anyone for him even though he surely knew where he was. Was this the excuse Mason had been looking for?

"Damn it!"

"Excuse me, sir?"

Twice. He had broken the rules twice and he was about to

pay the price. Twice dumped from the space program. Even this crap assignment was better than nothing. *Stupid, stupid, stupid!*

He spun to face the sergeant. "You want to do something for me?"

The sergeant looked around as if he were suddenly lost.

"It's not illegal and it won't jeopardize your career."

"What would you like me to do, sir?"

"I'm going back to my apartment. I want you to find the biggest bottle of vodka you can and bring it to me."

"It's not good to drink on an empty stomach, sir."

"How would you know?"

Jack stalked off toward the apartment he had shared with Jane. He entered the apartment and slammed the door. He pulled the sofa over so that it was directly in front of the large window and sat without moving, while purple darkness spread across the mountainside. The rail was lit, a sign of the impending launch. The string of lights reminded him of a nighttime ski lift, but this lift ended in space.

There was a knock at his door. He hadn't expected the sergeant to come through for him. He got up and walked over to open it. It was Doctor Smith-Jones.

"Aren't you going to invite me in?" Kate asked.

"I'm in no mood for company."

"Maybe this will change your mind." She brought her hand around from behind her back to reveal a liter of Russian vodka. "Ran into a sergeant out there. He asked me to bring it up."

Jack reached for it, but she pulled it away.

"Ah, ah, ah," she said with a grin. "If you want this very good vodka, you'll have to invite me in."

"Come in then," Jack snapped and stepped back.

She handed him the bottle and wandered over to the window.

He unscrewed the cap and took a swig straight from the bottle. It burnt all the way to his stomach.

"What do you want, Doctor?"

"Kate, remember?"

He nodded, "Kate. What are you doing here?"

"Came over for a visit. Missed you at the meeting today."

Jack's knees felt weak, but he had to ask. "Am I out?"

"To be truthful, Mason was fuming mad, but a big guy, Pie something or other, came in and they had a talk. I think you're still part of the team."

Thank God. He took another gulp of the fiery liquid before sitting on the sofa.

Kate looked around the darkened room. "Saving on electricity?"

"How astute."

She sat down on the sofa and reached over to jerk the bottle out of his grip. She studied the label. "A good year."

"Vodka doesn't—"

"Where's your sense of humor? Do you have a glass?"

"No."

"You're not a very gracious host."

"I didn't invite you in."

"Exactly."

He could just make her out in the faint light. She raised the bottle to her lips and took a large gulp. There was no sipping with her.

"A very good year," she declared. She wiped her lips with the back of her hand and patted the sofa next to her. "Move over. I won't bite, unless you want me to."

He remained where he was.

She chuckled.

"Why did you come here?" he asked.

"Came to watch the show. They have me on the ground floor in the back, not nearly as nice as this. This is married housing, isn't it?"

"Yes."

"I heard you're divorced."

She handed the bottle to him. He tipped the bottle up and felt the burn.

"It wasn't a total loss," she continued, "at least you got the good view."

"You guessed it. I married her so I could live in this palace."

"I heard Director Mason married her. An interesting turn of events."

"Interesting? That conniving asshole plotted, kept me out of the way, and all the time was using her in projects that kept them working together. He sabotaged my marriage. The bastard!"

"It takes two to tango."

"It does not!"

"I stand corrected. It takes one to tango."

She took the bottle and had hardly swallowed when he took the bottle back.

"I want you to leave," he said.

"Are you going to throw me out? I hear you have a nasty temper."

"I do not! Who told you that?"

"Just heard, that's all."

"Then, aren't you afraid to be here with me, all alone?"

"I don't believe everything I hear. Are you going to drink or just hold it? Didn't your mom teach you to share?"

He allowed her to take the bottle. His mom. So little to remember, soft skin, the fragrance of lilacs. So very little.

They sat in the dark, passing the bottle. She was much easier to be with when she simply sat with him, silently sharing the night. He was secretly glad he didn't have to spend the evening alone.

The lights on the slope began a pattern of flashing, an illusion of light rushing up the mountain, a special effect with no purpose, unless it was to impress visiting dignitaries. It wouldn't be long now. By the time the scramjet shot out of the underground tunnel, it would already be traveling at fifteen hundred kilometers per hour.

He felt the sonic boom before he heard it. There was a blur, the fleeting shape of the debris sled followed by the ship, a flash of movement with no perceptible shape. It's hard to appreciate how fast fifteen hundred kilometers per hour is unless seen from a sofa.

"That's it?" Kate asked.

He didn't recall getting to his feet. "We'll see how you feel about it when you're being squeezed until you can't even breathe and then get ejected into space."

"You don't scare me. You sound excited."

"It won't kill you."

"How reassuring."

The string of lights returned to a steady glow, pearls of light stretching up the mountainside. He sat down on the sofa.

"Do you think Colonel Patterson is a good pilot?" she asked.

"It's kind of a misnomer. The time intervals and forces involved are too complex for a human to control. Your question should be, do we have excellent computers and software?"

"Do we?"

"Yes. I've ridden the rail many times in preparation for...well...."

"You were supposed to have commanded the second Mars mission, weren't you?"

He nodded. "I know the Mars Explorer inside and out. We were to finish setting up the base and go exploring. Roger Slater and I were going to walk on Mars. We talked about it all the time, but only Roger...."

"You must feel lucky as hell not to have gone."

Jack sat in silence. He couldn't answer that question, even for himself.

"I've been told you broke Mason's nose." Her speech was becoming slurred.

"I did a hell of a lot more than that. The media only reported a broken nose, but I also broke his cheekbone and jaw."

"You sound pleased."

"Not really. I stopped too soon."

He took another gulp before handing the bottle back to her.

"So, did you come to any conclusions about the cause of their deaths?" he asked.

She shook her head. "But I did remember what their pathology reminded me of. Before monoclonal therapy was perfected, cancer was treated with poisons, which had their greatest affect on cells with a rapid turnover. They called it chemotherapy."

"You think they were poisoned?"

"No, I said it reminded me of it. If it were that simple, they wouldn't have needed me."

"Think pretty highly of yourself, don't you?"

She nodded and took another swig.

"In ways, you remind me of someone else I met recently."

"Is that good or bad?"

"Good." He took the bottle back. "You know what I think?"

She slumped a little lower in the sofa.

He continued. "It's obvious. Those alien artifacts killed them."

"Perhaps. But to jump to a conclusion without data is dangerous. And, if the artifacts caused them to die, how did they cause them to die? One must consider all possibilities." Her speech was thick. "Speaking of possibilities, do you know what I'm thinking about?"

"Not a clue."

"Sex. I like it."

"Sounds like a normal, healthy appetite."

"No, I mean I *really* like sex. Are you interested?" She looked at him through eyelids that were alcohol limp.

Jack studied her. She was robust, a bit like a man in build, but still attractive. He shook his head. "Not tonight. I've had a tough day, but I do consider it a compliment."

"You shouldn't. I'm so horny right about now that a banana is beginning to look handsome."

"I think you've had too much to drink."

"In your dreams." She took another swig and was about to take another when he pulled the bottle away from her. "Hey, is that any way to treat a guest?"

He got up to visit the bathroom. When he returned she was sprawled on the sofa. He shook her shoulder and her eyes opened.

"Change your mind?" she mumbled.

He decided she'd be okay. He looked at the bottle; it was nearly empty. He let it drop to the floor and weaved his way into the bedroom. In the morning, he'd have to apologize to Mason. That thought made his stomach burn, or maybe it was the alcohol. He flopped onto his bed without bothering to get undressed.

CHAPTER 5

Ten days of intensive preparation passed. Pie managed to negotiate the return of most of the station crew, but not before the Mars Explorer had docked at the International Space Station. By this time, all the partner nations of the WSA had been informed of the disaster, along with a strong advisement to keep it a secret. The agreement included acquiescence to Russia's demand that the returning stationers land at the alternate site, Star City. The advantage of having the debriefing and rehab in Russia wasn't obvious. It was probably one more example of governmental posturing.

After spending the last ten days with Colonel Patterson, Jack began to have serious doubts about the man; he seemed to become more extreme in his views with each passing day. Jack had mentioned it to Pie, but Pie wasn't concerned; Patterson had an impeccable record.

On the other hand, Kate had been a delight. When given the choice, it was Kate he spent his time with, but they didn't repeat their night of drinking; space flight and vodka don't mix.

The team had a final meeting with Pie before they boarded the scramjet. Politics remained an issue; one of the two stationers who refused to leave was the stationmaster. Pie had instructed them to work out that issue in person and to use discretion.

With the closure of the entry hatch, the team was sealed inside the scramjet. The forward shields slid into place. The only light in their dim little world was from the monitor screens.

Jack adjusted his seat restraints. If it weren't for the fresh memory of having to tell the families about the death aboard the Mars Explorer, he'd be feeling happy with the prospect of returning to space. He'd had no choice; Mason had demanded it as his punishment for the missed meeting, or at least that was the rationale Mason had given. He couldn't keep Slater's wife and son out of his mind. She had taken the shocking news with such dignity, but the boy's reaction had been bizarre; he just sat there and nodded, didn't cry, didn't do anything except nod. He remembered Sandra Slater's look as she was led away; she had not only lost her husband, but was now under house arrest. Jack shifted his weight in search of comfort and readjusted his restraint harness. She blamed him. Pie had told him he was being ridiculous, but he had seen it in her eyes.

Next to Jack, Kate sat rigidly still. Her hands grasped the ends of the armrests. Beyond her was Colonel Patterson. His arms also rested on the armrests, but his fingers were touching the control pads. One might think he was doing nothing, but the small tracings of his fingers across the pads represented essential communication with the scramjet and the control room.

Jack's fingers were also tracing the patterns that would result in activation of the mag-drive and full engagement of computer control, but his pad was offline. He returned his hands to his lap and watched the lines on a monitor bend toward intersection. Status lights above the monitors turned from red to green.

The countdown proceeded. They were thirty seconds away from the point of no return.

Jack heard noisy swallowing and turned to Kate. "You doing okay?"

She nodded, but continued to stare straight ahead.

"Nothing more than one hell of a roller coaster ride, with a special kick at the end."

She nodded again.

The lines on the monitor screen converged; it was the moment of release, t-minus zero. The scramjet began moving. It wasn't the bone-rattling liftoff of outdated rockets; it was a gentle beginning.

Jack again looked to Kate. "Breathe. Don't hold your breath."

The acceleration increased. The scramjet climbed the tunnel, pulled along by mag-drivers.

"This isn't so bad," Kate declared.

Jack said nothing. The only limit to the mag-drivers was how much stress the human body could tolerate. He could imagine them breaking out of the tunnel, a ghostly specter as the ship shot along the rail, climbing the mountain. The sonic boom was left far behind.

The acceleration increased; it was a pressure. The pressure increased until it was painful.

Jack could no longer turn to check on Kate. The debris sled fell away and the ship shot into the atmosphere where the scramjet engines ignited and added their thrust. His eyes felt as if someone was pressing their thumbs into them, pushing them into their sockets; the monitors became a teary-eyed blur. There was nothing to do except put one's faith in software and the ship's computers. If there were to be a serious problem, they would never be aware of it, going directly from substance to vapor. He ignored the innate body sense that told him he was dying and felt the jitters of an adrenaline rush. The scramjets shut down and the ship passed the Kámán line, then the rocket boosters fired. His vision was a red glow.

Suddenly, the pressure was gone; the acceleration ended so abruptly it felt as if there was a malfunction. His vision cleared and he immediately attended to the monitors, reading the lines that curved across the screens as easily as most people read text. All was nominal.

The shields retracted. The stars appeared: bright specks and fuzzy nebulas, the Milky Way in all its splendor, unlike anything visible from Earth.

Kate's eyes fluttered open. "I think I'm going to be sick," she whispered.

"Aren't you wearing your patches?" Jack asked.

"Yes," she moaned. "They aren't helping."

"Take care of that," the Colonel ordered, but kept his attention focused on the monitors, while his fingers appeared to caress the control pads.

Jack opened the medical kit on the side of his seat. "Keep your mind on your own business. I'll take care of Kate." He pealed open a paper, took out the blue dot and applied it to her arm. "Take some deep breaths. No vomiting allowed. The med-patch will help in a minute. Deep breaths. You're a doctor. You know how to do this."

"A sick doctor," she groaned.

"Don't worry. The hard part is over."

"I thought you said it wasn't so bad."

"I never said that. I said it wouldn't kill you."

"Well, it did."

Jack smiled.

The medication began to work. She gazed in his direction

and returned his smile with a wan smile of her own. "You have bulbar conjunctival hemorrhages," she said without concern.

"If you're talking about the burst blood vessels in the whites of our eyes, we all do. It's natural."

"I wouldn't call it natural." She shifted her attention to the forward viewing windows and took an audible breath. "My God, it's beautiful."

The ship began a slow roll and Kate held on as if she were about to be tossed out of her seat. The sunlit Earth came into view.

"Kate."

"What?"

"Open your eyes."

She opened one, just a slit, and then opened both eyes.

The Mediterranean Sea was a deep blue. The boot of Italy was obvious, and to the west, the Iberian Peninsula. To the east was the Balkan Peninsula and across the sea was the Ivory Coast. The islands of Sardinia, Corsica and Cypress were clearly visible. It was an incredibly detailed map, but there were no words to identify cities and no lines to mark borders.

"I'm speechless," she declared.

Jack nodded. "Isn't it amazing? From space, the Earth is a single place. We _are_ all brothers and sisters."

The spectacle of Earth was more than enough to occupy them and then, as the scramjet rotated, the Earth drifted out of view.

The lines on the monitors twisted and curved, seeking the one best path, at the only acceptable velocity. The International Space Station swung into view. It had grown through the years; more modules had been added, more solar panels. It was a giant dragonfly with silver wings, bright against the crisp blackness of space and the speckling of uncountable stars.

A palpable change in direction occurred when the ship's computers fired a short burst from a navigation jet.

Jack glanced at the monitors. "We're on course," he said for Kate's benefit.

"Is that it?" she asked, pointing.

"Yes, that's it."

The Mars Explorer looked like it had been cobbled together

in a junkyard. It was in its "T" configuration, with the ship proper the cross at the top of "T". The base of the "T" consisted of huge cylinders connected by a spine to a bulbous engine. Struts and girders held the assemblage together. To some, it might have looked like an ugly parasite had attached itself to an elegant dragonfly, but to Jack, the Mars Explorer was beautiful. In the next moment, the pleasure was replaced with dread. He imagined the dead crew within, had seen them, and knew exactly where they were. It was a death ship they had come to investigate.

As the lifting body Galileo, now spaceship Galileo, approached the station, the station computers assumed control and began their mating calculations. The Galileo slowed in relation to the station and rolled to position itself for docking, both traveling at more than 25,000 kilometers per hour relative to the Earth. It was at moments like this that Jack was in awe of the accomplishments of his fellow humans, the engineers who remained Earth bound. The docking port grew and then rotated out of sight.

"Is everything okay?" Kate asked with a tightness that stole all musicality from her voice.

"Fine, everything is just peachy fine." Jack watched the monitor as a blue line snaked across, searching for the yellow line that was reaching across from the opposite side. The docking port neared the belly of the craft, ten meters, five, one, slowing, gently approaching, and then a barely perceptible contact. The line stretched straight across the monitor and turned red. The ship and station clamped together and sealed. They had arrived.

The Galileo's speakers broadcast greetings from the station crew, the two who had refused to evacuate. Neither China, nor France had insisted they leave, probably had insisted they stay. The greetings were in English, the default language of space.

It won't be long now, Jack thought. He would soon see the death aboard the Explorer firsthand.

"Is there a problem? Is everything okay?" Kate asked.

Jack forced the thought from his mind and manufactured a smile for her. "Just peachy. Be careful until you get your space legs. No need for cute little bumps to appear on your scalp. Is your stomach doing better?"

"Yes, haven't felt like barfing for over fifteen seconds now."

Jack released his straps and drifted away from his seat. It was always an adjustment; his mind insisted he was falling.

There was a "clang" and then a "hiss".

"What's that?" Kate grabbed onto Jack.

He swung around to face her. "Just the lock equilibrating."

"I'll go first for visual confirmation," Colonel Patterson declared.

"My God, he speaks," Kate said.

"Watch your language, Doctor," Patterson ordered. "I've warned you about that before."

Patterson drifted past, toward the airlock in the belly of the craft. The status light was green; the seal was intact, pressures had equalized. He opened the protection plate and pushed the button. The hatch swung inward.

"Let's join him," Jack suggested.

"Right. I sure as hell didn't come all this way to sit in this God-awful seat."

Jack helped her with her straps and took her by the arm.

"What about the cargo?" she asked with a glance toward the rear of the craft.

"We'll unload later. You've got to let go of the chair, or we'll be staying here."

She released one hand and then the other. It was a test of will and trust and she passed.

Jack pushed off head first, with Kate in tow. They sailed down the tube that pierced the belly of the craft. Patterson waved them through the airlock. The station air was tainted with body odor; the air scrubbers were efficient, but the residual odor was stronger than most would tolerate in their homes.

A woman awaited them. Her dark eyes were accented with epicanthic folds and her black hair was woven into a braid that floated away from her head like a tail.

"Mei Li, I presume?" Jack said.

She smiled. "Captain Nichols and Doctor Smith-Jones, welcome to the International Space Station." She drifted aside to allow passage down the cylindrical module.

Jack released his grip on Kate. He was no neophyte to space and intended to prove it. He sailed toward the second person, an angular-faced man, with dull brown hair pulled into a ponytail, and who seemed to have no body fat and little muscle.

"And you must be Gustave Theriot."

The Frenchman nodded with a toothy smile. "Follow me." With two words, his French accent was evident.

Jack looked over his shoulder. Kate held onto the handrail and pulled herself along. She was flushed but had a determined grin. Satisfied, he followed Gustave into the biggest component of the station, big enough to accommodate them all with plenty of room to spare. Two men had died constructing this module, the last to die in space, until... Jack tasted acidity and swallowed. He would not disgrace himself. No way.

"Grab a spot," Gustave suggested as he rotated until he appeared to be standing on his head.

Jack drifted over to one of the harnesses and strapped in, claiming his personal space from among the row of cubicles that lined the bulkhead. The sides of his shallow cubicle were darkly stained from the touch of former crewmembers; the space station was no longer new. Above him were monitor screens on the curved surface designated as a ceiling. All station function could be seen from this room, and controlled, if need be, but, for the most part, it was the meeting room, dining room and sleeping quarters.

Kate floated into the room and was re-directed by Gustave so that she landed in the cubicle next to Jack. She missed her grab at the harness and was about to rebound into the room when Jack caught her arm and pulled her into contact. Her face was pale and her skin moist. Jack reached across to strap her in.

"I've never seen a reaction this severe. Are you okay?" Jack asked.

"It'll pass," she said, but had to take a breath before she could continue. "Meniere's. Once in a blue moon I get an attack of vertigo. Just my luck to have it happen now."

"Guess you forgot to tell the WSA about that little detail, huh?"

"Did you tell them about your nightmares?"

"No need to get nasty. Why don't you put on another patch?" he suggested.

She shook her head and tiny droplets of sweat drifted into their communal air supply. "I already feel so doped up. I don't want anything more. It'll pass."

Jack continued to watch her while Colonel Patterson sailed across the room and expertly caught the harness to pull into one of the shallow cubicles.

Gustave studied Kate for a moment. "Another patch wouldn't hurt you."

"No." Kate gulped air, a body waste calamity in the making.

"Put on a patch, now!" Patterson commanded.

"Eat shit," she replied in a whisper, which wasn't far from the potential truth.

Gustave reached overhead and unclipped a device that looked like a vacuum cleaner. No one wanted to suffer a chemical pneumonitis from someone else's vomit. He watched her closely while she clung tightly to her straps. Her eyes were shut; she seemed to be coping, for the moment.

Mei Li was last to drift into the living quarters with the grace of a cat and took in the newcomers with a sweeping glance. All the while, she displayed her tiny smile, which seemed to be a permanent fixture on her lips, even when she surveyed Kate's struggle.

"Greetings and welcome," Mei Li said as she drifted without concern. "There will be time for us to get know each other better, but there are a few issues that need to be addressed at the outset." She spoke with a British accent and took pleasure in annunciating each word. "I am commander of the station. My word is law while you are here. And that includes you, Colonel Patterson."

"Now just a damn minute! I can't agree to that! None of us can."

"Speak for yourself," Jack said.

"Shut up!" He glared at Jack before redirecting his gaze to Mei Li.

She continued to smile. "If you would like, you can refer to the International Space Treaty that governs the station. I doubt that your superiors would be pleased if you caused an international incident."

He eyed her like a predatory bird.

Mei Li continued, "You will be directing the investigation of the tragedy aboard the Mars Explorer."

"What tragedy?" Patterson asked.

"Please do not patronize me. The Explorer has been docked for over a week. Our governments have apprised us of the situation, but it was already obvious to the station crew. When we tried to communicate with the crew aboard the Explorer, there was no response. Dead people do not talk."

Patterson continued to scowl, but didn't object further.

"As is true of all newcomers and even experienced visitors," she nodded toward Jack, "there will be a period of acclimation before any useful work can be done. Gustave and I will begin off-loading supplies. We will—"

"Wait," Kate interjected. "There is some very delicate equipment aboard as well as laboratory animals. I need to be involved."

Mei Li surveyed her with that smile of contentment, in itself enough to settle most concerns. "We are all members of the WSA team, as much as you Americans seem to have difficulty remembering it," she added in that sweet voice, and then bowed her head as if she had actually paid them a compliment.

That brought a smile to Gustave's face, revealing deep dimples in both cheeks.

Mei Li raised her face. "We have been informed of the contents of your cargo and are aware of the special treatment that portions of it require. We must work together, otherwise, I am afraid," she added softly, "this will be a difficult time for all of us and less productive than it could be. There needs to be trust among us. Gustave and I have been on station for a year now. Trust us." She smiled, lips only, with no display of teeth.

"What should we be doing?" Kate asked, indicating that she had accepted Mei Li's advice.

"You will practice moving about the station. Familiarize yourself with the modules. This is an unforgiving environment. A mistake will very likely not only kill you, but all of us. Make use of this time. In all probability, your duties will not allow another time like this. There is a spectacular view of Earth from the M-1 module. I never tire of that view."

"I'll go with you to supervise," Patterson insisted.

"You will not. You will stay here." She waited a moment. When Patterson didn't respond, she continued. "I would suggest that you begin by practicing in this cylinder. We call it the commons. In a short while, Gustave or I will be back to escort you around the station." With a flick of her foot, she propelled herself down the tubular corridor.

"Can you handle this?" Gustave asked.

Jack nodded.

Gustave sailed the vacuum device in his direction and

pushed off, with as much grace as Mei Li, to follow after her.

"Well, that was different," Kate said as soon as they were gone.

"Indeed," Jack agreed. "I'm glad they decided to stay aboard."

"Damn foreigners," Patterson declared. "We don't need, or want them meddling in this. They'll just get in the way."

"You know, Colonel—" Jack began.

"My name is James."

"I'll call you James when you start acting like James and not like Colonel James Patterson."

"What does that mean?"

"I guess that's part of the problem, isn't it? We're going to be living so close we might as well be wearing the same clothes. We have to accommodate one another."

"I'm here to do a job."

"And what is that job, Colonel? As if we don't all know, including Gustave and Mei Li."

"I'm here to maintain the chain of command. That is something you claim to understand, Captain."

"It sounds so innocent."

The Colonel's face screwed up with an impressive scowl.

Jack turned to Kate. She looked much better with color in her lips.

"What do you think so far?" Jack asked.

"Fabulous. More than I ever imagined. God, it's so wonderful!"

"I will not tolerate your profanity," Patterson growled.

Both Jack and Kate focused on him.

"I won't tolerate anyone taking the Lord's name in vain."

Jack shrugged and returned his attention to Kate. "Ready for a solo flight?"

She nodded. Her cropped hair was perfect for space.

"Just remember," Jack added, "you may be weightless, but you do have mass. If you bang your head on the corner of a monitor, it'll hurt like hell." He waited a second, but Patterson said nothing. "I think I've got it now. Damn is okay. Hell is okay. But God, Christ and Jesus are not. Right, Colonel?"

"Your disrespect is appalling," Patterson said.

"Tolerance, Colonel. It's the only way to survive in space."

"Are you being tolerant of me?"

Jack considered Patterson's remark and then nodded. "I'll

be more careful in the future."

"See to it that you are."

"Wheee...!"

Jack turned in time to see Kate sail across the chamber. She'd do just fine.

CHAPTER 6

Despite Mason's disinformation campaign and the release of additional fabricated sound bites, supposedly originating from the Mars Explorer, speculation grew. The tabloid press was publishing pictures of slim, gray-skinned aliens with black, almond-shaped eyes, claiming they had taken over the ship and were preparing for an invasion. Even the legitimate press was conjecturing that something had gone terribly wrong.

Mason pushed to accelerate the timetable. Despite the urgency, it took the crew a week to set up the decontamination equipment in the airlock of the Mars Explorer. Gustave had space-walked a cable over to the Explorer, which sped the transport of Kate's equipment, while Kate stayed aboard the station with Mei Li, preparing the station's airlock to insure there would be no contamination. The extra precautions were made at Kate's insistence when it would've been so easy to enter the docked ship through its primary airlock which, though sealed, was coupled with the space station.

On the eighth day, the team donned their hazmat suits and then their specially designed spacesuits. They were crowded into the airlock when it began cycling.

Jack heard his own heavy breathing in the confines of his helmet. He was remembering the men who had died and their families, and remembering the videos of the derelict spaceship they were about to visit.

"Are you all right, Jack?" It was sweetness that greeted his ears. "I'm getting some readings."

"I'm fine, Mei Li. Just putting some memories in order. I'll be okay."

"Then is everybody ready?" she asked.

"Ready," Patterson said.

"Ready." Kate's voice was high and tight.

Mei Li saw it in Kate's biometrics. She began talking in tones that could quench a fire. "You are lucky, Kate. You are about to see the naked universe, a privilege very few humans have had, or ever will."

They all heard a deep breath and then Kate's voice, "I wouldn't miss it for the world."

"All right, Colonel," Mei Li continued, "Gustave and I will continue to monitor, but the rest of the show is yours. Best of luck."

"We'll proceed as planned," Patterson said matter-of-factly. "I'll go first, then you Doctor, and finally Captain Nichols. I'm opening the lock."

The door parted in the middle and revealed the bottomless, limitless universe, dressed with sparks of bright light, some red, some blue, most a harsh white, and beyond the sparks of light was the misty cloud of more than two-hundred billion stars.

The Colonel reached out and clipped his safety cord onto the cable, immediately pulling himself into the void. Kate fumbled and stepped back against Jack. He took her hand and guided it to the cable, clipping her on.

"Go, Kate."

She reached up and pulled herself out of the lock. There was nothing beneath her but the endless universe. She froze.

"Kate."

There was no answer.

"Kate, can you hear me?" Jack asked.

"Yes." Her voice was small.

"Don't you think we should catch up with the Colonel?"

Patterson twisted on his cord until he was oriented toward Kate. His face was hidden within a mirror-faced helmet; his suit was white, but not as brilliant as the blinding white of the Mars Explorer, which was crisscrossed with sharp-edged, obsidian-black shadows cast by girders.

Kate clung to the cord with both hands.

"Doctor, you have a duty. I order you to do it!" The mirror-like finish of Patterson's helmet hid his expression, but his voice was as sharp as his command.

Jack saw Kate reach for the cable and begin to pull herself along it. She'd be all right. The first time was always intimidating.

Patterson was in the airlock when Kate arrived. He caught her arm, swung her in, and unclipped the cord for her. When Jack arrived at the Explorer, he too felt the strength in the Colonel's grip as he was pulled into the lock.

Jack was about to face a reality that matched his

nightmares, something he'd never have shared with the psychologists and still expect to remain part of the program. The only difference was that in his dreams it was his own face he saw on the dead bodies.

The lock closed and began to pressurize. With the return to a human-sized space, Kate found her voice.

She laughed self-consciously. "Sorry about that. It won't happen again." When she continued her voice was steady, without a trace of the wonder and terror she had just experienced. "We'll remove our spacesuits and put them in the sterilization cabinets. We've practiced wearing these hazmat suits at Copper Mountain, but be careful. They are level A military grade, but it is possible to tear a hole in it and if you do...well, just don't. Any last questions?"

"Get on with it, Doctor."

"As you wish, Colonel."

They stripped off their spacesuits, leaving them dressed in state of the art hazmat suits, covered from head to feet and self-contained. The inner door slid open to reveal the interior of man's first interplanetary spaceship. A motionless man was strapped into the command chair. As if drawn to the sight, Jack pushed past Kate and floated over until he could look Slater in the face. The spaceman wore his jumpsuit, but within the suit was something else; it reminded Jack of an Egyptian mummy.

Slater's darkened skin was tight across his cheekbones. His lips were stretched, drawing his mouth into a grin of exposed teeth. His eyes had shriveled until they were dull nuggets. The same leathery skin covered his hands, tight against bones, and his fingers were like claws tipped with long fingernails. His frozen right hand clutched a picture.

Jack stared at the dead man. If it weren't for the embroidered name on Slater's uniform, he wouldn't have been certain it was Slater.

Kate studied the corpse from the other side.

"Interesting," she declared.

While holding onto the back of the seat, she reached down and pried at Slater's fingers; his hand broke off at the wrist with an audible "snap", sending a small cloud of dust into the air. She was left holding his hand, which still clasped the picture. It was Slater's wife and son, a formal portrait, much as Slater had been a formal man.

"Did you like him?" she asked.

"What?"

"You heard me."

"Well, yes, I did."

"Not all that much."

"Roger wasn't the kind of person you could joke with, but he was steady, dependable. He was a good teammate. He shared with me the..." Jack's voice caught. "We shared the dream of walking on the surface of Mars. In that sense, he was my brother."

Kate took out a bag, put the hand in it, along with the picture, and sealed it.

"What're you doing?" Jack asked.

"After I finish getting a good look at it, I'm going to look closer, microscopically, and then even closer, molecular. I'm going to find out what happened to them. Let's take a look at the others."

She reached up for the pole that ran the length of the ship and pulled herself along it.

Jack also grabbed hold and pulled, but then released his grip so that he passed her to sail toward the shaft that led to the sleeping quarters. It was strange being aboard again, a grisly homecoming, with the specter of death scattered about the ship.

Renshaw was strapped into his web-bed, with his arm still attached to an empty infusion set, the last of the blood substitute. If it weren't for a few wisps of sandy-blond hair, he could've been Slater's twin, the same leathery, mahogany-hued skin, and the same death rictus. They looked much more alike in death than they ever had in life, shaped by the bones of their bodies, their muscles wasted to almost nothing.

Patterson was attending to Renshaw's personal cubby and overrode the security code. The cubby popped open.

"Hey!" Jack drifted over and grabbed hold of the webbing of the bed. "That's Ben's private stuff."

Patterson gave Jack a cold look, easily visible through the transparent plastic of his helmet, and then returned to sorting through the cubby. The contents floated upward: a silver-beaded rosary with the cross swimming before it, his lucky silver dollar, a picture of his pregnant wife. His little girl was now a toddler. He never had the chance to hold her. And then commercial cubes with naked women pictured on their surfaces floated up, followed by the helmet that would make the sex seem so real.

"That's Ben's stuff," Jack repeated.

"Captain, he's dead. I'm going to learn all I can about these men. When I'm finished, the agency will return the contents to their families."

"Not all of it." Jack declared. Renshaw's wife had cried out when he'd told her about the death aboard the Explorer. She had screamed with pain while she held her daughter.

"This time I agree with you." Patterson held one of the porno-cubes. "This trash needs to be jettisoned into space."

A pair of gloves floated up, perhaps a souvenir for his daughter. There was a trace of orange dust on them. Jack could not take his eyes off the gloves. In an unexpected way, it was the final proof that his crew had made the trip, without him. Unless they returned to Earth with answers, it could mean the end of the space program for everyone. The Mars base would never be inhabited.

Dodd hung in midair, half in, half out of the commode room, with his foot trapped behind a conduit. The skin of his bald scalp was tight, revealing the suture lines between the bones of his skull. There was a black stain on the deck and bulkhead around him. Kate pulled the body upright; although his skin was ebony, it was characterized by the same glossy hardness that made them all grotesque brothers and his face displayed the same sardonic grin.

Jack grabbed hold of the pole and pushed off. He swam down the tube, past the exercise chamber and into the hydroponics laboratory; the cylinder was still rotating, designed to never stop. He took hold of the central ladder to climb outward. The ladder accelerated until it matched the spin of the chamber. He twisted and released his hold to land on his feet. The blue liquid that fed the plants was visible beneath the grating, but the plants had withered. Ben Renshaw had insisted that flowers be included in the hydroponics experiment, but Jack could see no remaining color, nothing to differentiate one dried husk from another.

He took hold of a rung and, as the ladder decelerated, climbed back to the center of rotation. He released his grip, to push off again, into storage. It wasn't the supplies that he focused on; it was the viewing port on the rear bulkhead. He grasped the ring attached to the wall and hung in front of the port. Sealed aluminum canisters containing samples of Martian soil were secured in a rack and a dozen golden globes were strapped to the deck with netting. Beyond them was a dull-gold slab of the alien ship's hull, the size of a tabletop. He pressed close to the port window and looked to the side; the lock that led to the lander was closed.

When Jack returned to the command module, Patterson was helping Kate tether Slater's rigid body to the deck. Jack tried to ignore the gruesome scene while he settled into the second command chair and strapped in. He powered up the console to repeat the tests done by remote, rechecking systems. Life support was intact. He recalibrated and checked the monitors; there was no evidence of malfunction. It was as he had expected, but it had to be done, the basics confirmed. He heard Kate and Patterson talking, but he wasn't listening; he remained focused on his task. There was no evidence of toxic gases and the water supply was pure. Out of curiosity, he checked the huge storage drums that contained the water used as a propellant by the fission engine; there was plenty left.

When he had finished he stared at the screens. All was functioning. Everything was to specs. There was no evidence of excessive radiation exposure, nothing.

From a transport pack that Patterson had carried over, Kate withdrew a white rat with pink, beady eyes and put it into a cage. She was smiling. It was obvious the death around her had no impact on how she felt.

When she noticed Jack was watching, she spoke. "This is a cloned Sprague-Dawley, designed to be sensitive to toxins and diseases. They'll be our early warning system. You know, like the parakeets miners used to take into the coal mines, because they were more susceptible."

"No, not familiar with that."

"This rat is our parakeet. It's being exposed to the air of the ship. Next time we come, I'll bring a rat that will drink water from the ship, but not breath its air. Too bad we can't move in here. It'd make our work go so much faster."

Jack felt tired, more tired than he had any right to be. He dragged the memories of these men around with him like boulders in a backpack and he couldn't let go.

Patterson checked his air supply gauge. "That's about as much work as we can get done today," he declared.

"Just a little longer?" Kate begged.

Jack unstrapped and pushed out of the command chair. "The Colonel's right. Let's go back." He was first in the lock and waited impatiently for the others.

Once the inner door closed, they were bathed in ultraviolet light and then the lock was filled with toxic gas, colored red so they could see it. After the gas was sucked into space and replaced with air from the station's supply, they removed their spacesuits from the cabinets.

Kate did much better on the trip back, only needing help when it came time to detach the cord.

To Jack, the universe didn't seem nearly as spectacular as it had on the way over. As soon as he removed his suit, he headed for the farthest corner of the station, without talking to anyone. He sat in front of the viewing port of the M-1 module and watched nighttime swallow the Earth. A huge storm over the Amazon lit the atmosphere with splashes of lightening.

"How are you doing?" Mei Li asked.

Jack swung around, irritated that she had chosen to invade his privacy, something he would never have expected from a veteran stationer.

"I will leave, if you would like." Her ever-present smile was, for once, nowhere to be seen, but her voice retained that soothing sweetness.

"I wouldn't mind if you stayed a while."

She floated over to the middle seat and strapped in. She said nothing for a time and watched one of the many glorious views the Earth had to offer, a night storm.

"The Earth is so beautiful," she finally said. "It is a pity that every human cannot see it like this."

Jack nodded. "I don't think I'm going to find anything wrong with the ship."

"I think you will."

"It's going to turn out to be some kind of infection and that'll be the end of humanity's exploration of space." He sighed.

"I disagree. I do not think their deaths were caused by infection."

Jack studied her face, a mask of peace; there were no lines to mar the perfection of her complexion, no evidence of internal doubts.

"Why do you say that?" he asked.

"It is what I believe."

"But...is it just wishful thinking? Or do you know something you're not telling me?"

She smiled. "Things will be okay. I have news. We have been granted a special treat by the space authority."

"Oh?"

She nodded. "After weeks of silence, we will be allowed to talk with our families tomorrow. Of course, we must be careful what we say. The guidelines they have sent are rather restrictive, but still, it is better than nothing." She watched him for a response; he seemed as grim as ever. "No family?" she asked.

"No."

"There must be someone special waiting for you down there. I need to send a list so the encryption equipment can be set up."

"No, no one."

"If you think of someone, tell me, but I need to know within the next hour or so. When you are ready, come up to the commons. I am preparing a special meal." She displayed her minimal smile and pushed off to sail up the tube.

Jack stared at the Earth and thought about the people down there, trying to think of someone who'd like to hear from him. Pie was always busy. Not Jane, that was a definite. He wondered if she had delivered, if she was doing all right, if the baby was healthy. His mind turned to another woman, one with red hair and a fiery personality to match, Roxanne. He smiled with the memory of their single night together. He stayed in the observation module until he was certain he had missed the deadline and then ascended.

It was night cycle; the lighting was dim as he drifted down the tube. A hand caught him and he swung around, barely avoiding a collision with the bulkhead.

"My apologies." Mei Li released her grip. "I was waiting for you. I need to send the list. Did you think of anybody?"

"Maybe."

"Do you have something to lose?"

"Her name is Roxanne Wiley."

"Does the Space Agency have her on file?"

"I imagine. I tried to contact her from Copper Mountain."

"Very good." She handed him a warm squeeze-bottle. "It's

one of my specialties. Tubular Kung Pow Chicken. Goodnight, Jack."

"Goodnight."

He watched her sail off and then his attention was drawn to the warm bottle. He inspected the brown contents and decided to try it; his appetite had returned. He squeezed the warm mush into his mouth. Not bad, not bad at all. By the time he swam into the commons, everyone was strapped into their web-beds and asleep, except for Gustave, who was on duty. Jack settled into his cove, strapped in, and fell asleep. He dreamed of his fifth birthday party, a time from before his parents' death; he played hide and seek with a friendly giant named Pie Traynor and a pirate named Roxanne.

CHAPTER 7

Kate and Jack floated near the entrance to the communication cylinder, like two corks in a calm pond, not even thinking it was unnatural; adaptation was complete. They waited for their turn at the encrypted monitor and listened, but not really eavesdropping, mostly because they couldn't understand what was being said. It was Mei Li's turn and she was chattering away in Mandarin. It sounded like a little boy or girl was answering.

Jack clamped his hands together and squeezed as another wave of doubt passed through him. Why would Roxanne want to talk with him? After all, they had only spent one night together; it could hardly be considered a relationship. His mind was elsewhere, but his eyes were fixed on Kate's blond hair, which glowed from the light behind her; her hair was beginning to grow out.

"What are you looking at?" she asked.

"What? Oh, nothing." Jack smiled and released his clasped hands. "So, how are things going aboard the Explorer?"

"We're getting there. The Colonel has been a tremendous help."

"I'll be able to return to the ship in a few days. I've pretty much got the hang of operating the crawlies, but there is a lot of ship to inspect. I'd be there otherwise."

"Okay."

"You know that, right? It's not as if I'm staying—"

"I believe you. Jeez, don't get all sensitive on me. The one I don't get is the Colonel. Do you know what his expertise was in the Special Forces?"

"No."

"Cyber warfare. He's an expert in computer programming. I've never had a better assistant. His skill with instrumentation is amazing and he's always right there when I'm doing something."

"I bet."

"What do you mean by that?"

"A good spy makes himself useful."

Patterson swam into view and then pulled to an expert stop, grabbing onto a handrail. "You were saying?"

Jack smiled sheepishly. "Hi James. Kate was just telling me about how much help you've been."

"We each have our responsibilities, Captain." He swung around to face Kate. "I'll do what I can to assist you, but my primary responsibility is to be the eyes and ears of authority back on Earth."

"Ah hah!" Jack exclaimed

"I've never hid my mission."

Jack relaxed. "No...you haven't. I guess I owe you an apology."

"Why?" Patterson looked genuinely puzzled.

Mei Li appeared in the entryway. Her smile was wide enough to reveal her small, regular teeth. "It's so energizing to talk with family. Family is—" She looked to Jack and closed her mouth before turning to Patterson. "You're next, Colonel."

Patterson swam into the cylinder and out of sight. Neither Kate nor Jack had any intention of moving.

Mei Li gave them a look, a crease at the base of her nose; she was a master at showing her feelings with tiny changes in her face, but her silent disapproval was not enough to budge them. She shook her head, causing her long braid to wag, and pushed off.

Kate ran her hand across her hair. Static electricity made it appear that she had just been shocked. "Doesn't anyone cut their hair up here? Is it a tradition or something?"

"You can use an exfoliative cream like I use for my beard if you want to go for the bald look. Or, you can try to cut it while wearing the vacuum hood, but it doesn't work very well. And it's not a good idea to have tiny strands of indigestible protein flying around until the scrubbers clear it. Very irritating to eyes, throat and lungs. Worse than hair in your food. In fact—"

"Okay, okay, I get it. So, are you going to wear a ponytail like Gustave, or are you going to braid it like Mei Li?"

"Depends. How long do you think it'll be before you come up with an answer?" He wanted to add, "if ever", but kept the thought to himself.

"Hard to tell. I could get a breakthrough tomorrow, or it could—"

They heard Patterson yelling and swung to face the communication cylinder.

"You tell Patrick that if he doesn't start obeying you, I'll give him a whipping he'll never forget!"

The response was from a woman with a bird-like voice. "But, James, he's only seven years old. I was just trying to tell you what was happening. He's a good boy."

"Seven years is old enough. He better behave himself. I expect him to show a little leadership."

"Yes, James."

"Where is he?"

"In his tree house."

"Didn't he know I was calling? Why didn't you tell him?"

There was a moment of silence and then the bird voice again. "I did, James."

The silence stretched on until the Colonel finally broke it. "Guess I'm going to sign off then. Ellen?"

"Yes, James?"

"I'd like to talk with Patrick the next time I call. Will you tell him that? And that he's in my prayers every night. Will you tell him for me?"

"Yes, James."

"The Lord be with you, Ellen."

"And with you, James."

Both Kate and Jack wished they had followed Mei Li's advice, but Patterson saved them the need to talk and coasted past without looking at either of them.

"You're next," Jack said.

"Are you going to listen to me too?"

"No."

She smiled. "You dog. I know you are." She pushed off, through the hatch and into the adjacent cylinder.

After a few minutes, Jack heard her talking.

"Hey, Jones, getting any?" Kate asked.

Her question was answered by easy laughter. "Yeah, as a matter of fact. How about you Smith?"

"Slim pickings I'm afraid."

"Too bad. Boy, this is really crazy. Here I am in the middle of the Amazon and a WSA helicopter swoops in and drops off this equipment. Well, not exactly drops it off, there's a squad of nasty looking soldiers standing around the hut. Man, I wish I could keep it."

"Why don't you buy it?"

"Can't afford to."

"The hell you can't. I'm your wife, remember? I know how rich you are."

"Oh yeah, I remember now. You're that blond woman I see a few times a year."

"Very funny, Dickey."

"Seriously, Kate, we need to spend more time together. I miss you. I hate to admit it, but I'm beginning to tire of these youngsters with their breasts sticking straight out and their nipples staring with wide-eyed wonder, with brains to match."

Kate laughed. "You're too much, Dickey. I miss you too."

"How are things going up there? I can see your little home. It's brighter than a star."

"That's crap. I can see the clouds over the Amazon. You can't see a damn thing."

"That's one of the things I love about you, dear. Could never put one over on you. It's been raining like hell down here. So tell me, why are you up there anyway? I mean, if the oxygen went bad, what more is there to say, except, adios amigos?"

"I'm not supposed to talk about it."

"Why not? This stuff has got to be encrypted up the ying yang."

"But you aren't."

"Got me there."

Kate changed the subject. "How's the dig going? Find a new Machu Picchu yet?"

"Nah, just mud and bugs so far. But, I have hopes. There's this big guy next to me with all kinds of buttons and a big gun. Hey, nice gun," he said as an aside. "He's giving me this signal, you know, the finger across the throat one. What do you think he's trying to tell me? That my time's up, or he's about to cut off my head?"

"Dickey, I love you."

"I love you too, dear. And I'm dead serious about getting together as soon as you get back down here. Is it a date?"

"Wouldn't miss it for the world."

The screen went black. Kate unstrapped and pushed off. She drifted through the hatch and saw Jack hanging there, as she knew she would.

"What do you mean, 'slim pickings'?" Jack asked with a

grin.

Her smile widened. "Is that a proposition, Captain?"

"You and your husband have an unusual relationship."

"It works for us. So, what do you say? Want to make the three-hundred-kilometer-high-club?"

"Already have."

"You have? Say, weren't you married then?"

His face flushed red.

"Stop it. You're such a prude. It's your turn. Who is this Roxanne babe anyway?"

"How do you know about that?"

"Come on, Jack, you know you can't even pass a silent one in here without everyone knowing. You better get on with it. It would be pretty embarrassing for you to call from space and then stand her up. Are you nervous or something? You look nervous."

"I am not."

"Jack, I've never met anyone more transparent than you. Time's a wasting."

"All right."

"Well, don't sound so happy about it."

He twisted toward her as he drifted backward, toward the communication cylinder. "You're not going to wait out here are you?"

"Of course not," she lied.

Jack settled into the console chair; the seat was still warm from Kate. His fingers felt cold as he fumbled with the straps, finally getting them secured. He pushed the send button and there she was, instantly, and in perfect clarity. The wall behind her was plain. He couldn't place where she was; it didn't look like her farmhouse. She was smiling, her lips curled up at the corners. He had forgotten how sensuous they were.

"Aren't you going to say anything?" she said with a wide grin. "Or are you just going to sit there and stare?"

"It's good to see you again."

"Same here, but I must admit I'm surprised. I expected a call from you, or a message, or something, and then I read in the newscasts about you going to the space station and now you call, from space of all places."

"I couldn't call before now."

"Broken earphone?"

"Very funny. I wasn't permitted to."

"Okay...if you say so. At any rate, I'm glad."

"You are?"

"Yes, I wanted to thank you. Things have really been moving down here. After the NIH approval, it's like the door to heaven's money opened up. The pharmaceutical giant GLF has signed an agreement with the University. I have so much money, I'm not sure I'll even know how to spend it. And Rathburn, he's been walking around with his chest puffed out as if this was his idea all along. You know something else?" She didn't wait for him to answer. "There's been talk going around that this is Nobel Prize material. Imagine, Roxanne Wiley, Noble Prize winner. Just kidding. Not really. Why are you so quiet?"

"Well...."

"That's okay. Why *did* you decide to contact me? You're a good-looking guy. You probably have any number of women you could've contacted."

He bowed his head. "Not really," he said softly.

"I didn't quite catch that. What did you say?"

"Well...."

"Yes?"

"Well, I chose to call you because...." Hell's bells, he wasn't some school kid.

She nodded and smiled. Those lips seemed to suck him right in.

"I agree, Jack. I think we might have to try that evening again. Why don't you look me up when you get back? A nice dinner and then...who knows? You might even get a chance to drive my car, so to speak."

Jack grinned. "Sounds good to me. Where are you?"

"Oh, that's another thing." She laughed. "The government has put me up in a suite at the Gardston. Claimed the power supply for this equipment was inadequate at the farm. What the hell? I think they just didn't like it. Anyway, the government is paying for everything. It's great!"

"How's your work coming along?"

"Progressing, but I'm having a problem. The active molecule is particularly complex and elusive. Most unusual. But, at this level of support, it shouldn't take much longer. Anyway, it stops the propagation of both bacteria and DNA based viruses, almost immediately. Every single one we've tested it on. We're onto something big. They're pushing for my first paper to go into the next edition of the New England Journal. Pressing for immediate peer review. How's your work going?"

Jack thought about his dead comrades, being sliced, diced and analyzed by Kate. It wasn't a picture he wanted in his mind.

"Afraid to say anything about it? I was under the impression that this was a very private line."

"It is, except for two or three hundred security people around the world who are listening and watching."

"How exciting. Guess what."

"I have no idea."

"I even got a sample of mammoth muscle to analyze." She snapped her fingers. "Just like that. By the time you get back, I'll probably have my own research institute. I have to thank you, Jack, for believing in me. You've no idea how much that means to me. I'll thank you in person when we get the chance. Well, I guess our time is up. That's what they're telling me anyway."

"Roxanne...."

"Yes?"

"Would you mind if I contacted you again?"

"Not at all. I get to stay in this luxurious hotel. People do my laundry and pick up after me. Yeah, great. I'll look forward to it."

"Okay then...until later."

"Right. Later."

The screen went black and Jack sat there. She was grateful, but that wasn't what he wanted from her. He shook his head. He'd gone too far with his fantasy of this woman. What could he honestly expect? After all, they had only shared dinner and part of a night. Maybe it hadn't meant as much to her. She probably did that kind of thing all the time.

"Jack, are you done?"

He twisted around to see Kate in the passageway.

"Are you okay?" she asked.

"Of course I am. Why wouldn't I be?" He undid the belt and pushed off. "I have work to do."

He propelled himself past her and headed for the robotic lab, intending to send out another half dozen crawlies and monitor them as they inched along the girders and across the skin of the Explorer, searching for any anomaly. When he swam through the portal he stuck out his hand to grab a rail and swung to a stop.

Gustave looked up from where he was working on one of the repair remotes, the one he called "Big Dog". "Come on in. Plenty of room."

"Thanks, but I just thought of something I have to do."

Gustave shrugged and returned to the open cowling.

Jack glided down the central corridor of the station. He considered and then rejected the M-1 module, finally deciding on the computer center. He was pleased to find it empty; Mei Li was almost always there. With Kate and Patterson going back aboard the Explorer, he'd have some time to himself.

He settled in and connected to the main frame. His work began to scroll across the screen. He called up the history of the air scrubbers and watched the spikes grow on the screen. The yellow spike arose abruptly, two weeks after lift off from Mars. Biological substances were being extracted from the air. He called up a breakdown of the spike: the components of blood and skin, followed by excrement. He could imagine them, too ill to attend to themselves. There was a line that sloped off to nothing, epidermis cells. They must have lost their outer layer of skin and leaked whatever body fluids remained, like a second-degree burn, painful, exposing their entire bodies to infection.

It was a graphic representation of the crew's death. They had died within weeks of lift off, not months. Those bastards at WSA knew they had died ten months before they told anybody, at least anyone Jack had asked about it. Perhaps Pie knew. He suppressed the thought. Pie was his friend. He considered broadcasting his findings to Earth, to all of Earth, but then settled back into his seat. It would mean the end of the space program. He was restless with guilt. He would've kept their deaths a secret too. He shifted, trying to find comfort against the straps that held him. If they could only find the problem and fix it. There had to be another trip to Mars, and somehow, he had to be one of those chosen to go.

He switched to the data on the Martian soil samples and sat forward, pulling against his straps. Sample twenty-three was showing evidence of biological activity. It was the clue they had been searching for.

He patched into the Explorer. "Kate, you've got to see this! Access the soil data. There is evidence of life in one of the samples!"

CHAPTER 8

On Earth, it was every time of day, but on the International Space Station it was midnight. The entire crew had gathered in the commons. Mei Li had decided that it was time to talk, to share.

They were strapped into their sleep cocoons, Jack next to Kate, next to Patterson. Across the cylinder were Mei Li and Gustave. Seven of the cocoons were empty. They had eaten another of Mei's special meals; somehow she managed to make food in squeeze bottles taste like a treat. She had told them that part of the secret was in the spices, but insisted the most important ingredient was a good attitude.

They were each quiet with their own thoughts, but the station was not silent. There were the usual "clicks" of opening and closing valves and the "ping" of metal being stretched or shrunk by heat or cold. Occasionally there was a louder "cracking", a sound that promised someday the station would be destroyed by the stresses on it, but not today, not for many years.

Mei Li focused on Jack and smiled; her dark eyes were visible as sparks of reflected light. "Jack, why don't you start," she suggested in a voice as peaceful as a summer breeze.

Jack nodded. "Kate and I have additional data on soil specimen twenty-three. There is trace evidence of simple molecules with hydrogen-carbon bonds. PCR and electron chemical evaluation of the specimen did not reveal any evidence of human contamination. Our preliminary conclusion is that the active substrate is not of Earth. However, the chemical signature of mellitic acid is present which can, in combination with lime, cause the release of carbon dioxide and benzene."

"Despite the presence of mellitic acid, is there still the possibility of life?" Mei Li asked Jack.

"We were unable to detect any complex organic molecules. I doubt it."

"But it remains a possibility," Mei Li suggested.

Kate shook her head. "Highly unlikely, at least in sample twenty-three."

Mei Li focused on Kate. "Would you bring us up to date on your findings?"

"All of the crewmen died of the same cause. There were the expected findings, such as bone demineralization, but the unexpected pathology was the complete shutdown of their bone marrow, as severe an aplastic anemia as possible. At the same time, there was a general breakdown of their gut and skin, resulting in bleeding as well as the loss of other body fluids. They died of hemorrhagic shock. Yet, their bodies were well-preserved." She looked around the cylinder before directing her gaze back to Mei Li. "Perhaps the most amazing thing about their bodies is the complete lack of putrefaction. Their native bacteria should've caused decomposition. The fact is, I can detect no evidence of life aboard the Explorer, not even microbial."

There was quiet in the cylinder, so quiet that Jack could hear the breathing of his companions.

"So," Mei Li finally said, "what are the questions that need to be answered?"

"We still need to determine the source of the problem," Gustave said. "Did it come from the Martian soil, or the alien ship, or something that we haven't thought of, some third factor? Jack has already told us that there was no malfunction in the ship. Was there an oversight in its design? What do you think, Jack?"

Jack heard him, but was still thinking about the crew, bleeding to death. When he looked up, they were looking back at him. He shook his head. "I don't think the answer lies in a design flaw."

"I don't even know why we're talking about this," Patterson said into the following quiet. "It's the so-called alien artifacts and everything that implies. The truth has been revealed to us."

Jack turned to him. "There was a time when I would've whole-heartedly agreed with you. But, the more I've thought about it, the less likely it seems. I knew these men. They were careful, professional scientists. They knew the risks. They wouldn't have exposed themselves to the crash site and would've kept the globes contained, just as they did with the soil samples."

"How much exposure would it take?" Gustave asked, looking to Kate. "I mean, if it's some kind of infection, it must take time for the infection to spread. It can't happen in a few seconds, right?"

"It's not likely that an infectious agent could contaminate the Explorer after a few seconds of exposure, but I wouldn't call it impossible."

"But it's very unlikely, right? You said there was no evidence of any life on the Explorer."

"It's a moot point," Jack interjected. "The ship is intact and the specimen bay is sealed away from the crew compartment."

"Did they have the capability to take the precautions that Kate has instituted?" Mei Li asked.

"No," Jack answered, "but they would've had their suits on and the suits were kept stored in the lock. They would've been very careful not to—"

They waited.

When Jack didn't continue, it was Kate who prodded him. "What is it? Did you think of something?"

Jack thought about the gloves in Renshaw's personal cubby. He would hate to admit that their deaths had been caused by the failure to follow elementary procedures. Not his crew. Maybe Dodd, but not his crew.

"It is important that you tell us what you are thinking," Mei Li added.

Jack nodded. "I saw a pair of gloves in Renshaw's cubby. They were of the type worn outside. They should be checked to see if there is any indication of Martian soil or other contaminant."

"Why didn't you tell us that before?" Kate asked.

"Yes," Gustave agreed. "Why didn't you?"

"Please," Mei Li said, "we are not trying to find fault. We are trying to find answers."

"Stop this drivel!" Patterson looked from face to face. "It's time to face the truth. There are no aliens. Never were. That's delusional. Ninety years of SETI has taught us that we're alone in the universe. We've been investigating this for over a month and what have we found? Nothing. And do you know why?" No one said anything. "I'll tell you why. That ship is evil. There are no aliens. This is the work of the devil."

Jack looked for signs that Patterson had finally made a joke, but there was no humor in the Colonel's stern face; he was dead serious.

Finally, Gustave laughed. He didn't sound joyful, but it was a response. "Are you talking about _the_ devil, Beelzebub?" Patterson glared across the cylinder at him. "The Godless shall perish. This is the beginning of the Second Coming."

"Wasn't there supposed to be fire," Kate asked with an impish smile, "or brimstone, or something a little more biblical than gold balls?"

"You will live to regret your Godlessness. That ship is cursed," Patterson declared. "It's been subverted to the will of the antichrist. If you want to look for a cause, you need look no further than the hubris of humanity. The Lord our God created the Earth for humanity, but humanity wasn't satisfied. Some among us wanted more. Greed and hubris. We can blame no one but ourselves. We've opened the forbidden door and allowed Lucifer to come among us. Our only hope is to launch that ship into the sun, destroy it before it's too late, if it's not already too late."

Jack looked to Mei Li, but for once the woman seemed to be without guidance. Jack's toes and fingers began to ache. It was the first time he could recall that the station felt too cold.

When Mei Li finally spoke, they all looked to her. She wasn't smiling and her voice was barely audible. "I may not agree with your rationale, Colonel, but you may be right about what we should do with the ship."

"What do you mean?" Kate pushed forward, straining against the straps that held her in place. "Are you actually suggesting that we destroy the first evidence of alien life we've ever found?" Kate was truly astounded and turned her gaze to Gustave.

He shrugged. "There are more artifacts on Mars. I've learned to trust the stationmaster. She has good instincts."

Kate retreated into her cocoon and then peeked around at Jack. "And you, do you think we should simply destroy it?"

"No," he said on a long exhalation. "I think we need to come to terms with it. I don't believe we should be forced to cower on our planet, afraid to even reach out to our nearest neighboring world. This is our solar system."

"Even if it means risking humanity?" Mei Li asked.

"I don't see any evidence we're risking humanity. So far, three men have died. We're the only ones at risk. And, if Kate is as good as I think she is, then we're not even at risk."

"Thank you, Jack," Kate said.

"We need to know," he added. "Not knowing is the real risk to humanity."

"That ship needs to be destroyed!" Patterson yelled.

Jack turned to him. "Colonel, you are under orders. You don't have the authority to destroy that ship. None of us do."

The Colonel's only response was to stare. His eyelids were rimmed with red.

Jack looked to the others, but no one said anything. So, he continued, "Let there be no doubt in anyone's mind. What you're suggesting means that we'll never be allowed to return to Earth. Isn't that right, Patterson?"

The Colonel said nothing.

"That's ridiculous," Gustave declared. "My government would never tolerate such a barbaric measure."

"What do you think, Mei Li?" Jack asked.

She directed her gaze at the deck and didn't reply.

Jack turned his attention to Kate.

Kate shook her head and looked to Paterson. "You're not going to do anything crazy, are you?" She raked her gaze across the others and finally came to rest on the dark eyes of Mei Li. "Are you?"

"No," Mei Li answered, "but let us not close off our options. Let us learn what we can and then we will revisit this discussion. Is that fair enough?"

"Not really," Kate replied. "This conversation has gotten really scary." She shivered. "We're scientists. Let's approach this as scientists. Evaluate, gather information, make hypotheses, test them. I propose that we expose a rat to one of the globes and another to the soil. At least that might help us determine where the danger lies."

"What if the danger is only to humans, not rats?" Gustave asked.

"I guess that's what we need to find out, isn't it? That's what we're here for, for God's sake."

"Don't!" Patterson growled.

She shook her head. "Oh jeez, what the...okay, Colonel. You stay aboard the station. Jack will help on the Explorer." She turned to Jack who, after a few seconds, consented with a slow nod. "You're not going bonkers on me too, are you, Jack?

"No one is going bonkers," Gustave said, "as you so quaintly put it. This has been a very interesting discussion. I suggest we drop it for now. And from now on, hold nightly meetings so that we can all assess what is happening and decide our next step. Don't you agree?"

Clearly Kate did not agree.

"We will follow Gustave's suggestion," Mei Li stated. "Do any of you have an objection?" she asked, facing Kate.

Kate scowled.

"Well, Kate?"

"Oh, all right."

"Very good. Then for now, the investigation will continue, but we all expect to be kept current on any discoveries." She accepted Kate's silence as agreement. "On a lighter note, you will all be glad to know that we have been granted the right to increased communication with our loved ones. Not for a good reason, I might add. There has been a leak. The entire world has been informed about our problem up here and the alien surprise the Explorer crew found on Mars. I understand there is some disturbance below, both among the people and those who govern. We may not have much more time before our little group will be joined by others, so I suggest we use our time wisely."

"What do you mean disturbance?" Jack asked

"Some below, like the good Colonel here, believe this is a sign." She looked pointedly at the Colonel. "But, we are professionals, are we not?" She continued her stare until the Colonel nodded. "Get some sleep so we will be fresh for tomorrow. We will have access to the communication network at ten, station time. I did not have time to consult you, so I asked that the same contacts be made."

Mei Li waited a moment. When she heard no further comments, she dimmed the lighting. "I will be taking night watch."

"It's my turn," Patterson stated.

"I am stationmaster and I have decided I will take the watch. You should be pleased. I have never had a crewmember complain about the chance to get a little extra sleep."

"I'm not a crewmember."

"You are while you are aboard this station, mister."

Jack looked to Kate and saw the white around her eyes, staring back at him, but he'd had enough for one night. More than enough. He closed his eyes and feigned sleep, unaware when his masquerade became the real thing.

CHAPTER 9

Jack was waiting for Kate to return from the Explorer. He'd requested that she tidy up, pack up the autopsy remains, before he ventured into the ship. She clearly thought he was being absurd, but had ultimately agreed.

He was watching Mei Li while she sat at a console, wearing a helmet that covered her entire head. He watched as the feathery touch of her fingers traced across the blank panel in front of her; she was seeing things through the eyes of a crawly as it crept along outside the station, inspecting pipes and fittings, all the everyday things that kept the station alive and well. She slipped the helmet off and rubbed her eyes before turning in his direction, not surprised by his presence, as if she knew he was there all along.

"Good morning." The song was back in her voice. That alone helped the ache in his gut more than the patch he had applied to his arm.

"Good morning." He drifted closer and grabbed onto a handhold. "What are you up to?"

"Just checking things." She waited.

Jack had the feeling that she could probably wait for hours, an amazingly placid woman. Finally, he asked. "How are things going?"

"Good."

"Seen the Colonel?"

"He's down in communications talking with his wife."

"How is he this morning?"

"The same."

Jack nodded as if he knew what that meant. "Did you speak with your family yet?"

"Yes."

"Are they well?"

"Yes."

"Okay." Jack nodded. "Good. Mei, there's something that's been bothering me. I don't know how to ask this."

"Ask."

"Well, I've had this worry, I know it's silly, but—" Jack turned to see Patterson drifting down the tube toward them. "Good morning, James."

Patterson looked at him as if he were a stranger and continued down the corridor.

"It's your turn, Jack," Mei Li said, smiling.

"Sometime I'd like to talk with you about when the Explorer first arrived. Before we got here."

She nodded. "Anytime. I am not hard to find."

"Okay then. See you later."

He sailed down the tube to the communication module and settled into the seat in front of the monitor. A man's face appeared on the screen; he had closely cut hair, a stranger, but no stranger in ways. Jack had seen such men and women many times during his military career.

"Are you ready, Captain?"

"Ready."

Roxanne's face replaced the stranger's

"Hello," he said.

"Hi." She was wearing a nightgown with a plunging neckline.

"Just getting up?"

"It's not morning. It's night. Three in the morning as a matter of fact."

"Sorry about that. It's easy to lose track of time when you're sealed away in a can."

"I imagine."

"I don't want to impose. If you want to go back to bed...."

"Captain Jack." She shook her head; her hair fell around her face and when she looked up he saw those green eyes. She smiled and her lips seemed to swell. "Don't you want to know how things are going?"

"How are things going?"

"Slow. I'm going to have to rename my genome. Can't call it the primordial genome anymore. You remember that sample of mammoth muscle that was sent to my lab?"

"Yes."

"Well, guess what? No primordial genome. I don't quite know what to make of that."

"Causing you trouble?"

"A little. I've begun testing the extract on rats. So far so good. It cures them of infection within hours. Truly incredible. GLP pharmaceuticals is practically salivating. But there was an odd side effect. It may also be the key to the elusive male birth control pill. Sperm counts dropped dramatically."

"Really. I didn't know you would even be checking sperm counts. How do you do that? Little hand jobs?"

The moment he said it, he wished he hadn't, but she only smiled. "How did you guess?"

"Sorry."

"Getting kind of horny up there?"

"Well...."

"Oh, I know, all those hundreds of security agents are listening and they're inhibiting you, aren't they?"

"Well...."

"It's okay. I like shy. I've been thinking about you, a lot."

"You have?"

"Don't sound so surprised. You come into my life. All barriers fall to my research. I become queen of the campus and a handsome spaceman starts calling me from orbit. It may surprise you, but those things don't happen to me all the time. Are you always that good in bed?"

"Well...." He felt the heat of a flush.

"'Well' seems to be your favorite word. Well what?"

"I guess the proof is in the pudding, so to speak."

"An odd analogy, but I accept. Did you hear that, all you hundreds of voyeurs? The Captain and I have just made a date to have sexual intercourse. Isn't that right, Captain?"

He loved that smile.

"Roxanne."

She drew close to her monitor, until her face filled the screen. "Yes?"

"I may have to cut my work short up here. I feel a tremendous urge to return to my home planet."

"I'll be here, Jack. In the meantime, take care of yourself. There's been quite a bit of worrisome speculation about the death of the Mars Explorer crew. It would screw up our relationship if something happened to you before we could really test each other out."

"I agree. That would be a real pity. You motivate me to remain in good health."

"Until later then."

"Until later."

The screen went blank, but the vision of Roxanne remained before his mind's eye.

"Superb."

Jack turned in his seat; it was Gustave.

"How long have you been there?" Jack demanded.

"You're one hell of a lucky man. Not my image of a molecular biologist," Gustave added.

"She's kind of a free spirit, but very bright. She deserves...."

"You know, she might be too much for one man to handle." He laughed. "You should see your face. I was only kidding. You've really got it bad for this woman, don't you? How long have you known her?"

The frown disappeared and Jack smiled. "We've spent about six hours together, more or less."

"Six whole hours?"

"I was with her when I was called back to Copper Mountain."

"I see. Coitus interruptus."

This time he failed to get a rise. Jack only smiled.

"Kate's waiting for you aboard the Explorer."

The abrupt change of subject to death and dissection erased any lingering feeling of eroticism.

"Thanks."

Jack pushed up and kicked off. As he turned into the cylinder that led to the airlock, he passed by Mei Li; she was digging around in the medical kit. He pulled up. Any reason to delay was a good reason.

"What happened?" Jack asked.

Mei looked up with her contained smile. "That scrolly thing, you know that Art Nouveau thing around the entry to cylinder Liberate? It sticks out. I've been meaning to remove it for months. Frenchmen. Always needing to embellish." She applied the sealing glue to the laceration on her forearm.

"I know what you mean." Jack held up his forearm, revealing the pink stripe of a healing wound. "So, who's going to fix it?"

"Let's leave that to Gustave. Isn't Kate waiting for you?"

"Shit, does everybody know everything that happens up here?"

Mei Li shook her head. "Gustave hasn't told me how your cyber date with Roxanne went...yet."

"Don't believe anything he says."

"All right." Her smile said otherwise.

He pushed off and rounded the corner. After entering the airlock, he put on his hazmat suit and then his spacesuit. The inner hatch closed and then the outer hatch opened to space. There was the full moon. It was so crisp that the blacks, grays and whites gave it palpable dimension. The mountains arose from the surface and the rims of craters cast shadows that gave them depth. He felt drawn forward. He could push off and float away to drift in space for years before Earth reclaimed him. He legs felt wobbly and he took a step back, away from the abyss. That thought scared him, that he even had such a thought scared him; one wrong impulse meant death and he wasn't ready, not by a long ways. He smiled as he thought about Roxanne. No, he was not ready. He clipped on to the line and pushed off with confidence, following the cable to the lock of the Explorer.

He waited in the lock until it pressurized and then put his spacesuit in the locker, next to Kate's. He opened the inner lock and Kate turned. She quickly covered something up and he didn't try to see what it was. Instead, he looked over at the rats; they seemed content enough, swimming around their cages as if they had been born in space.

"Jack."

He returned his attention to her. "I'm all right."

"For crap's sake, I expect you to be all right. Come over here."

Jack pushed off in the relatively spacious command deck of the Explorer and swung around on the pole so he was looking down from above her. There were two new cages, two new rats.

"I need you to get a sample from soil specimen twenty-three and one of the golden balls."

The recent temptation to float away into space gave him the willies and made his stomach feel hollow.

"What's bothering you now?" Kate asked.

"Why didn't you tell me what you needed so I could have gone directly—oh, never mind."

Jack reentered the lock and resuited for space. He strapped on a jetpack, just in case, and leaned out of the hatch. He avoided gazing into infinity and took hold of a strut. Hand over hand he worked his way back to the lander and then entered through the lock.

For the first time, the dozen golden balls were within touching distance. He felt a moment of hesitation; the first to touch one was Dodd and now he was dead, all of them were. The globes were stacked in a net in front of the table-sized fragment of hull. He stared at the globes and shivered; they were made by an alien species for...what were they for? He pulled back the mesh and picked up one of the globes. They had mass, but not what one would expect from a solid, metallic globe; it was probably hollow. He pushed the globe into a transport container and sealed it. Next, he pushed the button that would deposit a portion of soil from specimen twenty-three into the other container. He placed both on the work counter and then, out of curiosity, opened the drawer. There was a piece of the hull in it, about the size of a dinner plate. He looked at the edge and studied the rainbow shimmer. He remembered the video of Michael Dodd slicing off a piece and presenting the shimmering edge to the camera. He scanned the drawer, looking for the second piece, when his comm-unit came to life.

"Jack, what's taking so long?"

"Did Patterson put up with this kind of harassment? I'm thinking about filing a complaint with the labor relations board."

"Come on, Jack. I'm not good at thumb twiddling."

"All right. I'll be there in a few minutes."

He replaced the piece in the drawer and headed for the lock.

When he reentered the command module, Kate was waiting, hands out, wanting the container with the golden globe first. She turned the container over as she inspected the globe. It was reflective and smooth, not a mark on it, a hollow, golden ball, perfect, as if made by a jeweler.

"You know something, Jack?"

"What?"

"Dickey, you know, my husband?"

"Yes."

"Well, Dickey told me something interesting today. He said that when he heard about the golden balls brought back from Mars, it reminded him of something. There was this anthropologist named Timmins who found a golden ball when he was excavating in Kenya, but it was in a layer previously established to be about four thousand years old. Well before mankind began working with metals like this and certainly before such a perfectly shaped sphere could be produced. It was considered to be a hoax, but he sent it back to England anyway. It's probably somewhere in storage at the British

Museum of Natural History. I think I should mention that to someone, although it's hard to see what the relationship is."

"I wouldn't worry about it. By now the WSA is already rummaging through boxes looking for it."

"You mean, they were listening in?"

"Gee, what do you think, Kate?"

"You don't have to be sarcastic with me." She turned away and attached the container with the golden globe to a rat's self-contained cage and then did the same with the compacted soil sample.

While she was working, Jack drifted back down to the living quarters. Renshaw's body was gone from the sleeping web and Dodd was no longer drifting half in and half out of the head. The lumps secured under the plastic tarp in the command module attested to where they had gone. He opened Renshaw's cubby. It was empty.

He called out. "Kate, what happened to that glove I mentioned?"

"Patterson took it."

"He wouldn't take it back to the station, would he?"

"Don't be ridiculous. He's got a lock box in the Explorer where he's been saving things like a squirrel gathering nuts. It's probably in there. I'll have to get the key from him so I can analyze it."

Jack pushed off and sailed through the exercise cylinder to the hydroponics module. He stared at the spinning cylinder. Its outer surface was a whirling yellow of dried crusts. A half formed thought skitted across his mind and was gone. He pushed off and sailed back through central tunnel to the command module.

"Kate."

"Yes?" She straightened and swung around to face him.

"If we can identify the cause, will you be able to devise a treatment?"

"Probably not."

Jack floated in front of her.

"Don't worry," she continued, "if we can identify the cause, I have enough specialized equipment on board to send a molecular analysis down below. They'll be able to develop a treatment."

"Are you sure?"

"What's all this negativity about? Did Roxanne dump you?"

"What is it with you people? Don't you have a life of your own?"

"As a matter of fact, yes. Have you reconsidered my request to be inducted into the three-hundred-kilometer-high-club?"

"There are dead bodies in here."

"Don't play stupid. I didn't mean here."

"Kate...it's not that. It's just...."

"Okay, your loss."

Jack looked away, at the original rat cages; one of the rats was floating without leg movements. He swam over until his faceplate was against the transparent cage. The rat didn't move; it wasn't breathing.

"Kate, come here. It was okay a few minutes ago."

Kate arrived at his side a few seconds later. She immediately pushed off and swung into one of the command chairs where she accessed the ship's computer. While she was working, Jack glanced over at the other cage and saw bright red blood pouring out of the second rat's mouth to be whisked away by the cage's suction cleaner. The rat shook a couple of times and then was as still as the first.

Kate spoke as she read the output from the monitor. "There's a peak in iron containing proteins, looks like blood."

"Oh, I think so."

"Why—" She saw the second dead rat. Both rats had died, one exposed to the air of the Explorer and the other to the water.

Jack glanced over at the sealed cage with the golden ball and then at the red-orange pellet of soil in the second cage. "Good luck."

"What?"

"I was talking to the rats."

"This may be a good thing."

"Right."

"I may be able to isolate the agent that caused this bleeding. I've got work to do. You can go back to the station, if you'd like."

He shook his head. "I'll stay with you."

She smiled. "Thanks."

She carefully transferred the first dead rat into her diagnostic cabinet, keeping it safe from cross contamination. She slid her hands into the glove holes and expertly dissected the rat, taking tissue specimen as well as cultures. After flash freezing tissue, she used a microtone to make razor-thin slices and sterilized these specimens before she removed them to insert them into an automated analyzer. When she had completed the job with the second rat, she turned to Jack. "We'll be getting some data by this evening. Should we?" She motioned toward the lock.

This time Jack didn't mind waiting for the decontamination process, almost wishing that Kate had added even more safeguards.

CHAPTER 10

Roxanne was on the screen. To Jack, she could not look less than sexy; it was the way nature had formed her, but she was not her usual, over-the-top self. She appeared tired.

"Hello, Roxanne."

"You can call me Roxy, if you want. That's what my sister calls me and I seem to be talking with you more than anyone else these days."

"You have a sister?"

"Don't look so surprised."

"There's more than one of you?"

"Nope, there's only one of me. How are things in space?"

"Not so good."

She shook her head. "Not good here either. First of all, it's more complex than I thought. I haven't found the true trigger, but I have been able to stimulate the gene cluster to transcribe, at least temporarily. I've discovered it codes for more than one protein and all of them seem to be repressors. Kind of like a master gene, or more exactly, a master operon. I think I've found the key to controlling the entire genome. In ways, it scares the hell out of me. I can now truly appreciate the terrible conflict experienced by the scientists who participated in the Manhattan Project. Don't you dare roll your eyes at me!"

"I wasn't rolling my eyes."

"Yes, you were! Jack, I'm not kidding. This is an incredibly powerful discovery. It could be wonderful, or terribly dangerous. And I don't feel like I have control of the situation. You know those rats that I tested the anti-infection protein on?"

"Yes."

"They all died."

"Aplastic crisis?"

Roxanne's eyes opened wider. "Well, yes, that was a part of it, plus ulceration of the GI tract. They bled to death. How did you know that?"

"Our rats died too."

"What happened?"

"Same as yours."

Her gaze drifted away from the monitor, not looking at anything in particular. "I don't know what to make of this," she murmured and then looked up. "It must be a coincidence. There are many causes of aplastic crises. The Mars Explorer has been kept under strict quarantine, right?"

"That's right."

"Still, it does seem like a weird coincidence. Anything else you can tell me?"

The security agents had allowed the conversation to progress this far. Apparently they considered Roxanne to be within the information loop and had a need to know.

"Yes," Jack said. "There is one other thing that's been bothering me. Renshaw's flowers died."

She raised one questioning eyebrow.

"The hydroponics tanks were functioning the way they'd been designed to. It's an automated system. The plants didn't require attention, but all of them were dead."

"Let me see. Let me think." She raked her fingers through her hair. "Plants, rats, humans." Her fingers stopped and she stared at him.

"They all do have something in common, don't they?" he said.

"The genome," she whispered. "My God. The project has grown so large. I have good, careful people working for me. I'm certain they follow containment protocol." She arose and stripped off her nightgown to begin dressing. "I have to go."

"Where to? It's midnight down there."

"Have to check on some things. Contact me again tomorrow, would you?"

"Yes."

The screen went black. The pleasure of seeing a naked Roxanne faded quickly. Jack felt heavy in the weightlessness of space, but he pushed himself up to allow Mei Li her turn.

She swung around the corner with her usual grace and waited with one hand on a hold. The wound on her forearm was dressed with a bloodstained bandage.

"I see you gashed yourself again," Jack said. "I'm going to remove that scroll work right now."

Mei glanced at her arm. "No, it just has not healed yet and do not worry about fixing it. I shamed Gustave into doing it."

Jack remained in the communication chair. "I need to talk with you."

"Yes, yes, I know. You already said that. Can I have my turn now?"

"Now."

"Come on, Jack. You know they only give us a few minutes. Move."

She was obviously eager to speak with her little boy and her husband. She had been at the station far longer than expected.

"Sure." Jack unbuckled and pushed out of the seat. "Say hello to them for me."

She smiled. "I will do that."

Jack rounded the corner and swam down the central tube to the living quarters.

Patterson was hanging in front of Kate. He held onto a rail with one hand and, to make a point, swung his other hand in a fist above his head. She wasn't afraid; it was just the Colonel being the Colonel. She looked past him to Jack and Patterson twirled around to face him.

"So," Jack began, "what are you up to, James? Haven't seen much of you lately. Been taking space walks I hear. Sightseeing?"

Patterson fixed him with a brittle look.

"Well?" Jack urged with as friendly a smile as he could manufacture.

"I've been checking the integrity of the outer lines."

"Isn't that what the crawlies are for?"

"I don't have to explain myself to you." He pushed off and glided past.

Jack looked back to Kate with a shrug.

"Glad you showed up," Kate said. "Man, that guy is going off the deep end."

"What do you mean?"

"He was quoting bible passages to me about how all this was predicted. He truly believes there are no aliens. His logic is that man was made in the image of God and therefore those globes were made by not-man, which only leaves the devil."

Jack hated to come to Patterson's defense, but.... "You don't get to be a Colonel in the Special Forces without discipline and a strong sense of duty. He may bluster but he won't do anything counter to his orders, or that would jeopardize the mission. We don't have to worry about him."

"Oh, I see. By golly, that's really reassuring. Did I tell you he's crazy? Say, did you read the memo from Copper Mountain yet?"

"No."

"Well, you were right. I didn't have to tell them about the globe in the museum. They're listening to everything we say, aren't they?"

"Yes."

"Even now?"

"Probably."

"So...is that why you said what you did about the Colonel. Kissing up?"

"Stop it, Kate. I've something important to discuss with you."

"Do they have video feed too?"

"If they want. Why?"

"Oh, my God." She chuckled.

"What?"

"Nothing. What did you want to say?"

"Have you discovered the cause of the rat's deaths?" Jack asked.

"No. There are a hell of a lot of molecules to sort through."

"There's something happening on Earth that may be related to our problem up here."

"No kidding."

"Just stop and listen for a minute will you?" When she said nothing he continued. "Are you familiar with Roxanne Wiley's work?"

"A little. Something about primordial genome bull shit."

"It's not bull shit and it's not a primordial genome. It's possible that this...she called it an operon, began appearing in the gene pool less than five thousand years ago."

"Only bacteria have operons."

"I'm not a macromolecular biologist. I'm only repeating what she told me."

"Are you trying to relate this to the memo?"

"I told you I haven't read it yet. Listen to me, Kate. The genome was not present in tissue that dates to about five thousand years ago."

"Are you suggesting that the globe Timmins found has something to do with this primordial gene thing?"

"I'm just trying to tell you what I found out."

"How much data does Wiley have? There can't be that much DNA available for analysis from five thousand years ago."

"I don't know. The important thing is that Roxanne has identified some proteins that caused the death of her test animals and her animals died…just like ours. You may want to have her send up the amino acid sequences. It might simplify your search."

"Thanks. I'll do that, but I hope to hell it doesn't match anything we've got up here."

"That's the damned truth. There's one more thing. Did you notice that wound on Mei Li's arm?"

"Yeah, so?"

"It's just a hunch, but I think you should do a sperm count on Patterson, Gustave and me."

"So, you think a rogue sperm attacked her, huh?"

"Damn it! This is serious. Just do it."

"Relax. I already did Gustave."

"You did?"

"Jealous?"

"What do you mean?"

"The dumb game again, huh? Although it is a little disconcerting to think that maybe hundreds, or thousands of people were watching. It wasn't my best performance."

"Performance?"

"Gustave strapped us into a sleeping web and we did the deed. I must admit it was disappointing. For every action there is an equal and opposite reaction, awkward. I missed that earthly sense of pressure. When he—did you swallow something that tasted bad?"

"Spare me the details. Just check the sperm counts will you?"

"Sure. You first."

"All right. In a little while."

Kate shook her head. "You're such a prude. It's so much more fun being a pervert. Are you blushing?"

"I'm going to take a look at the memo."

"You do that. But I expect your sperm back here before supper."

"Yes, well, okay."

He pushed off and headed for communications, where he

settled into a seat and strapped in. There were two messages; the first was from Copper Mountain. He entered the "continue" command. The message was in text only: "The globe that was discovered in Kenya has been found to be highly unusual. It consists of molecular thin layers of a gold alloy, alternating with what appears to be a degraded organic substance. The globe was found to be capable of conducting heat around itself and then shedding it. As it cooled, microscopic pores appeared and then, as it cooled further, the pores closed. The inside of the globe was empty. Attempts at dating it have failed."

Jack leaned back. A globe that was sealed when hot or cold, but at just the right temperature opened to form pores. A perfect tool to seed with, it would seem. He had to tell Roxanne about this.

The second message was from Mason and began with a request for Jack to enter his security code. He entered his code and the message continued. "For your eyes only." He looked toward the entry hatch; no one was around. "A serious issue has arisen. The psychological profiling team has become increasingly concerned about Colonel Patterson. If it is determined that he is a threat to the mission, you will be instructed to take him out. Be prepared."

Take him out?

Mei Li flew into the cylinder, breathless. "The Colonel. He's taken the Explorer!"

"What?"

"He's already a kilometer away from the station."

"Damn it to hell." He turned back to the console. "Connect to the Mars Explorer."

A vision of Colonel James Patterson appeared. He was sitting in the first command chair, dressed in his station jumpsuit, wearing no protective gear.

"James." Jack began.

Patterson ignored him while he finished making some adjustments on his finger pad.

"James, we need to talk."

Patterson made a few last adjustments and then looked directly into the screen. Jack had never seen his eyes so bright.

"Colonel, you need to bring the ship back. We need it. We have to understand what has happened so we can protect the

Earth."

Patterson nodded. "In that respect, we are the same, you and I."

Jack was not about to agree.

He continued. "You may as well save your breath. General Clark has already tried to alter my decision and, if he couldn't do it, you certainly cannot."

"Why are you doing this?"

"For the very reason you stated. My life is little payment for saving the Earth from the evil aboard this ship. I give it gladly for the Earth and for God."

"But, we need that ship. We're rational men. We can figure out what the danger is and then nullify it."

"The arrogance of man. I reviewed your service record before I agreed to accept you on my team. Seal Team Six, to say nothing of that firefight in Mexico. Other than for that tiff with Mitchell Mason, it's quite impressive and that's saying a lot, coming from me. However, you also embody all the bad qualities of our current Godless society. You are loyal, but arrogant. Humility, my good Captain, learn humility before God."

"Colonel, you know the WSA will take control of the ship and bring it back. Come back now, before it's too late. I'll stand up for you."

"How generous. I truly appreciate your offer, but you're wrong. I have disabled all connection with the WSA. I control this ship and I *will* do the right thing."

"How do I get you to understand? You may be destroying our only chance of defeating this threat. Don't you realize that if that ship crashes into the Earth you could cause a terrible epidemic?"

"I do realize that. I'm taking the ship out of orbit. I've plotted a course for Venus and from there the ship will be slung toward the sun."

"Colonel, you *are* courageous and I believe you think you're doing the right thing, but you're dead wrong."

Patterson smiled, thin-lipped. "Dead is right, but not wrong."

"What about your family? Your wife and son?"

"This I'll ask of you. I made a video chip. You'll see it clipped to the side of the monitor. I'd appreciate it, if you would make sure my family receives it. As one military man to another, I believe I can count on you for that. Take care, Captain Nichols, and when you return to Earth, take some time and search for the truth in the Book of God. You will find the way you have lost. God bless you all." The screen went blank.

"Reconnect to the Mars Explorer." Nothing happened. "Connect to Copper Mountain."

A security woman appeared on screen.

"I need to speak with Mitchell Mason. Now!"

"Sir, he is unavailable."

"Damn it, this is an emergency! Patterson has taken the Explorer and is headed into space."

"Sir, we're aware of the situation and we're working on it." The screen went blank again.

"Can they send a scramjet from Earth?" Mei Li asked.

Jack shook his head. "Not enough time."

"What about your scramjet?"

"Maybe. Computer, reconnect with Copper Mountain."

The security woman reappeared.

"Request navigational support to intercept the Explorer using the scramjet Galileo."

"Negative, Captain. The Colonel has disabled the scramjet. We will contact you when a plan of action has been developed."

"You do that. By that time he'll be half way to the moon!" The screen went blank.

"They will not try to destroy the Explorer," Mei Li said.

Jack nodded. "They wouldn't want to risk any of those globes falling back to Earth. Probably, some below are relieved that Patterson has taken control of the Explore and is leaving Earth orbit. Out of sight. Out of mind."

"What can we do?"

"I don't know, probably nothing." He picked up the video chip and slid it into the reader.

Patterson had his hands clasped before him, his fingers interlaced. He appeared more at peace than he had in weeks. "Ellen, this will be the last time we can speak on this earthly plain, but I wanted you to know how much I love you and the boy. Patrick must be made to understand that I did not desert my duty, but that I'm obeying a higher authority. You know I'm not an impulsive man. I've given this a lot of thought and I've prayed on it. I'm doing the work of God. I hope Patrick doesn't grow up hating me. I tried to be a good husband and father. I know I didn't always succeed, but God knows I tried. Tell my son that his father loves him and will always be watching over him. Tell him to obey you as if I were still there, still part of the family. Ellen, I'll miss you most of all. I love you. May God always be with you." He blew a kiss at the screen and the short video ended.

The silence drifted on with both of them staring at the now blank monitor.

It was Mei Li who broke the silence. "I guess that is that. We may as well return to Earth."

Jack twisted in his seat to look up at her. "You know that's not possible."

"What do you mean? The ship is gone, along with the artifacts."

"You chose to stay, Mei. You were asked to leave along with the others, but you chose to stay. No one is going anywhere."

"I am not going to stay up here forever. I have a family, a life to live. I will be appointed the president of a university when I return to China. My family will prosper. If they refuse to send a scramjet for us, we can use the crew rescue vehicle."

Jack glanced at the sore on Mei Li's arm and then turned back to the console with a sigh. "Mei, we solve this problem with our stored data, or we die here."

"That is a lie."

Jack twisted around with enough force that he lifted away from the console and found himself face to face with the petite woman. "Is it really? Tell me, Mei. Why isn't your cut healing?" He held up his own arm with the pink wound still visible, but fading. "We are not going to risk infecting the Earth."

The perfect sphere of an escaped tear floated in the space between them. She pushed off.

Jack didn't follow. He was drifting aimlessly in the communication cylinder, an accurate reflection of his state of mind, when Kate appeared in the hatch. She hadn't looked this pale since her first day in space. Her lips trembled.

"Jack."

He grabbed a handhold to meet her gaze.

"Jack, I've just been down in storage to check on the remaining rats and..." She looked away.

Jack finished the sentence for her. "They're all dead."

"How did you know?"

"The station is contaminated, Kate. We're as good as dead."

She shook her head. "I'm so sorry. God, I am so sorry. I thought I could keep the infection from spreading, if that's what it turned out to be. I really did. Do you believe me? Please believe me."

He pushed off and gathered her in his arms. They began a slow motion twirl.

"It's not your fault," he whispered into her hair.

She sobbed against his shoulder and he continued to hold her; it was all he had to offer.

CHAPTER 11

The stationers were in the commons, strapped into their webbed cocoons. No one wanted the insecurity of freely floating around the cylinder. No one wanted to be there at all. For once, it was not Mei Li who led the discussion. She was quiet and her face was silent, no smile and no sense of serenity; there was a distance, so that when Jack called her name, he had to repeat it before she looked in his direction.

"It's time for truth," Jack declared and no one objected to the assertion that the complete truth had yet to be spoken. "Tell us the truth, Mei Li."

She nodded. "The truth. When the Explorer docked and we were waiting for the scramjets to take those back to Earth who had agreed to go, we decided we had a right to take a peek inside the Explorer. It did not belong to the United States. It belonged to the entire world." She waited for Jack to object, but when he said nothing, she continued, in a voice that was so quiet that it was barely louder than the "creaks" and "pings" of the station. "We sent in a crawly. The hatch was only open for a few seconds, not long enough to allow any cross contamination, or at least that's what we thought and we did have two medically trained personnel aboard, Trejo from Brazil and Tito from Russia. Both said it would be all right. Just a few seconds and another few seconds when the crawly was retrieved. I swear it could not have been more than twenty seconds in total."

Jack had suspected as much. Those bastards at the WSA had to have known. He looked to Kate. "It's not your fault."

Kate answered Jack's continued gaze with an anemic smile. "It's no one's fault. I've already told Dickey. I've never seen him cry before. God it was awful." Her eyes began to glitter with tears, but not enough to release droplets into the air of the cabin. "I—" Her voice caught and she shut her mouth.

Jack refocused on Mei Li. "Did one of you remove a souvenir? A small piece of the alien ship's hull from the work counter drawer in the isolation room aboard the Explorer?"

"No."

"Tell me the truth. It has to be somewhere."

"Leave her alone," Gustave said. "Nothing was removed from the Explorer."

Jack focused his attention on the Frenchman, waiting.

"What?" Gustave asked. "What do you want? Some kind of confession? Well you're not going to get it. I will not die begging for forgiveness. I'll die with dignity."

"With dignity? Do you think bleeding to death through your ass is dignified?"

Gustave dropped his gaze. "Jack, believe me, if I'd known...."

The bunched muscles in Jack's shoulders relaxed. "I know. It's just so damn difficult to come to terms with."

"Maybe the best place for that accursed ship is the center of the Sun," Gustave said.

"It was senseless," Kate said bitterly. "I don't know if I have enough data or not. It's probably too late anyway," she added, and then paused to gather enough breath to speak the thought on everyone's mind. "We're all infected or contaminated or whatever it is. That means that every stationer who evacuated is probably also infected and spreading the infection on Earth. We should notify the WSA. They need to be picked up and put into strict quarantine. The only real solution that occurs to me is so gruesome, it almost seems that death is preferable. They could nuke the cities they returned to. Maybe that would stop it."

Mei Li named the cities. "Star City and from there they went home to Moscow, Rio de Janeiro, Osaka, Miami, London, Jerusalem and Kansas City."

The names of the cities hung in the air.

Jack shook his head. "It wouldn't make any difference in the end. The infection is able to be transmitted by other species."

"Only rats," Kate said.

"You're wrong. It killed the bacteria in the crew and it killed the plants in the hydroponics ring aboard the Explorer. If the infection is somehow related to the gene sequence that Roxanne Wiley discovered, and I believe it is, then every living thing on Earth is susceptible. Any bird could've been infected. We've been up here for two months. How far can a bird fly in two months? How far can a fish swim? How many people have boarded aircraft to spread it elsewhere?"

"Maybe the stationers who returned to Earth weren't infected," Mei Li said.

"What do you think, Kate?" Jack asked. "The lock was only open twenty seconds."

"We'll know soon enough." Kate had to pause and take a deep breath before continuing. "Why did they do it? What would make a sentient, highly evolved species want to destroy our world?"

"Maybe the Colonel was right," Gustave said. "Maybe they are devils."

"I've been giving this some thought," Jack said. "They sent an infectious agent that inserted a gene sequence into every living creature and then gave it time to spread throughout every niche. Then they sent the trigger, but it crashed on Mars. It took stupidity, bad luck, and the Mars Explorer to bring it to Earth. Which means they're ready for the next step."

"And that would be?" Kate asked.

"The seeding of a sterile world with their own flora, their own microbes. If any human did manage to survive, they would find that they were the aliens, that the Earth no longer belongs to our biology. I don't even really think it was aimed at us. I think we're only collateral damage. I think it was the microbial and plant kingdoms that were of greatest concern. Then, at some time in the future, when the Earth belongs to them, they'll come and the planet will be ready, their own plants, their own insects and bacteria. A place as friendly to them as their home world."

"But they must have known there were sapient beings on Earth," Kate said. "At the very least, they should've known that a sapient species would develop, if allowed to."

"It just doesn't make sense," Mei Li said. "There are millions of worlds out there."

"Maybe so," Jack replied, "but maybe the world needs to be the perfect size, the sun perfect, the distance perfect, the moon perfect. Maybe the perfect conditions to produce a planet like Earth are rare. Ninety years of listening and we've heard nothing from the universe. Not a peep. If there are so damned many great planets out there, where are they? We may have been more fortunate than we ever imagined, more special. And our world one among millions."

"No one knows how long the wreck has been on Mars,"

Mei added. "They could be coming tomorrow, or maybe in a thousand years, or maybe never, if something happened to their culture before they could follow through." She cleared her throat and looked to Kate. "How much time do you think Gustave and I have before we die?" Her voice was surprisingly strong.

"There is no absolute answer to that," Kate answered. "We cannot know how long the crew was exposed before they died. If we assume they were infected on the first visit to the wreck site, then they lived an additional three months. That's the maximum, it could be less."

"That would mean Gustave and I have less than a month to live, with luck."

"With transfusions," Kate added.

"Yes," Mei said in her soft voice, "with transfusions."

"What caused them to die?" Gustave asked, taking courage from Mei Li. "Did they just run out of blood?"

"That's part of it," Kate replied. "But once the lining of your intestine breaks down, there will be no stopping the blood and fluid loss. It'll be impossible to keep up. You'll have terrible thirst and be unable to catch your breath. And when your epidermis is shed, your skin will burn as if it's on fire."

"Was that really necessary?" Jack asked.

"He wanted to know."

"I doubt it."

The cylinder was quiet, but for the sounds of the station and the breathing of those who were trying not to contemplate the inevitable. Death had come much earlier than any of them had expected.

"Can you find a solution?" Gustave asked. "We'll help."

Kate answered. "It's a very complex biological problem, one that resides within our genes. We've been genetically modified. But, we're not alone." It was a realization that was easy to forget as they orbited above the Earth. "I'm sure all of humanity's resources will be directed at this problem. Jack's friend, Roxanne Wiley, has a head start on it, even though she didn't realize what she'd found."

"That's right," Gustave added with a smile. "We're not whipped. We'll have a surprise for those bastards when they get here."

Jack released his webbing and pushed off.

"Where are you going?" Kate called after him.

He ignored her. He swung around the corner and flew down the cylinder until he was in the one place where he could see the Earth, serene in its blue and white, hanging in space. He tried not to think of it as a dead world, where there was only dirt and rocks and an empty sea washing against sterile beaches.

"Jack." It was Kate.

"Go away." He refused to turn, was angry she had come. This was supposed to be a place of privacy. He wiped his eyes on the sleeve of his jumpsuit, ashamed that she had caught him like this, the real source of his anger.

"I received the amino acid sequences from Roxanne's lab."

He turned to face her.

"Jack, we can't give up. With this new information I'll be able to identify the infectious trigger-agent."

"That's great, Kate," He said in a flat voice and returned to staring at the Earth. When he looked over his shoulder, she was gone.

He sat before the window for another hour, focused on the Earth, and then pushed off to float down the cylinder. He swung into the hatch of the communication cylinder, where Mei Li brushed past him without a word.

There isn't enough room in this damn can to die in peace.

He kicked off and swung into the chair, not knowing what he really wanted to do. He faced the monitor. "Connect me with Director Mitchell Mason."

The face of a stern, young man appeared. "Captain, the Director is not available. Can I be of assistance?"

"Yes, you can tell Mason that he's a piece of shit, a God damned lying, son of a bitch."

The young man's lips tightened and his cheeks took on a rosy color. "I cannot do that, sir."

Jack relaxed again. It seemed like he was a rubber band, tight one moment and, in the next, so loose he would have floated out of the seat if he hadn't strapped himself in. "Why don't you connect me with Assistant Director Traynor then? Would that be acceptable?"

The young man didn't move.

"Go ahead," Jack encouraged. "He won't give you a hard time. He's my friend," Jack added in a nearly inaudible voice.

The man touched something out of view and his lips moved, but the sound wasn't transmitted. He turned his attention to

Jack with a smile that could only be described as pleased with himself.

"Assistant Director Traynor will speak with you."

The young man's face was replaced with Traynor's big nose and dumb appearing face. The face of someone he could always trust, until now.

"You knew about it, didn't you?" Jack began. "You bastard. You're just like all the—"

"Hold on there, Jack. If you're talking about the crawly entering the Explorer, yes, of course, but if you think we knew the station was contaminated, then the answer is 'no'. Think about it. Would we have allowed those others to return to Earth?"

Jack tilted his head back and took a big breath before leaning forward to face his friend. "No, I guess not, but, damn it! How could you all be so stupid?"

"It was analyzed by the best medical minds in the WSA and they passed on it."

"Talk about malpractice. They killed the Earth. What a bunch of stupid idiots." Jack hoped that Pie would refute his assertion, but he said nothing. "I suppose you've been listening," Jack said into the silence.

"I suppose, but we're about twenty-four hours ahead of you. The government has annexed Roxanne Wiley's lab. She and all her people are being moved to Copper Mountain."

"That's good."

"We've also just completed a series of high ranking talks."

"Wow, high ranking talks. I guess that'll take care of the problem."

"Stop it, Jack!"

Jack sat a little straighter; in all their years of friendship, his soft-spoken friend had never spoken to him in that tone.

"Stop wallowing in self-pity," Pie continued. "The whole damn Earth is dying, not just you."

"So...the infection did make its way to Earth."

"Public Health and the CDC have sent out alerts for the mandatory reporting of any cases of aplastic anemia. The reports are coming in. The incidence is spiking with no end in sight. We are getting similar reports from the WHO."

He couldn't recall a time in his life when he felt smaller. He couldn't think of what to say. "Is Jane okay?"

"Fine, healthy baby boy."

"I mean, has Copper Mountain been sealed off from exposure?"

"We're moving on numerous fronts."

"Are measures being taken to contain it? Have you told everyone to stay indoors, or something?"

"Our epidemiologists have told us that containment is no longer possible. Do you remember reading about that habitat that was constructed down in Texas years ago? We talked about it. Remember?"

"Yes."

"We're in the process of building habitats throughout the nation and in other parts of the world."

Jack shook his head. "Too slow."

"Maybe not. At any rate we're not going to sit on our duffs. We're not going out without a fight."

"What about the news media. Does the general public know?"

"They know the Explorer has left the station, any bozo with a telescope could tell that, but they don't know why."

"Are you going to tell them? Or are you just going to let them puke their guts out and die in front of one another with no idea it's coming?"

"No decision on that yet. We can't handle anarchy and still accomplish what we need to do."

"Take care of Jane, will you?"

"Mason is quite capable—yeah, sure. I'll stop by and check on her. Should I say hello for you?"

"No."

"Jack."

"Yes?"

"I'll do what I can for you. It may not be much, but I'll do what I can. I'm sending up a scramjet to deliver blood, cloned, perfect matches for all of you. It should be enough to...well, it should be enough."

"Thanks. You be careful down there, Pie. And damn it, don't let this happen!"

"I'll do my best and you do the same."

"Later."

"Right."

The screen went blank. He waited for his heart to settle, until he felt he was secure within that part of him which had been trained to accept anything, even death, but not the death of the entire world. His heart began pounding again.

He took another deep breath and then spoke. "Connect with Roxanne Wiley."

The minutes drifted past. The blinking signal indicated that his request had been received and then a face came on. It was Roxanne, but her hair was hanging in tangled strands.

"Jack, all hell's breaking out down here. The government's taking over my lab and moving us. I have to get back to make sure they don't break anything, or lose something vital. I don't have much time. What's happening?"

"I don't have much time either."

"Then maybe you should contact me later."

"If you have to go, then go."

She paused with the memory of their evening together and rewarded him with one of her luscious smiles. "I'd like to stay, but...." She shrugged. "I have to, you know?"

Jack nodded. "Take good care of yourself."

She studied him for a moment. "What's happening, Jack? Are you doing okay?" Then she looked off screen and yelled, "All right! I'll be there right away." And then returned her attention to Jack. "I really have to go."

"I understand."

"Later, Jack."

The screen went blank.

"Bye, Roxy," he said to blank screen.

He felt such emptiness, so alone. He needed something, somebody. *Who else?* Maybe Blas Uribe. They had roomed together at Annapolis. *There was no one else.* He saw movement and glanced to the side. It was Gustave, waiting for his turn.

Jack released his belt and pushed off. As Mei Li had done, he passed the Frenchman without speaking. The sense of doom was washed away by anger as he approached the computer lab. *Damn it! This was not going to happen!*

He turned the corner. Kate's fingers were busy while she worked at a monitor. He swam over and gave her a hug.

She looked up at him. "Your timing is bad. I don't really feel like it right now, maybe later."

"Hells bells, Kate." He released his hold on her and smiled sheepishly. "I'm just happy to see you, that's all."

She smiled. "We've got work to do. I want you to help me search for molecules that should not be in the cell of a rat.

Help me find the parts that aren't rat. Okay?"

"You bet." He slipped into the seat next to her and buckled himself in.

"What's Mei doing?"

"Don't know."

"Gustave?"

"Down in communications."

"Okay then, it's you and me."

"You and me," Jack agreed with a nod.

CHAPTER 12

Two weeks of searching had revealed fragments of the infectious agent, but no intact specimen, simply clues as to the complexity of the capsule that allowed it access to every organism on Earth. One fact became obvious; the universal contagion was designed by a species that was advanced far beyond the capabilities of human biotechnology.

Jack sat with his back to the monitor and watched his headset rotate around its center of mass. "And it's a cure for cancer too," he said out of nowhere.

Kate stretched her arms over her head and, with a satisfying "pop", returned them to her sides. "The illusive universal cure, if you consider death a cure. I knew there were risks, but I was so confident I could make us safe. That sooner or later, even if we didn't find a solution, the WSA would get tired of us circling overhead and bring us back down."

"And I saw this as a second chance, a chance to earn a place on the next Mars expedition. It never occurred to me that the Mars program was over, done, kaput. It's so hard to believe that it might be over for all of us, for all of Earth. Do you really think the aliens knew what they were doing, or was it just a mistake? Oops, we didn't know there were humans on Earth."

"I think that beings advanced enough to design such a devastating life weapon, must have known that a sapient being already existed on Earth. I think that's why they designed it to be an abrupt, catastrophic event. They expected us to be dead before we even knew what hit us. That's what I think."

"Unless sapient life is another anomaly of cosmic proportions, like the Earth itself. But...I guess we'll never know the answers to those questions, will we?"

"I guess not. I sent the last data to Copper Mountain, to Roxanne Wiley to be specific. They've been able to develop a screen to determine who is infected and who isn't. I've gotten to know her and I like her. And, we talk about you."

"Me?"

"I think you've made a conquest."

He was speechless.

"I can see that you like that idea," Kate added with a grin.

"Ridiculous." He thought about being with Roxanne again and then the happy glow died. There was no future. "Do you think they'll be able to come up with something?"

"Don't know. Wouldn't hold my breath if I were you, for whatever difference that makes. Wouldn't it be great to be back on Earth? For some crazy reason, I have this overwhelming desire to swing from the thick limb of an oak tree. My swing 'creeks' each time I fly back and forth. I see myself kicking my legs out, pulling back, and then sailing toward the sky, seeing the clouds, and then swinging back to see the worn patch of dirt that is found beneath any self-respecting swing."

"You know what I'd like? I'd like to walk down a country road, with cornfields on either side. I can hear the raspy sound of leaves scraping against one another and then I come across a surprise. Maybe a little rodeo with lots of straw and palomino ponies, or maybe a forgotten waterfall, a small one, near an abandoned mill."

"Did you ever see those things?"

"Yes, when I was boy, and I'd love to see them again."

They were quiet as they tried to keep their imaginings alive within the metal skin of the station, with hard vacuum just a few meters away.

Jack was first to fail. "The scramjet dropped off the package. The pilot did nothing but discuss the technical details of the package and its attachment to the hull of the station. Didn't really want to talk with me, one of the condemned. Apparently, even within the WSA not everyone is aware of the true situation. He'll be dead within months along with his wife, his children, his friends, everyone he knows."

"You sure know how to paint a grim picture."

"Do you think it's inaccurate?"

Kate shook her head. "No." And then added softly, "I hope Dickey is okay. I asked Mason to try to get him into one of those habitats they're building...if he's not already infected."

"How's Mei Li doing?"

"About the same as Gustave. You can smell the blood, even here."

Jack nodded.

"We've exhausted the supply of artificial blood. The package contains ten units of cloned blood for each of us. When it's gone, that's it. Goodnight."

"Have you noticed anything yet?" Jack asked.

Kate looked down at her long fingers and nodded. "Afraid so. And you?"

"Me too. Let's go check on them."

Kate followed Jack out as they headed for the commons and the foul odor of partially digested blood. Both Mei Li and Gustave looked ghastly, pale and drawn, as they floated in their cocoon harnesses.

Jack turned around and swam for the lock to dress in a space suit. They desperately needed that blood from Earth.

When he returned, Kate helped him prepare the blood for transfusion. Mei Li was unconscious when Jack hooked up the blood to the catheter; Kate had placed a subclavian line in each of them. While Jack pumped four units into her, Kate did the same for Gustave. By the time the third unit was in, they were both awake. They were no longer pale to the point of yellow; there was some color in their lips.

It was senseless to urge them to eat; they couldn't tolerate it.

Jack had experienced terrible heartburn with the blandest food they had, rice paste, no spices, nothing to give it taste. Even the thought of spices made Jack's chest burn. His skin itched, but he tried not to rub it.

Mei Li's luxurious braid was gone; she wore a scarf to cover her bald scalp. "Hello, Jack," she said. "I think I will go speak with my family now. I apologize for the mess. I cannot control it."

"I know, Mei," Jack said.

He released the webbing for her. He was certain, had there been any gravity, she wouldn't have been able to make it on her own. He didn't follow her, trying not to infringe on the little time she had left.

Gustave was also awake. His breathing had slowed with the oxygen hunger temporarily appeased. He managed one of those big, toothy smiles. "Have you ever been to the French Riviera, either of you?"

Jack nodded. He remembered a rough coast, with sheer, stony hillsides, craggy. The natural beaches were covered with large rocks. The water of the Mediterranean was cold. It reminded him of California without sandy beaches.

"Beautiful, isn't it? Have you ever seen a more beautiful place on earth?"

"Beautiful, Gustave."

"Go on. Say it. You Americans are always so afraid to admit that there is somewhere better than America. Don't be afraid to admit it. Say it, the most beautiful place on Earth."

"The most beautiful place on Earth."

"Yes-s," Gustave hissed and nodded. His eyes were no longer focused on Jack; they were looking elsewhere, to his memories. "I have a little cottage there, in a village called Eze, perfume country, flower country. I intended to return there, the rich and famous astronaut, and settle down with Marie and have children. We were meant for each other. A beautiful woman with dark eyes and hair, as only a French woman can be beautiful. You Americans always think bigger is better, but her breasts were perfect. A perfect fit for my hands." His eyes focused on Kate. "Not that there aren't beautiful American women as well. It was good, wasn't it, Kate? Our little tryst?"

"I now know what it means to be taken by a Frenchman. What more could a woman want?"

"Indeed, indeed. Well, I imagine Mei is about done. I think I'll talk with Mon Cherrie." Jack drifted toward Gustave's cocoon, but Gustave waved him off.

"I can do it myself."

Jack waited and watched as Gustave's feeble efforts finally succeeded.

He then looked up at Jack and nodded. "You've been as good a pair of crewmates as a man could ever wish. When we return to Earth, you'll have to visit me on the Riviera, both of you. I'll show you France as only a Frenchman can."

"We may yet have that opportunity," Jack said without conviction. "They're working on it down below. Very hard."

Gustave smiled again and touched his fingers to his forehead in a salute. "Until later, my friends. Please give me the courtesy of saying goodbye to Marie in private."

"Sure," Jack said and Kate nodded.

When Gustave drifted past, the foul odor of blood drifted with him. His cocoon was stained a black-maroon. Jack reached overhead to pull out the suction cleaner and began working on the mess while Kate attended to Mei Li's cocoon. When they had finished, they waited, expecting Mei to float through the hatch at any moment, but time passed and she didn't reappear. They honored Gustave's request for privacy but, after another thirty minutes, Jack could wait no longer.

"We better go check on them. Don't you think?"

Kate frowned. "He asked for privacy and Mei will come back when she decides to."

"I'm going to check."

He pushed off and drifted down the central corridor. Grabbing a handhold, he changed direction and sailed into the communication cylinder. It was vacant.

"Kate", he yelled, "they aren't here!"

Kate swam into view a few seconds later. "I know where they are."

"Where?"

"They're in cylinder Liberate. They've closed the hatch and sealed it from the inside."

Jack pushed off on a trajectory for Liberate. He pulled up in front of the hatch. It was closed as Kate had reported. He tried to open the hatch, but it was locked. He rapped on the metal with his knuckles.

"What are you doing in there?" Jack yelled. "It's not time to give up. While we still have blood, we have time."

"Hello, Jack." Mei Li's voice was broadcast throughout the station. "We have decided we will suffer no more. It is our right. We do not want you to be forced to witness our deaths. It is only common decency."

"Mei, with the blood, we can keep you alive, maybe long enough for Earth to find an answer. Don't give up, please."

"You are a sweet man, Jack Nichols. We wish you tranquility as the truth unfolds. You and Kate have cared for us as a brother and sister would have and for that we are deeply grateful. Now it is time to say goodbye. Goodbye, Jack. Goodbye, Kate."

"Just a minute. We didn't ask for you to leave us. You are *not* a burden. Don't shut us out." Jack waited, but there was only silence. "Mei Li, answer me, damn it!"

Nothing.

"Gustave, I expect more out of you. Show me that French spirit. Talk to me at least."

There was nothing but Kate's heavy breathing behind him.

"Damn it," he said quietly. "And damn those alien bastards.

Damn it to hell! They will pay. I swear it." He felt Kate's hand on his shoulder and he released his grip on the hatch, allowing himself to be pulled away. He twisted around until he was face to face with her. "You're not going to leave me too, are you?"

"No, Jack. We'll keep each other company until the end. I don't want to die by myself."

"It's not time for that kind of talk. If we attend to our needs, we'll be able to live another...." His voice dwindled to nothing.

Kate nodded. "Come on. You can come with me while I talk with Dickey. I don't mind."

He shook his head. "You go ahead. I'll take my turn after you're done."

He floated in midair. The instrument filled bulkhead swung past his eyes. He was still drifting when Kate returned.

"Jack."

He looked to her.

"Give her a call."

"I don't know. She seems so busy. She has a lot on her mind. I don't want to interrupt her every time I get a little homesick."

"Contact her. It'll do you good and I know she wants to hear from you."

He told himself he didn't need to contact her, but found he was drifting toward communications. With a small additional effort, he found himself in the cylinder. The odor of blood was there as well, but he could see that Kate had spent time cleaning up; she was a stronger person than he, that was his opinion. He strapped into the chair.

"Request connection with Roxanne Wiley."

A first lieutenant came onto the screen, might have been the same one as last time. It was difficult to tell; they all seemed the same. Jack didn't like the look the man gave him. He wanted no pity from a stranger.

"Well, Lieutenant?" Jack said in a robust voice, far different from the collapsed feeling in his gut where both pain and sadness mingled.

"A moment please."

The lieutenant worked his board, searching for a connect with Roxanne and then, suddenly, she was there.

He didn't remember the creases being so deep in her

forehead, running across that scar, or darkness beneath her eyes.

She smiled for him. "Hey, Jack, how are things going?"

"Not very well."

"What's happened?"

"What makes you think something's happened?"

Roxanne waited for him to continue.

"Mei Li and Gustave are dead."

"Oh, Jack...." Those lips pulled into as straight a line as he'd ever seen. "I'm so sorry to hear that. From everything you've told me, I feel like I knew them."

There was silence that stretched on until Jack spoke again. "How are things going on your end?"

"We've been processing the information that Kate sent. It was very helpful."

"It was?" Hope made him lean closer.

"Yes, we've been able to get samples from newly infected serviceman and, using the protein strands Kate provided, we've been able to identify the capsule. It's very complex. We're mapping it right now. Should be done in a few days."

"What then?"

"We have some ideas."

"Some ideas?"

"It's a little premature for me to discuss them. It's new ground for us."

"I see." Jack pushed back into the seat. People walked behind her, sexless and ageless in their hazmat suits. "Why aren't you wearing one of those suits?"

"I'm outside the containment unit." She glanced over her shoulder. "Unbreakable glass. It's amazing in some ways. I would've expected the bureaucracy to respond slowly, but someone powerful is pulling strings. Seed samples, samples of every living thing we can get our hands on are being sealed away at containment centers around the world. I understand there are entire habitat bubbles going up. There's a big one outside San Francisco and another outside Chicago."

"What's the news like?"

"You don't want to know."

"Is the public aware?"

"Not officially, but martial law has been declared. All travel has been banned. It's horrible out there. Society and all the niceties of law are breaking down so fast, it makes a person wonder what held it together in the first place. It's hell out there."

"How about your sister?"

"I've been told that she and her family are secure in the McGill bubble. I'm really worried about her, but I have to focus on the task at hand and that part has been remarkable. People that I only knew by reputation are here, from all over the country. To be honest, these are researchers that I feel a certain awe for and I'm directing the whole shebang. It's been intimidating, but as I get to know them better, we've really come together, very close."

"Close?"

"Working together like never before. God, Jack, how can you possibly think of sex at a time like this?"

"That isn't what I meant."

"The hell it wasn't."

Jack had to grin. "How are Jane and her baby doing?"

"Jane? Oh...her. I have no idea. I don't have time to keep track of your ex-wives."

"Ex-wife. Only one."

"Seriously, Jack, how are you?"

"As good as can be expected."

"Have you needed to be transfused?"

"I'd rather not talk about that right now."

"We're all busting our butts down here."

"I know. Roxy, if you ever need anything, have any trouble, I want you to ask for Pie Traynor. He's a friend of mine and is the Assistant Director at Copper Mountain. Remember the name 'Pie Traynor'."

"Why are you telling me that now?"

"I...I just want to know that you are well, and not alone."

She nodded and their eyes met. There was moment of silence. It seemed to Jack that understanding passed between them, of many things left unspoken.

Jack took a deep breath and released it before continuing. "I hate to interfere with your work or what little sleep you seem to be getting."

"Am I looking that bad?" She formed her lips into a pout.

Jack shook his head. "Always fishing for a compliment aren't you? Well, the truth is, you look great. If...well anyway, you look great."

A man in a lab coat came up behind her and she turned to

speak with him. Jack could see that there were others in the room who were also waiting to speak with her. She finished her business with the first man and returned to the screen.

"I can see you're busy," Jack said. "I better let you go. I'll be thinking about you."

"I'll be thinking about you too. Contact me again, soon. Anytime you want."

"Bye, Roxy."

"Bye, Jack."

The screen went blank.

Kate hung in the hatch between cylinders. "Hope you don't mind that I stayed."

"Not at all." He unbuckled and pushed out of the seat. "I need to see the Earth. Want to go down to M-1 with me for a while?"

"I'd love to, but I don't want any funny business. I have my reputation to protect."

Jack smiled. "You're a terrific woman, Kate."

"Why thank you, Captain Nichols. Should we?"

Jack pushed off and drifted after her. They settled into seats next to one another and, when Kate put her hand in his, he clasped it with affection and need. The Earth was beautiful in sunlight. Somehow, Jack swore to himself, he had to live long enough to kill those alien bastards. He just had to live, for that reason alone.

CHAPTER 13

Jack and Kate were strapped into their web-beds with infusers hanging in front of them, pumping in the last of their blood supply. It wasn't enough. They were too weak to clean up after themselves and had packed their cocoons with absorbent sheets. The smell of blood was so constant, that even that penetrating odor didn't register strongly.

They hadn't requested additional blood and Copper Mountain medical hadn't sent any on their own. Neither he nor Kate wanted to prolong this torture. They were dying; they knew it and the decision-makers at Copper Mountain knew it.

Jack now understood Mei Li and Gustave's choice as only one who was following in their footsteps could. He brushed his hand across his smooth scalp. He ached, in his bones, in his chest. He glanced toward Kate; she looked haggard and pale. Her blond hair was gone.

He had opened the communication channel so they could monitor it in the commons. At first he thought it was his imagination.

"Do you hear that?" Kate asked.

He listened hard, trying to hear through the static, and heard a faint voice. His mind drifted.

He hadn't spoken with Roxanne in over a week. He stared at the blood tubing, filled with black-red blood that was being pumped into the catheter beneath his collarbone. That they even bothered was a mild surprise to Jack; hope had proven harder to kill than he ever imagined it would be, pushing them to tolerate the intolerable. Perhaps the hints from Roxanne had helped, a suggestion that progress was being made. The protein sequences Kate had identified had speeded their recovery of the infective microbe, if it could be called a microbe. Roxanne said they were trying out an experimental vaccine, but she never suggested it was a treatment, only a preventative.

The bell on the infuser chimed; his last unit was in. He

detached the tubing from the catheter, cleaned it and capped it, even though there would be no further use for it; there was no more blood. Life had come down to hours, perhaps a day, but not more. The static increased with the ghostly sound of a voice mixed in.

"What the hell is that?" Jack asked, not expecting an answer.

"I think it's Patterson," Kate whispered, all that remained of her voice.

"What? You think he's still alive?"

"He was a stubborn cuss. You have to at least grant him that."

The static grew stronger and the ghostly voice was no longer heard.

"I should go down to communications," Jack said. "I can probably boost the signal strength."

Kate looked over at him. Her lips were a faint pink, only a suggestion of color, even after four units of blood. It wasn't just the blood loss. They could no longer eat and the bone pain was terrible, even with the use of blocking agents.

Kate spoke in her coarse whisper. "I think the removal of the euphoric properties from analgesics was a mistake. Don't you?"

"If there's anything I could use right now, euphoria would be near the top of my wish list. I'm going down to communications. That poor bastard is all alone out there. That he could still be alive amazes me, but he must be near death."

Kate closed her eyes without responding. She appeared to be dozing, but Jack knew she was just trying to focus the remainder of her will, to cope.

He unbuckled his web straps and pushed off, once again thankful for zero-G. He drifted across the cylinder. "Don't go anywhere."

"I'll try not to."

Jack looked over his shoulder; her eyes were closed and her breathing was faster than natural. He grasped a handhold. "Don't you dare go anywhere without me."

She opened her eyes and smiled. "Say hello to the Colonel for me, will you?"

"Sure. I'll be right back."

He pushed off, gliding through air. He passed the closed

cylinder that contained the bodies of Mei Li and Gustave and nodded in their direction. "We'll be joining you shortly," he murmured.

He drifted into the communication cylinder and missed his handhold, hitting the bulkhead with his shoulder. The lancinating pain would have brought tears to his eyes if he wasn't so dehydrated, but they had already used the last of their intravenous fluids. He licked his dry lips, trying to draw out enough saliva to allow him to speak in a voice that could be heard. When he finally managed to maneuver himself into the seat, he had barely enough strength to buckle in.

Static crackled away in the background.

He forced his head up and directed the receiver to fix on the signal and amplify.

"International Space Station, this is the Mars Explorer. Come in."

"Hello, Colonel, this is the Station. Jack Nichols at your service."

There was a pause. When the Colonel's voice returned the static rose in intensity so that Jack couldn't make out what he was saying.

"Please repeat. Reception is poor," Jack said.

There was a long pause before the Colonel's voice returned.

"Did my family get the video chip?"

"Yes, I forwarded the contents to the WSA. I'm sure they did."

There was another long pause.

"Good, I—" Static interfered. "—running out of everything here. I do not regret"—static—"It was worth it. Why are you"—static—"are they punishing you for what I did?"

"Everything is fine here, Colonel. You were successful. Your sacrifice has saved humanity. You were right all along."

The Mars Explorer must be quite distant. Jack thought about doing the calculation, but it was too much effort.

"Thank God. It was a gamble but"—static—"I am ready to meet my maker. Not afraid to"—static—"" am about"—static—"kilometers past Earth. The ship is all but dead, as am I. God bless you all. I"—static.

"Come again."

There was only a crackling hiss.

"Kate sends her best."

Jack waited, straining to hear a voice, but there was nothing.

"Mars Explorer, please repeat last message."

He increased the gain to maximum, until the static was a roar, but there was no voice to be heard. The Colonel was again alone in his last moments, but then again, maybe not. Maybe the Colonel was the only one equipped to accept his death with equanimity.

He waited a few minutes, but there was nothing more. He unbuckled and pushed off, rounding the corners with as much grace as his aching bones could tolerate. When he entered the commons, he floated directly toward Kate, studying her, making sure she was still breathing. He didn't want to be the last to die.

She opened her eyes. "What did the Colonel have to say?"

"Not much. Blessed us and so forth. Seemed to be at peace with his fate."

"Did you tell him it was all for nothing?" She smiled when Jack looked away. "That's good. A good lie. I'm proud of you."

He met her gaze; the blue of her eyes seemed even more intense, set in her ghostly white face.

"Do you believe in God?" he asked.

"I'd like to. It's hard to think we're on our own, lonely. If there is a God, I hope she has a wild side and won't toss me out on my butt without a second thought."

"If there is a God and you get tossed out, I don't want to go to heaven."

"Better be careful what you wish for, Jack."

"I just wish I'd taken you up on your offer. To have inducted you into the three-hundred-kilometer-high-club would've been an honor."

"An honor? Hell, Jack, that's a slap in the face. It was supposed to be a thrilling, erotic experience, not an honor. Gustave did his best, but I wish it had been you. I'm afraid it's a bit beyond me in my current state. The spirit is willing but the flesh is weak."

"If that's a biblical quotation, I think you might have warped its meaning a bit."

"The story of my life, warped biblical quotations. Did you contact Roxanne?"

"No. I don't know what to say anymore. I'm afraid I'll just break down and beg for help, or something. How about you? Do you want me to help you down there so you can talk with Dickey?"

"No. We've said our good-byes."

Jack hung in front of her. Her brief burst of energy ebbed; she closed her eyes.

"Kate?"

Her eyes fluttered open and then shut.

"Kate!" he said as loudly as his hoarse voice would allow.

"What does a woman have to do to get a little rest around here?"

"I want to see the blue sky again. I want to see the Earth again before I die. Do you?"

"Oh sure, Jack. Why not? And perhaps we could take in a play and then dine at a gourmet restaurant. That would be nice. Now leave me alone for a while, will you? I've got a few thoughts I need to put in order." She opened her eyes. "I mean it."

"Just be ready."

She closed her eyes and Jack pushed off. When he arrived at the communications center, he managed to buckle into the seat.

"Connect me with Director Mason."

This time it was a young woman who came on screen. Other than for the cut of her hair and softer facial features, she could have been the twin sister of any of the young security agents he had contact with, all of them with medium everything. Where are the big noses? That brought a picture of Pie Traynor to his mind. He smiled. Pie Traynor, a species onto himself, ugly as shit.

"Sir, did you hear me? Would you like me to repeat?"

He looked at the woman. Her face was devoid of emotion. Was that the current recommendation for dealing with the living dead?

"Sir, would you like me to repeat?"

"Sure, have at it."

"Sir, Director Mason is not available."

"That's okay. I didn't really want to talk with him anyway. Connect me with Assistant Director Traynor. I need to see a big nose."

This brought out a frown on the woman.

Jack smiled. He had found her weakness, big noses.

"Would you like me to repeat?" he asked.

"No, sir, that won't be necessary."

The lieutenant did something with her hand. Her lips

moved and she nodded in answer to a response that wasn't being shared with him.

"I haven't got all day you know. I've got things to do. For one, I have to die."

She focused on him. "I know, sir."

Traynor's big-nosed, goofy face came on screen.

"Hello, Jack."

"How are things going?"

"We've made some real breakthroughs. Doctor Wiley's team has completed testing of the modified infectious agent on varicella-zoster. The test was successful. The viruses survived."

"Varicella? God, that's great news, Pie. You've managed to save chickenpox. Hallelujah."

The quip didn't even bring a smile to Pie's normally expressive face. "We've already begun human trials."

"Where did you ever find anyone stupid enough to volunteer for that?"

Pie answered with a stare.

"I see. I didn't really mean stupid, but couldn't you have found someone a little less vital to try it on first?"

"Everyone is vital."

"Sure, Pie. Whatever. Are you okay?"

"I feel fine."

"That's good, because I've made a decision."

Pie gave him his full attention.

"I've decided to die on Earth."

"Now, just a minute. Have you thought this through?"

"Not really and I don't intend to, no time. The WSA owes us for the colossal blunder of sending us to a contaminated station. I don't intend to make things worse, but I swear Kate and I are coming down as our last willful act and don't give me any of that shit about bravery and self sacrifice. The Earth is already infected. It won't make a damn bit of difference to anyone on Earth, but it'll make a hell of a lot of difference to Kate and me. You can shoot us out of the sky as we come down, but that'll have to be your decision. I'm giving you fair warning and will even come down where you recommend, for easier targeting."

To Jack's surprise, Pie didn't argue.

"Outside Wichita would be a reasonable landing site. Stationer Lopez spent only enough time to infect most of

Florida before he flew to Kansas City and then on to Wichita to see his family. The area is a hot bed of infection."

Jack nodded. "Wichita it is. Thanks, Pie. If Roxanne Wiley comes to you for help, please do what you can for her and...give Jane my best, will you?"

"Of course."

"And take good care of yourself. Stay well. If anyone can pull Earth out of this nosedive, it's you."

"I'll do my best. Until later, buddy."

"Right...until later."

Jack pushed the interrupt button and the screen went blank. It sounded like a stupid idea when he had told Pie about it, but it was better than sitting around while the last of his blood hemorrhaged away. When he released the harness, his fingers were tingling. He was breathing too fast, or maybe it was just fast enough to sustain him.

He swam to the computer cylinder and began to load in data to program the escape vehicle, but his mind was fuzzy. He found himself repeating commands and had to start over. It was hopeless. He was about to give up when the finished program scrolled across his screen.

"Thank you, Pie," he whispered fervently.

He rounded the corner into the commons. Kate's head was tipped to the side. He stopped within a hand's breath of her face. She was still breathing. "Kate!"

She didn't respond.

"Kate, we're getting out of here. We're not going to die in this can."

He released the straps of her web and she floated free.

"Dickey, what're you doing?" she asked with her head lolling on her neck.

"We're going home."

"Home? We are home. You aren't leaving are you? I want you to stay. I need you, Dickey."

He pulled her along behind him. He dragged her through the next cylinders and was able to push her into one of the seats of the crew return vehicle. He closed the hatch. While he was securing her restraint harness she looked up at him with a big smile.

"I love you, Dickey," she said.

Jack nodded. "I love you too, Kate. Let's take a little ride, should we?"

"That would be nice." She closed her eyes, still smiling.

Jack keyed in the activation sequence and waited for the computer to dictate when and at what angle the CRV would be ejected from the station. There was nothing more to do; he finally allowed himself to surrender to the illness that was eating him.

Neither of them was conscious when the rescue vehicle was released. Neither was aware of the buffeting of re-entry, nor were they aware when the parasail opened. The CRV drifted through sunlit sky on a bright red parachute. There was no one to take control, no one to pilot it to a soft landing on its skids. Neither of them stirred when the rescue vehicle slammed into a Kansas wheat field.

A fire blossomed around the craft. Black smoke rose into the autumn sky.

CHAPTER 14

Roxanne leaned against Pie with familiarity. They stood on the other side of a one-way window and watched Jack's face contort with pain; his mouth opened wide with an unheard scream. A doctor rushed into hospital room and increased the infusion of pain medication. Jack's face relaxed into blankness.

"I don't know." Her gaze was fixed on Jack; most of his body was submerged beneath the blue surface of the gel bed. "Despite everything we've accomplished, chances are he won't survive. He's septic."

"He'll survive," Pie declared in his rumbling voice.

"I hope you're right."

"Then the hard part comes. I'm going to have to do something to make him really angry. Something that will make him get up and get going."

She pushed away. "If by some miracle he does survive, you're not going to tell him about us, are you?"

"Do you care?"

She stared at him.

"I guess you do." Pie folded his massive arms across his chest. "No, that wasn't what I had in mind. I'm going to lay it on the line about his injuries. He has to know the truth so he can focus on making the best of his recovery."

"Are you sure? That sounds like it'd push him over the edge."

"When he sets his mind to do something, there's no stopping him. He told me he was five years old when he decided he'd go to Mars, same year his parents died in a plane crash. After being passed around like a hot potato, an elderly uncle took him in, a retired drill sergeant. I've heard stories about Sergeant Nichols. Strict is too weak a word to describe him, but when Jack talks about him, it's always with affection. His uncle passed away the day he graduated from high school, but he never gave up on his dream to go to Mars."

"He didn't make it."

"Believe me, he hasn't given up," Pie said.

Roxanne glanced at the critically ill man beyond the glass and shrugged. "If you say so. It was kind of a rough childhood, wasn't it?"

"Yeah, but no worse than yours. Raising your sister by yourself in the toughest part of Detroit and then going on to accomplish what you have. Well...that's nothing short of extraordinary."

"Bullshit. Are you making moon-eyes at me?"

"Moon-eyes?"

"You know what I mean."

"It wasn't his child—"

"Changing the subject, huh?" She gave him a playful jab on the chest.

He cleared his voice and then continued. "The blow that almost destroyed him was when Jane divorced him. He believes that when two people commit to one another, that's that. End of story. A man of extremes. He has no idea what the word 'moderation' means."

"I understand that perfectly."

"Do you?"

Roxanne met Pie's gaze and then again looked through the window to stare at the man who fought death with such determination.

"Absolutely," she said.

"Moderation isn't a bad quality, you know."

She continued to stare through the window.

"Don't you agree?" Pie persisted.

"I suppose," she said absently and then returned her attention to Pie and smiled. "Moderation is not a bad quality."

"I should say not," Pie declared with a nod of his head.

"You seem to know an awfully lot about him."

"I should. Before we joined the space program, we were part of an advance team, covert operations."

"You were spies?"

"I prefer the term 'special ops'. He has this gift of taking odd pieces of information and putting them together in a way that defies logic. The bastard. I miss him."

She returned to studying the dying man in the gel bed. "We talked a lot when he was on the space station, but I wish I could've gotten to know him even better."

"Let's get something straight. We are _not_ going to give up on him. He stuck with me no matter what. One time, over

Chihuahua, Mexico, our plane was shot down. He pulled me and four others from the burning wreckage and drove away the rebels, single-handedly, even though he too was seriously wounded." This time it was Pie who stared at the motionless figure beyond the glass. When he continued his voice was soft. "He saved my life."

"Is that where he got those scars? During the fight?"

Pie chuckled. "Yeah. When someone asks him how he got them, he tells them he was attacked by a pack of Chihuahuas and then laughs. What a stupid joke."

Roxanne nodded and was quiet as she relived her own memories. Memories of a night that had taken on proportions she would never have believed possible at the time.

Pie continued. "He was awarded the Navy Cross. If it had been up to me it would've been the Medal of Honor."

"The Navy Cross is a big deal, right?"

"Yeah, it's a big deal."

Roxanne was quiet for a moment and then spoke. "What does it look like?"

"The Navy Cross?"

"Yes."

"It's a blue ribbon with a vertical white stripe and a bronze cross beneath it. Why?"

"He wore it on the night of our big date. I think I made fun of it."

"He wore it? Now that is surprising. He must have been trying to impress you."

"Yeah, I guess so."

"How's Angie?" Pie asked.

She smiled. "She is such a gift, so sweet. She's crawling now. You haven't been over in a while."

"It's not that I wanted to stay away. I've been incredibly busy."

She looked into his hazel eyes, the only thing about him that could be called beautiful. "Why don't you come over and see her this evening?"

He nodded. "It's a date. I can hardly wait to see her again...and you," he added with a big smile.

"Great. See you tonight."

He bent forward to give her a kiss but she had turned away and was again focused on the man beyond the glass, the one who was fighting for his life.

CHAPTER 15

There was no sense of time. The days of darkness slipped past. There was no awareness; he was gone, no longer within his body or anywhere else, simply gone from the universe. But, there came a day when the white light returned. It seemed like it had only been a moment since the last time. He remembered and was afraid, afraid of the pain and the red glow, afraid of the fire that would consume him.

He was staring at it for some time before he knew what it was. He stopped trembling as he focused his attention. It was a face, with lips that were moving. There were sounds, words, his name.

"Jack, can you hear me? Don't just stare like that. Say something."

He heard a rattling croak, the remnants of his voice.

The face nodded. He knew that face.

"Good, Jack." A hand held a glass of water for him to sip from. "Try again. What's my name?"

Jack's gaze was fixed on her, mesmerized by those lips. "Roxy."

"Hey, great job! I knew it would take more than a killer gene to keep my Captain Jack down."

"I'm dead."

"Nope. Want to try again?"

"I'm not dead."

"There you go." She smiled.

"You're not dead."

"Hey, big fellow, let's not push the envelope."

He took a deep breath. He could smell her, not a perfume, but a body sweetness. The flow of his sedative was adjusted and he drifted back into his dark world of not being.

There were more non-days, until the dose of sedative was decreased. He drifted toward awareness and broke through the surface. The ceiling was white and bright. It hurt his eyes. He turned his head. Numbers and red lights on monitors flickered as they tracked his progress.

He began to comprehend. He was in a room and he was alive, but he was alone.

"Help!"

No one came. Everyone was dead except him. The Earth was dead.

"Oh God."

Tears filled his eyes so that when the door did open, he couldn't make out the figure. He tried to raise his hand to brush away the tears, but his arm collapsed back against the bed. He closed his eyes and this time he slept.

When he awakened he felt better. His arm trembled with weakness when he raised his hand to inspect it; the muscles had melted away. It was the bony hand of an old person. Had he slept for forty years? He heard the door as it slid open. There were footsteps.

"Hello, Jack."

He turned his head and saw the lopsided face of Pie Traynor.

"Hello, Pie."

"I imagine you have a few questions."

Jack switched his attention to the man who stood next to Pie. The man's face was stern; he had a skinny neck that suggested he was an exercise fanatic and that he was always careful what he ate.

Pie gestured in the man's direction. "This is Doctor Lyons. He and his colleagues saved your life, along with extensive help from the genomics research team."

Jack focused on the ceiling. "Why save me when the world is dead?"

"Always thinking of yourself." Pie had Jack's attention again. "Glad to see you can still scowl. That would've been a real loss. The Doctor said I should go slow with you, but he doesn't know how resilient you are."

Resilient? A lie. He was weak. He had abandoned the station and— "Where's Kate?"

Pie's crooked smile faded. "Kate is dead. We weren't able to save her. When we reached the CRV, she was dead and you weren't far from it."

"Dead," Jack whispered and looked back to the bright, white ceiling. He could picture her unruly blond hair and her smile, boasting of life. "She can't be."

"I assure you, she is. I was there."

"What about Dickey, her husband?"

"He was offered refuge, but declined. Last I heard he planned to sail his boat around the world."

"Did he make it?"

"I doubt it."

"Perhaps that's enough for today," the doctor suggested.

"What about Patterson's wife and son?"

"Same. We offered her refuge, but she told me she'd rather put her trust in God."

"How long...what month is it?"

"November."

"I've been unconscious for two months?"

"Not exactly. You came down last year. It's been fourteen months."

"Fourteen?" Jack's voice was a lost whisper.

"That's enough," the doctor insisted.

Pie shook his head. "I don't think so. He needs to know how things are." He returned his attention to Jack. "The genomics research group was able to construct a counter virus, one that blocks the trigger for the death gene. We've all been infected with the counter virus, but those who were infected by the trigger died. You're the only one who was saved."

"Why bother." Jack continued to stare at the ceiling.

"We're in a fight to save the Earth and we will not just roll over. We'll save any life we can."

"Even mine."

"Yeah, you asshole, even yours." Pie waited a moment for a spark of defiance, but his comment had no effect. "Okay, as long as you are in a mood to feel sorry for yourself, you might as well know the rest." The doctor put a restraining hand on Pie's shoulder, but Pie ignored the warning. "Your guts were beyond repair. Most of your intestines had to be removed or you would've died at once. Your legs were smashed. They would never have healed so they were amputated below the knees. You're sterile and always will be, but, on a brighter note, you will heal if cut, your immune system has been resurrected and you do make your own blood. You have hair and skin that regenerates. All major accomplishments of the research team."

"You didn't save me. I'm dead."

"In a way, you're right. It's up to you save yourself. Think about it."

Jack didn't reply.

"I'll see you later," Pie said. He stood, and waited a moment, before he walked away.

The doctor reached down to pat Jack on his arm.

"Get away from me," Jack growled.

The doctor withdrew his hand, but remained next to the bed.

"I told you to get out of here!"

The doctor nodded. "If that's what you really want."

"It's what I really want."

"If you need anything, I can always be reached."

"Get out!"

Jack watched the doctor walk away. When the door shut, he began to shake and wrapped his arms across his chest, but the shaking wouldn't stop.

CHAPTER 16

Days turned into weeks. The support equipment was withdrawn and the monitors were turned off. Jack was moved to a room in the rehabilitation wing of the Copper Mountain infirmary. This room too was equipped for his special needs.

He had learned to transfer from bed to wheelchair, wheelchair to commode. The professional staff had been just that, professional, saying the right things and attending to his bodily needs, but he remained desolate. He wanted, needed, the one person he truly trusted, but Pie hadn't returned. Jack was not about to beg, that would surely have been the end of him.

There was a large monitor on the wall. He had stared at the black rectangle and the words to activate it had been thought, but never voiced. He was uncertain if he wanted to know what the monitor would reveal.

He sat in his wheelchair with his fingers poised over the control pad; the chair awaited his command to take him elsewhere, but there was nowhere he wanted to go. It seemed right that he stay sequestered, hidden from sight.

A chime sounded; there was someone at his door. He had just eaten, if you could call it eating, so it wasn't someone bringing his next meal. He had sent the psychs away in no uncertain terms. He doubted they would return any time soon. The chime repeated. It was an obvious attempt to suggest that he actually had control over some part of his life. They didn't need his permission to enter; everyone in the complex had the right to enter his room, at least that's the way it seemed to him. The chime sounded again. That was odd; they always entered after the second request was ignored.

"Open." Jack swiveled in his chair to face the door. A blanket covered his amputated legs.

Roxanne stood in the doorway. "May I come in?"

"Suit yourself."

There were times when simply the sight of her face had been enough to stimulate sexual excitement, but not now, no longer. His libido was another part of him that hadn't survived.

She walked into the room and looked around. The walls were bare. There was nothing but the most basic functionality, a hospital room without the monitoring equipment. The light was muted, half strength. There was one hard-back chair, used only by his psychiatrist.

"May I?" she said indicating the chair.

He shrugged.

It was enough of an invitation.

He was relieved she didn't try to encourage him with a display of artificial happiness or optimism. Although he felt no sexual stirring, from an esthetic viewpoint, he could still appreciate the good fortune of her face: her lips and mouth, high cheekbones, straight nose and green eyes. Her figure didn't appear as crispy molded as he recalled, but it was obvious she had continued to care for herself. She returned his gaze and he refused to look away. He wanted to shock her, to let the blanket fall to the floor and reveal legs that ended in stumps just below his knees, but didn't have the courage to act on the impulse, not in front of her. He could sit in silence forever. He'd done it often enough with his psychiatrist. If that was her plan, it wouldn't work.

"How are you doing?" she finally asked.

He viewed it as a small victory, but it wasn't a perfunctory question. There were lines in her face, new lines around her eyes and across her forehead.

He cleared his throat and nodded. "All right."

"I've been busy lately." The slump of her posture confirmed that she wasn't exaggerating. "Everybody has," she added.

"Not me."

She looked at the bed; it had side rails that could be raised. Her gaze didn't speak of seduction, but of the profound desire to rest, to close her eyes. Which she did.

A sense of concern arose. It was a shock to discover that caring hadn't gone completely from his life.

Her breathing became regular and her head slowly bent forward.

He wished he could somehow lift her and lay her on the bed. *Pure fantasy.* His greatest accomplishment was brushing his teeth. He drove his wheelchair closer, in case she began to slip from the chair, although how he could actually help her was unclear. For a second time, a sense of caring sneaked past his depression. He was glad she was here. That realization was more than he could cope with. Tears filled his lids and dripped down his face. His breath caught with a sob. In complete humiliation, he turned his chair away from her.

He pulled at the edge of the blanket and wiped his face, certain that she had heard his crying, that she had awakened. He searched for that deadly plain of depression, where he was nothing more than a husk of a man, but couldn't find it. The tears wouldn't stop. He began to sob. *Oh God, not that.* He had no control; the pain had found his hiding place. He couldn't escape. He wiped his face and prepared to swivel his chair to witness her scorn.

She had not hugged him. That thought broke his feeble control and he buried his face in his hands. He felt his chair being pushed and looked up; his face was as flushed and wet as that of any heart-broken child.

"Don't say a thing," she ordered. She rolled the chair over to the bed, which was just big enough for two people, if they held one another. "Get onto the bed."

"I can't...."

"You do it every day. Don't expect me to lift you."

"I mean...well, I...I can't...."

"Shit, Jack. Don't you ever think of anything besides sex?"

He smiled, a miracle. He raised himself up with his arms and swung his body around until he was on the bed. He felt the bed give and the warmth of a body pressed against his back, the special heat of another human. He held perfectly still, waiting for whatever disaster was to follow, and then heard her begin to snore. He relaxed, not to sleep, but to feel the warmth of her nearness. His shoulders began to ache, but he wasn't about to awaken her. It was a pleasure. He had forgotten all about pleasure.

As he rested, a burning pain replaced the pleasure. It was a familiar pain; his legs and feet felt as if they were still there and on fire. He tried to be still, but couldn't. The pain was unbearable. When he moved, he felt her awaken and then the loss of touch when she got out of the bed. He hid his face in the pillow.

"You're in pain, aren't you?"

"No, I'm not," he gritted through clenched teeth.

"Let me call a doctor."

"You're a doctor."

She nodded. "But I've never practiced. I'm a researcher, a macromolecular biologist. I don't know much about taking care of patients. Sorry." She rested her hand on his shoulder, but it only made the pain worse.

"In the drawer."

There was an assortment of medicated patches in the drawer of the nightstand. He held his breath while she sorted through them. It seemed to take her forever to select a small red dot and apply it to the skin of his shoulder. After a few minutes, the vice of pain eased and he looked up at her.

"I hate using those. It numbs my mind."

"Isn't that the point?"

"It numbs everything. I feel like I'm losing control. I don't want to be gone again, like I've been for the last year. Never again."

"Is it helping?"

"Yes."

"Good. Mason is making an address It's almost over. Boy, I must've been tired." She brushed her red hair back with her fingers. "I want to hear it."

He frowned, but suppressed his objection. He wanted her to stay even more than he didn't want Mason in his sight.

The screen came to life for the first time since he'd taken up residence in this room, his universe, as much space as he could cope with.

Mason was in mid-sentence and appeared serious. "—and that brings me to propose three objectives. The first is the construction of a true space station, a city in space. The second is the development and construction of a starship capable of establishing a colony elsewhere. The third is the full implementation of mass cloning to revitalize our species and all the life we've managed to save."

A square on the screen opened to reveal a woman with curly gray hair who disdained all cosmetics. The words "Stanford-San Jose" appeared beneath her portion of the screen. "There is much that needs to be attended to on Earth. With the fires and the collapse of life, the temperature has risen. The ice caps are melting. We must first focus on the Earth."

A man's face replaced hers. His dark hair was cut close; his features were coarse and the blackness of his shaved beard was a mask across his lower face. The word "St.

Petersburg" was under his square. The words from the translator did not match the movement of his lips. "I agree with Director Mason. Whoever sent this plague will be following. We aren't in a position to defend ourselves against a superior technology. We must find another home for mankind. We'll need the space station to construct the starship and to maintain a strong presence in space."

The woman's face returned; she was composed as she responded. It was a civilized exchange.

Jack stopped listening to the words. It was the bland tone of the discussion that shocked him. He couldn't believe these people were discussing the future of humanity.

"So, as you can see, we don't have the resources to undertake such a project," the woman concluded.

Mason, who had remained on the screen in his own secure square, answered. "I disagree, Marta. This is the only time we *will* have the resources. Key personnel have been saved. The entire Earth is available for our use. There will be no competition for resources and it's all there, in warehouses, stockpiles, manufacturing plants, but there will be a time in the near future when mankind's knowledge will be in jeopardy. We have the people now. We need to use them because in two or three generations, well...there is a regression toward the mean."

A laugh accompanied the appearance of a thin-framed man who spoke with a British accent. "We won't become dimwitted simply because the population base has been devastated. There are plenty left to maintain the gene pool, an improved one, no doubt."

Jack shook his head. If this man's kooky arrogance was an example of the remaining gene pool, he had doubts about its viability.

Mason smiled.

Did they all know something he didn't? Jack wondered. How could there be room for levity? Were things not as bad as he suspected, so bad he'd been afraid to ask about it?

"Charles," Mason said with an amused shake of his head, "I'm sure you'll do your best to propagate your genes. At any rate, I'm making these proposals now so you can discuss them among yourselves. We cannot afford to miss this unparalleled opportunity of worldwide cooperation. We can at least thank this catastrophe for finally bringing us together.

I have one last announcement. At the website CopperMountain.com/infectedman, you'll be able to review the data we've gathered during our efforts to salvage an infected person."

Jack pushed himself up on his elbows.

"You'll find that the effort was very expensive in terms of resources consumed and that the end result was questionable at best. However, we did learn a lot that your own medical teams may find useful."

Jack lowered himself back onto the bed.

"Our next meeting will be on Wednesday, fifteen hundred, Greenwich time."

The screen faded to black.

"Jack?"

He looked over at her.

"Are you okay?" she asked.

"Just peachy."

"Jack, I know this is going to sound like an odd question but, if you could have either your legs, or your intestines back, what would you choose?"

He glared at her.

"I guess it's kind of a hard question to answer. Anyway, don't take Mason so personally. He doesn't represent the team and he's like that to everyone, but he has provided a desperately needed sense of direction."

"He's a real special fellow. Sounds like you've been talking with Pie Traynor. Have you?"

"Pie Traynor?"

"Yes, have you met him?"

She hesitated and then said, "I've met him."

"Have you seen him lately?"

"Why...no. Why do you ask?"

"I was just wondering because—never mind."

"I think he's been away from Copper Mountain because I haven't...seen him lately. He's been busy."

"Right. He's been busy. You've been busy. Everybody's been busy."

"It's the truth." She stood and glanced at her watch before looking back to him. "What did you say?"

"I didn't say anything."

"Would you like me to stay a while longer?"

"No."

"Are you sure?"

"I'm sure. Thanks for stopping by."

"I'll be back. I have things I need to attend to."

"No doubt. See you."

"Okay."

Her lips did that pouting thing, but it failed to arouse even a trace of a lascivious thought.

As soon as the door closed, Jack transferred from the bed to his chair. He drove the chair over to the wall screen. "Connect with CopperMountain.com/infectedman."

He could hardly recognize himself. Bright lights illuminated an operating table. On the table, amongst a crowd of doctors and nurses, was a naked, bloodied body. He heard his moaning, an unconscious agony, and saw his crushed legs. Numerous tubes connected him to bundles of bags, some containing dark-red blood, others clear liquids. A narrator began to detail each of his injuries. Jack fast-forwarded.

The view shifted to a laboratory where a young man in a white coat explained with great enthusiasm about how Jack's DNA had been harvested from stored blood and tissue samples. He went on to explain how the shell of the alien microbe had provided the perfect vehicle to reestablish Jack's immune system. The report described further enhancements over a period of months and concluded with a view of Jack's comatose body. He was completely exposed; his legs had been amputated and the midline abdominal incision that had been used to remove the majority of his intestines was still pink.

A man came on, with a trimmed mustache and dignified stance. Rathburn insisted that the effort had been worth it, that it had led to great advances in cloning and the technique of genetic modification. The greatest failure, Rathburn asserted, was in the infected-man's ability to cope. He went on to suggest that this failure was most likely due to an inherent weakness of the subject, an inability to appreciate what had been done for him, or to become a productive member of society. Rathburn declared that there was nothing more to be learned from this experiment. He extended his arm and the view expanded to include a room full of men and women, many jockeying for position so that their faces could be seen.

Jack searched for Roxanne, but didn't see her.

"The team," Rathburn announced and began clapping; those who had worked on the project joined him. Rathburn bowed toward the team to accept his due praise and then faced the screen. "The technical details can be downloaded. Simply request the articles you'd like to review." Rathburn's face with its self-satisfied smile faded and was replaced by the slowly scrolling titles of various aspects of the project.

"Monitor off." Jack stared at the blank screen.

Time had again become unmeasurable when his door chimed. He arranged his blanket to cover the stumps of his legs. It chimed a second time, followed within seconds by the entry of a young woman, one of his caretakers. It was part of an effort that was no longer worthwhile, according to those who made such decisions. Jack could find no argument with their conclusion.

The young woman, a girl actually, set up his tray and placed his "food" on it.

"Can I do anything for you?" she asked sweetly.

"Shoot me."

The girl's too-happy-smile froze and she backed nervously from the room.

Jack drove his chair over to his food, a thick, yellow liquid in a wide-mouthed carafe. It was all his truncated intestine could absorb, a well-balanced, predigested concoction, the essential components of life. It tasted faintly of dust and soybeans. He knew what would happen when he drank it; thirty minutes later he would have to be sitting on the commode, never more than forty. He stared at the so-called food. If he could only get his hands on some real food, that alone would probably kill him. He could visualize Rathburn's addendum to the report. "Today, the sole survivor of the death microbe was unable to cope and killed himself with a hot dog."

He picked up the carafe and threw it. The contents splattered across the wall and began to ooze down it. He swiveled his chair toward the opposite wall. He waited for time to stop, but the minutes continued to creep past. He directed his chair to the nightstand and opened the drawer. He used the dots of transdermal medication to make a happy face on his chest. While applying them in a row up his arm, he fell to the floor, unconscious.

CHAPTER 17

Jack opened his eyes. It had all been a terrible nightmare. He stretched and then turned his head. Lines wove their way across monitor screens. He reached down to feel the knobs of his amputated legs. It was no nightmare. It was much worse; it was reality.

The door slid open, but he didn't even look in that direction. "Why," he said, "are you wasting more resources on me? It's stupid. Let me die."

He closed his eyes and waited for a response, but all he heard was the "creak" of a chair when someone lowered his weight onto it.

"Go away."

"The trouble with you is that you've got no guts." It was Pie Traynor.

Jack's eyes shot open.

"That's a damn mean thing to say." He stared at his friend, or was it former friend?

"No guts," Pie repeated.

"All right, damn it! You've made your point. I'm a cowardly piece of shit. Anything else?"

"That's not what I mean. I mean you need some guts, you know, some intestines. I've seen what you've been eating. A man cannot live on mush alone. I figure, if we can get some real food into you, maybe you'll get up out of that bed and give us a hand. We could sure use it."

"I watched CopperMountain.com/infected man."

"Is that the one with two blondes and—"

"Stop it, Pie. I appreciate what you're trying to do, but I'm not...."

"Not what?"

"Not anything."

"I didn't risk my neck to gather up your broken carcass so you could come back here and lounge around on an extended holiday."

"I wish you'd let me die."

"Too late for that. I guess you're going to have to live. Oh, by the way, tomorrow you get your legs."

"Legs? You...I would never expect such mean, vicious—"

"They may not be as good as your old ones, but in some ways they'll be better."

"What are you saying?"

"Biomechanical."

"That's bullshit. After what I heard on the monitor yesterday? The experiment is over."

"You mean a week ago?"

"Whatever." Then Jack nodded. "Now I understand. I get it. On to the next phase of messing around with the infected-man."

"I guess you could look at it that way. Or, you could get your ass out of bed and begin walking around."

"Why?"

"Jack, you had what it takes before...before, well, you know, before everything. I want you to be my assistant, if you don't find it too demeaning."

"Not at all, boss. Make sure your clothes are set out, wipe your butt. Sounds like a career anyone would die for."

"I can hardly wait until you're up and around again, because I feel the need to knock you onto your ass, whack that little head of yours until it rings." Pie took a deep breath and exhaled with a smile. "That sounds so good."

Jack could withhold his sense of desertion no longer. "Where have you been?"

"Well, let me see. I've been to St. Petersburg, Berlin, Cambridge, Jerusalem, Taipei, Kobe, Paris, Padua, Cape Town, Bogotá—"

"All right."

"I'm not finished. I'm only getting started. I have been to every bubble, every dome, every underground, every outpost where humans are struggling to survive."

"Why?"

"Sometimes video conferencing isn't enough. Sometimes there is a need for person to person contact for real ties to develop."

"For Mason."

"You still don't get it do you? I'm doing whatever the hell I can to somehow help humanity survive and I expect the same of you."

Jack returned his gaze to the ceiling.

"Any other burning questions?" Pie asked.

Jack remained silent.

"Until later then." He punched Jack on the shoulder. It was not a light tap; it sent pain shooting down Jack's arm. He grabbed his shoulder and began rubbing it.

Pie began to laugh in that belly rumbling way of his.

Jack stared at him, incredulous. "You can't do that."

"I'll tell you this my little friend, until you get out of that bed and begin defending yourself, I'm going to come in and beat you up a little every day. Think of it as my contribution to your mental health." Pie smiled. "It felt good, didn't it?"

To Jack's surprise he found himself nodding.

"Okay, till tomorrow then."

CHAPTER 18

The pain of regenerating nerves was special only because it was the pain that was freshest in Jack's memory. The subliminal learning tapes had helped but, in the end, rehabilitation hadn't changed all that much; it had been a daily grind.

Jack walked down the hall. He avoided the eyes of those he passed. He didn't want to see pity or curiosity or answer any questions about how he felt. He'd had enough of that from his doctors.

His mechanical feet clicked against the floor despite the shoes he wore. He needed the hard contact for feedback. Although he had regained a sense of position, it wasn't natural enough that he could ignore his new legs; walking required his attention. At least he was no longer afraid he was going to fall; that had been a major hurdle.

He clicked down the hall with a faint "whirring" which he thought everyone could hear but, in reality, only he could; the sound was transmitted up metal pins and plates into the bones of his body. He rounded a corner and saw Pie up ahead. Pie waved and Jack smiled, more grateful for the support of his old friend than he could ever express.

"Hey, Jack, how goes it, my mechanical man?"

He wished everyone could be as matter of fact as his friend.

"I'm fine," Jack said as he drew close. "I'm thinking about playing a little B-ball this afternoon. Care to join me?"

"Wouldn't be fair."

Jack frowned.

"I imagine you could jump through the ceiling with those mechanical legs," Pie added with a rumbling laugh.

Jack grinned. It had been so long since he had felt any emotion akin to happiness.

Pie clapped him on the shoulder, hard enough that Jack's knees almost buckled, but he could take it. Pie had that effect on him.

Pie kept his hold on Jack's shoulder. "Are you ready?"

Jack nodded, a little grimmer. He had accepted the position Pie had offered. He was now the assistant to the Assistant Director of Copper Mountain, which had become for all practical purposes the capital of the world. Pie was the Assistant Director of the world; yet, he carried the responsibility as if it were nothing more than a job. Jack studied his friend and saw the redness of his eyes and the sagging skin beneath them.

"Do I have a pimple or something?" Pie asked.

Jack smiled. "No, you're the same handsome bastard as always." Pie was feeling the pressure; he just had too much pride to show it.

Pie entered the elevator with Jack behind him.

When the door closed he looked to Jack. "You know Mason will be there, right?"

Jack nodded. "I know. I'll behave."

"Good."

Mason's new office was fronted by an anteroom filled with people, some working in front of monitors and others gathered in hushed discussions of apparent grave import. They were so focused that not a single person gave them anything other than a cursory glance as they walked through the room.

"Where's Sam?" Jack asked.

"A field agent. Too useful to keep at a desk any longer."

With a sense of relief, Jack nodded. He didn't want to hear about one more death.

An armed guard opened the door for them. They entered a conference room that was large enough to seat twenty people around an elliptical table. Most of the chairs were already taken. Pie led Jack to a couple of empty chairs near the front of the room.

After they were seated Jack leaned toward Pie. "Where's Roxanne Wiley? You've met her, haven't you?"

"Yes...we've met."

"Isn't she a member of the executive council?"

Pie shook his head.

Jack recognized the flight operations director, but no one else. All of them were men and most were graying or balding or both; all were dressed in suits with tight collars. There was a subversive feel to the group. No one met his eyes as he looked around the room; some studied portable monitors, while others were in solemn conversations with their neighbors. No one was smiling. There was no sense of camaraderie.

"Why isn't she here?"

"Wasn't invited."

Jack took another frowning look around the room and saw one more person he recognized. The man was well groomed, with a closely trimmed mustache and a full head of hair, touched with gray at the temples. It was not an unfriendly gaze that returned Jack's stare, more a look of self-congratulation. Though it was an effort, Jack managed not to give him the finger.

"I see Rathburn is here."

"You know him?"

"Not really. I spoke briefly to him a long time ago and then there is that wonderful infected-man piece. Roxanne Wiley told me some things about him. She should be here, not him."

"I agree, but it's Mason's show and these are the people he has chosen to work with."

"What an ass—"

"Careful." The word was spoken harshly. "No matter what your personal feelings are, or mine for that matter, Mason has been working non-stop, providing the leadership the world needs. He is one of the main reasons the Earth is not even worse off than it is. He deserves credit."

Jack clenched his teeth and stared at the mahogany tabletop.

"I mean it, Jack."

Jack refused to meet Pie's gaze and slid a little deeper into his seat. He heard the door open and then a voice that made his gut tighten.

"We'll get right to it," Mason said as he walked toward Jack, "but first I want to welcome the newest member of our little group, Captain Jack Nichols. Jack will be assisting Pie in special projects."

The room was quiet with stares. No friendly words of welcome were spoken.

Jack didn't look up, but could feel the heat is his face. This is the man who was responsible for sending them into a contaminated station, of bringing the infection back to Earth, of Gustave, Mei Li and Kate's deaths. He stiffened when he felt Mason's hand on his shoulder and turned to stare at it as if were a dead rat.

"As you all know, Jack survived the microbe, the only human to have survived. A major effort was required, but a great deal of the success belongs to Jack. He's a fighter, a survivor, the kind of man that we want on our team as we attack the problems that confront us."

Jack felt the rat squeeze his shoulder, but refused to look up, afraid of what he might do if he saw Mason's smiling face.

"Anything to say, Jack?" Mason asked.

Jack could feel Pie's stare without looking in his direction. "I'll do the best I can." He was grateful to feel the rat-grip ease and leave his shoulder.

"That's all any of us can do."

He finally took a normal breath, while Mason made his way back to the front of the room and took his seat.

"Let's keep the reports brief. Larson."

The fat man's eyes were dark slits. Sweat glistened on his upper lip despite the air conditioning. "The first section of the station's cylinder is completed and ready for transport into space. Plans for the starship are proceeding and on schedule."

Mason switched his gaze to a man who was sitting with the rigidity of a soldier and the man responded. "Crews are ready. Scramjets are ready. We can begin construction of the station today, if need be."

"Good, very good. Life Science?"

Rathburn glanced briefly at Jack before directing his gaze to Mason. "Preliminary reports indicate that the anti-microbe seeding of the oceans is going to be a success. The kills washing to shore have begun to abate and there is evidence of continued life in the sea, including plankton. This was vital for replenishing oxygen and deserves celebration."

Mason began a measured clapping and most joined him, stopping the moment he stopped.

Rathburn smiled, revealing his stark-white, too-perfect teeth. "So true. It ensures a renewable atmosphere. Our success on land has been less evident. However, due to your early and decisive leadership—" He nodded toward Mason. "—we haven't lost our capability to restock land flora and fauna. Unfortunately, a number of holdings have lost all their rescued specimens. Therefore, I recommend the continued isolation of most specimens. We've had major successes in cloning and research is progressing on a universal uterus."

A universal uterus? What the hell? Jack looked to Pie, but Pie didn't respond.

"Patel." Mason said.

"Humanity section is coping."

Jack fought an unacceptable urge to laugh.

"Suicide rate is dropping—"

The urge to laugh was gone.

"—and the birth rate is climbing. Also, as I understand it, advances in cloning could result in the salvage of much of the genetic heritage of those who have killed themselves." He gestured in Rathburn's direction, as if Rathburn alone was responsible for the successes of the Life Science section. "There is a growing sense of mission which has helped tremendously." This time he inclined his head toward Mason.

"Worthington?"

"Material levels are excellent when it comes to industrial supplies, but food will become a problem within the next year. Better food, fresh food, would go a long way to helping moral, in my opinion."

Patel nodded. "I agree, good point."

Mason looked to Rathburn.

"We won't starve. Using the penetrating microbe, we're close to designing organisms that can produce all the nutrition we'll need."

Mason nodded. "That's good, but we were talking about identifiable food."

His comment was met with a tempered chuckle from around the table.

Rathburn continued, "Attempts at growing food outside have not met with success. The ultraviolet radiation is too intense. And we haven't been able to promote animal life to the point it can be used for food. When the sea has fully recovered, it may provide us with our best source of animal protein."

"General Clark, field ops?"

"There continues to be a remarkable level of cooperation around the world and an acceptance of our leadership here at Copper Mountain. I've begun to recruit operatives at the most important sites. So far we're on course. As you know, there is one major problem. JPL-Caltech has gone off-line. They don't respond. Satellite surveillance reveals none of the usual activity outside the dome cluster, but the domes themselves appear intact."

Pie spoke. "I'm going to investigate in person."

"Is that a wise decision?" Mason asked. "We need you

here. Why don't you send Jack? Unless, of course, you don't think he's ready."

Jack scowled and for the first time looked Mason in the face. His retort remained unvoiced. Mason looked ten years older. His hair had heavy streaks of gray and his face had a pasty appearance with dark crescents under his eyes.

Mason returned Jack's gaze. "Do you think you're up to it?"

Pie answered, "I don't know, Mitch, I—"

"Yes," Jack said over Pie. "I'm ready."

Mason continued to measure him with his eyes and finally nodded. "Very well. The next full council meeting will be in seven days. You can give us a report then. Pie can reach me if you need to contact me before then." He turned his attention to the room. "I'm going to skip the rest of the reports so I can prepare for the general meeting tonight. I'd like you all to be here. There are going to be some problems with Pyongyang and Shanghai. Meeting's adjourned."

As the men arose Mason spoke to Jack. "Stay a moment, will you? You too, Pie." He waited for the room to empty and then sat back, resting with his eyes shut for a minute. He opened his bloodshot eyes and sat forward. "Glad to see you up and around, Jack."

"I hope it was worth the tremendous effort." The bitterness would not go away.

"I hope so too."

Jack was about to respond, but Mason stopped him.

"Jane asked me to say hello and to tell you that she hopes you're doing well."

The rage wilted. "How is she?"

"Doing as well as any of us."

"And the boy?"

"Thanks for asking. His name is Joshua. He's one and half now and, to be perfectly blunt, he's one of the main reasons I keep going."

"I can imagine," Jack said in a flat voice.

"It's been hard for all of us. I don't want to push you into something you're not ready for. Do you feel up to a mission?"

Jack nodded.

"All right then. One of General Clark's aides will brief you." He pushed himself up as if he weighed twice as much and walked out of the room.

Pie turned to Jack. "There's a major problem going on and I haven't had the time to look into the details. Do you really feel up it?"

"Damn it! Why does everyone keep asking me that?" Of all people, Pie's question was the only one that shook his confidence. "Don't *you* think I'm ready?"

"I think you are."

"Damn right."

"Then you better go up to field ops. You'll be leaving the day after tomorrow."

CHAPTER 19

It was apparent that General Clark had reservations about Jack. Even though Jack had trained as a pilot in preparation for the Mars mission, he wasn't chosen to pilot or copilot the aircraft; he was a passenger, the only passenger. However, the choice of pilot was a good one and had Pie's fingerprints all over it. Jack had known Blas Uribe since their academy days.

When Blas had learned they were to be teamed up, he and his wife had dropped by Jack's apartment for a visit. Maria was the same jovial, warm-hearted person Jack remembered, but she had certainly filled out. Having five children could do that to a person. She had insisted that Jack come over for a home-cooked meal of tamales and beans when they returned.

Jack looked out the window of the aircraft and shifted to get more comfortable in his seat; he had the feeling that she hadn't believed him when he told her he couldn't eat food anymore. She hadn't come right out and said it, but he could see it in her face.

"Hey, Blas."

"Go ahead, Jack."

"Maria believed me when I told her I couldn't eat food, didn't she?"

"What?"

"Never mind." He would stop by when they got home, just to make sure.

The co-pilot was a different story altogether. Jack was still irritated with him for calling his food "baby formula" and then laughing like a jackass. Everyone who made that joke thought they were being so clever. The co-pilot was one those people who thought everything he said was so damned funny and never noticed he was the only one laughing. He insisted that everyone call him Timmy. Whoever heard of an adult named Timmy? He was young and stupid, Jack told himself, suggesting that he would change with maturity, but not really believing it.

Jack stared out the window as they completed their descent. They broke through dirty gray clouds and the clouds were revealed for what they actually were: the gritty smoke from hundreds of fires. The cities of Earth were burning and there was no one to extinguish the blaze.

The aircraft banked and approached the flaming city from the ocean. The coastline was altered. The ocean was rising. The world was in an oven heated by its own conflagration. The sea had flooded the low-lying coast; tall buildings protruded from the water with white surf crashing against their walls. It wouldn't take long for the ocean to complete the destruction.

When they approached the San Gabriel Mountains, Uribe flew the aircraft lower and slowed as they neared Pasadena. He increased the pitch of the jets so that the aircraft drifted along, above Colorado Avenue. Entire blocks were gutted, with orphan walls standing by themselves, charred and black. Caltech was a ruin. Those who had been invited, and heeded the early warning, had fled to the bubble refuge that had been built at JPL and that was their destination as well. To the left was the empty Rose Bowl, thousands of vacant seats with a field of muddy brown at its center. The craft banked to the right revealing the bubble-city, two-dozen Bucky-bubbles made rigid by repeating triangles of aluminum tubes. The bubbles were joined by covered walkways, a giant hamster habitat where humans were the hamsters.

The aircraft descended to hover ten meters above what had been a grassy field; it was now mud. There was no green. Along the perimeter, the bare bones of tree trunks stuck out of the earth, their brittle branches snapped off by wind.

Jack arose to stand behind Blas and look out the cockpit window. The stark-white domes in the rain etched field of mud appeared deserted. The roar of the jet engines had to be audible in every dome, but no one came out to greet them.

Blas twisted in his seat and looked to Jack for direction.

"Take her down."

He nodded and returned to his console. The aircraft touched down with a barely perceptible bob, attesting to another skill humanity was at risk of losing. There was so much that needed to be saved; one essential missing piece and humanity's tottering civilization could come tumbling down, perhaps leading to the extinction of mankind.

To Jack, it already looked like the end of the world. There

were no birds, nothing but mud and rocks. No bomb could cause devastation as vast as this. This was Armageddon and he had lived to see it.

Blas shut down the engines and there was quiet. Again he turned to Jack. "Want help putting on your suit?"

Jack shook his head and walked to the rear of the aircraft. He took out the hazmat suit and held it. He could imagine Kate, ready to join him, but that would never again be possible.

"Changed your mind?" Timmy asked. "Because I think you're right. We should get the hell out of here."

In answer, Jack stepped into the legs of his suit. It was better to be prepared for the worst than bring something unwanted back to Copper Mountain.

Timmy reluctantly followed Jack's example.

While Jack was sealing the helmet, he had a thought. Wouldn't they feel ridiculous when the people in the bubble met them in t-shirts and jeans? He paused. They wouldn't shoot first and ask questions later, would they? He watched as Timmy strapped the latest incarnation of a Gatling gun to his thigh; it was nasty looking and as long as his forearm. He had intended to insist that Timmy leave it behind, but now he wasn't so sure. He looked past Timmy, through the front windshield of the aircraft; no one had stepped out of the domes. There was no sign of life.

"Did you try to raise them?" Jack asked, his voice loud in the confines of the suit.

"I've been trying for the last five hundred kilometers," Blas replied. "Nothing. Not even a squawk."

"We should ask for back-up," Timmy suggested.

Jack heard them through his comm-unit; the only other thing he could hear was his own breathing. "We were sent here to find out what happened and retrieve data and that's exactly what we're going to do."

Timmy's expression was visible through the faceplate of his helmet. There was little chance of another joke.

Jack opened the aircraft door and waited for the ladder to extend to the ground. Climbing down ladders wasn't a skill he had practiced. With no sensation in his mechanical feet, it required deliberate placement of his feet on each rung. His progress was slow, but he managed without falling. He stepped onto the mud and looked down, peering through his faceplate. There was nothing, not a stray weed, not a blade of grass, nothing but clay-marbled mud. He glanced up to see Timmy climbing down and waited for him before proceeding.

Jack pointed to the biggest dome and Timmy nodded with his hand resting on the butt of his gun. As they slogged through the mud, a light rain began to fall. Jack looked up; his faceplate darkened to protect him from ultraviolet radiation, which was intense despite the cloud cover. He lowered his gaze and the faceplate lightened to again reveal the gray light of a rainy day and the dark orange of wet clay swirled into the black mud of topsoil.

He slowed as he approached the lock to the main bubble, still expecting someone to open the door and welcome them to "sunny California". He waited at the door with Timmy, who had drawn his weapon.

Above the door was a camera. "Hello in there," Jack said, broadcasting from his suit. "We're from Copper Mountain." He pushed on the handle; it was locked. He saw movement out of the corner of his eyes and walked around to the side of the short entrance tunnel. There was a rent in the material where the tunnel met the dome; it was flapping in the breeze.

"Do you want me to shoot the latch off?" Timmy asked.

To say "yes" meant the acceptance that a catastrophe had befallen JPL.

"Let me take a look at this first."

Jack walked along the length of the entry tube and stared at the flapping material. He grabbed hold and pulled it back. There was an inner layer. He stepped into the space and saw another tear.

"It looks like they've had a breech in their barrier," Jack said. "The microbe must have gotten in."

"Negative," the eavesdropping Blas responded. "They would've been dead a year ago. They were immunized."

Jack nodded. *Stupid.* He needed to be better than that.

"Maybe a marauding band of criminals broke in," Timmy suggested.

Jack shook his head. There was no marauding anything out there. Anything that survived, survived within a dome; the seeding of land with the anti-microbe had been a failure. He reached down and pulled at the material; it was synthetic and tough. He felt his shoulder being tapped and swiveled overly fast.

"Want a knife?" Timmy asked.

Jack took the knife and began sawing away at the fabric until the hole was large enough for them to enter.

They stopped just inside. They were standing in a rotunda. Other than for a water stain at their feet, the dome appeared untouched. There was still power. Overhead lights lit the entire dome, which had been sectioned into cubicles, all of them open to the ceiling. There were monitors on a wall in front of a console; the chairs were tipped back, some had been upended, but there were no people, no bodies.

"Where do you think they went?" Timmy continued to hold his weapon at the ready.

Jack walked around to the front of the monitor array and touched an activator pad. One of the monitors revealed the stubby-winged aircraft sitting in the muddy field with steam rising from where the engines were pointed at the earth. Another monitor revealed the front entrance, where they had been standing, and others showed various views outside the complex. Nothing moved.

"I don't know how to access the internal monitors," Jack said.

"If there are any," Timmy added.

"True." The little privacy they had was probably guarded as closely as it was in Copper Mountain. "Blas, are you getting all this?"

"Loud and clear. Good audio and video from both of you. Be careful out there."

"We plan to."

Jack led Timmy down a hallway, opening doors as he went. The rooms were empty. There was no sign of a struggle; it was as if the people of JPL had simply vanished.

They returned to the main concourse and Jack eyed the tunnels that led to other domes. None were labeled; the people who lived here were few enough that everyone knew where every tunnel led. He picked one at random.

The tunnel was dimly lit by feeble sunlight diffusing through the double layer of the dome material. Crates and metal drums were stored in the tunnel.

"What were they working on here? Do you know?" Timmy asked.

"A number of things, but the information we need to retrieve has something to do with the starship. Something about a stasis cylinder."

The hazmat suits isolated them from sounds and from each other. Only their voices were broadcast with clarity; it was tempting to keep talking. The opening to the next dome lay ahead. There was light.

Jack stepped through the doorway. The overhead lighting was as bright as a sunny day. On the concrete floor of the dome were rows of bubbling tanks. Hydroponics. He stepped forward to inspect one of the tanks. It did not lack for nutrient fluid, but there was nothing there. He walked to the next and then the next. All were empty.

"It looks like they took their plants with them. Wherever they went." Timmy clipped his gun onto his thigh.

Jack led the way back to the main dome. This time he walked all the way around the dome before entering another tunnel. The end of this tunnel was different; the doorway was blocked off. Heavy cabinets were visible as dark shapes behind a layer of fabric.

They stood side by side staring at it.

"Looks like they were trying to keep something out," Timmy said.

"Or something in," Jack added.

"Maybe so." Timmy unclipped his weapon. "Should we go in?"

"I think we need to." Jack took a couple of steps back.

Timmy aimed the Gatling gun at the barricade and pressed the button. The gun vibrated, firing a spray of a hundred explosive pellets a second. The fabric and cabinets disintegrated. He held his gun ready, with the whirring of the spinning cylinders the only sound, but nothing came at them through the cloud of cabinetry and material. The dust settled to reveal a large hole, attesting to the firepower he held in his hands.

This time Timmy led the way into the dome. He picked his footing to avoid twisted metal.

"Look at this!" Timmy yelled. He swept his weapon across the dome, but held his fire. Nothing moved.

Jack stepped around him to inspect the human skeleton that was lying on the concrete.

"This fellow's been dead for a while," Jack said. "Very strange."

"Uh-huh, this place gives me the creeps. Let's find that data and get the hell out of here."

"We don't know what happened. That's one of the reasons we were sent here."

"I don't like the feel of this place," Timmy said.

"Me either, but we have a mission to complete."

Jack walked down the hallway, around the circumference of the dome, and tried to open the first door. It was barricaded from the inside. He got down on his hands and knees to peer through the ventilation space at the bottom of the door. There was no movement. He stood and again began pushing against the door.

"Come on, Timmy, I could use a little help here," Jack said.

Together, they were able to open the door far enough for Jack to squeeze through. There were more skeletons. Seven. In the corner, there was an adult-sized skeleton collapsed on top of a smaller one, as if trying to shield a child. The room appeared otherwise untouched, except for the desk and table that had been pushed up against the door. He knelt next to a skeleton; it was bare bones other than for a metallic belt clasp that looked as if it had been held together by leather at one time. This was not right. JPL had gone silent within the last week, not long enough for bacteria to have digested their remains.

Jack began to tremble; it was the Mars Explorer all over again, a new and even more terrible disease. He squeezed back into the hallway. Timmy was standing with his back to him, focused on the entrance to the tunnel with his weapon in hand.

"Did you hear that?" Timmy asked.

It was difficult to hear much of anything within their suits. Jack increased the gain on the suit's microphones. "What did you hear?"

"A sound, like a clicking, but many times over, small sounds like...."

Now Jack heard the sound as well. "Like sand against glass."

"It's time for you two to get out of there," Blas said.

"In a minute," Jack replied. "We still need to find and retrieve the data."

The dome darkened and they looked up. A shadow was passing over the material, as if a black cloud was blocking out the weak sunlight of a rainy day. They activated their headlights, casting harsh shadows.

They both heard Blas over their comm-units. "I don't know what's happening out there but there is something black spreading over the domes. It doesn't look good. Get the hell out of there, now!"

Timmy ran down the tunnel, holding his weapon out in front, and Jack hurried after him.

The metallic "clicking" grew louder and was accompanied by a "chittering". The sound was coming from the main dome.

Timmy stopped and looked back to Jack. "I'm going to blast our way out of here."

"Do it."

Timmy raked the tunnel wall with his weapon; explosive bursts tore an opening to the outside. Without waiting, he charged through and was immediately engulfed in blackness that fell off the fabric. He stumbled into the muddy field and lost his weapon as he swatted at the blackness.

"My God! What is it?" Jack asked. All he heard in response was Timmy's heavy breathing.

Jack stood within the ragged opening and saw the blackness crawl around the edge of the hole. Huge black beetles dropped to the floor with the sound of pebbles striking concrete and scurried toward him. One opened its shell to reveal wings and flew at him. He slapped it out of the air as he retreated and then looked back to the living quarters; there were only skeletons in that direction. He ran down the tunnel toward the main dome, with Timmy's voice in his ears, crying and screaming, begging for help.

Jack slowed and looked back in the direction he had come. There was nothing he could do for Timmy. He ran to the exit tunnel and stopped. A black, seething mass of scarab beetles oozed through the hole in the fabric. They sensed meat and were coming for him as they had for all who had lived at JPL. He heard a whimpering from Timmy and then nothing.

"Timmy?" It was Blas. "Jack?"

"I'm here." Jack's voice sounded thin in his own ears. He backed away, along the circumference of the main dome, trying to see in every direction at once.

"What's happening in there?" Blas transmitted. "Where's Timmy? I've lost his audio and video feed. His biometrics have flat lined."

"He went outside and was engulfed by beetles. He's dead."

"There's a black cloud heading toward the aircraft. Jack...I don't know how long I can wait. If they plug the intake manifold, that'll be all she wrote. It's vital I get this information back to Copper Mountain."

"Wait, for God's sake! I'll find a way out." Jack pushed against the tough fabric, but it barely dented with the effort. He wished he still had Timmy's knife and looked around for something sharp, anything.

"Forgive me, Jack. Can't wait. If I don't lift off now, I won't be able to. Forgive me, my friend."

Jack stopped his frantic search. He heard the whine of the engines as they wound up for lift off. The first black beetles made their way around the curve and scuttled toward him. He retreated along the circumference of the dome. He would soon be out of running room and then.... He shivered with the thought.

Chitinous bodies clicked as they jostled against one another. The sound was coming from all sides. It wouldn't be long.

Suddenly, Jack was blown off his feet. The fabric of the dome was torn away and the interior walls were knocked down. He lay on the concrete floor looking up at gray clouds, while raindrops pelted him. His mind was a fuzzy jumble, until a beetle crawled onto to his faceplate. Its black carapace glistened with shimmers of bright green and its sharp mandibles scratched against the clear acrylic as it tried to cut its way through to his face.

He jumped to his feet and swatted away the few beetles that had made their way to him. The dome was shredded and beyond it was a carpet of beetles, but they weren't all dead. There was movement. He ran onto the mud, slipped and fell, as if he'd forgotten all he'd learned about his mechanical legs. He struggled to his feet and ran again, until the muddy field was in full view. The aircraft had exploded and its ruptured fuel tanks fed a blue flame that spread outward from the wreckage across the muddy field. There was no possibility that Blas had survived.

The ground was black around him, a seething mass that was closing in. As he ran he heard the "crunching" of beetles, transmitted through his metal legs. If he fell again, he would never get up. He didn't look down, but knew that beetles clung to the legs of his suit and were crawling upward, working on the fabric, cutting their way in. He kept his vision fixed on the fire and ran into it. His boots and pants caught on fire, exposing the metal of his feet and legs. When he exited the flames, he shed his smoldering outfit. He ran through the warm, fat raindrops. Even though his sides ached and his throat was raw, he continued to run.

CHAPTER 20

Jack hurried down the hill. He didn't look behind to witness the writhing mass of beetles feeding on the dead. He staggered to a stop when he heard a sharp "crack". A pine tree collapsed to the muddy earth and exploded in a cloud of yellow dust, its wood eaten away by a swarm of red bugs.

He ran and stumbled onto a street, but didn't stop; his soot-blackened metallic legs carried him on. His helmet was all that remained of his hazmat suit, the faceplate warped by the heat; he threw it away. He ran until he could run no more and finally turned to look. There was no black cloud in pursuit. He began walking down the street, glancing behind from time to time, but was never reassured.

Abandoned buses and occasional cars were scattered along the street, their power cells long dead. He saw more skeletons and began running again until he found a bicycle shop. All the windows were broken. It had been looted during the first days of anarchy, but there was so much to take, too much, even for the greediest of thieves.

The shop window was nothing more than a rectangle of air, but he entered through the door. There was a mountain bike, more than one. He chose a bike at random and found a pump to reinflate the tires, all the while watching the street, looking for bug sign. Before he left, he put on a long-sleeved riding outfit, gloves, helmet and dark glasses. His skin was already hot from the sunburn he had sustained while running away from the dome.

Once on the street, he pedaled and found a freeway entrance. His way was not impeded; there were a few vehicles, an occasional truck, a bus, a car, but he carefully avoided looking into them. Whenever he approached a fallen tree, he pedaled as fast as he could and then looked over his shoulder, expecting to see a black cloud of carnivorous beetles. The insects had been there; the skeletal remains along the roadway were proof of that.

He pedaled on, sweltering in his suit but afraid to take it

off; the sun would burn him to death with ultraviolet rays, the likes of which hadn't been seen on Earth for millions of years. Clouds of halogenated hydrocarbons had arisen from the burning cities and had consumed the ozone layer. He was thirsty but didn't stop. There seemed to be no end to bug sign, the skeletons of dogs and people, usually not far from an abandoned car or truck.

He pedaled north, the only moving object from horizon to horizon, toward Ventura, until he could no longer force his tortured thighs to push his mechanical legs. He coasted down an off-ramp and into the parking lot of a minimart. He let his bike fall as he got off and stumbled toward the store.

He peered through the smashed window and then tried the door; it was locked. The owner had planned to return, not knowing that death awaited him and everyone he knew. There was too much quiet, too much loss.

While he leaned against the door, a stab of pain shot up his arm. He looked down in time to see a wasp as big as his thumb fly away. The sleeve of his riding shirt was stained with blood. It was time to get a move on. He broke away the sharp triangles of glass that lined the windowsill and climbed in, ignoring the throbbing pain in his arm. The shelves were empty except for a small assortment of unidentifiable can goods, their paper labels eaten away; the bugs had been there before him. He found some bottled water and guzzled it. His stomach threatened to rebel, but he clamped his jaw shut as he climbed back out the window.

A swarm of wasps was approaching; he jumped on his bike and began pedaling furiously up the ramp to the freeway. He peddled as fast and hard as he could, his metal legs didn't complain, but his thighs burned with fatigue.

The sun had long set, but he pedaled on in the dim light of a baleful moon, until he saw a sign that announced he was entering Santa Barbara. Although bare of leaves, bark still clung to the tree trunks. Finally, it seemed safe to rest; there was enough food between him and the beetles to keep their ravenous appetites satisfied, at least for a while.

The freeway was washed out ahead. Booming breakers crashed over it, white foam in the moonlight. He sat on his bike and looked out to sea. Debris was piled high where the ocean met land. It was as if the city had crashed into the sea and its splintered parts were washing ashore. He exited the freeway and road uphill, into the old city of Santa Barbara. He pedaled along a residential street with large homes visible beyond wrought iron gates.

He was hungry and thirsty. He stopped in front of a gate; a Spanish-style house loomed beyond the driveway, set amidst dark mud. The grass was long dead and washed away, but the trees still had bark, a sign he was beginning to appreciate. He leaned his bike against the gate and climbed over the brick wall, to land feet first in the brittle remnants of a bush.

He walked toward the two-story stucco house with its red clay roof tiles. The windows were dark; it was dead and abandoned, as was all he had seen during his ride. It seemed like he was the last man on Earth. He felt a convulsive squeeze in his throat that felt like it could've choked him, if he hadn't been so mind-numbing tired.

The double door had a knocker, but he didn't bother. He pushed the latch; it was locked. He picked up an exposed rock from the raw earth and heaved it at the nearest window. The sharp "crack" of shattering glass was the only sound other than the whisper of a breeze through the web-like branches of dead trees.

He climbed in. In the moonlit room, he could see the vague outline of pictures on the walls and the bulky shape of furniture. Everything was in its place, as if the owners had simply gone on vacation. His metallic shin struck a chair; it didn't even register in his mind. He flung his helmet into the room and shed his gloves and riding shirt, gingerly pulling it off his swollen arm. He found the kitchen and then the dark pantry. It was stocked with canned food and there were dried vegetables, shrunken and hard. After knocking cans and boxes off the shelves, he gave up the effort. He didn't even know what he was searching for.

He unlocked the back door and stepped outside. The surface of a flowerpot glittered in the moonlight. He knelt down and sipped the water; it was reasonably free of grit and definitely free of bacteria.

He reentered the house and closed the door, but didn't bother to lock it. On the other side of the living room, he found a staircase and climbed it. There was a dark hallway at the top. He felt along the wall until he found a door and opened it.

The windows were lit with pale moonlight on filmy drapes.

There was a white desk on one side of the room and a bed with a white canopy on the other. The bed was made and there was no dark lump of a dead body.

This was as far as he could go. He crawled on top of the bed and sneezed from the dust that had gathered on the plush comforter. He struggled with the ache of hunger, but his fatigue overcame him and he fell asleep.

CHAPTER 21

Jack awakened to bright sunlight. The room was cheerful in sunlight. The overhead canopy had tiny blue flowers stitched onto it; the workmanship was fine and delicate. He turned his head and saw a framed picture on the bedside table; it showed a smiling, curly-haired teenage girl with her lean brother standing next to her. A pretty woman, with the same curly hair, and a handsome man stood protectively on either side of them. He had to look away. Across the room was a monitor desk and, above it, bookshelves with real books. On the upper most shelf was a row of smiling dolls, dressed in outfits of times past. They appeared smug. He threw the picture at them, but missed; they continued to smile as if nothing had happened.

He looked toward the window; sunlight slanted across the maple wood floor. It was mid-afternoon. It had been a day and half since he'd eaten, since he'd drunk a bottle of his special food, his baby formula as Timmy had called it. He shied away from the memory of Timmy's agonizing screams while being eaten alive. Should he have done something to save him? Could he have done something?

He couldn't lie there a moment longer. He got up and reentered the hallway. Sunlight spilled through the open door of the girl's room. There were double doors at the end of the hall. He imagined what he might see on the other side of those doors: a dead family, huddled together or abandoning each other in the last moments of their life, perhaps hiding their death behind the closed door of a bathroom to save their children from the sight. He knew what they'd look like, like Slater aboard the Mars Explorer, dried and shrunken. All of them with the same macabre grin. He hurried down the stairs and tried to clear these pictures from his mind.

He searched the pantry and this time found beef bouillon cubes as well as sugar and salt, all untouched, a reassuring sign. But, it would not be long before the insects found their way north and consumed everything in their path. He put the food in plastic bags, which he stuffed into his pockets, and returned to the living room to stand by the front window. As long as the sun was up, he dare not expose himself further; he had water blisters on his sunburned face and his swollen arm ached from the wasp venom. He sat down on the sofa to wait.

At dusk, dark clouds rolled in from the ocean. It was time. He hurried across the muddy yard and climbed the wall. His bicycle was still there. He almost wished that someone had stolen it, evidence that there was someone else alive in this devastated world. He lowered his tender buttocks onto the seat and began coasting downhill.

He had no choice; he had to go scavenging again. He needed proper clothing. He pedaled until he spotted a shopping center. The mall door was broken and inside it was dark. He listened, but could only hear the faint patter of rain. He crept forward and his insensitive feet tripped on something, sending him sprawling. It was a dried, dead body. He pushed himself away and arose to his feet, backing away until he was against the wall. He felt dizzy and weak. He eased away from the dark shape of the body and wandered farther into the mall, not able to tell one store from another until he was upon it.

Finally, in a sporting goods store, he found a flashlight that could be charged by shaking it. Among the mounds of merchandise that were strewn on the floor, he found a pith helmet, sunglasses, a long-sleeved shirt and gloves. He stuffed a rain slicker and a knife into a backpack and considered looking for a gun, but gave up on the idea; he couldn't shoot the bugs and there was nothing else alive, it seemed, in the whole world. Insect repellant? The thought almost made him laugh. He didn't want to make himself any tastier than he already was. He continued to wander around until he found a compass and added that to his backpack before he reentered the hall.

He looked up. The skylights flared bright with bursts of lightening, followed by booming thunder. The flashes made the deserted mall even more ominous; every shadow appeared to be another body, more death. He put on his rain slicker and hurried along the wall until he found the broken door. He climbed aboard his bike and headed downhill, toward the sea.

He heard the crashing waves before he saw the white line curling out of the darkness. When he arrived at what had been a marina, he sat back on his bike. The rising ocean had freed the boats and then had crushed them against the shore. There was no sandy beach, it was under water, only a shoreline piled high with collapsed homes and pieces of shattered boats tumbled together by the surf.

He got off his bike and sat down on an overturned dinghy which had a large hole gouged in its hull. Near his feet was an ice chest with the lid torn off. He touched his finger to the water in the bottom of the chest and tasted it. Rainwater. From his backpack, he dug out a glass and scooped water into it. He then poured in some sugar. He hesitated, not knowing the effect it would have on his damaged gut, but there was no real choice; it was eat or die. He took a sip and felt nauseated, but forced himself to drink the entire glass and then waited. His abdomen cramped and he expected more, but the grumbling and gripping of his gut subsided, only a mild protest.

The night sky was dark, without moon or stars. He looked to the south and wondered where the insects were, how fast they were advancing. He twisted to take in the wreckage of the marina. He wouldn't be able to sail his way north; it was ride the bike or stay and be eaten. For a while, he sat and listened to the rain patter against the hood of his rain slicker, a solitary figure. Then, with a measure of determination, he climbed onto his bike and began the long trip up the coast.

CHAPTER 22

Jack slowed at the top of the hill and coasted to a stop. He leaned on the handlebars to take in the sight below; there were lights and a green field and people, playing baseball, and others sitting next to one another on a small bleacher, socializing, being human. Even though his intellect had told him otherwise, emotionally he had come to believe there was no one left in the world. The death, the dead and dried people, dogs, cats, squirrels, horses, birds, the dead land he had ridden through, all of it had beaten upon him. He had continued only because he knew he must not believe his eyes or his heart. There had to be someone else and they had to be told about the insects. And here they were, live people, the ones he had been searching for.

A cheer arose with the "crack" of the bat hitting the hardball, a white speck, lit by bulbs hung on lines stretched between poles. Beyond the ball field were domes, not white like JPL, but painted the colors of a child's rainbow, carnival like. He took a breath and rubbed his chest. There was little left of him, bones and starved flesh; he had been living on sugar water alone, after an unfortunate experiment with beef broth. That memory by itself was enough to cause his tortured guts to cramp.

He cleared his mind. It was downhill, not so hard. He eased his raw buttocks onto the seat and coasted. He was within fifty meters before anyone noticed his approach. A graying man and woman began walking toward him, hand in hand, as if a bicyclist coming out of the dark was an everyday occurrence. The game continued; the players played and the crowd cheered them on.

Jack braked the bike and nearly fell from exhaustion, but refused, not after coming this far. He straightened in the seat and waited.

The benign smile of the graying gentleman disappeared within his extravagant mustache. He whispered something to the woman and she nodded. They stopped ten meters away, not as friendly as they had appeared at a distance.

"You're not from the Berkley bubble," the man said. He turned without waiting for a response and waved to a couple of sturdy looking men near the fringe of the spectators.

"I'm from Copper Mountain," Jack said.

"I see, Copper Mountain. Kind of a long bike ride, isn't it?" The woman shifted her gaze to Jack's legs as the two men joined them, each carrying a baseball bat, not an official weapon, but it would do.

Jack felt an almost overwhelming urge to laugh. They didn't need baseball bats to knock him over; a toothpick would suffice. He looked down, to where the woman was staring, and felt exposed; the metal of his leg was visible through a tear in his pants, but he was too exhausted to make the effort to hide it.

"I was on a mission," Jack began, "to investigate JPL—"

"I know who you are." The mustached man's gaze wasn't quite as stern as it had been, but the smile hadn't returned. "You're rather famous, the only survivor of the death gene. Your anatomy is all over the net. Interesting." He nodded as he inspected Jack more closely. "We heard you were killed, along with a couple of other men."

"You heard?" It was too much. His ride had been for nothing. He slipped off his bike and sat on the dirt. He wished he could lie on the green grass of the field, the most beautiful sight he had seen since…he couldn't recall a more beautiful sight.

"Looks like you could use a little help," the woman said.

"There are bugs south of here." Jack looked up at the man and woman.

The man nodded. "Cooper Mountain sent a complete report."

It was more than Jack could take. He collapsed. From flat against the dirt, the field disappeared. His eyes closed. He tried to open them and thought he succeeded.

When he awakened, his mind slid sideways. He was back in the hospital. It had the look, the monitors, and the fluid in the bag that was dripping into tubing stuck in his arm, but he did notice differences. There were landscape pictures on the walls and the domed ceiling was a pinwheel of colors, muted to pastels by a translucent inner lining of white.

It didn't have the look of Copper Mountain. He had ridden up the coast to warn them and…. He struggled to a sitting position, but then fell back onto the bed as his mind took another jump. *They already knew. Everyone knew.* Blas must have succeeded in up-linking before the aircraft exploded. He had done nothing but save himself, again, a feat that was becoming tiresome at best.

A middle-aged woman entered the room. She was the one who had been walking with the mustached man, the man who had authority.

"Good to see you awake!"

She was overly cheerful, offensively cheerful. He turned his head away, but she wouldn't be denied; she walked around to the other side of the bed.

"My name's Doctor Barken, but you can call me Marta, everyone does. How are you feeling?"

"Just peachy fine."

She nodded. "Glad to hear it. It's a good thing you made it when you did. Metabolically, you were a wreck."

"I'm more of a wreck than you think."

"None of that now. Director Mason was quite pleased to hear you had survived."

"I bet."

"It is remarkable. You'll have to tell me about it, when you feel up to it. It must be quite a story. That's a nasty wound on your arm."

Jack glanced at his red and swollen arm. "Wasp."

"Wasp? All right, if you say so. You also have a severe sunburn. You must remember never to go into sunlight without protection."

"What a wonderful piece of advice. Next time I'm running for my life, I assure you I'll stop and put on sunscreen first."

"You're being sarcastic."

"How astute of you, Doctor."

"Although you probably already know this, it's worth reiterating. Sunscreen—"

"I didn't even know you iterated."

"A sense of humor is a good sign. Sunscreen is not adequate. You need to cover up with a hat and long sleeves, every bit of exposed skin must be covered and you must protect your eyes, or you'll get cancer and cataracts."

Jack tried to ignore the chatter and stared at the triangles that made up the colorful ceiling. She rested her hand on his chest and he felt the urge to bite it, but tightened his jaw instead.

"Copper Mountain has sent us the formula for your food. I'm sure you'll feel better once you've eaten. Take it slow at first."

He said nothing.

"It appears that you could use some more time to gather yourself. I'm sure I would too."

He looked at her. She had honest creases across her forehead and laugh lines radiating away from the corners of her eyes. Her eyes were brown and clear, intelligent. She seemed likeable. Why did he feel like hitting her?

"Have you begun to prepare for the bugs?" he asked. "They're coming."

She sighed, but then lifted her shoulders and her smile found its place. "Just when it seems like we're making progress, something else comes up. Well, we'll just have to deal with it. No choice. We've been working on the problem for about three weeks. We'll be ready. You get some rest. I'll be back later with some of your food to sip. And later, if you feel up to it, I'll show you around." She patted him on the chest and finally withdrew the hand that Jack found so inexplicably offensive.

He heard the door shut and lifted his head high enough to ensure that there were no other merry-makers lurking in the room. He lay back in the bed and shifted his position. His buttocks felt like they would never recover from the pounding on the bicycle seat. He never wanted to ride one again, a torture device.

Three weeks? Her words finally reached his mind. One week to get up the coast. Had he been unconscious for two weeks? Another slice of his life gone?

"Hello. Can anyone hear me?"

He managed to push himself to a sitting position; the room felt like it was twirling. He forced the nausea to subside. Vomiting was to be avoided at all costs; after the beef broth he never wanted to retch again. He collapsed back onto the bed and a moment later heard the door open. He expected to see Doctor Marta, but it was a young man, an adolescent with acne; a problem that society had decided was no longer a priority but, from the way the boy hid his face, it was a big problem for him.

"Where do you want this?" the boy asked, his voice cracking.

He was gawky looking, not yet with the full flesh of an adult, or the assurance. Jack caught him trying to get a glimpse of his metal legs.

"Just put it down. What's your name?"

"Casey...Casey Conklin."

"Well, Casey Casey Conklin, how long have I been here?"

The boy-man put the glass on the bedside table. "Two days."

"I mean, when did I get here? How long has it been?"

He grinned, too many teeth, too big; his face was overwhelmed by teeth. "Two days."

"Two days?"

He nodded, but Jack was no longer looking at him.

"If you need anything, just speak up. I'll be outside, but I'll be able to hear you."

"Yes, fine."

The boy-man waited a moment more, as if there must be more to be said, but Jack continued to stare at the ceiling. He left the room, not quite as cheerful as he had been when he entered it.

Two weeks? No, two days. Two days. He closed his eyes and slept.

When he awakened he was alone. His formula was still on the bedside table. He managed to take a few sips and then waited. When nothing gastrointestinal happened, he drank the rest. His mind returned to what he'd been told. Two days. That couldn't be, unless.... He nodded. *It could be. Mason!* He was going to kill him, even if he had to ride that damn bike all the way to Copper Mountain. He pushed himself to a sitting position and was rewarded by the appearance of Casey Conklin.

The boy's inflamed face scrunched with impermanent creases. He glanced behind, looking for help, before he returned his gaze to Jack. "You shouldn't be up. Doctor Marta told me you need to stay in bed."

"Screw Doctor Marta."

Casey drew in a deep breath; he looked as if he might explode. He opened his mouth, but no words found their way out.

Jack stood, fell back onto the bed, and stood again, giving Casey such a look that the boy's first step forward was not followed by a second.

"Get me a cane, Boy."

"A cane?"

"To hell with it." Jack tore the intravenous line from the

vein in his arm and stumbled forward. He swayed and then locked his knees, that which was metal held; it was the rest of him that wasn't cooperating. He managed to reach the doorway and was met by Doctor Marta. She was smiling. It made Jack feel more like a boy than the boy he had chased from his room. He leaned against the wall, as breathless as if he'd been running.

"Good to see you up," she said.

Jack was prepared for the next instruction, "Return to bed", but it didn't come.

"Casey, put a dressing on that IV site so he doesn't drip blood all over the floor." She waited and then turned her attention to Jack. "Follow me."

She walked off down the hall, leaving Jack to his own feeble power, toddling along after her, hoping there was a chair somewhere up ahead. He rounded the corner; the doctor was nowhere in sight. He pushed on. So much for sympathy and assistance. he didn't want it, but did want the opportunity to turn it down.

There was a well-lit room around the next curve, but no windows. It could be either night or day; he had no idea as he staggered into the room and flopped into the first chair. The graying, mustached man nodded toward him and then continued talking with Doctor Marta and a thin man. The thin man used his hands to accent each word and shuffled his feet. Too much caffeine, Jack surmised as he sat in the chair, waiting.

The graying man and doctor both laughed at something the hyperthyroid man said, just before he hurried off. Only then did they turn their attention to Jack, pulling two chairs over so they could sit facing him.

"Good to see you up and about," the born statesman said.

Jack tolerated a pat on his arm.

"Last time I saw you, you looked like you were two steps this side of death."

"Been there, didn't like it."

The statesman rewarded him with a smile. "Copper Mountain is sending an aircraft for you. Should be here before morning."

"What time is it?"

"About eight P.M. I guess you military types would call it twenty hundred. Ever since the ozone layer disappeared we've become nocturnal. Would you like to see around a bit?"

"Not really."

The statesman shrugged. "Okay, that's up to you. Well, I've got to be off." He stood.

"A minute, please," Jack said.

"Yes."

"What have you done to protect yourselves from the bugs?"

"Not that it's any of your business, but we've designed multiple levels of response. We've dug a pit around the compound that can be flooded with gasoline and we have nets that can be dropped. If any manage to penetrate this outer defense, we'll have swivel guns that can spray clouds of potent insecticide. We'll be okay. Thanks for asking." He began to walk off.

"You're dead."

He stopped and turned back to Jack.

"Why do you say that?" he asked and stared at Jack as if he were a bug himself.

"That won't stop them. I've seen them. They'll just keep coming until you're overwhelmed and your defenses are depleted."

"What would you suggest?" he asked with a condescending smile.

"I'd suggest that you seal yourself away, pour as much concrete between you and them as you can."

"Thanks for your advice." He walked off without giving Jack another glance.

Jack turned his attention to Doctor Marta. "And how about you? What do you think?"

"We've dispatched watchers down the coast, an early warning system. They have radios and motorcycles."

"What good will that do?"

"When—if they come this far north—we'll have time to gather everyone into the domes."

"The bugs will appreciate that. They won't have to scrounge around."

"You've been through a lot," Dr. Marta said.

"What's that supposed to mean?"

"You have an anger that needs to be healed."

"I know exactly what to do about that and it doesn't involve healing. And what about you, Doctor Feel-Good? Is everything really so wonderful?"

She answered his comment with a pleasant smile.

"Sorry about that," Jack added. "What you have to understand is that I rode all the way here to warn you and then find out you already knew. It was a shock to me. You see, Mason may have told you about the bugs, but he forgot to tell my crew and myself and now they're dead. That bastard!"

"We're not fond of him either."

That got Jack's attention.

"We have our own organization on the West Coast, which used to include JPL. Such a tragedy." She dropped her gaze to her hands, the skin raw from scrubbing. "Wonderful people. Gone." She looked up as she regained her train of thought. "But, we still have seven bubble communities. Mason is taking too much on himself. He's not the director of the world, as he seems to believe."

"Damn right."

"The Governor and a few senators survived. They're living in the Davis bubble. They're the legitimate officials of this state."

Jack leaned back in his chair. "What bullshit."

"Our way of life and democracy are not bullshit. I won't accept that."

"Whatever."

"Are you a proponent of anarchy?"

"I don't know what I am. I used to think that if you followed the rules, everything would turn out all right. I think I'm a man who should've died."

"Depression." Doctor Marta shook her head. "We must guard against that."

"Doctor Marta."

"Yes?"

"Cram it up your ass." He looked for a response, but nothing happened. What was it with this woman? "I want to go out and sit on the grass."

"Very well."

She raised her hand and Casey came forward with a wheelchair.

"But it's not grass," she continued. "It's artificial turf. Nothing can withstand the ultraviolet as it is now. At least there's one good thing about these bugs."

"And what could that possibly be?"

"They are keeping some hydrocarbons out of the

atmosphere."

"That's just great. I'm sure those people down at JPL were pleased as hell that they got eaten instead of burned."

"I wasn't talking about them. You're in serious need of help. I'm worried about you."

"Really."

She nodded. "Yes, really."

"Where did you get the artificial turf?"

"There's a nearby domed stadium. Professional sports, you know."

Jack sat forward, causing the Doctor to lean back. He grabbed her hand and Casey hurried toward them, as if he was about to defend her.

"Listen to me, Doctor," Jack said. "If you have any influence around here, convince that arrogant man who runs this place to prepare the stadium. Seal it and reinforce it. And once you're there, prepare to stay there, because you won't be able to go outside again for a long time, maybe not for the rest of your lives."

"That's rather grim." She managed to withdraw her hand from his grip.

"Do it, Doctor. I've seen them. Believe me, please."

"Since you put it so nicely, I will discuss it with that arrogant man, also known as Professor Bertrand Barnhard, my husband."

"You do that. You tell old Bert what I said. I don't want to be sent out from Copper Mountain to collect your data from among your bones because you and your people have become bug food."

She stood with her smile fully restored and nodded toward Casey. "Casey will attend to you. I have other duties. Perhaps we'll get a chance to talk again."

"Perhaps."

After she had walked away, Casey positioned the wheelchair for him.

"Get away. Leave me alone."

Casey frowned.

"Is there something wrong with your hearing?" Jack asked.

Casey shook his head.

"Then get out of here."

"But...but, Doctor Marta told me I should watch out for you. Help you."

"Do you always do what Doctor Marta tells you to?"

He nodded. "She's a wonderful person."

"Are you in love with her?"

"No! Why would you say that?" Casey's face got even redder.

Jack took a breath and leaned back in the chair. "It's all right, son. It's just me. I'm in kind of a foul mood. If you've chosen her as the person you most look up to, I think you've chosen well."

Casey grinned, showing his big teeth. "I want to be just like her. She's training me to be a doctor and I'm going on the starship. She said she'd help me, if that's what I really want. And I do. I've made up my mind," he added earnestly.

"The starship. Okay. Well, I wish you luck then."

"Thank you." Casey looked at the concrete floor. "When you get back to Copper Mountain, if you could put in a word for me, I'd really appreciate it."

Jack shook his head.

"You won't help me?"

"Sure, Casey. I'll do what I can." It was a crazy idea, but the boy's passion reminded him of his own dream, of going to Mars.

Casey looked up with his big-toothed grin. "Thank you so much!"

"You know, I've had a few hard days and I just want to sit here, all by myself for a while. You can understand that, can't you?"

Casey nodded.

"You should say 'yes', not just nod when you are in agreement."

"Yes, Mister—I mean Captain Nichols."

"Goodbye, Casey" Jack waved his fingers. When the boy did nothing, Jack added, "Go!"

He startled, but then gathered himself and stood tall. Jack saw a glimpse of the man he would become. He smiled at Jack and pushed the wheelchair away, turning to wave before he disappeared around a corner.

The moment the boy was gone, the smile on Jack's face vanished. He was looking forward to his return to Copper Mountain. He was going to strangle Mason and enjoy witnessing his last gurgling breath.

CHAPTER 23

Jack leaned his cheek against the cold window of the aircraft. The surface of the world was far below. The arid mountains looked pasty-yellow and inhospitable. Only the inhospitable seemed untouched by the Earth's devastation. There would be no patchwork fields of green, only dirt and death, no magical splashes of city lights, only darkness and clouds of smoke.

"What do you see, Jack?"

He lifted his head from the window as if were a heavy stone and turned to look across the aisle at his friend, Pie Traynor, who was impervious, it seemed.

"Don't you feel it? The death, the loss?" Jack asked.

Pie nodded. "We all feel it." He studied Jack. "You look as if you don't believe me."

"Why am I the only one who is melting away from it? I look in a mirror and I can barely recognize myself, old, bony. I have to move my head back and forth to convince myself that it really is me, not just some horror show villain. Did you see the way the pilot looked at me?"

"You always think people are looking at you, judging you. That's baloney. And besides, you don't look that bad. A little under weight, but that happens when a person doesn't eat for a while."

"Bullshit."

"Bullshit yourself."

Only Pie could get away with a response like that without raising a hint of anger. Jack felt a thin smile on his face, but no joy in his heart.

Pie cleared his throat and in his rumbling voice began reciting:

"A red marble is floating
Across a green pond
Caught between muck and air!
But suspicious
Of waves and black water bugs."

"Are you accusing me of being a red marble?"

"You know what I think?" Pie leaned toward Jack with an earnest expression.

Jack leaned away. This was not going to be pleasant.

"You need to look outside of yourself. Look to others and perhaps you won't find yourself looking into a mirror so much."

"You think I'm just feeling sorry for myself."

"I said what I had to say." Pie sat back in his seat.

"What have you lost? I've lost my legs. I can't eat or drink, except this damn pabulum." Jack knocked the bottle onto the floor. "I've lost my wife to—"

"That's it, isn't it?"

Pie stared at Jack until he was forced to look away, out the window at the world he no longer wanted to see.

Pie continued. "You didn't lose her. You pushed her away."

Jack swung around, rising against his seatbelt, as if he could physically threaten the giant who sat across from him, the one person who he knew still cared for him.

"If you had shown a tenth of the interest you're showing now, she'd still be with you. You only want things when you can't have them."

Jack unbuckled his seatbelt and lunged at Pie, but was pushed back into his seat as if he was nothing more than a poorly behaved child.

Pie unbuckled and stood to lean over Jack. "Now you shut up and listen!"

Jack had never seen anger on his friend's face before; it was both horrifying and a curiosity.

"Everybody has lost someone. Everybody! And that sure as hell includes me. I lost my parents and two sisters. I've lost friends. You aren't my only friend, Jack."

Jack's shoulders slumped.

"You've lost your legs and eat special food. Poor, Jack."

"Shut up!" Jack managed to knock Pie back. "So my parents were already dead and I didn't have a brother or sister. So what?"

"As much as I like you, as much as I've seen you behave with gallantry in the past, right now you disgust me. Selfish...." Pie shook his head and sat back down in his seat.

Jack hid his face in his hands. He turned away and slammed his fist into the bulkhead. The silence stretched on until Jack spoke again. "Everyone around me dies, but I keep living. Why?"

"Do you believe in fate?"

"No!"

"It was only a question. What do you want, Jack?"

He waited for his eyes to clear, hoping Pie wouldn't notice. "I'll tell you what I want. I want to get back to Copper Mountain. And when I do, I'm going to find Mason and kill him with my bare hands."

"Why?"

Jack expected more of a response than that. He took a few seconds to gather his thoughts.

"Mason sent us up to a contaminated station. He is the one who caused me to become a cripple. He is the one who caused Kate's death and all the others. He sent us to JPL, knowing full well there was a problem with bugs. He warned Stanford, but not us. Why?" Pie was about to answer when Jack raised his hand to silence him. "I'll tell you why. Because he wants me dead. He knows Jane still wants me and this is the only way to get rid of his competition."

"Is that all?"

"All? Well, no.... He's an egomaniac, acts like he's emperor of the world. And I'm not the only one who thinks he's a crackpot dictator. Doctor Marta and I had an interesting chat before you arrived."

"That's nice."

"Damn it! If you don't believe me, ask her yourself. Ask that Professor Bertrand."

"Mason may be a lot of things, I would never consider him a friend, but he is one of the main reasons that humanity hasn't already sunk to oblivion. He was the one who sent out the warning about the microbe. He directed the building of the survival bubbles. He is the one they all turn to when they need something. He finds it. He has it delivered. He has a plan and by God it might work. If humanity survives, and I know how much you hate to hear this, it'll be due to a great part because of Mitchell Mason. So I'd take those complaints you've heard with a grain of salt."

"Then why is he trying to kill me?"

"He's not. I was there, remember? He didn't want you to go, didn't think you were ready, but you insisted you were and I was the one who made it possible. If you're going to blame someone, blame me, or better yet, blame yourself. As for the insects, Langley reported a problem with bugs and Mason had the information passed on, around the world, but it was nothing like the situation you ran into and Virginia is a hell of a long way from Southern California."

"If he could tell every other God forsaken human in this world, he could've told us. What the hell did he think happened? They went on vacation? Langley reports bugs and a week later JPL goes silent. It doesn't take a genius to connect the dots."

"General Clark was the one who briefed you."

"Bullshit. You know damn well those people on his puppet council don't even take a crap unless Mason gives the okay."

"I'm on the Executive Council."

"You know what I'm talking about and don't even try to deny it."

"It was an oversight on his part."

"An oversight? The supreme architect of our survival goofed. Is that what you're telling me?"

"We all make mistakes."

"Well, all his mistakes are aimed at me. It's enough to make a person wonder."

"Leave him alone, Jack. We need him."

"Much more than you need a guy with no intestines and no legs."

Pie sighed. "We do need you."

"Right."

"I was talking with Roxy the other day and she—"

"Roxy? Not Roxanne. It's 'Roxy' now?"

"An incredible woman, more courage than anyone I know and smarter than both of us put together." Pie smiled.

"So, it's you and Roxy now, is it?"

"Shut up, Jack. Sometimes you make me feel like beating the living hell out of you."

"Feeling guilty?"

"No. Hell no. There's only one reason you act like a cripple and that's because you want to."

"Changing the subject, aren't you?"

"Back off. Do you have some kind of claim on her? When she came by to visit you during your rehab you always found an excuse to send her away."

"How would you know?"

"You haven't said more than ten words to her in the last

two months. Is it because someone else might be interested in her that you're suddenly concerned? What the hell do you want, Jack?"

"I guess that answers my question."

He turned away and looked out the window. The view of the world was a perfect match for his soul. He couldn't wait for the aircraft to land, anything to escape this cabin and his so-called friend. He had no friends, no one. Why didn't he just die?

Not another word was said during the remainder of the flight. By the time the aircraft landed and taxied to a stop at Copper Mountain, the sun had set.

Pie offered his hand. "Come on, Jack. Let's go."

Jack turned away to stare out the window.

"Suit yourself."

Pie walked down the aisle to the exit, but Jack remained in his seat, not moving.

Finally, the pilot walked back. "Do you need assistance?"

He didn't acknowledge the pilot, but did unbuckle his belt and stand. He held onto the rail when he descended the steps to the tarmac. He walked away from the lights of the runway and looked up. The stars were still there, bright and unchanged, but then he saw a ribbon of magenta and blue wiggle it's away across the sky; the aurora borealis was everywhere now. It was one more reminder of the death grip that was squeezing the life out of the Earth. A woman walked toward him.

"What do think, Captain Jack? It's beautiful, isn't it?"

The colors flared and danced across Roxanne's face, making her lips look purple.

"Some people might think so."

"I guess you're not one of those people."

She studied his face. "I'm so glad to see you. It was such a relief to hear you were okay. We thought you were dead."

"I don't die. I just experience death, over and over."

"What does that mean?"

"You figure it out."

"Jack...are you angry with me? Because, if you are—"

"I know, get over it."

"That's not what I was going to say. If you are, I want to know why."

"I'm not angry."

"You sure sound like you are. Pie and I were planning to come over to your place this evening. Do you think you're up to it?"

"You and Pie?"

"Uh-huh. I can see why you value his friendship. You told me to call on him if I ever needed anything. One of the best pieces of advice I've ever received."

"Did he satisfy your need?"

"Yes, he's helped me with that meddling, incompetent Rathburn on more than one occasion."

"He is quite an extraordinary person." Jack had meant for it to be sarcastic, but the truth of his belief came out instead. He grunted a laugh.

"What's so funny?"

"Absolutely nothing."

"Where is Pie anyway? I thought he'd be with you."

"Sorry to disappoint you."

"You're acting strange."

He looked up; the stars were no longer the champions of the night; instead, it was ribbons of rainbow light. "If you like this, you better come out at night often, because it won't be long before mankind will be trapped indoors, day and night."

"Why do you say that?"

"The land seeding of the anti-microbe wasn't a total failure. There are bugs out there. Giant black beetles that love to eat meat and wasps that are big enough to kill." He absently rubbed his arm, which was still swollen and painful.

He saw her shiver, despite the unnaturally balmy night air. He didn't even attempt to wrap his arms around her.

"Would you like some visitors this evening?" she asked.

"No."

"Well...all right. We're not trying to intrude. Do you really want to be alone tonight?"

"Yes." He returned his attention to the glowing night sky.

"I guess I'll say goodnight, then."

"Goodnight."

Only after she began walking away, did he lower his gaze. He watched her; she was as appealing from the rear as she was face on, with body curves that proclaimed her womanhood.

He started across the parade grounds and noticed two people walking toward him. At first, he thought they were sentries, but then the truth was thrown in his face; they were lovers, taking a stroll beneath the newly majestic night sky. There was no need for guards when there was nothing but specks of humanity separated by vast tracts of devastated land, nothing alive, other than the bugs, eating their way north. How long, he wondered, before they made their way to Copper Mountain and tried for another snack of human flesh?

He headed toward the apartment buildings and saw the specter of a scramjet skimming along the rail; it was out of sight before he heard the sonic boom. When he reached the building, he climbed the stairs to the apartment he had shared with Jane.

He tried the door handle, expecting to find it locked; it was the human way, but the latch "clicked" and the door swung inward. He touched the light pad; nothing happened. The housing units were a ghost village, sitting atop the real city, a city of ten thousand subterranean inhabitants crammed into every corner imaginable, some living where they worked, the biggest city left on Earth.

The room was lit by spectral light streaming through the window. The sofa was still there, the one he had shared with Kate. His foot bumped something, a metallic "clink" against glass. He could make out the shape of an empty vodka bottle. If there had been anything in it, he would've drunk it, despite the pain it would've caused.

He sat on the sofa and faced the window, waiting for the next launch. The rail had never been busier than now, serving Mason's two projects, the space station and the Starship Pinnacle. *The Pinnacle of what? Mankind running for cover?*

He wished he had accepted Roxy's offer. He wanted to be with her, to talk with her, to talk with his friend, to be with other humans, but he couldn't. Not now, after he'd refused. He wouldn't go begging for companionship.

His thoughts returned to his conversation with Pie. *What do I want? What is left for me to want?*

He wandered into the bedroom; the bed was still there. Dust billowed up when he fell onto it. It reminded him of the death houses he'd taken refuge in during his long ride up the coast. He felt cold. He'd never tell Roxanne and Pie about it. He'd spare them that, keep the terror bundled deep inside, along with all the other nightmares his life had become. Was there a chance for him to strike a balance? Which was it to be: find a purpose, a fate, as Pie had put it, or live to suffer?

He rolled over and waited for the sneezing to subside before he closed his eyes.

CHAPTER 24

Jack awakened. Bright light streamed through the doorway and lit up the faded picture of the F-35. He had a headache and was hungry and thirsty. He tried the faucet in the kitchen, but the water was turned off; everything was turned off.

The door that led to the hallway was closed; no one had come looking for him. With that realization, Jack sat down on the sofa. His stomach demanded food, but he was trapped in the deserted building by the power of raw sunlight. He could've thrown a blanket over his head and rushed to the entrance of the underground, but he simply ground his teeth, molar against molar.

He felt more than saw the scramjet as it disappeared up the rail, a faint afterimage on his eyes. It seemed everyone knew their place in this time of devastation; everyone was displaying the most admirable qualities of self-sacrifice for the good of mankind, everyone that was except him. He looked at his hands, nothing but bones and the cords of tendons. He was wasting away with nothing to show for it, a wasted man, a wasted life. Jane had been right to leave him and Pie had been right about everything. It was too late.

He pushed the sofa away from the window. He didn't want any more pain, didn't want to fry his skin in the light that was coming through. That seemed to be what he wanted: not to want. He massaged his scalp, trying to rub away the chaos that gave him no peace. He looked up to see another scramjet shoot up the rail with near invisibility. Mason was going ahead with his plans and everyone seemed to have bought in, regardless of what they said. *Thank you very much, Doctor Marta.*

He sat on the sofa and waited.

When the sun had set and twilight darkened the world outside his window, he pushed to his feet. He swayed with weakness and braced himself against the sofa until he felt he was ready to try the door, the stairs and, finally, the grounds.

He approached the doorway to the underground and was

again surprised that there was no guard. The sense never seemed to leave him that the world was still there, somewhere, hiding, that humanity couldn't have been reduced to tiny islands of tenuous existence, surrounded by vast stretches of dead earth. Had the others truly grasped the magnitude of death, were they stronger, or was there something wrong with him?

He stood with his hand on the push bar, paralyzed by despair, until he noticed that someone was staring at him through the window of the door. Her lips always seemed to be smiling, smirking when closed. Still, she was there, waiting for him. That had to mean something.

He pushed the bar and the door opened. He stepped inside and leaned back against it. It was not his mechanical legs that were failing; it was the rest of him.

"We were worried about you," Roxanne said as she studied his face. "Glad you didn't do anything really stupid."

"I try to do only moderately stupid things."

"Well, you're quite successful. Come on." She held out her hand.

For a moment he refused, wanted to and didn't want to, but she continued to hold her hand out. He took it. Her hand was warm and soft. Her fragrance filled his nose with sweetness, mingled with spice. She led him to the elevator, like a small boy being led home by an indulgent parent, but he didn't have the strength to reject her touch.

"Who is we?" he asked and felt the flush of foolishness.

"What are you talking about?"

"Nothing." It was so obvious he was fishing for signs of concern. How weak he must appear, exactly the kind of man Roxanne would toss away like any other useless piece of trash. He stared at the polished wall of the elevator as it descended; his cheekbones were made prominent by the hollows beneath them.

"Where are we going?" he asked.

"You are going to your room. You are going to eat. Later, Pie and I will be stopping by for a visit."

He released his clasp on her hand, but she didn't loosen the grip she held on his now limp hand. Limp, whatever else, this he would not be. He pulled his hand out of her grip.

"What's bothering you now?" she asked.

"Nothing."

She shrugged and stood at his side.

When the door opened, Jack refused her offered hand and stumbled forward. He preferred to fall, which he would've had the wall not come up against his shoulder.

"You know something?" she said as she watched him regain his balance. She waited until he looked her in the face. "You're the most bullheaded son of a bitch I've ever met."

He smiled.

"So, you like that, huh?" she asked.

"I'm not saying I agree."

"Since you obviously intend to make it on your own, I've got things to do. Can you make it on your own?"

"I didn't ask you—" He took a breath and nodded. "Thank you. I can make it."

"You have potential," she said with that smile that could, in better times, have turned him on from across a room.

While she walked away, he leaned on the wall. He waited until she was out of sight and then staggered along, keeping contact with the wall until he found his two-room apartment. He had Pie to thank for a private apartment, as small as it was; most residents had to share.

He entered and stopped. There was a colorful banner stuck to the wall: "Happy Birthday". He thought about collapsing into the chair, but knew he needed food and wasn't certain he could get back up. He tottered into the kitchenette and opened the refrigerator. It was well stocked with his formula. He took out a bottle and drank. Even though his appetite was gone after the first sip of the soybean-smelling concoction, he forced the second bottle down, followed by two glasses of water. After a brief discussion with his stomach, he was reasonably certain it wouldn't come back up.

He stumbled back into the small living area and flopped into the over-stuffed chair, his one luxury, again thanks to Pie.

"Thanks to Pie," he said out loud. Saved his life and took his woman, or had he pushed her away? He stared at the banner. The party he had skipped had been his own.

He shook his head. *What an asshole I am. It's amazing I still have two people who care about me.* He slowed his breathing and tried to reassure himself. They still cared. After all, Roxanne had been waiting at the door. He relaxed into the chair and despite his mind, which insisted on twisting everything into a knot, he dozed.

Something awakened him. He was momentarily confused; he'd been dreaming that he was hiding in that home in Santa Barbara, the one with the Spanish tile roof and the bed with the tiny blue flowers stitched onto the fabric. The bed was surrounded by smiling dolls and beyond them was the dead family, all of them grinning with that ghoulish smile of the dead. There was a knock at his door. The knock repeated, louder. He shook the nightmare off and pushed himself up to walk over to the door. He opened it. It was Pie and Roxanne.

"What took you so long?" Pie brushed past him, nearly knocking him down.

Jack stepped back and Roxanne entered.

Pie walked over to the refrigerator and looked inside. "It's a good thing we brought our own." He set the sack on the table and took out a bottle of vodka and a bag of chips. "Picked them up in San Jose." He looked at the bag. "Sell by August 16. Hmmm. Doesn't say what year. Oh well. Don't keep like Spam but I'm sure they're still good." He turned back to Jack, who continued to stand by the door. "Where are your glasses?"

Jack shrugged.

Pie began opening and slamming cupboard doors until he found some plastic cups. "I don't suppose you have any ice?"

"I don't know."

"Do you live here or not?" He found some ice cubes in the freezer and poured the vodka into two cups before turning back to Jack and Roxanne.

"Go ahead, sit down, make yourselves at home," Pie said.

Jack indicated the soft chair for Roxanne, but she shook her head and sat down on the small sofa.

This was the first time she'd been in Jack's apartment. She looked around. The walls were off-white and plain, except for the banner Pie had hung yesterday. The gray tiled floor was bare and the sofa appeared to have been confiscated from a bus stop. There were no pictures, no decorations, no personal items.

"I like what you've done with the place," she said. "I see you've gone for the penitentiary look. Very nice."

"Sorry about that," Jack replied, "my interior decorator died. Come to think of it, everyone died."

Pie met Roxanne's gaze. Neither of them responded. Pie handed Roxanne the drink and sat down next to her, completely filling the remainder of the sofa.

"So," Pie began, "after all our planning, you refused to come to your party last night, preferring to mope around your old place."

"I didn't know you had planned a party." Jack looked at the single banner. "Sorry to have put you out."

"Oh, shut up. You're in desperate need of a kick in the ass."

"Is that what you got me for my birthday?"

Pie chuckled. "No, I brought you this." He tossed the joint to Jack. "I understand it's bad for you but, being that you can't imbibe in the socially accepted drug, we'll do the best we can."

Jack held it in his fingers and looked up.

"It's medicinal," Pie added with a wink.

Jack lit the joint and inhaled, coughing until tears came to his eyes.

Pie raised his cup to touch Roxanne's. "Cheers and happy birthday!" He downed the cup in a single, throat-burning gulp and filled their cups again. "Smoke it, damn it. That might be the last pot in the world."

"Really?" Jack looked at the large joint.

"No."

Jack took another toke with less coughing.

"Now it's time for the birthday song." Pie cleared his voice and Roxanne joined him.

Jack couldn't help but smile. Neither of them could carry a tune. If it hadn't been for the words, it would've been unrecognizable. He took another toke and settled deeper into the chair. His feet tried to rise off the floor. He was becoming weightless.

"Now it's time for my present," Roxanne said and leaned forward to hand Jack a manila envelope.

He opened it. It contained a picture. He turned it one-way and then another. It looked like a whitish ribbon or something.

"Hope you like it," Roxanne said. "It took all of Pie's considerable influence to free up the resources." She punched Pie playfully in the arm.

Jack wished it were his arm that she had punched with such easy familiarity. "Thank you," he said and took another toke.

"You do know what it is, don't you?" Roxanne asked.

"Sure. It's a tapeworm."

Pie and Roxanne started laughing.

Jack wanted to take offense, but laughter ruled. He laughed until his face ached. When he finally regained control, Roxanne was wiping tears of laughter from her eyes.

She looked to him. "Why in the world would I give you a tapeworm? That's ridiculous. That's a picture of your new intestines."

Jack studied the picture. "My new intestines?"

"Uh-huh, grew them in my own little lab." She raised her hand and wiggled her fingers. "With my own little hands. That alien microbe has made things much easier. A great tool."

"I don't want to hear that!" Jack yelled, surprising even himself. When he continued, his voice was softer. "They killed us and when I get my hands on them I'm going to return the favor."

"There is a committee discussing that very issue," Pie said. "Would you like to be included?"

"A committee?"

"Yeah, you know, a bunch of people sitting around, talking about everything and doing nothing."

Jack smiled. "Sounds enticing."

"Very well. I'll see that you're included." Pie turned to Roxanne. "Now this lady is something else. She doesn't need a committee. Give her a problem and she solves it."

"Go on now, you're going to turn my head." She smiled.

"Brilliant cloning. You're one incredible woman," Pie said.

"Couldn't have done it without you. Convincing Mason, that was the hard part."

Jack sat holding the picture while Roxanne and Pie beamed good will at one another. He felt alone again.

Pie returned his attention to Jack. "Well, what do you say? It's not without risk. It's a major and never before attempted surgery." There was no trace of a smile on his face. He rested his meaty hands on his knees. "It could kill you."

Jack's smile was no deeper than his lips. "I don't care about that. I just don't want to wake up with another part missing."

Pie nodded. "Tomorrow morning."

"Tomorrow morning?"

"Got something better to do?"

Jack shook his head.

Pie continued. "In a couple of weeks, there's a transport heading into Denver to pick up supplies. You should be up and around by then. Want to go shopping with us?"

"No, I've seen as much as I care to. That trip up the coast was horrible, death everywhere, every house. I'll never be able to get it out of my mind. I saw—" He stopped himself.

"What did you see?" Roxanne asked.

"Nothing. I don't want to talk about it."

"We don't go into residential areas, only large stores and warehouses," Pie said.

Jack shook his head. "I don't want to go."

"Anything you want us to bring back for you?"

"No." He looked at the picture that to him still looked like a tapeworm. "I've got everything I want right here." He looked up, first to Pie and then his gaze lingered on Roxanne. "Bugs?" he asked with concern.

"No," Pie answered. "It'll probably be a years before they make it this far north. The cooler weather is expected to slow their progress. We can also delay their advance with insecticides but, from what we've learned, ultimately, I don't see any stopping them. They mutate so quickly they become resistant within days. Had quite a chat with Professor Barnhard and Doctor Marta at the Stanford dome. I have a feeling she's the real authority in that facility, but Barnhard did have a good idea. They plan to move the bubble city into a nearby sport's stadium, enclosed and easily fortified."

"Gee, he sure is smart. That's a great idea," Jack said.

Pie frowned but didn't pursue it. "JPL was a horrible loss. Those poor people. Goddard and Lawrence-Livermore are being hardened. We're recommending that they all move into the closest domed stadium."

"How are things going otherwise?" Jack asked.

"Actually, better than expected. We were able to retrieve the data from JPL and it's expected that the starship will be completed in about ten rather than twenty years. The space station is progressing. It should be ready for habitation within the year. You've got to hand it to Mason."

"I'd rather not."

"You're not still hell bent on killing him are you?"

"No."

"That's a start."

Jack took another toke and held his breath before exhaling.

This was the first time he'd been relaxed since...his mind drifted back to that night he had spent with Roxanne at her farmhouse. He looked at the two who sat on the sofa.

"This is the best birthday party I've had in many a year," he said.

"And next time, we'll celebrate in the traditional fashion, with cake as well as vodka." Pie boomed his laugh and then glanced down at his bare forearm, as if he were looking at a watch, and declared he had to be off.

In Jack's fogged mind he didn't even notice. He pushed himself to his feet. He swayed and his heart pounded but, for once, he didn't feel the weight of the world. He expected Roxanne to follow after Pie, but she remained sitting. All Jack could think was that he was alone with Roxanne, feeling every teenage anxiety that he had ever felt.

She smiled and patted the sofa next to her. "Come here and sit. It's time we get reacquainted. Don't you agree, Captain Jack?"

"Roxy, I...." He couldn't look her in the eyes. "I...have been...oh hell." He met her green eyes. "Roxy, I don't like the way I look."

"I'll keep my eyes shut."

"Roxy, please. You have no idea how hard this is."

"How hard what is?"

"Are you trying to make a joke out of this?"

"Do you want me to leave, or do you want me to stay?"

Jack took a deep breath and the slowly exhaled. "I want you to stay."

"Now, was that so difficult?" She arose and took his hand. "I promise I'll behave myself, but *you* have to promise *me* that there will be no shenanigans."

"What do you mean?"

"Last time I shared your bed, you tried to kill yourself. That's kind of hard on a woman's ego."

"It wasn't—I won't try to kill myself."

"Wonderful. Let's go to bed."

If the pot hadn't stolen his judgment, he'd never have agreed. He let her lead him into the small bedroom. He lay down on top of the covers and watched her strip off her blouse and then drop her skirt to the floor. She was wearing nothing beneath it. She was beautiful.

"Aren't you going to get undressed?" she asked as she

stood before him, hiding nothing.

"No."

"Have it your way."

She walked around behind him and he felt her climb onto the bed. She snuggled up against him. He could feel the warm length of her body and the softness of her breasts against his back.

"I trust you," he said, afraid his inadequacy was about to be tested.

"Good."

Her hand slipped around his side. He took hold of it and pulled her arm up until it was across his chest. When she did nothing more than hold him, he finally relaxed, luxuriating in her warmth, feeling safe as he drifted off to sleep.

CHAPTER 25

Jack sat next to Pie at the conference table. The section leaders filled the remainder of the table, including Roxanne's supervisor, Jonathan Rathburn. Baskets of crackers, salvaged from who knows where, and bowls of yellowish dip were set at intervals around the tabletop. Pie had called the yellow paste, cheese dip, but Jack knew genetically tailored bacteria had produced it.

He rubbed his stomach and thought about his new intestines. The incision could hardly be seen, but his first exposures to food had brought on mighty cramps. His abdominal wall didn't hurt anymore, even when he worked out at the gym. The thing that had really surprised him was the pain he'd felt a little lower. He'd told Pie it felt like he'd been kicked in the balls. Although it hadn't resulted in sympathy, at least it had served to amuse his old friend.

He resisted the ersatz cheese, but did begin munching on a cracker and couldn't help but notice Rathburn watching him. Rathburn nodded and smiled. Jack almost felt like giving into the nausea and vomiting the crackers onto the table, just to see the expression on Rathburn's face.

The door opened and Mason entered. Jack expected him to have continued that accelerated aging, would've taken that as payment for unsettled debts, but he looked younger, not older. Maybe it was because he was getting fat. Jack smiled with a degree of satisfaction.

Pie leaned toward Jack. "Behave yourself."

Jack nodded, but continued to stare at Mason as he settled into the chair at the head of the table, and then switched his gaze to the boy who had followed Mason in and who now sat at Mason's side. The boy seemed familiar, but Jack couldn't quite place him. He appeared to be in early puberty, but his face already had the angular qualities of an adult, with a sharp, straight nose. He looked like he would become a strikingly handsome man.

When the boy's gaze met Jack's, his mouth twisted into a

smirk.

Mason looked around the table, skipping over Jack, as if to emphasize that Jack was only there as Pie's assistant.

Assistant-what, Jack had not yet determined, probably just one more act of charity. His mood began to darken as his self-worth plunged.

"I've called this special meeting because I have news of grave importance." Mason paused and scanned the faces of the men who sat around the table.

In a time before the Death, Jack would've called this calculated melodrama, but no more.

Mason continued. "Goddard has reported the discovery of a near Mars object that is over two kilometers long and a quarter-kilometer in diameter. Visuals have been obtained." He handed out pictures to be passed around.

Pie and Jack were expected to share. Jack studied the picture in Pie's hands. The object was reflective and smooth, shaped to penetrate an atmosphere.

Mason spoke again. "As you can all see, the object is some sort of spaceship." He paused, allowing the momentous news to percolate a little deeper and then continued. "There is no visible means of propulsion, yet the object has shifted course and has gone into orbit around Mars." Again he paused. "I'm open for comments."

There was silence, until Jack spoke. "This is—"

Mason cut him off. "What do you think, Professor Timken?"

The elderly man appeared as if his mind was on the verge of leaving his body. His gaze darted around the room and then came to rest as he stared at the empty table in front of him. "There are two possibilities. One, we are about to be visited by the species that caused the Death. Or, it's the third phase of the invasion, the seeding of the Earth's biosphere with alien flora, fauna, and most importantly, microbes, to transform the Earth into a world that is truly natural for the invaders when they do arrive. Of these possibilities, the second is the more likely."

Mason nodded. "Why do you suppose it's in orbit around Mars?"

"It's homing in on the crashed ship," Jack said without preamble.

Mason turned his gaze to Jack. "And why would it do that?"

"Perhaps there's a distress signal being broadcast from the crashed ship and the ship that followed is on automatic, commanded by some sort of AI, too far from the home world for the aliens to communicate with it. A smart ship, coming to the rescue."

"Apparently not that smart," Rathburn quipped.

"This question is for the rest of you," Mason said. "Nichols, you be quiet. You're not a member of the Council. If scenario two is the correct one, how long do you think it'll take the alien ship to evaluate the situation and correct its choice of planets?"

"We need to destroy the damn thing," General Clark declared. "It can't be allowed to reach Earth. That would be the final blow for mankind." His eyes glinted with anger as he stared across the table at Jack, as if it were Jack's fault that the new ship had arrived.

Jack was about to respond to the look, when Pie rested his hand on Jack's arm.

"How would you propose we do that, General?" Mason asked.

"Missiles, nukes. There are plenty out there for the taking."

Jack couldn't resist. "Are there any capable of traveling to Mars and hitting a target that far away?"

"Don't be an idiot," Clark replied. "Of course not, but there are nuclear subs at New London. We can harvest their assets and send the rockets into space aboard scramjets. Get ready. When the ship approaches, we blow it to hell."

"What if the ship has defenses?" Pie asked. "It has successfully traversed interstellar space to arrive here."

"They expect this planet to be barren," the General answered. "They expect us to be dead, but they're in for the surprise of their lives."

"I agree." Mason said. "We'll begin planning at once, but I think it would be prudent to get more data."

"How do you propose to do that?" the General asked.

"We need to send someone to Mars," Mason answered.

"Perhaps we could send a reconnaissance probe," Timken speculated.

Mason responded. "I don't think so. The one advantage we have is the ability to make adjustments as a situation demands. There is no computer that can compete with a human being when it comes to adaptability."

"That's a relief," Jack said dryly. "I was beginning to think the aliens were a mystery to us."

"Shut up, Jack." Mason redirected his attention to the others. "We need to send a man."

Jack was about to respond when he felt Pie's firm grip on his thigh. He relaxed and focused his attention on the coffered ceiling of scavenged cheery wood.

"Terrible idea," the General grumbled with a shake of his head. "It'll tip our hand. We'll lose the element of surprise."

Mason pressed on. "If the ship is inhabited by aliens, there will be no surprise. We haven't been able to shield our communications. Radio waves have been traveling into space since the Death began. We had to communicate with one another. Even if it is some sort of self-directed computer-ship, it will already have detected the radio waves. I don't know. I'll have to think about it."

"Aren't you forgetting something?" Timken said, never meeting anyone's eyes. "We don't have a Mars ship anymore. The Explorer is somewhere near Venus by now."

"We could rig a scramjet to get there," Mason said. "Unfortunately, whoever we sent would not be able to return." He let that thought hang in the air.

"There are people who are willing to make the sacrifice," Rathburn declared.

"Are you volunteering for the mission?" Mason asked with the hint of a smile.

Rathburn's lips blanched against the artificial tan of his face. "I...." He took out a freshly starched handkerchief and wiped his forehead. "I...."

Mason's smile grew. "I couldn't possibly accept your brave offer. You're too valuable here. But...perhaps it would be sensible to ask for volunteers, in case this possibility becomes a part of our overall strategy. I want all of you to think about it. I'll be contacting the other bubbles to inform them of the alien ship and I'll be asking for their advice. But—" He pointed his thumb at his chest. "—in the end, it'll be up to us to decide. We'll meet again tomorrow to discuss our options and make some decisions. The departmental reports can wait. You're excused."

The general cleared his throat. When he had their attention, he spoke. "I want to go on record as being opposed to sending a reconnaissance ship to Mars. Anyone with any military training would agree that it's a terrible waste of a tactical advantage." He nodded toward Jack. "I'm sure even Captain Nichols would agree with me."

"Yes, I'm sure he would," Mason interjected before Jack could respond. "I, on the other hand, believe there is a considerable chance of success."

"Success at what?" Clark asked.

"For one, success at probing the alien's defenses. Your objection is duly noted. This meeting is adjourned."

Pie didn't get up, so neither did Jack. The section heads hurried from the room, rushing to spread the news. It was only a moment before the room was empty, other than for Mason and the boy who sat at his side.

"Jack, leave us," Mason ordered.

"I want him to stay," Pie said.

"Very well, if you insist. What do you think?" Mason asked.

"I'd like to volunteer," Pie said.

"No way. I need you here."

Pie studied the Director before responding. "You're going to send a modified scramjet with a nuclear payload and no return ticket, aren't you?"

Mason smiled. "See, I told you I needed you. I've found it's good to allow a discussion before the obvious hard solution is reached. I will grant that there is no chance at all of sneaking up on the alien ship. On the other hand, there would be no reason for a computer run drone ship to be programmed to defend itself from an active attack when it is assumed that the native species has already been destroyed."

"You're only guessing at the alien ship's capabilities," Pie replied.

"True, but, at the very least it would provide us with some idea of how the ship will respond to an attack. It's crucial information that we'll need should the alien ship retarget and travel to Earth. In that case, we'll be forced to make our last stand here."

"As I understand it, if the alien ship does travel to Earth and it is able to bombard us with its cargo, then the war for survival will have been lost, even if we do manage to destroy the ship," Pie countered.

"So, you agree that we must do our best to make sure that it is destroyed far from Earth. Do you have a better plan?"

Pie said nothing.

Mason continued, "You've made my argument for me. I expect your full support when I present it."

"I volunteer to go," Jack said. "I won't need my legs. I'll leave them behind to allow for a greater payload."

"Can I have them, Uncle Mitch?" the boy asked with bright eagerness.

Mason reached over to tousle his hair and chuckled, before returning his attention to Jack. He stared at Jack as if dissecting him. "You *have* established a remarkable record...of failing to achieve mission objectives. In fact, the only extraordinary thing about you is your amazing, well, for lack of a better word, we'll call it luck. You manage to save your own hide when everyone around you is dying. I wonder why that is? Before Uribe's aircraft exploded, he was transmitting real time to Copper Mountain. I've viewed the video record of Timmy Sullivan's death, recorded from your own helmet cam. Poor Timmy. What did you do to save him?"

"You bastard!", Jack began to rise out of his chair, but was held in place by Pie.

Pie spoke. "That's not a fair description of what Jack has had to endure, or of Sullivan's death, and you damn well know it. I'd trust Jack with my life, have trusted him with my life."

Mason smiled. "People change, but...perhaps you're right. My apologies, Jack."

"Apologies? You're the reason— You are a sick bastard," Jack added quietly.

The boy took it all in with a nasty smile. Jack wanted to reach across the table and slap that smirk right off his face.

"I can see one benefit in sending you," Mason mused. "You, among all of us, seem to have no usefulness."

"I object," Pie snapped. "What the hell do you think you're doing?"

Mason held up a hand that was becoming thick with fat. "I know. Jack is your special do-good project. You've been trying to build up his self-esteem, even to the point of assigning pretend-work, but—"

"Pretend work!" Jack pulled his arm out of Pie's grip.

"Mason." Pie gave him a threatening look.

"I apologize again. See, I'm a reasonable man." Mason turned his attention to Jack. "Perhaps you could be of some use as a scramjet pilot. We can always use more of those and it was part of your training, as I recall."

"I want to get as far away from you as I can. I volunteer for that starship you're building."

"The feeling is mutual, but you're not qualified. You certainly don't expect us to pin mankind's future on a man with no legs and secondhand intestines."

The boy laughed. It was a surprisingly adult sound and as shallow as his teeth.

Jack pointed his finger at the boy. "You shut up. You need a spanking."

"Uncle Mitch?" The boy looked to Mason with a sad face and scooted closer.

Mason focused on Jack. "Control yourself. If I say the word, my personal guard will appear so fast it'll make your head spin and I can assure you they'll do far more than spank you."

"Call them, Uncle Mitch. He's going to hurt me."

Mason put his arm around the boy. "Not a chance. And as far as the starship goes, the crew will be selected from the best candidates from around the world, from all the bubbles. They'll be in their early twenties when the ship is ready so they'll arrive with plenty of life left, preserved by the technology you failed to retrieve from JPL. I had to send another team to clean up after you."

"Did you send them in paper-thin hazmat suits, or were they in full combat armor?" Jack stood and was about to charge when Pie positioned himself between them.

Pie looked over his shoulder at Mason. "Why are you baiting him?"

"I'm not baiting him. How picturesque. I didn't even want him here. You're the one who insisted he stay."

Pie took hold of Jack's arm, a no nonsense grip. "Come on."

As Pie led Jack from the room, Mason spoke. "Jane's pregnant again."

Both men paused and looked back to Mason, who still had his arm around the boy.

"Congratulations," Pie said.

Jack wanted to ask about her, but could say nothing and allowed Pie to lead him out of the room. Neither man spoke until they were walking down the main hallway.

"Pie, can I ask you question?"

"Shoot."

"Do you think I could've done something to save Timmy?"

"Hell no. Hell no! I saw that video. Unless you think dying with him would've helped."

"Maybe I should have."

"That's exactly what Mason wants you to think. He's an expert at manipulating people, getting into their heads. He's a cruel son of a bitch. Don't let him get to you. Do you hear me?"

Jack took a deep breath and slowly let it out. "I hear you...I guess. I don't see how you can work with that bastard. What an asshole. And what is it with that kid? I expect kids to act inappropriate, but he's a monster. Is Mason really his uncle?"

"No. His name is Geoffrey Slater, Roger Slater's son."

Jack remembered. He was the boy who had sat next to his mother and simply nodded when Jack had informed them that Roger was dead. "How's his mother?"

"That's part of the tragedy. She stuck a gun in her mouth and blew her head off, right in front of the boy."

"That's terrible."

"No doubt about that. For some reason Mason has taken a special interest in the boy. The kid doesn't live with them, but he might as well. I think Mason is grooming him to be the commander of the starship."

"My God." Jack shook his head. "What a horrible choice by a horrible man. How can you tolerate him?"

"He gets results. I can't think of anyone who could replace him."

"What about you?"

"No, not me. He has to make decisions that I'd find impossible, but it has to be done. He doesn't treat everyone like he treats you. I shouldn't have brought you back into contact with him. It was a mistake. It brings out the worst in him."

"It's because of Jane. He knows she still loves me."

"I suspect it has more to do with the fact that you broke nearly every bone in his face. You nearly killed him. As for Jane, get over it."

Jack grabbed his much bigger friend by the arm and tried to twist him around, without success.

"Get over it?" Jack yelled.

Pie turned of his own will. Those in the hall stopped to

look.

"Get over it?" Jack's voice went up another notch. "To hell with you too!" He turned away and stalked off down the hall, his metal feet "clicking" with each angry step.

CHAPTER 26

Roxanne was leaning over a monitor, pointing to something as she discussed an issue with two of her colleagues; they paid close attention to what she was saying. When she had finished, they both nodded.

She saw Pie standing nearby and brushed her hair out of her face. She smiled and walked toward him. "Why so serious?" She folded her arms across her chest and waited.

"Things are going to hell. You'll learn about it soon enough anyway. Another spaceship has been detected, in orbit around Mars. The third phase of the invasion is about to begin."

She nodded. "I expected it. But it's not the third, it's the fourth."

"Fourth?"

"Before they could genetically alter us, they had to know about our biology. That means that they had to have sent an initial ship to define our genetics and then somehow get the information back to their home world. Who knows how many thousands of years they've been working toward their goal."

"Well, they're not infallible. They missed RNA viruses altogether."

"Not really. Viruses require a DNA based host to survive. They're obligate parasites. There's no knowing how long that crashed ship has been on Mars. I believe the initial estimates of fifty to a hundred years were way off. It's a testament to their incredibly advanced technology that the trigger organism remained viable. If they had managed to seed the Earth with the many thousands of golden spheres that must be aboard that crashed starship, we would be dead. As it is, we barely survived the seven stationers who returned to Earth. Seven. I believe the crashed starship has been there for a thousand years or more, long enough for them to assume that the Earth is ready for seeding. Overkill is the word."

"That's basically what Professor Timken said."

"That old loony bird occasionally gets it right. Now that the Earth is supposedly sterilized, they'll want to establish their own bacteria and viruses, maybe even animals and plants."

"You don't think it's the invaders themselves?"

"No way. Not yet. Want some coffee? Freeze dried. Picked it up in Denver."

"Sure."

She walked toward her office and Pie followed, an ogre trailing after a princess.

The office was in its typical condition; there were papers, folders and books everywhere. Pie had given up trying to convince her of the merits of an electronic record. For once, the single visitor's chair had nothing piled on it. Pie looked to her.

"I'm taking steps to improve myself," she said.

Pie took in the stacks of papers and books, which covered every flat surface.

"Small steps," she added with a smile.

He sat and accepted the coffee mug from her. The mug said "Mother of the Year".

"Did Angie get this for you?" Pie asked with a confused frown.

Roxanne's face colored and she smiled. "Of course not. I did. But, she would've if she wasn't unemployed."

Pie returned her smile. "I have noticed a high rate of unemployment among toddlers. We'll have to do something about that." He took a sip; it hardly qualified as coffee but at least it was hot.

Roxanne rested her elbow on the desk with her chin within her palm as she studied the big man, who could only be described as an oaf, until one got to know him. In her estimation, he was a remarkable man, affectionate, bright, assured, and effective. Not for the first time, she wondered if it was his appearance that stood between them. That had never been on her list of "must haves". No, that wasn't it. It was Jack Nichols.

"Had another blow up with Jack today," Pie said after taking another sip.

Roxanne sat up with a start. For a second she wondered if she'd been thinking out loud. "What now?"

"Same old stuff. I wish you'd known him before, I guess before he met Jane. She was never right for him. He needed someone who was more of a free spirit, a rebel." He looked steadily at Roxanne.

"Are you accusing me of being a rebel?"

"That and much more. He was such a prankster, but if you ever needed somebody, there wasn't a better person to have at your back. Did I tell you about that fight in Kabul?"

Roxanne nodded. "And many others. It's amazing you two are still in one piece."

"Now that you've gotten his guts in order, he should be okay. He is okay with his biomechanical legs. Never heard him complain about them. No, that's not it. There's something eating at him, and it's not losing Jane, and it's not the hatred he has for Mason. It's something else. Are you planning on seeing him soon?"

"This evening, if he doesn't blow it off. He's supposed to come over to my apartment for a home cooked meal."

"Do you cook?" Pie asked with interest.

"I can make this...." She stared at him with a deadpan look. "I guess not...but I know someone who does." She continued to stare at him.

Pie set his coffee down. "Now, just a minute. The end of the world is entering its final chapter. I've got things to do."

She nodded and smiled.

He sighed. "I wouldn't do this for anyone but you two. Is Italian okay?"

"Great."

"What time?"

"Seventeen hundred should be about right. I'll put it in the oven. Is that what you do?"

"I'll drop it off, along with instructions." He leaned forward as if he was about to stand and then relaxed back into the chair.

"Yes?" Roxanne gave him her full attention. "What is it?"

"Are you going to tell Jack about Angie tonight?"

"Maybe, depends on him. I'll feel him out a little first."

"You know, Jack is a different kind of guy. If he commits to a person, that's it, end of story. It's all or nothing. Probably why he has so few friends."

"You've told me that before. People have accused me of the same thing."

"I'm not saying it's bad. What I'm trying to say is...are you...I mean...."

"Stringing him along?"

"I guess that's one way to put it. Are you interested in him only because he's so needy?"

"You're a good friend, Pie."

"I don't know about that. We've had issues lately."

"Pie."

"Yes."

"Do you believe human beings are susceptible to pheromones?"

"Is that a polite way to tell me I stink?"

She smiled. "I was just wondering. Trying to understand...well, I guess it's not important."

"It's pretty clear, what—who you've been thinking about. I've decided to start wearing a little eau de Jack. What do you think?"

"I think eau de Pie smells just fine. I wouldn't want you to change a thing."

He looked down to hide a pleased smile. "If things don't go well," he said without looking up, "I'm ready to step in. I'd be honored to adopt Angie."

"Are you suggesting I need help?"

He looked up. "Everyone—"

"You can go to hell, Pie Traynor. I don't need you or any man. I'm perfectly capable of taking care of Angie and myself. If I do decide on a permanent relationship, it'll be because I want it, not because I need it."

"Okay, okay, I was only offering to help." He held up his big hands in surrender.

"I don't need your or anybody else's help."

He stood. "I get the picture. Sorry I offered."

"You should be."

He looked down at her.

"Did you have something else to say?" she asked.

"Not a thing." He turned to leave.

"Pie."

He turned back to her.

"You *are* still going to help me with the cooking, aren't you?"

"Of course, but I hesitate to call it help. Let's call it a coordinated effort in nutrition."

She smiled.

"I've got some end of the world cooking to do. Later."

"Later, Pie."

CHAPTER 27

Jack stood in the deserted hallway. He began to walk away, but then stopped and returned to the door. He looked up and down the hall, glad that no one had been watching while he had approached and then retreated from the door three times. Finally, he brought up his knuckles and rapped on it.

It seemed quiet in there; she had probably forgotten. He was turning away when the door opened.

Roxanne held a toddler, who glared at him. Roxanne's red hair seemed even redder when compared to the black hair of the girl child she held.

She smiled. "Aren't you coming in?"

There was an appealing aroma in the apartment and he was hungry. He stepped in far enough for her to close the door. Her apartment had the same layout as his, yet it was so different. There were toys scattered around, dolls, stuffed animals and blocks. In the corner, the trashcan was lying on its side; something yellow had seeped out of it and onto the Persian rug. His gaze fixed with surprise on a picture above the sofa; it was his reproduction of "Nighthawks". How in the world?

"Did you take that from…." He walked closer, astounded at what he was seeing.

"I didn't exactly take it. Much of the art had been vandalized, but I found this hidden in a closet at the Chicago Art Institute. Do you like it? It's one of my favorites."

He nodded, his eyes fixed on the painting. "It's absolutely fantastic." The greens were so much richer than in any reproduction.

"Go ahead and sit down. Make yourself at home." She pointed at the sofa.

There was little of the paisley fabric that wasn't covered by books or discarded clothing. He stood there for a moment before he looked back to her.

"You know what to do. Just put the stuff on the floor." She laughed and lowered the toddler to the rug.

He frowned. *How sanitary could it be for a toddler to be allowed on this floor?*

Roxanne disappeared into the kitchenette.

He stacked some of the books in a neat pile, just enough to allow him a place to sit. He sat with his legs together, hands in his lap, as if to take up as little space as was possible.

The little girl watched him.

Her lashes were as dark as her hair and her big eyes were pale blue. He couldn't see much of Roxy in her, except for the fair skin. He looked for a suggestion of Roxanne's lips, or her nose or something.

She stared back at him with unknowable thoughts, and then she toddled toward him. She grabbed onto his trouser leg and wobbled, but held on.

She seemed serious for such a little girl. *Is this the way little kids act?*

"Awfully quiet in there," Roxanne said from the kitchenette. "Is everything going okay?"

"Sure. We're okay." He was trying to remember the little girl's name and was too embarrassed to admit that he'd forgotten it.

The little girl smiled. She had two front teeth and she showed them when she began jabbering.

Roxanne peeked around the corner. "Pick her up. She won't bite."

The girl jabbered more insistently; it sounded like a demand. Jack put out his hand and expected her to retreat across the room, but she grabbed his fingers. He lifted her onto his lap. She smiled and pointed at his face. It was impossible not to return that smile. She climbed up his chest and put her pudgy arm around his neck. She smelled good, not a smell he could identify, sweet, personal, good. He kissed her on the cheek and was more surprised than she was. Evidently, she was used to being kissed on every occasion.

Roxanne looked around the corner. "That's better. Dinner will be ready in a few minutes."

The toddler was jabbering again; it seemed like she was saying something important. He lifted her above him and she giggled. When he lowered her, she pushed with her feet and raised her arms; she wanted to be lifted again, so he did, again and again, until he thought there would be no end to it.

"Time to eat," Roxanne called.

Jack held the girl against his chest as he stood, concerned about his metallic legs for the first time in months, afraid he might fall with her in his arms. He managed to make it to the small table, which was set for three. While he strapped her into her highchair, Roxanne hurried over to pull the chair out for him.

"Do you think I can't do it for myself?" Jack asked.

"I'm sure you can. It was meant as a courtesy, not as a comment on your gender."

"My gender? I thought—I get it." He chuckled. "In that case, thank you very much. Good manners are always appreciated, even old fashioned ones."

"Oddly enough, I've developed a taste for the old fashioned."

She returned to the kitchenette and brought out spaghetti and meatballs. It had a familiar aroma. A moment later she returned with a bottle of wine and took the seat across from him.

"Very good Chianti," she announced. "We should have enough wine for a few generations." She sliced up a small portion of spaghetti and blew on it before putting it on her daughter's plate.

Jack couldn't stop staring at Roxanne; she was beautiful, everything about her, from her rosy cheeks, to her wild red hair and green eyes.

"Is there something wrong?" she asked. "Don't you like spaghetti?"

"I like it a lot."

"You're awfully quiet. Care to share your thoughts?"

"Umm, it smells good." He took a bite.

She watched him chew and swallow.

"Do you like it?" she asked

"Absolutely. Pie's spaghetti is one of my favorites."

"Pie's? Why I—"

He looked up at her.

"All right, so he helped me a little."

He smiled.

"I *can* cook, you know."

He continued to smile. "No doubt about it."

He took a sip of the wine and then another. It went straight to his head, the first alcohol he had drunk in over two years. He felt good as he ate: happy to be sitting across the table from Roxy and the little girl.

Jack nodded toward the toddler. "She's very friendly."

"Not as friendly as you might think. Pie calls her the prosecutor."

Pie. Jack nodded and kept his attention focused on his plate. Of course Pie had been here. He looked up, just as Roxanne sucked in a noodle.

She laughed. "Do you remember our first date? Or, I guess we should call it a business dinner."

"I remember that green dress you were wearing. I'm surprised you didn't have every man in that hotel following you around."

"What makes you think they weren't?"

He remembered that man in the expensive suit, hanging all over her. "Do you still have that dress?"

"Yes, but it doesn't fit like it used to. Not after Angie."

"You're still the most beautiful woman I've ever met."

"Thank you."

"And humble too?"

"I'm working on it. Do you remember what you said when that couple walked past singing the alphabet song?"

"No. What did I say?"

"It's not important. You know, you looked really great. I loved that military tux. When I saw you, it literally made my legs go weak."

"You didn't act like it."

"I couldn't, not with things the way they were. Did you enjoy going to that restaurant with me? Bijon's. I don't see how you could have. I was irritated with the world that night and with men in particular."

He nodded. "It was like rubbing up against sandpaper."

"That's me. Gritty as hell."

"And I remember the visit to your farmhouse." He was surprised to see Roxanne's cheeks flush and felt an answering warmth in his own face. He looked away, to the little girl who had spaghetti sauce smeared from ear to ear. "You have a beautiful daughter." He wondered who her father was, wondered how many men Roxanne had slept with. He began to massage his forehead, as if he could the rub the thoughts out of his mind.

"Are you okay? Is the food too rich for you?"

He lowered his hand to his lap. "No, it's good."

"Would you like some more?"

"No thanks." And he shook his head to an offer of more wine. "I suppose you've heard the news."

"About the ship in orbit around Mars?"

He nodded.

"I imagine Mason plans to send a scramjet to blow it up."

Jack stared at her.

"Oh come on. We both know him. It won't work, of course."

"Why do you say that?"

"Here is this starship. It has come from God knows where without a problem. Now, if we ignore the other ship for a moment, the crashed one, what likelihood is there that it won't be able to defend itself? It must have cost a hell of a lot, no matter what the aliens use for money. They're not just going to send it out with best wishes. Do you think?"

Jack found himself nodding. Somehow he had forgotten how bright she was. It was so easy to do when looking into her eyes. He hated to admit it, but she was probably smarter than he was.

"Is that a grimace or a smile?" she asked.

"It just seems that you should be the section leader not that Nobel Prize prick, Rathburn."

"You're right of course—what are you smiling about now?"

"Nothing."

The little girl was evidently getting bored and began to throw the reminder of her food on the floor.

"Angie, don't do that!"

Angie. That was it.

Roxanne used a towel to clean Angie's face before setting her on the floor. She watched for a moment, as Angie ran over to her favorite doll, and then retook her seat.

Roxanne picked up where she'd left off. "It seems society, what's left of it anyway, has begun to drift back into bad habits. It's becoming a man's world again. Did you know that Mason has issued a policy statement that all woman are to become pregnant as soon as possible, that it's their duty?"

"No." He sat forward, feeling possessive for no reason he could pinpoint.

She nodded. "Oh, yeah. And you know how civic minded I am."

"What do you mean?"

"I'm going to seduce the next man I see."

Jack's mouth dropped open.

"Just joking." She laughed. "Gotcha."

"Sure did."

"Aren't you ready for a child?" she asked, her hands suddenly still.

"This is no world to bring a child into." He regretted it immediately. "I'm sorry, I didn't mean—"

"I could give a shit what you think, Jack Nichols. I choose what I do. Not you and sure as hell not Mason."

Jack glanced over at the little girl and she smiled, her cheeks stained orange from spaghetti sauce. He looked back to Roxanne. "I'm really sorry, Roxy. Sometimes, I...I don't know. I have to go." He stood.

"Not before you do the dishes."

"What?"

"You don't expect to come in here and eat and not do a damn thing, do you?"

He nodded. "All right." He walked over to the sink, which was piled with dishes, many with caked on food, not tonight's dishes; it looked like a week's worth.

Roxanne leaned back in her chair and watched him while he stared at the dishes. "All of them."

He returned her gaze and had to meet her broad smile with one of his own. "All right, all the dishes." He started scrubbing while Roxanne got Angie ready for bed. He was nearly half done when Roxanne approached with the little girl in her arms.

"She wants to say goodnight."

Jack was about to comment on how ridiculous that claim was; he had heard her jabbering. But, when he turned and saw the little girl, he bent forward and gave her a hug and a kiss.

"Goodnight, sweetheart," he said.

She waved to him with her plump, dimpled hand.

He returned to the dishes and listened to Roxanne read a bedtime story to her daughter. He had just finished when Roxanne returned from the bedroom.

"She's asleep," she said.

Jack nodded as he dried his waterlogged hands and then froze when he felt Roxanne's hand on his buttocks.

She stood on her tiptoes, until her mouth was a centimeter from his ear. "Care to join me in the bedroom?"

Jack turned to her.

"What's the problem now?"

"She's in there."

"You mean Angie?"

"Yes, Angie."

"She's only a baby."

"It doesn't seem right."

"My God you're up tight. Is the floor okay?"

Jack looked around at the floor, at the scattered toys, books, and papers and then focused on that unidentifiable yellow goo.

"You don't need to be afraid of me," she said as she pressed against him.

He twisted away. "I'm not afraid!"

"Then, what *is* the problem?"

"Look at this place."

She glanced around the room and then met his eyes. "That's just an excuse. But, if that's how you feel, then I'm glad I found out before it was too late."

She began to turn away and he reached out to grip her arm.

She jerked her arm out of his grasp and turned to face him. "No one touches me without my permission. If you ever do that again, you better mean it, because I'll make you wish I never put you back together again."

"Sorry. It's just that...I don't know. I was sick. I can understand you have needs—I mean—who is Angie's father?"

"You have no claim on me. I don't see how that's any business of yours. You're right. It *is* time for you to leave."

He walked the few steps to the door and opened it. While he held the door open, he turned back to her. "Roxanne, I...I think you're beautiful."

"So what?"

"It's more than that...it's...well...."

"If you have something to say, spit it out."

"I just wanted to say, thanks. I enjoyed being with you. The meal was delicious and it was really great seeing Angie. She's wonderful."

Roxanne managed a smile. "Yes, she is wonderful. Goodnight, Jack."

"Goodnight, Roxanne."

Jack closed the door and walked slowly to the elevator. He descended to the administrative offices and entered the computer lab where he found the person he'd been searching for and sat down next to him.

Pie looked up from his monitor. "Did you go to see Roxanne?"

Jack nodded, looking for a sign, a frown, a twitch, some evidence of distress on his friend's face, but there was nothing as he stared back at Jack.

"Anything interesting happen?" Pie asked.

"No."

"Called it a night kind of early, didn't you? What happened?"

"Nothing. By the way, your spaghetti sauce was delicious, as usual."

"Mine? Why would you—"

Jack cut him off with a look.

"Well, thanks. But she heated it up."

"Yes, she's damn good at heating things up."

"What did you think about Angie? She's a little devil, isn't she?"

"No...why would you say such a thing?"

"I bet she hid and then screamed every time you came close. It took quite a while before she was willing to come within reach of me, but keep at it. I did and now she jumps into my arms. It just takes persistence. She'll come around, really a sweet little girl, once you get to know her."

"She's a wonderful little girl," Jack declared.

"Then, what happened?"

"I've been thinking."

"That sounds dangerous."

Jack ignored the comment. "Angie's about two years old. That means she must've been conceived shortly after I arrived at the space station. Do you know who Angie's father is and whether he survived the Death?"

Pie said nothing.

"You know, don't you, Pie."

"Jack, it's not for me to say. That's Roxanne's business."

"Are you and Roxanne...involved?"

Pie studied him for a moment and then came to a decision. "You were dying. As much as I told people you'd pull through, I guess I didn't really believe it myself."

"What exactly are you saying?" Jack ground out the words.

"I'm trying to tell you that we've had sex—are you going to hit me?"

Jack lowered his fist and sighed. "No."

"I wouldn't make too much of it. She sure as hell doesn't. It happened while you were in that coma, when it looked like you had finally given up the fight, before you rallied."

"I don't remember any of that."

"No, I don't suppose so. I know, for a virgin like yourself, this must come as quite a shock."

Jack rested his head on his arms on the desk. "No," he mumbled.

"Are you tired of her and ready to push her away like you know who?"

Jack sat straight up. "I'm not pushing Roxy away." He sighed. "At least, I didn't think I was. I better go back and talk with her."

"I wouldn't. I suspect you've used up her patience for tonight. Just try to be a little more demonstrative of your affection, if you have any." Pie studied him closely and then let his shoulders slump.

Jack nodded. "I will. Thanks."

Pie turned back to the screen and Jack followed his gaze. It was a recording of the alien starship as it went into orbit around Mars.

"Show me that again," Jack said

Pie ran the sequence again. The spindle-shaped craft shifted its direction and slid into orbit.

"Once more." Jack watched. "Does it seem to you that the ship is bending as it goes into orbit, almost as if it points its snout and the body of the ship curves to follow?"

"It does look that way, but it may be an illusion. I wonder how it moves? There is no sign of heat or radiation. It just moves."

"I wonder why the first one crashed on Mars."

"Don't we all." Pie sat back.

The sequence repeated; the golden ship glistened with reflected light as it established an orbit. It didn't look like an illusion.

"Roxy says Mason's plan to send an armed scramjet won't work."

"That was top secret."

"Take a break, Pie. I didn't tell her a damn thing. She figured it out on her own. Took her about five seconds."

Pie nodded. "I can believe it. She does have a remarkable

knack for being right about things, but she isn't infallible."
Pie took a sideways glance at Jack. "In fact, she's been wrong
so many times, I can hardly count—" Pie smiled. "Just joking.
If you feel that way about her, you better get your butt in
gear. In Copper Mountain alone, there are dozens of men who
are tripping over one another to get a chance at her."

"Damn it!" Jack pushed away from the table and stood,
glaring down at him.

"It's not me you have to worry about. Kind of odd to be in
that position, isn't it? I remember once, Jane asked me—"

"Shut up! Just shut up. Who is Angie's father? Are you
her father?"

"Not me. Beyond that, I suggest you ask Roxy."

"Is she still seeing him?"

"Rumor has it he's kind of a stubborn asshole, but he has
his good points."

"Then you do know! Tell me."

"That's Roxy's decision, not mine."

"When I find out who it is...."

"Aren't you glad she has Angie?"

"Of course I am. That doesn't have anything to do with it."

"Really?"

"I'm going to break every bone in his body."

"Should be interesting. Maybe I'll help."

"Sometimes you don't act like my friend."

"Sometimes you don't act like the man I've known. Take
charge of your life. It's time for you to move beyond the past.
I could use you at my side again, the way we used to be."

"Damn it! Damn it to hell!"

Pie shrugged and turned back to the screen.

Jack stood and pushed his chair back so hard it tipped
over. His metallic feet "clicked" across the floor and he slammed
the door on his way out.

CHAPTER 28

Roxanne looked up from her monitor and smiled when Pie entered her office. "Hi stranger, haven't seen you in a while. How goes the great attack?" she asked with a smirk.

Pie removed the books and printouts from the chair, looked at them as if he could put them on the floor in some kind of order and then just let them fall. "I see you're backsliding. Why do you persist in using all this paper? It gathers around you like the leaves of a tree."

"That's a pleasant way to put it. I rather like that."

"Oh yeah, well, it gathers around you like...."

"Give it up, Pie. How are Mason's plans progressing?"

"They're progressing."

"You don't look too happy about it. Are you beginning to believe me when I tell you it's futile."

"No."

Roxanne's eyes narrowed. "Has Mason changed his mind about sending Jack?"

"No, he still considers Jack to be the talisman of bad luck for the new society."

"New society?"

"Yeah, he seems to believe that he has the answer to all of mankind's problems, big or small."

"I warned you."

"Yeah...well. Speaking of our mutual friend, I gather Jack has opened up to you, or you to him, so to speak."

"A little crudely put, but true. Is there no in between with that man? First, I can't get him interested and now he won't give me a moment's peace. Everyday, he's there."

"Is that so bad?"

"I'm not Jane."

Pie shook his head. "No, that you're not. So he's crowding you a little, huh?"

"I wish he'd realize that. The more I try to get a little breathing room, the closer he pushes."

"Have your feelings about him changed?"

"No. I don't know. I don't think so. He gave me a present."

"I know. Mason was mad as hell when he heard that Jack made the pilot divert so he could be dropped off. Mad as hell."

"It was already mine, but still, it was a present. And he brought back chocolates for Angie. They were old. Don't keep like Spam, as you're so found of saying."

"But, you do have to appreciate the fact that he left Copper Mountain to get your car and then drove it back through the dead lands. You know how he feels about going out, after that bicycle trip up the coast."

She nodded. "I know and I do. He even had a special hand pump made to get gasoline."

"Did you thank him? As if I didn't know the answer to that one."

"Sure. At least, I think I did. Anyway, he knows I appreciated it."

"Ah, the telepathy approach to a relationship."

"Gee, thanks mom. I don't think I asked for your advice."

"Are you planning on telling him about Angie?" Pie asked

"I'm considering it, but I'm beginning to regret I ever told you."

"Okay, I'm backing off. Have you tried that new recipe I gave you for Spam fettuccini?"

"No, but I'm sure looking forward to it."

"Sarcasm doesn't become you——no, to be truthful, it does." She smiled.

"As for your problem with Jack, I don't think you have to be worried about being smothered for long."

"Why do you say that?" Roxanne asked.

"He's taken pilot refresher training and will be shuttling supplies to the space station."

"He didn't tell me about that. Is it dangerous?"

"We've only lost two so far."

"Two?"

"Yeah, and to hear Mason talk about it, you'd think they were traitors for wrecking two of the scramjets."

Roxanne sat still and frowned, while she absently twirled and caught her pen.

"Why hasn't he told me?" she finally asked.

"First you complain that he's crowding you and now you're complaining he doesn't tell you everything."

"Seriously."

"I am serious."

She shook her head, still frowning. "He's up to something."

"Maybe so. But he's been much happier lately. You're some woman."

"Cut the bullshit."

"And you have an excellent vocabulary."

"Get out of here before I poke you in the eye."

Pie stood. "Is it still on for tonight?"

"Of course, and that's one more thing. Do you know he's taken to cleaning up my place? I can't stand all those neat little stacks. I have the feeling that he's going to make us start sitting in alphabetical order."

"Not that!" Pie exclaimed. "Cleanliness and order?"

"Out!"

Pie grinned. "As much as I enjoy our little chats, I do have to be off. See you tonight."

"Right."

Roxanne felt restless and decided to go to her lab. She was not sitting at the molecular scanner for more than a moment when she felt a hand on her back. She shook it off and turned around, ready to punch the offender, but held her counterattack.

"Hi, Jack. What's up?" The adoring way he looked at her made her cringe.

"I just wanted to tell you how—" His eyes strayed to the monitor of the scanner. "What's that?"

"You were about to say something?" Maybe she was as bad as he was. That thought disturbed her.

"What's that on the monitor?"

"This is it. The villain of all villains. The little invader that can enter our cells at will and bring with it anything it wants, or now, anything we want it to."

He watched with rapt attention as the organism attached itself to the cell wall. The wall melded with it and then the invader injected its payload, which wiggled its way to the nucleus.

Roxanne followed his gaze to the screen. "Amazing, isn't it? If the cell wall is breached it simply dies, can't live with a hole in it, but this way the cell is changed and lives to do whatever the invading microbe wants it to. That's one advantage biological systems have over mechanical. They can heal. That which was cut can become whole again."

She waited for his usual tirade about how he was going to destroy those "damn aliens" but he was quiet as he studied the monitor.

"First time you've ever seen the little bastard in action?" That ought to please him.

He nodded.

She waved her hand in front of his eyes. "Hello, hello in there. What are you thinking about?"

"I get it now. I understand. On the Explorer, I thought there was a piece of the alien ship's hull missing, but it wasn't missing at all. It had healed."

"What? You're not making any sense. We're not talking about a ship's hull, we're talking about the trigger microbe."

"But, what about biomechanical? I can heal and I'm part machine. In fact, I can fix the mechanical parts if they go on the blink, replace a servomotor or whatever. Weren't those golden spheres a mixture of organic and mechanical? Maybe the same is true for the hull."

"I wouldn't know. That's not in my area of expertise. Look."

The spindle-shaped organism attached to the wall of the nucleus and then slithered inside. It was the ultimate invasion and no defense was mounted.

"It's able to sense where the DNA is and then insert it's genetic package. It's just as effective on prokaryotes, like Cyanobacteria."

"Cyanobacteria?"

"Blue-green algae. They've given us a tool we could only dream about." That should do it, she thought, and waited for the outburst.

"I have to go," he said.

"But, you just got here."

"See you tonight." He hurried away with purpose in his stride.

Roxanne stared after him. He was one damn infuriating man. Didn't even let her ask him about that scram-pilot thing. She smiled as she turned back to the monitor. But he does have a nice ass.

She continued to work with the newly inserted gene, accelerating the cell's reproduction, checking for perfect replication. It wasn't until the last of her staff walked past and said goodnight that she realized how late it was. She had to pick up Angie from daycare and she was late.

She was carrying Angie when she arrived at her apartment. The door was open a crack and there was a mouth-watering aroma. She toed the door open and saw the bulky body of Pie, with his back to her while he worked in the kitchen. As soon as she set Angie down, Angie ran across the room and attached herself to Pie's leg. Only if Jack were present would she have gone elsewhere.

She really should tell Jack about Angie, she thought as she watched Pie pick up the toddler and lift her to the ceiling.

"Want to bonk your head?" he asked the squealing girl and got a vigorous nod in response. He lifted her to the ceiling, touched her head against it, and then dropped her, catching her just in time, but without ever releasing his hands from her.

She giggled with delight. "Again."

"Not now darlin'. I've got a feast to prepare."

"Where's Jack?" Roxanne asked as she looked around her small apartment. She peeked into her bedroom.

"Don't know."

"Why don't you know?" she asked, unable to keep irritation from her voice.

Pie turned and leaned against the kitchen counter. "You may think I have nothing better to do than keep track of you two and your so very tangled affairs, but I actually do have responsibilities."

"I'm sorry. I don't know...I feel confused...."

"Then let me set you straight. I'm a very important person."

"I know. And that's the truth." She stepped forward and gave him a chaste hug.

He held her a little longer than was proper. She pushed lightly and he released his hug to attend to the stove.

After freshening up, she returned to the small dining area where Pie was already setting the table with Kung Pow chicken. Where he got the meat, she had no idea and didn't want to know. It looked and smelled delicious. It's a good thing Pie didn't cook every night. She'd be a blimp within a month. She sat down. She had to start working out more. In the gym, she added to herself.

Pie sat across from her. "What're you smiling about?"

She shook her head

"And such pretty pink cheeks too. I can guess."

"Shush, not in front of—" She nodded toward Angie.

"Oh yeah, I bet. If she has any memory at all, sex education won't be needed."

"Pie!"

"Yeah, right."

They sat with their hands in their laps, except for Angie who stuffed her mouth with Kung Pow, minus the peanuts and hot peppers. She too loved Uncle Pie's cooking.

Roxanne looked to the door and then back to Pie. "To hell with him. If he can't get here on time, he can eat by himself. I'm not going to let this get cold."

"Me either."

They ate in silence other than for Roxanne's compliments and Pie's agreement with her assessment. They were sipping what had been expensive wine, when there was such a thing as money, and still Jack hadn't appeared.

"Where the hell is he?" Roxanne asked.

"Hell" Angie repeated.

Pie shook his finger at Roxanne.

"She has to learn some time," Roxanne declared.

"Perhaps, but it probably shouldn't be among her first words."

"She knows lots of words!"

"Do you want me to go look for him?"

"No!" She stood abruptly and walked across the room, kicking over piles of neatly stacked books and scattering papers about.

Pie and Angie watched, both equally fascinated, until Roxanne turned to stare at them.

"Don't say a word," she warned Pie.

"Hell," Angie said.

The set of Roxanne's shoulders softened. "All right, Pie. Would you go find that lost soul?"

"Sure." He stood. "But that means you have to do the dishes."

"No it doesn't. Jack has to. He has to pay some penalty."

Pie glanced around the room. "Oh, I think he'll get the idea that he screwed up."

CHAPTER 29

Jack's face was lit by the glow of the monitor. He was focused on the screen as if watching the climax of a cliffhanger. He heard others in the room shift their chairs and looked up from the monitor. A dark silhouette was weaving his way through the room. There was no mistaking that physique.

When Pie stopped next to Jack's workstation a realization struck.

"Oh, no," Jack said.

"Oh, yes. You are in deep shit, my friend."

"But, I just skipped a meal."

"Don't be a dunce. There's a lot more going on here and you damn well know it. Why didn't you tell her you were going to be piloting a scramjet?"

"Are you mad at me?"

Pie took a breath and shook his head. "No." He laughed.

Jack could not help but wonder at his friend's behavior.

Pie gave him a friendly jab on the shoulder. "There's some food left over." He glanced at the screen. "What's that? Isn't that a trajectory? What is that, Jack?"

Jack's finger stabbed the off button and the monitor went black.

"What was that?" Pie asked.

"What was what?" Jack stood. "Come on. We have to go."

Pie stood where he was, causing Jack to pause.

"What was on the screen, Jack?"

"I was just practicing navigation vectors. You know. Boring stuff. Come on." He tugged on his big friend's arm. "I need you to be there."

Pie shook his head. "I don't think so. I've got work to do."

Jack nodded. "Thanks for coming for me."

"We'll see if you thank me tomorrow."

"She's pretty mad, huh?"

"Could be."

"I better go."

Pie said nothing.

Jack walked away but glanced back to see Pie staring at the now blank screen. He hurried down the main hall and entered the elevator. When he exited and approached Roxanne's apartment he slowed. He stopped before her door and tapped lightly. She might be sleeping, he told himself. She opened the door and stepped back, allowing him to enter without saying a word.

Jack glanced around the room. "It looks very nice. Everything's in order. For me?"

"Don't get too full of yourself. I had a lot of time on my hands."

"Uncle Jack!" Angie ran toward him and he bent to scoop her up.

He kissed her extravagantly on her cheeks and forehead, hugging her all the while. "I love you," he whispered to the little girl who rested her head on his shoulder. He reached up with a hand and she curled her fist around a finger.

Roxanne sat down on the sofa. "She refused to go to bed until you came to tuck her in. You dork."

He inhaled and his shoulders relaxed. "She smells so good. I'll just read her a tiny book," he said as he walked with her to the bedroom.

"Might as well. Your dinner couldn't get any colder."

Jacks voice was audible throughout the small apartment as was Angie's giggling. When all was quiet, he reentered the living area.

"It sounds like you enjoyed it," Roxanne said.

He took a deep breath and relaxed with a big smile. "There's something about holding her and doing things with her that just...I don't know. It feels good."

"Come sit by me." She patted the sofa. "I want to tell you something."

Jack looked to her and then at the food. He looked back to her. "What did you want to say?"

"Eat."

When he sat down at the table, he glanced briefly at Roxanne who seemed to be studying him. He returned his attention to his food. She had warmed it while he was with Angie and it hit the spot. When he had finished, he turned in his chair to face her.

She pointed at the sink. "Dishes."

He nodded. "Fair enough."

When he was drying the last plate, she spoke. "Where were you this evening?"

He smiled.

"A stupid smile is not going to do it. Where were you?"

"Studying."

"Studying what?"

"Brushing up on my skills."

"You've decided to become a scramjet pilot, haven't you?"

"Yes."

"Yes? That's all you have to say? What are you really up to?"

"Even though I have secondhand intestines and don't have legs, I'm going to do my part to save mankind."

"Oh shut up. Why didn't you tell me? Pie knew."

"He found out but I didn't tell him either."

"Truth?"

He nodded. "The truth."

"The whole truth?"

He walked over to sit next to her on the sofa. He put his arm around her and pulled her close, planting a kiss on her hair. "You're so wonderful," he whispered. "I...."

"You what?"

"I'm going to tell you something."

She stiffened in his embrace.

He continued, "I'm not useless or stupid, you know."

She relaxed. "That's your big news? Have I ever called you stupid?" She pulled away so that she could see his face.

"Only once or twice a day."

"I do not. I call you a dork." She formed her lips into a delicious pout.

"Don't do that. It's not fair."

"Don't do what?"

"You know damn well." He chuckled.

"What were you going to say?"

"Say? I'll tell you what I was going to say." He rolled onto her and began tickling.

"Don't," she begged between bouts of laughter.

The laughter was smothered as his lips met hers. Questions and answers faded away. The fear of closeness was gone. They could not get close enough; even their clothing was too much to be between them, only flesh touching flesh would do.

CHAPTER 30

Roxanne stood outside Pie's office and watched as he approached. She smiled but he didn't respond.

He stopped in front of her. "Is there a problem?"

"A problem? Why would you think that?"

"Are you telling me this is a social visit? You know the launch is scheduled for today, in two hours actually."

She glanced toward the door of his office but said nothing.

"Okay, Roxy, come on in."

A dozen technicians were busy at their terminals with a final review, too busy to even glance at them as they walked through to the inner office. Pie sat down in one of the two chairs in front of his desk. Roxanne sat in the other. She felt small, everyone did except Pie in his specially constructed, extra-large chairs. He began tapping on the arm of the chair with his fingers.

"I guess I came at a bad time," she said.

"I'm busy as hell."

"I better leave you to your work." She made as if to stand up, but it was obvious she expected Pie to stop her.

"Come on, Roxy. What's bothering you? Is it Jack?"

"Has he said anything to you?" She sat on the edge of her seat.

"Could you be more specific?" He couldn't help but look at the countdown clock on the wall.

"I hardly see him anymore."

"He's been requesting extra flights and the other pilots are more than happy to let him have as many as he wants."

"Why is he doing that?" Roxanne asked.

"I suggest you ask him."

"I have. I've also looked into the modifications they've made to increase the payload. The scramjets are only marginally stable. Jack says they require a lot of attention."

"I thought they were piloted by computers," Pie said.

"True, but it seems they now require both the computer and human pilot to make them work."

"Are you worried about him?"

She studied her hands. "My husband taught me that risk is part of life."

She hadn't mentioned him in a long time and Pie couldn't resist. "The dead one?"

She looked up with a glare.

"Sorry about that, but I do agree. Jack does have to make his own decisions."

"And when he's not piloting, he's in the computer lab." She waited, but when Pie said nothing, she continued. "You're not going to help me out here, are you?"

"I can't. I don't have any answers. Ask Jack."

"He insisted I get a babysitter for tonight. Said he had something important to tell me. Tell me if this rumor is true. Did Jane have a miscarriage?"

Pie pursed his lips and then answered. "Yes."

"There's more, isn't there?"

Pie shifted in his chair and glanced at the clock. "Roxy, I've really got to go. This is an important launch. Its success or failure will determine if we survive."

"That's bullshit. This mission is futile."

"Do you have a better idea?" Harshness had crept into his voice.

Roxanne shook her head. "Not a one. I assume, once the attack is launched, the alien ship will reorient toward Earth. Are you prepared for that?"

"You don't know that."

"Preparing for the expected is not enough, that's what my husband, *my dead husband*, used to tell me. Do you have a backup plan?"

"As much as you seem to think otherwise, you don't have clearance to know everything."

"Okay, Pie. Whatever."

She stood and walked past Pie and out of his office without a backward glance.

CHAPTER 31

Jack was a dark silhouette against the viewing window. The bastardized ship was on the launch platform, a double scramjet, one connected to the other, making the whole assemblage look ugly. It didn't inspire confidence.

Pie walked up to stand beside him.

"What do you think?" Pie asked.

"Not much." Jack watched the suicide pilot climb the steps to the cockpit. His name was Gordy Brinker. Jack had gotten to know him; there weren't that many scramjet pilots. Brinker was the only pilot, beside himself, who had no children and no wife. He was cocky, irritating, and insisted on calling him Jacko.

"A brave son of a bitch. We owe him," Pie said.

"I understand Mason has already taken care of that. Has promised him he'll be the first human cloned in the new program." He turned to Pie. "Would that make you feel better?"

"Not a hell of a lot."

"Me either." He glanced at the big board and then returned his attention to the launch platform.

"Roxy stopped by today," Pie said.

Jack nodded.

"You knew?"

"No."

"Curious?"

"Probably one last effort to stop the mission, as if anyone other than Mason has the power to do anything."

"Partly right. Have you been seeing Jane again? Since her miscarriage?"

Jack continued to stare at the last minute preparations below: lines being unhooked and a final inspection to ensure there was no loose metal in the room. The last thing the scramjet needed was a fragment of ferromagnetic metal being sucked toward it by the mag-driver, striking it like a bullet. The launch personnel hurried from the room.

"Promise me one thing, Pie. If something should happen

to me, and Mason begins to mistreat Jane, kill him."

"I can't make that kind of promise."

"I think he's treating her like a failure, a mission failure, failure to reproduce on schedule."

"He treats her with respect when I see them together."

"That's not what—" Jack closed his mouth.

"What Jane told you? So, you have been seeing her. Did you tell Roxy?"

Jack turned to face the giant man. "You know too damn much about my personal affairs."

"You're right, but that's the way it is. Roxy deserves better than this. If you don't tell her, I will."

Jack studied the big man with the big nose and coarse skin, while Pie found the view of the launch platform more to his liking.

"I know you love her, Pie."

"Nah," Pie shook his head.

"It's obvious. That's how I know I won't have to be worried about her if...."

"If what?" Pie asked.

"If something happens to me."

"If something happens to you? What are you talking about? What's going to happen to you?"

"The future is a strange and mysterious place."

Pie gave him a playful punch on the arm. "What a bullshit answer. Have you been smoking pot again?"

Jack smiled. "No."

"Are you worried you're going to have a scramjet accident?"

Jack shook his head.

All lights dimmed throughout the Copper Mountain space complex; energy was cut to everything that was not on a protected circuit so that the power hungry rail could be fed. The double ship began to move forward and then accelerated up the tunnel. By the time it broke through the surface and began riding the rail up the mountainside it would leave nothing but an impression that something had passed. The sonic boom echoed down the launch tunnel and rattled the viewing window.

Jack turned away from the window. Pie had a vacant look on his face; he was monitoring the flight via an implant.

"See you, Pie."

While Pie was oblivious to his surroundings, Jack walked

away. He descended the stairs to the deck below. He'd been spending time on the launch deck. The prep crew knew him as a light-hearted, backslapping guy. They were beginning to think of him as one of their own, a prep grunt. He pitched in to help roll up and store the hoses and cables.

When they had finished the necessary business, they gathered in the downstairs lounge and watched the mission monitors. The extra rocket engines of the booster scramjet were still firing. The tracking cameras had the doubled ship in view, sharp-edged against the blackness of space.

They drank coffee and watched, waiting for the moment. It was announced before it happened and everyone paused, cup half way to mouth, almost ready to sit or stand. It had been the engineer's plans, but it was their work that had made it a reality. A cheer went up as a bright flare at the rear of the lead ship blew the booster ship away and its own engines fired.

Jack took that moment to escape into the hallway. "Goodbye, Gordy, you brave, stupid bastard," he muttered as he made his way to the elevator.

It was evening. He felt like he and all of humanity had been turned into vampires, forever avoiding the searing light of day. After collecting some supplies from his apartment, he exited the elevator on Roxy's floor. He rapped on her door, his preference over the buzzer.

Roxy opened the door. She was wearing a forest-green dress that swooped low in the front, revealing cleavage, and then collected around her slim waist to flare over her pelvis, ending just above her knees.

"You are beautiful," he declared.

Roxy looked him over; he was dressed in a flannel shirt, workpants and hiking boots. He had a backpack slung over his shoulder.

"Did I misunderstand?" she asked.

"No, not at all. You look great." He waved to the middle-aged woman who was seated on the sofa; the woman responded with a modest smile. He looked back to Roxy and she answered his unspoken question.

"Angie's asleep. She's had a very long day. Played hard."

Jack nodded and looked to the doorway of Angie's room.

"No, you can't wake her up."

"Okay."

"At least let me change my shoes."

Without waiting for an answer, she disappeared into her bedroom. In the meantime, Jack and the babysitter studied each other. Roxy was back in a moment. Jack took her by the arm to lead her out. As soon as the door closed, he turned to her.

"Is that woman safe? I don't recognize her. Do you know anything about her?"

Roxanne smiled. "She's from my lab. I've known her from my university days and, yes, she's trustworthy. Don't worry about Angie. Where are we going?"

"Outside."

"Whoa, then I am dressed wrong." She pulled back.

"Not at all. Have you been out at night?"

"Yes."

"Really?"

"I do get to do things without you, don't I?" she asked.

"It depends on what they are."

"Oh stop it."

They entered the elevator and ascended to the surface. The night was dark, except for the usual phantasm of aurora borealis flares. No one could deny that it was beautiful, but it would've been so nice to step out and just see stars, moon and dark sky. At least it wasn't raining.

"What's in your backpack?"

"The usual."

"The usual?"

He took hold of her hand and led her up the lower slope of the mountain, up the paved road that ran parallel to the rail, and through a hole in the no longer electrified fence. They walked along a path and entered the woods. The trees were barren, as if it were the dead of winter, but it wasn't even chilly.

"Do you have any idea where you're going?" she asked.

"Absolutely. I've been there many times. We're almost there."

They rounded a bend and stopped. He opened his backpack to take out a blanket, which he spread out near a fire pit that was circled by small boulders.

The campsite was surrounded by truncated trees with stubby branches, snapped off by wind and the brittleness of death. Beyond the web of chaotic limbs were the red and

green ribbons of this night's display, weaving back and forth.
"You know, Jack, this is kind of spooky."

He looked up. "Those bastards are going to pay for what they did to us. I swear it. Do you want to go back inside?"

"No. But I doubt that they'll pay. Do Mason and the others really think their stupid plan is going to work?"

"The scramjet is able to accelerate faster than the Mars Explorer. We should know in about seven months, unless the alien ship leaves Mars before then."

He gathered branches from the abundance of deadfall scattered over the ground and stacked them in the fire pit atop ashes of former campfires he had made. He lit it. The fire grew quickly, crackling and popping with cherry-orange flames as it consumed the dry wood. They had to step back to avoid the heat.

He sat down on the blanket. "Come and sit next to me."

She sat and fixed her gaze on the fire.

"What are you thinking about?" he asked.

She hesitated, but then spoke. "I was remembering a time when my husband and I went on a canoeing trip in the Boundary Waters, north of Ely, Minnesota. It was early autumn. The air was so fresh, blue skies, wild life, the bright red leaves of maple trees and the green of pine, spruce and fir trees. We saw a bald eagle nesting in a white pine and a huge, old bull moose with antlers that must have been six feet from tip to tip." Her voice trailed off.

"You miss him," Jack said.

She nodded. "But, time passes. Things change. I've changed." She turned her attention to Jack.

"What do you think of me?" he asked and studied her closely.

"I think you wouldn't last a night if this was a real camping trip."

"I assume you're deflecting my question by attempting to make a joke. I've had extensive survival training. I could survive anywhere, but it's not the night, it's daytime I'd have to worry about."

Her shoulders slumped. "Yes." She rubbed her bare arms. "This is so bizarre."

"I'll take you back." He shifted his weight and began to stand.

"No, please. Sit down. I mean there are no crickets, no

croaking frogs, no sound but creaky trees about to fall from their own weight, no fear of bears or howling wolves, nothing, just nothing."

"Come here." He extended his arms and she scooted over until she was resting against him, her head on his shoulder. They sat like that and watched orange embers rise into the night sky.

After a while she spoke. "We might start a forest fire, you know."

"That's it. Enough."

He opened up the backpack and brought out two glasses and a bottle of wine that glowed ruby-red in the light of the campfire. He popped the cork and poured them both a glass.

"I don't want to hear anymore until you've had at least one glass," Jack said as he handed the crystal goblet to her. "Besides, what if we do start a fire? Do you think maybe it'll harm the environment? I think our friends from space have already done that. I just wish they'd show themselves. I'd love to strangle one, my hands around its neck."

"How do you know they have necks?"

"Well, squeezing wherever it hurts most then."

"I think I know where that is."

He smiled while he stared into the campfire but was aware her gaze was not on the fire; it was on him.

"Why did you bring me out here, Jack? Was it to tell me you and Jane are getting back together?"

His head jerked around to meet her eyes. "What? Well, I...I...." he sputtered. "Hell no."

She released a held breath. "Then why?"

"You're not going to laugh are you? Promise you won't laugh."

"I'll do my best."

"That's not very reassuring. I brought you out here because I wanted to take you to a romantic spot."

"Umm." Her generous lips pursed as she took in the barren landscape. "I guess it is kind of romantic, in a Frankensteinian sort of way."

"Frankensteinian is it?" He finished his glass and poured another.

"Two glasses of wine? Better be careful or I'll have to drive home."

"Roxy, please be serious for a second. Are you being

serious?"

"Quite." Her face was void of expression.

"There was a time when I thought I'd found the person who was going to be my soul mate, but—"

"Soul mate?"

"Please. I've tried this in my mind and every way I say it sounds corny, but I swear to you—" He stared into her eyes and then bent forward to press his lips against hers with a kiss that was beyond passion. "I swear to you that—"

"Hold it. Can I have another glass of wine?"

Jack took an audible breath, but then poured the wine for her, which she downed in one big gulp.

"Maybe this wasn't such a good idea. No, to hell with it." He took hold of her shoulders so that she couldn't look away. "Roxy, I love you."

He kissed her and she pressed forward until both wineglasses spilled. She was on top of him with her breath whispering into his mouth. He felt the pressure of her weight on him.

"I love you," he repeated.

"Shhh." She planted her delicious lips on his and there was not another word spoken.

Clothing gathered around their blanket in discarded piles. There was warmth, softness and hardness; the stirring in the mind that was beyond human resistance, more pleasure than any rationale being could ever expect their body to provide. They lay together as one, in a night of creaking branches and a kaleidoscope sky with the sweat of their bodies lit orange by the campfire.

In the languid afterglow, Jack gave her a feathery kiss on her neck and inhaled her spicy sweetness. "I really like that fragrance you wear."

She pulled away to look at him.

"I don't wear perfume." She leaned forward and kissed him softly on the lips. When their lips parted she said, "I like the fragrance you wear too."

"I don't use cologne," he declared indignantly.

"That's what you think."

"Sometimes I don't understand you."

"Same here."

He traced the scar on her forehead. "How did you get that?"

"When I was six years old, I told this boy I could fly and he called me a liar. So I climbed this big old tree, flapped my arms and jumped."

"Guess you failed."

"Not at all. I just didn't fly far. If that branch hadn't gotten in the way, I'm reasonably certain I'd still be soaring through the sky, touching the clouds. Anyway, for the rest of my childhood, everyone called me Birdie."

"Interesting."

"Yeah, right."

"I thought you grew up in Detroit."

"Do you think Detroit doesn't have trees?" She glanced at the broken trees around them. "At least it did."

"Don't you have any regrets?"

"Well...I suppose."

"Tell me."

"I don't believe in confessions."

"Come on, Roxy. Tell me."

"If you insist. Let me think. How about this? When I was a very young woman, I met this boy and he told me that he loved me and do you know what I did?"

"Can't imagine. Well, actually I can, but I prefer not to."

"Jealousy is not becoming. I scolded him. I told him he didn't know what he was saying. I never told him that I loved him."

"Did you love him?"

She turned over until their faces were so close their noses were touching. "I love you, Jack."

He pulled her close and held her. If time had ended and this moment was the one to go on for eternity, he would've been satisfied. He didn't have a thought in his mind, until the small stone under his back began to feel like a boulder. He shifted his position and they sat up. He poured the last of the wine and they sipped at it, while the warm wind dried their nude bodies.

Roxanne spoke. "I never thought I'd find anyone who could replace my husband, but here you are."

He smiled with pleasure and reached out to hold her hand.

"Jack, what's going on? Is there no in between with you, no moderation?"

"Nope, can't say there is. Is that a problem?"

"What I mean is, you avoided me for months and—"

"I was in a coma. What'd you expect?"

"Now look who's trying to be funny. I mean after that and then for a while you were sticking so close to me I could barely breathe and now I'm lucky to see you twice a week."

Jack nodded. "Sorry about that. I just couldn't stay away. Every time I'm around you, it feels like there is this gravitational attraction. When I sit next to you, I feel like the chair is tipping in your direction. I have to keep pushing back to keep from falling into your lap." He could feel his shoulders raising protectively. He understood Jane better now than he ever had when he was married to her, the desire to be close, to be near all the time.

"Well...it's true I am attractive, but I didn't know I had a measurable gravitational pull."

He chuckled and relaxed his shoulders. "You don't have to worry about me using up all the air in your vicinity. I think I've gotten things back under control."

"A little too much under control. What have you been up to?"

He looked up again, as if he could see beyond the web of black limbs, beyond the red and green curtain that was whipping and winding across the sky. "The space station and the starship are taking shape. I'm amazed to see the giant cylinder of the station becoming a reality. When it's finished, its rotation will create an artificial gravity. Don't ever tell anyone I said this, but Mason's vision of the future is really something. I'm almost glad I haven't killed him, yet."

She waved her hand. "And?"

"And what?"

"Are you just wrapped up in helping the projects come to a completion? Now that you've seen them?"

He continued to stare upward and nodded.

"Then why look so angry?"

"Angry?"

"You look like you're about ready to reach up there and...I don't know, do something violent. Pie told me you can be a very dangerous man. He said the only reason Mason is still alive is that you wanted to hurt him, not kill him. You're not going to sabotage either project are you?"

"That's ridiculous. I just told you how magnificent they are. As for killing Mason—" He shook his head. "—with all the death, I don't I have the heart to kill anybody or anything anymore. Except the aliens, of course. I could do that."

"I'm glad to hear that, Jack. Really glad. So, you've just been busy, huh? I understand how a person can get wrapped up in a project. It's happened to me many a time. Not so much since Angie, but before that, when I got into a groove, there was no stopping."

"Yes, I've been very busy. You know, on the flight back from the Stanford bubble, Pie—do you know what he said? He called me a red marble, floating but afraid of bugs, or something like that."

"Oh my, not that."

"I guess you had to be there. He was kind of hard on me. But he did say something that got me thinking. He asked me if I believed in fate. Do you believe in fate?" Jack asked.

"Not really. I believe in chaos. Do you believe in fate?"

"I didn't think I did, but now I don't know. My parents died, my uncle died, Kate, Mei Li and Gustave, the list goes on and on and...and I keep living. Why? Why do you think that is? I have to believe I was saved for a reason."

"And what reason would that be?"

"Well...." He shifted his attention to her. "Well, for one, to make love with you."

She slid close to him. "I told Wendy we'd be home before midnight."

He brushed his fingers lightly across her breasts. "I guess you were wrong."

He leaned forward and was met halfway.

CHAPTER 32

Roxanne sat in her office and twirled her pen. Jack was coming over that night and Pie was going to join them; that always meant an evening of good humor and interesting conversation. Angie would be beside herself with joy.

She was supposed to be mapping out the next phase of the cloning project. The shipment had arrived from the Buenos Aires bubble. They were going to clone a horse. Rathburn was such an idiot; if they were successful, where was he planning on keeping this horse? She smiled; her generous lips spread from their natural pout.

The door to her office was open; it always was. She watched as a uniformed man made his way through the maze of monitors, growth vats and freezer units, and wondered why one of those men would come to her lab. The serious man kept walking, straight toward her door. She stopped twirling her pen. The young man halted in her doorway, at attention.

She was not about to salute. "What do you want?"

"Message from Assistant Director Traynor." He took two steps forward and extended his arm to hand her a folded sheet of paper.

If Pie wanted to see her, he usually stopped by, or at least messaged her. She frowned as she took the paper from the man, who then resumed his rigid posture.

The paper said: "Come to my office at 14:00. Important." At least it was signed "Pie", not Assistant Director Traynor. That was a mild relief.

She looked up; the man was still there. "What do you want now?"

"Your answer."

"Do I have to write it down, or can you remember it?"

A flash of irritation crossed his face. "Your choice, Doctor Wiley."

"I'll come. Got that?"

He nodded and pivoted, before marching back through the maze of her lab. He couldn't be more than eighteen years old.

Someone had really done a job on him.

She tried to work on the project but, after several failed attempts, threw the pen onto her desk and got up. She was not going to wait until fourteen hundred.

She exited the elevator and walked toward Pie's office. Another young man stood at attention outside his door. It was impossible not to notice the large handgun clipped to his waist. She didn't know whether she should hope he did, or didn't know how to use it; either prospect seemed equally dangerous. When she approached, he held out his arm, preventing her from simply walking into the outer office as she had done so many times in the past.

"Name?" he demanded.

"Doctor Roxanne Wiley and yours?"

The young man was still as he listened through a cochlear implant. She could've tweaked him on the nose and he wouldn't have noticed, some guard.

"You may go in," he finally declared.

She eyed him as she walked past. Had she missed something? Where had these guys come from?

There was some activity in the outer office, but a surprising number of the communication technicians, or as Pie called them, gossips, sat idle at their consoles. The men ogled her as she walked through the room, while a small group laughed when one made an obscene gesture.

Not bothering to knock, she opened the door and walked in to see Pie standing behind his desk; he was talking loudly, with no one else present. He pointed toward a chair.

"All right!" he yelled. "I'll get as much information as I can and I'll be there."

She watched while he listened.

"No, not five minutes. I'll be there as soon as I can," he said.

He listened for a few seconds more.

"Mitch, I said I would be there. Goodbye. Disconnect."

Roxanne's eyebrows rose. "Did you just hang up on Mason?"

Pie nodded and sat down in his chair, with the desk between them. He'd never done that before and his complexion was ruddy.

Roxanne found herself gripping the arms of the chair.

"Heard anything from Jack?" he asked.

"Not today. We had a wonderful, I guess you could call it a date, but that was a week ago. He said he was going to be busy this week, but I'm sure he'll be there for our dinner party tonight. I decided to try your Spam fettuccini."

"I doubt it."

Roxanne frowned. "Well, I'll do the best I can. If you want something else, you can cook it yourself." She stood.

"Please, sit down." He waited for her before he continued. "When you had this date, did you say anything that might have upset him?"

"We had a wonderful time."

"Did you tell him he was Angie's father?"

Her grin was sheepish. "No, but I'm going to tonight. With you there. How do you think he'll take it?"

"He's not going to be there tonight."

"Why do you say that?"

Pie looked down at his desktop and then back up. There was no sense of the charming clown she loved so much. This was a different Pie; a man that could help rule a planet.

"He's not going to be there because he stole a scramjet." Pie shook his head. "It seems so obvious now. Damn it!" He pounded his fist on the desk, causing Roxanne to jump.

"Is he all right?"

"You're not going to pass out or something are you?"

"No!"

"You look kind of pale. Let me tell you what our friend has been up to and then you can tell me if you think he's going to be all right. He got to be good buddies with the workers down in scramjet prep and convinced them that he had been assigned to a special mission. He forged work orders, using my personal codes. How the hell he got those, I'll never know. Anyway, he had this special ship built right under our noses and managed a launch date. He took off at twenty hundred last night. It was not until this morning that it became clear to the jerk-off surveillance technicians that this was not an authorized mission and by then he was no longer in orbit."

"Mars?" The room began to spin. She found herself on the carpeted floor with Pie kneeling next to her.

"Just lie there for a few more seconds. I've sent for some water."

"I never pass out."

"That's not what I recall. You were falling all the over the place when you were pregnant with Angie."

"Oh, yeah, I guess there was that."

"I thought Jack was sterile."

She smiled.

"Okay, what have you done?"

"You remember that operation?"

"Go on."

"Well...I did a little extra fixing."

"You what?" he yelled. He stood from where he'd been kneeling and looked down at her. "Did you tell him? Why do I even ask? Of course you didn't."

"I was going to, but he was so beaten up. I was afraid it might be the meddling that he wouldn't be able to cope with."

"And what about you, Doctor Wiley? Don't you know how to control your own fertility?"

"I didn't say I was pregnant. You did."

"Are you saying you're not pregnant?"

"Pretty sure."

"Yeah, well, we'll see about that." He helped her back into the chair.

The water arrived and she took a sip.

When they were again alone, Pie picked up from where he had left off. "I've had the memory of the computer he's been using broken down and analyzed. He wiped the drives, but we've found enough traces to know that he's trying to rendezvous with the Mars Explorer."

"But...that's headed toward the sun."

"Not really. Colonel Patterson wasn't as good at astronavigation as he thought he was. He was going to use Venus to sling the Explorer into the sun, but he miscalculated. It swung in an elliptical orbit around the planet and headed out of the solar system. Now, two and a half years later, it's about to pass through the path of the Earth's orbit. So that damn asshole Nichols is trying to intercept it. What he plans to do after that is anyone's guess, assuming he can make the rendezvous, which is a major assumption. The Explorer is really moving. With expert astronavigation, he might get one shot at it, maybe none, and we both know he's no astronavigator."

Roxanne slumped deeper into her chair. "But, what about fuel and whatever?"

"He must have been planning this ever since he got back

from that abortive trip to the West Coast. He's carrying a load of water, enough to provide propulsion from the fission reactors aboard the Explorer, which are still active. God, the amazing thing is, he might just make it. Why didn't he ever talk to me about this? Damn it! I can't believe it. He's always followed the rules, considered rules sacred. What could have caused such a change in him?"

Roxanne stared at her hands.

"Doesn't matter now, I guess," Pie continued. "Damn his rotten ass!"

She sat in the chair and breathed; that was as much as she could manage for the moment.

Pie sat in the chair next to her and waited.

"Is he going to be okay?" she asked.

Pie got up and knelt next to her. "Roxanne," he said in the softest voice he had used all day, "you're a bright woman. What do you think?"

She hated crying. What was happening to her? She never cried.

Pie cradled her head on his shoulder and patted her back.

"I'm sorry," she whispered as she fought for composure. "How much water did he take with him?"

"If, by some miracle, he manages to rendezvous with the Explorer, he'll have enough to slow the ship and direct it toward Mars, but there is no possibility that he'll have enough to return."

"When will we know if he made it to the Explorer?"

"About three weeks."

"Will we be able to talk with him?"

"Theoretically, but so far he's failed to respond to any of our attempts at reaching him."

She looked up into Pie's hazel eyes.

"He's okay so far," Pie added. "He did hook up the medical monitoring equipment, everything by the book, except of course, everything. Do you know what he plans to do?"

She began to shake her head and then stopped.

"What is it, Roxy? Do you remember something?"

"Not really. He did talk about fate. Said you mentioned it to him."

"Me?"

"On the trip back from the West Coast. Something about a red marble."

"Red marble? What...oh that. I was just trying to get him out of that damn depression he was in. Trying to get him interested in something."

"I guess you succeeded."

"Oh no. Don't put this on me. I didn't tell him to steal a scramjet and take off on some crazy-assed mission. Do you remember anything else? Something a little more specific?"

She shook her head.

"Give it some thought. This situation is really out of hand. If—and that is a big 'if'—if he succeeds, he'll arrive at about the same time as the scramjet we sent to Mars. He may have screwed all our chances and that I'll never be able to forgive, assuming of course we live long enough to have any feelings at all."

One of the soldier boys arrived to stand at the door.

"What is it?" Pie growled.

"Director Mason is requesting your immediate attendance."

"Do you need some help getting back to your apartment, Roxy?" Pie asked.

"No, I'll be okay. I can manage. I don't know what's come over me."

"Yeah, right. You better check on that potential development I mentioned."

"I will."

"I have to go. I'll stop by tonight."

"All right," she said, even though now she was not looking forward to it.

CHAPTER 33

Pie strode down the hall. The guard outside Mason's offices held out his hand to stop him, but Pie slapped it aside, nearly knocking the guard to the floor.

He entered the conference room and took his usual seat. There was no one else there. He was beginning to wonder if he'd gone to the wrong place and then Mason entered, with that gangly Slater boy.

"Does that kid have to be here?" Pie asked.

Mason sat down, not next to Pie, but at the designated head of the table, as if the full council were present, and instructed the boy to sit next to him before turning his attention to Pie.

"Geoffrey has to learn. He'll have major responsibilities if he's to command the Pinnacle. I've been briefed about the theft of one of our scramjets and the criminal's probable destination. The chances of him succeeding are estimated to be less than five percent. Far too high for my liking. Have you discovered what his plan is?"

"No."

"Did you interrogate that molecular biology bitch, Wiley?"

"If you mean, Doctor Wiley, I've spoken with her."

"And?"

"She doesn't know anything. She was as shocked by the news as any of us."

Mason pointed his finger at Pie. "You bear a portion of responsibility for this, a big portion. If you hadn't intervened on more than one occasion, that psychopath would be dead by now, like he should be."

Pie focused on the boy. "Wipe that stupid grin off your face or I'll wipe it off for you." He refocused on Mason. "You'll have my letter of resignation within the hour."

"No." Mason smiled. "No, I don't want that. It's not really your fault for being blinded by loyalty to a friend. You consider me your friend, don't you?"

"No."

Mason continued to smile. "What do you think of me?"

Pie stared at the man. "I consider you the organizational focus of mankind."

Mason shrugged. "Good enough. Now down to business. I've discussed this with General Clark and he's running it through Goddard. If Nichols beats the odds, we need to have a plan. If the Explorer overtakes our scramjet, we'll have Brinker retarget one of the nuclear missiles and blow that son of a bitch out of the universe. What do you think?"

Pie tried to sort through his thoughts, tried to take his friendship for Jack out of the equation. "We don't know what Jack has in mind. It might be better to allow him to go ahead with his plan. If a nuclear weapon is used, it'll give the alien ship advanced warning that the scramjet is armed."

Mason nodded. "Yes...I've been wondering about that too. But we should make plans. Chances are we won't have to do anything, but it makes sense to have contingency plans. In the meantime, keep trying to find out what he has in mind. Try to learn more from that whore."

"I resent your slur. Her name is Doctor Wiley."

"Wiley may know something and not be aware of it. We're continuing to scan the drives on the computers he used. Something may show up there. Damn him! I was right when I kicked him off the Mars program. But then, if I hadn't, he would've died. I saved his life." Mason chuckled and the boy at his side giggled. "If I could only combine his luck with the loyalty of General Clark, we'd have a really great tool to work with. Do we have samples of his genome, if we decide to do a little genetic modification and try to get more of a team player next time?"

"I'm sure we do have his genome."

"Yes, I suppose so with all those guts and whatever that woman grew to stuff back into him. Talk with that Wiley woman again. We'll discuss the issue at full council tomorrow. For the rest of today, I'll be very busy, trying to explain to our partners what went wrong and how we're going to fix it. Damn it! Just when things were going so well."

"I wouldn't call an alien ship orbiting Mars as 'going so well'."

"We can handle that."

"Maybe."

"Are you starting to have doubts? After you get what you

can from that woman, I want you to stop spending time with her. She's beginning to corrupt your thinking."

"Is that all?"

"Yes, that's all, for now."

Pie got up and walked from the room.

CHAPTER 34

Roxanne sat in Pie's office.
"I suppose you've heard," Pie said.

She tried to read his expression. She shook her head and looked down at the gray, Berber carpet. "No."

"The bastard made it."

She looked up with a smile.

"This doesn't really change anything, you know. He's still on a one way trip to nowhere."

The smile faded and she nodded. "I know," she said quietly, "but I'm glad he didn't miss the rendezvous. That is amazing, isn't it?"

"It's more than amazing. It involved a very complex set of trajectories. He had to have had help." He stared at her.

She shook her head. "I told you I don't know anything about it. Don't you believe me? Besides, that's not something I know how to do."

"Yeah, I believe you." He leaned back in his chair, and then snapped his fingers and sat forward. "Now I get it. That explains a lot." He chuckled. "Damn it. And right under Mason's nose."

"What's so funny?"

"Do you know what Jane did before she took on the role of Mason's wife?"

She shook her head.

"Her specialty was astronavigation, and she was damn good, as you can see. None better."

"Jane? Why would she help him?"

"I guess I'll have to ask her. You don't have to be jealous. Jack—"

"Jealous? Not me."

"Yeah, right. As I was about to say, you don't have to be jealous, for many reasons, including the ultimate reason. He's gone, as gone as if he'd missed the rendezvous."

"He can return the Mars Explorer to Earth."

"He could have."

"What do you mean?"

"He has fired the engines, redirecting the Explorer toward Mars. He couldn't possibly turn the ship around at this point."

Roxanne's head listed to the side, as if too heavy to hold upright.

"I asked you a question a few weeks ago," Pie said.

"You asked me many questions."

Pie continued to stare at her. "You know what I mean."

She grinned. "It's incredible. Every time he gets stranded in space, I get pregnant."

Pie nodded. "If his future weren't so bleak, I'd have to laugh. Are you going to tell him?"

"I don't think I'll get the chance."

"I think you will. He hates to be alone. He'll reopen communications, now that he thinks he's beyond anything Mason can do. He thinks he's safe."

"Isn't he? At least as far as Mason goes?"

Pie sighed and leaned forward. "I shouldn't be telling you this, but—"

The door to Pie's office opened and a uniformed soldier stood there.

The soldier clicked his heals together and stood at rigid attention. "Director Mason commands your presence in his office, at once. Both of you."

Pie stood and walked around the desk to stand in front of the man. He looked down at the young soldier who took an involuntary step backward.

"Don't *ever* enter this office without knocking, without waiting for me to give you permission."

The soldier had no thoughts for the handgun he wore. "But, but Director—"

"Go outside and try it again and this time you damn well better knock. Go!"

The soldier backed out of the office and Pie slammed the door in his face.

There was a meek knock at the door and then a muffled, "May I come in?"

Pie looked to Roxanne. "I don't know what this is about. I have to go, but you don't."

"I'll go."

The knock repeated, no louder than the first time. "Can I please come in?"

Pie smiled. "Much better, don't you think? They just need a little training in manners. You may enter," he said in a louder voice.

The door slowly opened and the soldier stood there. He did not take one step into the room.

"Very good," Pie said and patted the soldier on the head. "Much better. Should we go?"

The soldier nodded as if he were a bobble-head doll.

"Stop that or your head's going to fall off."

Pie took Roxanne by the arm and escorted her past the soldier, who followed a respectful two steps behind.

The guard at the doorway to Mason's suite of offices remembered Pie from the last time and stepped aside to avoid the risk of having his arm torn from its socket. The outer office was empty, but the conference room was not. Mason was there, along with his shadow, the Slater boy. General Clark was present and there was a woman; she had auburn hair and warm brown eyes, high cheekbones and a pleasant nose. While not beautiful, there was no denying that she was pretty. She smiled at Roxanne and nodded a greeting.

"Hello, Jane," Pie said for Roxanne's benefit and then pulled out a chair. "Why don't you take a seat, Roxanne?"

Roxanne focused on the woman as she absently sat down in the chair Pie had provided for her.

Mason looked to Roxanne and then back to Jane as if expecting something more than a pleasant exchange of smiles. He turned his attention to Pie and Roxanne. "Nichols has *consented* to an interview, but insisted that you be present." He then nodded toward Jane. "I took the liberty of inviting my wife because I want all of you to try to talk some sense into him. It seems to be a preferable solution."

"Preferable to what?" Roxanne asked.

Mason smiled. "Just preferable. There will be no visual. The connection will commence now."

Other than for one snap of static, there was no obvious change.

"Hello, Jack," Mason began, his voice smarmy warm, "we were all so surprised by your unannounced trip."

"Are Pie and Roxanne present?"

"Of course, I always keep my word. And I brought a special guest. Say hello, Jane."

"Hello, Jack. Are you okay?" Her voice was sweet, girlish.

There was a pause beyond the brief distance delay. "I'm fine, Jane. How are you?"

"Good."

"Pie, are you and Roxanne there?"

"We're here," Pie answered.

"Very good," Mason continued, "just a friendly family gathering. Now tell us, Jack, what are you doing?"

"I'm going to Mars."

Mason laughed easily and Geoffrey followed suit with a giggle until Mason shut him up with a glare.

"We kind of figured that," Mason said. "What we want to know is, why are you going to Mars?"

"Pie, remember what I told you? Take care of, you know...."

Mason looked from Pie to Roxanne, who lowered her gaze.

"We *all* know what you mean, Jack. And if you really want her well cared for, you'll be a little more forthcoming."

"Is that a threat?"

"Jack, must you always be so confrontational? It should be obvious that I can be a good friend, or things can become difficult."

There was another pause. "Fuck you, Mason."

"Okay," Mason responded, "now that we have the usual formalities out of the way, we can get down to business. Your one friend, your former wife and your mistress are all asking you to return to Earth. We'll arrange an intercept to refuel the ship. All will be forgiven. You've provided us a great service by managing to save the Explorer. You'll be rewarded." He nodded toward Jane.

"Jack, I'll help you come back. Please do what Mitch has asked. We need you back here."

Next, Mason nodded to Pie.

"Jack, damn it anyway. There are rules, a chain of command. I shouldn't have to remind you about these things. You're Academy trained. If you have a plan, tell us about it. Maybe we can help. Maybe it's better than our plan, but we can't proceed in an orderly, organized fashion without you talking with us. Tell us your ideas."

Mason waited a moment but, when there was no response, he pointed to Roxanne.

"Jack, you piece of shit." She paused. "I miss you. But, do what you think is best. To hell with—"

"Wiley!" Mason shouted, rising from his seat.

"Don't worry about me, Jack. I can take care of—"

"Wiley, shut up!" Mason walked toward her, but Pie stood and blocked his advance.

"Thank you, Roxy," Jack said.

Pie leaned down and whispered in Roxanne's ear. She looked up with a frown. "No" she whispered in response. "That's my decision, not yours."

"What decision?" Mason asked as he peered around Pie.

Roxanne answered him with a glare.

Mason continued. "Jack, you're causing problems down here. Don't you care about these people? Are you that selfish?" He waited and then looked to the General who was monitoring the signal.

The General shook his head. "He's cut the connection."

Mason returned to his chair, sat down and folded his hands on the table, interlacing his fingers. "Dear," he said to Jane, "would you mind getting me a cup of coffee and one for anyone else who wants one?"

No one else wanted one. Jane stood without complaint.

Roxanne looked to Jane and met her eyes. Behind those eyes was an exceptionally bright mind, bright enough to calculate the course Jack was on. Roxanne couldn't help but wonder about her.

As Jane passed Roxanne, she patted her on the shoulder and left the room.

Mason immediately focused his attention on Roxanne. "Listen you two bit whore, if you don't get that bastard to change his mind within the next two days, it'll be too late, and I mean too late for him. I'll confiscate all his biologicals. There will be no clones, no extended life, nothing. Do I make myself clear? I'll purge him from humanity's genome and we'll all be the better for it."

Roxanne met his angry gaze with a fiery glare. "Mason, if there is a whore in this room, it's you. You are a son of a bitch! A God-damned—"

"Shut up! You have no idea what I can do to you."

Jane reentered with the cup of coffee.

Mason leaned back in his chair and smiled at her as he accepted it. "Thank you, sweetheart. So," he continued, "I guess that about does it for today. If you can help us at all, Doctor Wiley, you know how much we'd all appreciate it. Right, Jane?"

Jane nodded.

"Okay then. I'm sure you have much to think about."

Pie and Roxanne stood. They left the room with Pie's hand on Roxanne's back.

As soon as they were out of the room, she pulled away from his touch. "I can manage by myself."

Pie shook his head. "That's what Jack thought too. And now look. There's not a chance in hell he'll succeed in whatever crazy mission he's on. He's going to die and that'll be the end of it."

"You don't know that!"

"This is neither the time nor the place to discuss this."

"You brought it up!"

"All right, have it your way."

"I intend to."

She marched down the hall toward the elevators and Pie followed along at her side. They walked in silence.

When the door to the elevator closed, Pie spoke. "You've made yourself a powerful enemy."

"I've dealt with shit like him before."

Pie punched his code into the elevator and it came to a stop between floors. "I doubt it. Rathburn and Mason are not even in the same league. Mitchell Mason is, for all intents and purposes, Emperor of Earth and has been gathering an army to implement his wishes. There's a scramjet out there headed for Mars and that scramjet has four nuclear missiles. If one of those missiles were to be re-directed, say at an approaching spacecraft from Earth, there would still be plenty of firepower to obliterate the alien ship."

"Blow him up?" She unconsciously shielded her abdomen with her hand, as if the fetus might hear. "Why?" she whispered.

"Mason believes Jack might, on purpose or by accident, sabotage our best chance to destroy the alien starship."

"That's crazy. You have to stop him."

"Stop who?"

She stared at him. "Jack is your friend."

"I don't know what's right, or even what I can do."

"You can take over. Get rid of that bastard."

"Not so easy and probably not even right. He's holding the Federation together. I have a hand in it, but it's his vision. There's no one to replace him."

"You could."

Pie shook his head. "Not a chance. It takes a special kind of arrogance to do what he's doing. I don't have it. There's no room for doubt and I have doubts."

"Why didn't Mason tell Jack that he was going to blow him up if he didn't return to Earth?"

"I think he's deathly afraid of Jack. It's hard to take a beating like that and not be afraid on some level. We're not talking about a bloody nose here. Jack almost killed him. He doesn't want Jack to have any warning. Thinks that somehow Jack might find a way to avoid death, again."

"I'm going to tell Jack everything."

"Don't get cute with me. This is serious. That man can kill us all, including Angie, and believe me, if he thinks it'll help him get what he wants, he'll do it."

"Angie?" Roxanne extended her arm to brace herself against the elevator wall.

"Didn't think of that, did you? And one more thing, from now on you better be careful what you say and to whom you say it. You'll be under constant surveillance. Your apartment and lab will be bugged, if they aren't already, and don't even try to find them. These are military bugs. Not a chance in hell of finding them."

"And you support this man?"

"I've explained that. As abhorrent as he is, he's our best hope for survival as a species."

"Bullshit!"

"Why didn't you tell Jack about Angie and the new baby on the way? It's the one thing that might have gotten through to him."

Roxanne turned her back to him and he reactivated the elevator. Neither of them spoke until they were walking the deserted hall to Roxanne's apartment.

"You didn't answer my question," Pie persisted.

"It wasn't the right time to tell him."

"It never is the right time, is it Roxy? You know what I think? I think you're afraid he'll abandon you. You're scared. You'd rather have him stranded in space than run the risk of rejection. Is it because your father—"

Roxanne slugged him in the face as hard as she could.

Pie didn't try to deflect the blow. The "snap" of contact could be heard up and down the hall.

"You could've told him he was going to be blown up," Roxanne said while she rubbed her hand. "If he dies doing what he needs to do, that's one thing, but to get blown up? What's your excuse? Are you afraid of Mason? You slimy bastard!"

"That's a mean spirited thing to say. I'm shocked to hear such words coming from your mouth."

"And somehow what you said is better?"

"You're right. I apologize."

Tears welled up in her eyes and she turned away to hide them. He turned her back around and wrapped her up in his arms. He held her against his chest while he patted her on the back.

"Hormones," she whispered against his chest. "Sorry."

"Oh sure, it's the hormones."

"You know something? I think I could like Jane."

"Jane is a wonderful woman. When Jack lost her, discarded her really, I thought he'd made the biggest mistake of his life, but then he met you. Ignoring current developments, I think he's the luckiest man I've ever known."

Roxanne pushed back from Pie and looked up into his hazel eyes. "That was a nice thing to say."

"I'm not all bad."

She rested her hand against his chest, feeling the warmth. She had never before depended on a man for security. It was disconcerting.

"I have to protect Angie above all else," she said.

"Of course you do. Will you talk with Jack? Every second we delay makes the chances of saving him more remote."

"Can't you warn him?"

Pie shook his head.

"Why not? Is it because you agree with Mason?"

"I don't know what to think." When he saw the look on her face he took a step back. "You're not going to hit me again are you?"

"Depends."

"I could do more if he'd only tell us what his plans are. Is that asking too much?" He shook his head. "No, I think you're the only one who can convince him to abort his mission, or at least tell us what he's trying to do. I don't think he'd even believe anyone else, including me."

"Do you trust Mason? Is it even possible to send a rescue

ship?" Roxanne asked.

"I was watching Jane. I've known her for years. If it wasn't possible, I'm sure she would've signaled me in some way. However, Jack would have to use the remainder of his propellant to slow the Explorer."

"This goes against everything I believe in, about interfering in choices, even dangerous choices, risks, whatever. I'd be deserting him when he needs my support the most."

"Even if it kills him?"

She looked him straight in the eye; there were no more tears. "Even if it kills him."

"I wish you'd reconsider."

She sighed. "I'll think about it."

"You don't have much time. It won't be long before he's out of options. But, whatever your decision, I'll do what I can for him, and for you."

"I know. I'm sorry for what I said. You're a true friend."

"That I am," he replied. "I better get going." He bent and gave her a chaste kiss on her forehead.

Before entering her apartment, she watched him walk down the hall, and noticed with perverse satisfaction that he was rubbing his cheek. She would make it up to him somehow.

She entered her apartment and Angie ran over to her. Roxanne picked her up and kissed her before turning to the nanny.

"Thank you for watching her, Wendy."

"Always a pleasure, Doctor Wiley. She's a very sweet little girl."

After the sitter left, Roxanne continued to hold Angie, until the child became restless and began struggling to get down and play, but then the doorbell rang and Roxanne held her even tighter. No one used her doorbell. None of her friends, no one. The doorbell rang again.

Roxanne glanced around her small apartment; there was nowhere to run, nowhere to hide. She walked to the door with Angie in her arms and opened it a crack before opening it fully.

"Jane."

"Surprised to see me, I'm sure. May I come in?"

"Sure."

After Jane had entered, Roxanne closed the door and locked it. She put Angie down and Angie immediately ran over to her toy box where she pulled out her favorite toy, a now dirty and worn doll that Jack had given her.

"What a beautiful little girl," Jane said as she watched Angie. "I'm sure Jack is thrilled to have a daughter, despite his talk to the contrary when we were married. I wonder why he never told me about her?"

Roxanne attempted a laugh. "What a thing to say. She's not Jack's. Have a seat." She indicated the sofa and took a look at Angie herself. She always thought Angie looked like her, well, not Angie's dark hair or eyes, but mostly. She looked back to Jane who returned her gaze with a quizzical furrow of her brow.

"Would you like something to drink?" Roxanne asked.

"No, I don't have much time, but I just had to come and see you, to apologize."

"For what?" Roxanne sat down next to her and was surprised when Jane reached over and took Roxanne's hand in her own.

"It's all my fault," Jane said.

Roxanne waited for an explanation while holding hands with this stranger, as warm and womanly a person as she could recall, busty with a thin waist and exaggerated curves. From what she had learned, Jane was an intelligent and accomplished woman. Roxanne could see why Jack had married her. For some reason, that thought stuck in her throat. She cleared her throat as if it were a real obstruction.

"Would you like some water yourself?" Jane asked.

"I'm okay. What is your fault?"

"I've been feeling so terrible about this. I have to explain. You might not know about this, no reason you should, but I recently had a miscarriage."

"Actually...I did. I was sorry to hear about it."

"It was...kind of a hard time for me. And Mitch, well, he didn't show much understanding. I was spending all my time at home and, even though Joshua is as wonderful a son as anyone could ever want, it wasn't enough. And then Jack came along and told me about this problem that needed to be solved. It was a challenging one and gave me the opportunity to use my knowledge and skills. I dove right in, without thinking about the consequences. He told me he wanted to present the completed plan to Mitch, as a way of making up with him. I should've known it was pure fantasy. Jack wouldn't be out

there, facing death, if it hadn't been for me and I feel awful."
Her face was creased with genuine pain. "I still have feelings
for him. I hope that doesn't offend you."
Roxanne shook her head. "No, I understand."
"I don't see how you can. And if Mitch ever found out
about this...." Her hands grew noticeably cooler. "He has a
rather archaic attitude about woman."
"Does he hurt you?"
"He doesn't mean to. Nothing physical."
Roxanne remembered Pie's warning about listening devices
and began looking around the room. She slipped her hand
out of Jane's and began to feel around the edges of the sofa.
Jane watched her and finally asked. "What are you doing?"
"I don't want you to have trouble either. Someone warned
me about bugs."
"You mean spying devices?"
Roxanne nodded and heard Jane laugh. It was a deeper
laugh than she could've imagined, coming from this woman
with such a girlish voice.
"I may look like a baby machine," Jane said, "but I'm much
more than that." She pulled out a silver disk from her pocket
and shrugged with a little smile. "A jammer. If I press this
button, it's on. This one and it's off. It's top of the line military,
undetectable. Everyone should own one."
Roxanne nodded. "I agree."
"Mitch will be home soon and expect me to be there. He
really does love me and treats me with respect, most of the
time anyway. Can you forgive me?"
Roxanne leaned forward and gave her a hug. "It was Jack's
decision. Neither of us had the right to prevent it."
"Thank you, from the bottom of my heart. I only wish he'd
change his mind and return to Earth. Do you think you can
convince him?"
"Did your husband send you?"
"Why would you think that? If Mitch ever finds out about
my part in this mess, he'll...." She reached and took Roxanne's
hand again, squeezing until it hurt. "He's very affectionate
and protective, but he has a terrible temper. I can hardly
imagine." She released her grip. "I just want Jack to be okay."
"Jane, if things go badly for you, you're always welcome to
come here."
"You're not going to say anything are you?"

"Not a chance. I just wanted you to know that I'm here for you and Joshua."

"How sweet. One can never have too many friends. But, I'm probably not giving you a very accurate picture of my home life. For the most part, Mitch treats me like a queen. I love him and he loves me."

"I'm glad to hear that."

"I better be going. It wouldn't do to have Mitch find out I was visiting you."

Roxanne walked her to the door.

"Come back and see me again, when you can spend more time," Roxanne said.

"I wish I could, but I don't think I'll be able to. It could make things a little complicated at home. Be careful."

Roxanne nodded.

After Jane had left, she again locked the door. When she turned back to the room, she smiled. The silver disk of the jammer was lying on the sofa. It wasn't likely that Jane left it by accident.

CHAPTER 35

Jack stood on the deck of the command module. The deceleration force provided him with the equivalent of one-fifth of normal weight. It had been seven months since he left Earth, but it seemed even longer. The computers had just executed the command for the Explorer to rotate on the massive gimbal set within the girders of its framework. The maneuver had proceeded without a hitch so that the Mars Explorer now had the configuration of a "T" with its engines and massive water tanks leading the way.

Even though he had exercised as advised in the manual, he fatigued quickly. He sat down in the second command chair and glanced over at the first chair. In his mind, Colonel Patterson still sat there as he had found him, smiling like a ghoul, his hands frozen in a prayerful position with a picture of his wife and son propped up on the console in front of him. And beyond the chair had been the body bags, the autopsied remains of Slater, Dodd and Renshaw. He couldn't tolerate having any of them aboard and had set them free; that's how he preferred to think of it, free to drift through space. Even the rats had been "set free".

Although the cages had been jettisoned along with Kate's special tools, her handiwork was everywhere, at least in his mind. Sometimes he imagined Kate was with him, and then tried to laugh at the tricks his lonely mind played on him. It wasn't satisfying to laugh alone.

He had reopened a channel to Earth, but he didn't respond, didn't trust those behind the messages, or himself. He had toyed with the idea of telling all, got as far as rehearsing his arguments but, when he verbalized his plan, it sounded stupid, delusional. Saying it somehow made it seem impossible. If he had to convince only one person, Gordy Brinker, he could imagine success, but not if Mason became involved. And, if Pie were to question him...he couldn't take the chance. He had to believe in himself, in his fate.

Sometimes the transmissions from Earth sounded like

Roxanne's voice. The voice begged him to abort, to come home, as if he had special permission to disobey the laws of physics. The voices told him that if he altered his course, if he told Mason everything, a rescue crew would be sent. All would be forgiven. Sometimes it was Jane's voice and other times it was Pie's, but the message was always the same. He imagined that Mason was behind it all, like a spider, pulling the strings of marionettes. Usually he was certain that the voices were being artificially replicated, but there were times when he had doubts. The voices confused him; they sounded real.

While he sat in the second command chair, he listened to another Earth broadcast. It was Roxanne's voice. He liked that, even if it was synthesized. Pie had told him that Roxanne had run away from Copper Mountain, at least it had sounded like Pie's voice. She and Angie had sped away in her Aston Martin. If it was true, he had no doubt that Rathburn had been exposed as an incompetent lout and that Roxanne had been identified as the true genius behind the advances. If it was true, then it was equally likely that Mason had a team searching for her. Occasionally, Pie's voice had wanted to know where she might have gone, wanted to protect her, and asked Jack if he had any ideas. That worried him. If she had escaped, she had probably made her way to her sister's at the McGill Bubble. The Federation may cooperate with Mason, but they also resented him. They could be hiding her. He hoped so. It made him feel a little better.

He had been told so many conflicting stories that none of them were really true in his mind. His mind wandered as he listened to Roxanne's voice and imagined her face and the pleasure of her touch and her sweet fragrance that she claimed wasn't a perfume.

"Please, Jack, I'm told you're receiving. Are you injured or sick? Why won't you answer?"

He wanted to activate the send function, could've done so with a voice command, if his voice still worked. With his limited repertoire, he had given up singing a month ago; how many times could a person sing, "row row row your boat"? He wished the entertainment files hadn't become corrupted. They had offered to send anything he wanted, if he would answer a few simple questions.

He needed contact. He wondered about Brinker, no longer that far ahead and probably suffering from the same loneliness. Roxanne's voice continued. He wished the message hadn't become so strident. It certainly sounded like her, but a nice message was so much easier to listen to, like pleasant background music.

"Damn it, Jack, if you're still alive you'd better damn well begin transmitting. You have sixty more seconds. That's the most I can convince them to give me."

Jack began counting off the seconds; his voice was as raspy as if he had been yelling.

"All right, Jack, I don't know what else to say. This is Birdie signing off."

Jack sprung forward. "Open transmission. Roxanne?" He waited while the twenty-second delay passed: enough time for her to have received and for the answering transmission to have reached him. He bowed his head. He had missed his chance.

"So, you're not dead."

He sat up and smiled. "Not yet." He waited through the delay.

"Glad to hear it. There are some things you need to know."

"I'm listening." The delay was irritating.

"First, when you come within range, Brinker has been ordered to waste a missile on you, at least that's how Mason is portraying it."

"What? Why...."

Pause.

"You really should share your plan with Mason, if you actually have one."

"Of course I do. Do you think I would end my life for nothing?" While he waited the twenty seconds for her reply, his eyes strayed to the command chair in which he'd found the dead colonel.

"Then you better start talking. You might be able to change his mind about annihilating you."

"I'll consider it."

Pause.

"And...you need to know something. I want you to know."

The seconds passed. Jack anxiously looked to his monitors; the signal was still live.

"Jack, Angie is your daughter and you have a son on the way. He should be born in about two months."

"Sure I do." Jack nodded. It had been a trick after all.

"Whoever you are, you've made a big mistake. I'm sterile. Tell Mason to go hang himself." He thought about cutting off the transmission, but the seconds drifted by.

"Wrong, Jack. I fixed that little problem. Remember that special pain, down low?"

He did remember. How could he forget? "Then, tell me why you said your name was Birdie."

Pause.

"If that branch hadn't gotten in the way, I would still be flying."

"Oh my God. Roxy, why didn't you tell me before?"

Pause.

"Because you weren't acting like you were interested in having a child, or a substantial relationship, and in that case, neither of us needed you. And then you took me on that romantic trip into the dead woods. Apparently you didn't enjoy our honeymoon quite as much as I did."

"Why didn't you tell me?"

Pause.

"I was planning on telling you, but the next thing I knew you had blasted yourself into space on a one way trip. You didn't talk to me about it. You didn't tell me a damn thing."

"Roxy, I...I need some time to think about all this. I...I need to talk with you." He waited the twenty seconds.

"We are talking."

"No, I mean I need to talk with you after I've had a chance to get over the shock. I mean, Angie? My little girl? How could that be possible?"

Pause.

"The usual way. To be honest, I'd have to characterize it as a case of massive procrastination. By the time I got around to thinking about taking an abortant, there was all the death. I couldn't terminate the life that was growing in me. And thank God I didn't. I don't regret that decision, or non-decision, not even a tiny bit."

"And did you say you're pregnant? That is what you said, wasn't it?" He waited for her response.

"That's a definite."

"And I'm the father?" By the time he had thought better of that comment, her transmission had made it back to the Mars Explorer.

"Jack, you're really an asshole sometimes."

"I'm sorry. I...I'm speechless. I need to talk with you again."
Pause.

"Don't know when that'll be. Now that I've sent this little message, I'm sure Mason will be tracking me down. I'm going to have to hit the road again."

"But the mutated insects and you're pregnant. What about Angie? I can't let you do that." Jack squeezed his hands into fists while he waited for the delay.

"What makes you think you can, or cannot let me do anything? Even aside from the obvious fact that you're two hundred million kilometers away. The only reason I told you now was to try to save your damn hide. Make peace with Mason and do it now, before it's too late."

Seconds of silence trickled past, with the occasional "click" of static telling him that the line of communication was still live.

"Roxy, you do know it's already too late for me, don't you?"

The delay was longer than he could expect from the distance alone.

"Would you have stayed? Not taken this crazy, I don't even know what to call it, if I'd told you about Angie?"

"I had to take the chance. These alien bastards need to be stopped. If this new ship drops its cargo on Earth, it won't be our planet any longer."

Pause.

"Talk to Mason, please."

"Do you really think that would do any good?"

Pause.

"I don't know. But, if this plan of yours is truly worthwhile, it might. He's not stupid."

"I'll think about it, but at least you don't have to be afraid of him anymore. You're doing exactly what he wants you to do."

Pause.

"I don't trust him. I don't want him to use Angie or our son to control me. I need to protect them. I don't know if I'll be able to contact you again. If you can't convince Mason, then perhaps this will help."

A series of numbers began scrolling across his monitor, incoming data, possibly programming.

Damn, it was a trick after all. Jack jerked forward to engage the manual override.

"I love you, Jack."

He held his finger above the key, but couldn't press it.

"I've sent you the code to Brinker's ship. Talk with him. I don't know what crazy idea you have, but I want you to have the chance to implement it. I can't bear to think of you dying for no reason."

Jack sat back in his chair. Roxanne was not one to mince words. He was going to die. He knew it, but to have it confirmed by Roxanne was unnerving. "Thank you, Roxy. I love you too. When you see Pie again, give him my best and...I wish I could be there. Angie is a wonderful girl. I'm pleased beyond words."

He waited, but there was no response. He checked his monitors. There was still a signal, but the origination had changed.

"I love you, Jack. Tell Mason all about your plan. He will save you. He wants the same thing you do. Tell him now."

"Up yours, Mason." He pressed the interrupt.

Did Mason hear everything? If so, he would change the code to Brinker's scramjet.

"Computer, enter data received about outbound ship and connect."

The signal light indicated that the transmission had been successful. For how long was anyone's guess.

"Hey, Gordy, how goes it?"

"Is that you, Jacko?"

There was no delay; they were close.

"No one out here, except the two of us," Jack said.

"If I'd known you had your heart set on going, I'd have stepped aside. I'm not thrilled with the idea of slowly freezing to death, all by my lonesome."

"I agree. Why don't you feed me your coordinates? I have some fuel to spare. I could meet you for a nice little visit."

There was a silence.

"You still there, Gordy?"

"I'm here. You know the old saying about misery but, as much I'd like company, I don't think I should do that."

"Why?"

There was another silence.

"Hey, Gordy, we're both on the same side. Humans against the bastard aliens."

"I truly believe that, but...there's a problem."

"You've been spending too much time talking with Mason.

What's he been telling you?"

"For one thing, he warned me that you might find a way to sneak a message to me."

"Sneak? I don't think so. I'm simply broadcasting. I'm sure he and his little windups are listening right now. I've nothing to hide."

"I think I'll have to confirm that."

"Don't do that. I feel the need to talk. Don't you?"

"It's a directional beam, isn't it? You on that fancy Mars Explorer and me in this little rowboat of a spaceship, never meant to leave orbit. It's not fair."

"If you give me your coordinates, I can bring the Explorer to you. You can use the exercise equipment, take a shower, and sleep in a decent web-bed. Doesn't that sound good?"

"Jacko, I never knew you to be mean. Arrogant, but never mean."

"Arrogant? I don't understand."

"All the scram-pilots found you to be standoffish, but I had no complaints. You carried your load."

"I'm sorry you all felt that way, but my offer stands. Let me rendezvous with you."

"You know I can't do that."

"Why not?" Jack asked.

"I didn't volunteer for this mission because I have a death wish. I volunteered because I want to destroy them. They killed my mother and father and both brothers. I plan on paying them back, big time. Shove it up their ass and light the fuse."

"I'm right there with you on that."

"Mason told me that you took a low velocity handgun with you. Now what could a man possibly hope to do with a gun designed for use in a spaceship?"

"He's lying. He's a slimy lying bastard."

"Maybe, or maybe not. What if you killed me and aborted my mission? I can't take that chance, Jacko."

"Why would I do that?"

"Who knows? Maybe you're crazy. I've heard people talk about you that way."

"Listen to me, Gordy. I don't have a weapon. You're the one with the big guns. I just want to sit down and work something out with you. I'll explain what I'm going to do and we can coordinate our attack."

"What do you plan to attack with?"

"I was kind of hoping you'd loan me one of your missiles. You don't really need four. One should suffice. As I understand it, you were going to waste one anyway."

There was a long silence. Jack looked at his instruments; the connection was still live.

"What do you say?" Jack continued. "A little chat and then we attack as a team. Twice the chance of destroying them."

There was still silence.

"What do you say, Gordy? I've never lied to you before, have I?"

"Why did you bring a handgun with you?"

"I didn't! Mason is lying. I swear it. I just want to talk with you. How about it? Feed your coordinates into my computer."

"I'm really sorry. I can't. This mission is too important. More important than my life...or yours."

"I hope you're not saying what I think you are. You aren't really going to blow me to hell are you? What could that possibly accomplish?"

"Jack...I have my orders."

"Orders? We're beyond orders now. Isn't that why they sent you? To make adjustments as needed, on the spot?"

There was a pause. "You always were a smooth operator. I can't talk with you any longer. Believe me when I tell you I hate what I have to do. I'm signing off."

"Wait! Wait, Gordy, let's just talk. There's no harm in that. We can talk about anything you want."

There was silence and this time when Jack looked at his instruments, he knew what he would see; the link was down.

"Computer, reestablish connection with outbound ship."

He sat forward, against the seat straps, waiting for the connect signal, but the command began to cycle and then stopped.

"Unable to locate receiver," the deadpan voice of the computer stated.

He pushed back into his seat. How long did he have? It was one more week until he established orbit around Mars. Brinker must be less than a day away and, with the combination of his transmission to Earth and to Brinker's ship, Copper Mountain knew exactly where he was and, if Copper Mountain knew his coordinates, then so did Brinker.

Brinker had to be firing his engines to begin deceleration.

For all he knew, if he peeked out the window, he might see the flare of scramjet's engines, no more than a short space walk away. He resisted and then gave in. He peered out the porthole. He could see Earth, a spark of bright light, but in his current orientation he couldn't see Mars. He returned to the command console and activated video feed. Ruddy Mars came into view, but he couldn't see Brinker's scramjet, or the alien starship for that matter.

Brinker was going through with it; he was going to fire a missile at the Explorer and that would be it. On one level, as a military man, Jack could understand and respect Brinker's decision to follow orders. *But God damn! It was so stupid!* How much time did he have left? An hour, a day? Ten minutes? He had to have his chance! There was no other choice. He had to convince Mason.

"Computer, open communication with Copper Mountain."

When the board indicated connection, he spoke. "This is Captain Jack Nichols aboard the Mars Explorer. I request to speak with Director Mason."

While he waited, he stared at the forward facing video image, wondering if he would see the flash of a rocket, signaling the end. The delay was intolerable.

"This is Copper Mountain Command Center. Director Mason told us you would be transmitting to us and gave us a message to read to you. 'Jack Nichols, you have wasted your life and an important asset. The time for talking has passed. I have nothing against you, personally, but you have chosen to flaunt authority for the last time. This time you will pay the price. The reason for your insubordination is no longer important. We all mourn for another wasted life. This will be our final communication.'"

"Damn it, find the bastard! Didn't he leave instructions to be contacted the moment I opened a connection with Copper Mountain? He just tried to contact me a few minutes ago."

After a twenty-second delay: "No, sir, he did not. He specifically ordered us not to contact him."

Jack took a breath. "Okay, but I am asking that you contact the Director anyway. I'm sure he wants to know what I have to say. He's been trying to get me to tell him for the last seven months. This is important, for the survival of mankind. Damn it to hell! Contact him!" Jack waited without breathing.

"Sir, I have contacted General Clark. The Director is not to be disturbed."

"Connect me with Pie Traynor." Jack was immobile while the seconds ticked past, holding onto a glimmer of hope.

"I cannot do that, sir. I have strict instructions not to let you talk with anyone."

"Listen to me, you piece of shit! I'm about to be blown into atoms by a nuclear missile. I may not have more than a few minutes to live. This is life and death."

Pause.

"I...I know that, Captain. You *are* brave and I believe you thought you were doing the right thing, but you were wrong."

The words instantly transported Jack into the past. Was he just delusional? No better than crazy Patterson? Time passed.

"Sir, I must terminate this connection."

"Wait! Connect me with Brinker."

Pause.

"I have my orders. My heart goes out to you."

"To hell with that! I don't want your damned heart. I want...."

The monitor indicated that the connection was closed.

"Computer, connect me with Copper Mountain."

Jack waited, gripping the arm of the chair, leaning close to the monitor when the message came up. "Unable to locate receiver."

His grip lessened. He had waited too long. Maybe yesterday, or the day before...but, no. Mason had made up his mind the minute he had stolen the scramjet. He was not simply going to die; he was going to be executed.

"Computer, begin scanning files and connect with any Earth receiving station."

Jack's eyes were drawn to the video monitor; the red planet was stark against the blackness of space, and beyond it, was the star cloud of the Milky Way. Somewhere out there was a scramjet on a mission that was sure to fail. Jack felt certain of it and his own plan would never be given a chance.

He glanced down at the monitor when a message appeared. "Software Malfunction."

"Run diagnostic program and report."

Jack watched the results scroll across the screen. He knew what had happened. The message from Copper Mountain had carried a kill program that had frozen his communication software. Mason had been waiting for the connection to become active rather than passive, providing a doorway into the Explorer's communication system. Fortunately, the ship's other systems had remained unaffected; Patterson's firewalls had held.

Jack berated himself for holding out too long, but then shook his head. In all probability, Mason had never been interested, had only been waiting to spring the trap. And now he wasn't going to talk with anyone; Mason had made certain of that. Now that he wanted to tell everyone, it was no longer possible. He might be able to fix it, if he had a few days, which meant that he had little time left. He couldn't even send a farewell message to Roxanne. What had he said to her? Not enough, not nearly enough. It was up to Brinker now. The fate of the world was in the hands of a dedicated soldier about to carry out his duty and to hell with the consequences.

CHAPTER 36

Two days passed. The software block was far too
sophisticated for Jack to overcome. He had given up trying to
find a work around. Mars was close enough for Jack to not
only pick out the huge rift canyon of Valles Marineris, but
also the Tithonlum, Ius and Ophir Chasma. However, his mind
wasn't on the mottled surface of the burnt-orange planet; he
was thinking about Angie and Roxanne. He wanted to be back
on Earth, as ravaged as it was. He wanted to be with them.
They could make it, the three of them, four of them he reminded
himself.

The receiving function of the Mars Explorer still worked; it
was the sending function that was locked. If Brinker had
changed his mind, he could've contacted the Explorer. His
silence told the story. It shouldn't be long now. Maybe, at the
last minute, when it actually came down to launching the
missile, he'd change his mind.

Jack nodded. That was his best hope. He couldn't look
away from the monitor. He no longer tried to track the alien
ship; it had become irrelevant. Only the nuclear tipped missile
was important and there was no escape. A near hit would be
good enough to vaporize the ship and himself. The radiation
safe cylinder, while effective against solar storms, would be
like tissue to a nearby explosion.

Where was Brinker?

"Computer attempt contact with nearby ship on all bands."

"Processing," the screen reported.

He waited, knowing what the answer would be. He had
tried it numerous times with no success, but maybe this time—

"Software Malfunction." The red letters flashed on the
screen.

He felt like beating his fist against the console, almost did,
but then turned his attention to the video-scanning monitor.
He thought he'd seen a flash.

"Computer, do you detect an approaching object?" Jack
held his arms across his chest, a last attempt at protection,

an instinct having no basis in reality, while his gaze fixated on the monitor.

A message scrolled across the screen. "Object approaching. Estimated speed, twenty thousand kilometers per hour. Intercept time, fifty seconds."

Jack froze; his mind froze. He didn't move as the seconds ticked away. He probably wouldn't feel it. He would be here and then gone, nothing. The seconds continued their inexorable march.

He took another breath; he was still alive. He gritted his teeth and closed his eyes. He took another breath. "Computer, update information on approaching object."

He stared at the screen.

"Object is receding at twenty thousand kilometers per hour. Nearest approach, fifty-seven meters."

In another few seconds, it would be too far away, even if it did explode. The seconds passed and Jack smiled. A dud. A malfunction. But then he frowned. What about the other missiles? Had humanity lose its chance to destroy the alien ship because of obsolescence?

"Computer, calculate origin of object and plot a course to intercept."

The information scrolled across the screen. Brinker was three hundred kilometers away.

"Is there adequate fuel for intercept?"

"Fuel is adequate," the screen replied.

"Calculate for intercept and engage."

Jack strapped in. It was only a moment before he felt the change in the vector of acceleration. He looked at the monitor and waited. A second change in weight pressed against him while the Explorer rotated and decelerated. The shape of a scramjet appeared on the imaging screen. He began rehearsing what he would say to Brinker, how he would convince him to cooperate.

The engines continued to fire, slowing the Explorer until it hung in space next to the much smaller ship. He released his straps and floated toward the airlock where he put on a spacesuit, going through the checklist in his mind. When he was satisfied, he entered the airlock where he struggled into a jetpack. It was so much easier with help, everything was.

He cycled the lock and it opened to space. This time it was not Earth; it was Mars that dominated the cosmos. The red planet was surrounded by the halo of its thin atmosphere. His breath caught in his throat; he saw the alien ship, glittering-gold, spindle-shaped, beautiful in its other-worldness. There didn't seem to be a back or front, pure bilateral symmetry.

He jetted into space and oriented toward the scramjet. He fired small bursts to approach the ship. The contour of the scramjet was not the one he was familiar with. There were rocket pods fused onto the fuselage and he could see the tip of the missiles, that is, all except one.

Brinker must know he was outside.

"Just a few minutes to talk," Jack offered as a prayer to no one in particular.

Brinker had already committed to killing Jack. How difficult would it be to make a second effort?

He wasn't going to return to the Explorer without meeting with Brinker in person. *It'll make all the difference,* he told himself.

He tried to contact Brinker on the short-range radio, but there was no response, not a good sign. He approached the airlock and clamped on. Brinker had to have heard that, but there was still no response. Maybe Brinker had a gun and was going to blast him as soon as the airlock cycled.

Jack flipped open the emergency cover and keyed in the entrance code. Nothing happened. *Damn him! He's disabled the lock.* Stupid. It just makes for more work.

Jack activated a tool and unscrewed the plate that allowed for manual opening. He let the plate drift away and reached into the recess. The suit air conditioner became a loud "whir" as he worked to crank the handle. When the iris lock was open enough for him to slide through, he swam inside and waited a moment. Still nothing.

He tried to key the iris shut, but that too was nonfunctional. He worked on the inner crank until the lock was sealed. He expected the "okay" light to signal him once the lock was closed, but the panel was dead.

He knocked on the inner lock with the butt of his tool and then knocked harder. He felt a chill. *This was not right, not right at all.* He pried off the manual plate and cranked open the inner iris; there was a reassuring rush of air as it whistled through the small opening until the pressure equalized. The air sparkled with ice crystals.

When the inner iris was open to the size of grapefruit,

Jack peered through it. It was dark inside, completely dark. Was Brinker waiting in ambush?

He began cranking again until the lock was fully open. The spotlight of his helmet lit up the cockpit of the scramjet. It was tiny. Despite his turmoil, he felt admiration for the man and what he had given for humanity. He remained in the lock and directed his light around the small cabin until he saw Brinker, floating with his eyes open.

Jack raised his arms to ward off a blow, but then lowered them. Brinker was floating freely; there was no movement. He checked his suit monitors. There was oxygen. He unlatched his helmet and set it aside to float in the lock. The air was cold enough that his breath was a fog.

"Gordy?" He watched the man floating near the overhead. Brinker looked dead.

Jack pushed off and entered the small cabin. He reached up to grab hold of Brinker's arm; his flesh was hard and cold. There was no reason to check further; he was obviously dead. Jack released his grip on the body and surveyed the rest of the cabin. The monitors were black. He drifted over until he hung above the control panel where he pushed the emergency power button. There was no power, no life, nothing. It was as if the energy of the ship and everything in it had been sucked empty.

This wasn't simple power failure; this was something else altogether. Jack thought about the golden spindle. Somehow it had attacked Brinker's ship after he'd fired the missile and the missile had failed as well.

Jack felt an urgent need to escape before he too was killed. He pushed off for the lock and with nervous fingers fumbled with the latches on his helmet until it was secured. He hurried to crank open the outer iris, forgetting that the inner lock was still open. Air rushed past him and he was knocked against the bulkhead by a heavy object, Brinker's body. When the air supply of the ship was exhausted, Jack pushed the body away and cranked until the iris was wide enough to allow escape. He pushed into space and saw a wondrous site; it was as if a billion fireflies had gathered outside the lock. At first he thought that the aliens had come for him, but then recognized it for what it was, crystallized water vapor.

Using the directional jets on his suit, he approached the airlock of the Explorer. He mentally prepared himself to discover that his ship was as dead as the scramjet, but the finder light was blinking cheerfully at him, at least that's the way it felt. He keyed the lock and was grateful to see it slide open. His ship, his wonderful ship, hadn't deserted him.

He entered the lock and cycled it closed. When he was inside the Explorer, he felt like he had returned home after a harrowing escape. There was light and heat, but for how long?

He buckled into the command chair. He wanted to put distance between himself and the dead scramjet. He almost issued the command, but then began thinking. He had heard no distress call. The attack had been quick and total, perhaps the moment Brinker had launched the rocket at the Explorer. But, why had the alien ship disabled the missile?

He began reviewing his theories about the alien ship and then stopped in mid-thought, feeling a surge of exhilaration. He was right!

The alien ship was for practical purposes alive; it was protecting the downed ship on the surface of Mars and now it was protecting the Explorer because...because of the golden spheres in its storage bay.

Jack nodded. It might work. His crazy plan might actually work.

"Computer, open a channel to Copper Mountain."

Jack watched as the monitor indicated that data was being received, a software fix. He waited until the computer indicated that a connect had been made. So, they were willing to talk again. They must know Brinker was dead; their bio-monitors would have confirmed that and they hadn't detected a nuclear explosion signaling the end of himself.

Eat shit, Mason.

"This is Copper Mountain Command Center. Identify yourself."

Jack smiled. Who did they think it was? "This is Captain Jack Nichols of the Mars Explorer. I want to file a grievance. Scram-pilot Brinker fired a nuclear weapon at my ship. I demand an immediate connection with that bastard known as Director Mason."

There was a long pause and then a disgusting, but familiar voice. "Hello, Jack. Apparently you are indestructible."

Jack began talking while the message was still coming in. "You son of a bitch, just shut up and listen."

"Glad to hear you're okay. Can you give us an update? We

seem to have lost contact with Brinker. I have Roxanne Wiley and your little girl. She is such a sweet child. I would sure hate to see—"

Jack's last message reached earth. Ten seconds later the response resumed.

"—there's no reason for that kind of talk."

"Shut up, Mason, you lying bastard. I don't believe a damn thing you say, so you might as well shut up and listen. The alien craft attacked Brinker's scramjet. It's dead, along with Brinker. None of the missiles were fired, except for one of course. What I need is for you to send me instructions on how to jury rig one of the warheads."

Twenty seconds later, the reply: "How do we know you didn't kill Brinker?"

"I don't have time for this bullshit. You know damn well I was at least three hundred kilometers away when Brinker died."

Jack waited.

"What do you have in mind?"

"What the hell difference does it make? I'm your last and only chance. I'm not going to waste my breath explaining anything to an asshole like you. If you had wanted to know, you would've patched me through to you a couple of days ago. I'll tell you what I need and you do it. I need exact instructions on how to rig one of those nuclear warheads so it'll explode."

After the pause: "What's wrong with them?"

"They don't work. I believe the electronics have been fried."

The wait between each exchange was aggravating.

"What happened to Brinker?"

"He died."

Jack drummed his fingers on the console.

"How?"

"How the hell should I know? The alien ship killed him and disabled his scramjet. Somehow it sucked all the energy out of it. I strongly doubt that we have the technology to be able to mount a defense. So, what do you say? Do you want to sit there and watch little alien globes rain down on Earth, or are you going to give me my chance?"

Pause.

"Why are you still alive?"

"Because I know what I'm doing."

Pause.

"I hope you're right about that. I must admit you do have the luck, or whatever. I *am* impressed."

"I don't give a damn what you think. Are you going to do it or not?"

Pause.

"I'll consult with my section leaders."

"Screw that worthless council. You make the decisions. Make one. It's my ass out here."

Jack waited while the seconds crept past. He should tell him everything. *No, he would never consent, would call it a crackpot idea. Mason had no imagination.*

"All right, Jack. I'll see what I can do. I guess I'll have to take your word for what happened."

"Must be hard for you. But, you have to remember that not everyone is a lying, conniving son of a bitch like you."

Pause.

"Pushing it, aren't you, Jack?"

"Not really. You're a pragmatist above all else, as long as it's not your ass hanging out."

Pause.

"I'll get back to you."

"Don't wait too long. The alien ship may decide to investigate our little planet now that you've fired a weapon."

Jack waited until the monitor indicated that the connection was no longer active. He had work to do. He suited up and took another space walk, but didn't reenter the scramjet. He cut away at the protective tube outside the craft until he had one of the missiles exposed and then cut around it to free the warhead, hoping he wouldn't accidentally set it off.

He connected a tether and pulled the warhead into the airlock of the Explorer. After pushing it into the command module, he opened the radiation shield cylinder where he deposited it. He left it drifting in there and rotated the cylinder shut. When he swam toward the console he noticed there was a message waiting for him. He activated receive; technical data flowed across the screen and into the databank. He scrolled through it, and then again, slower. It looked like an insane mathematician had written it, nothing he could use.

"Computer, connect me with Copper Mountain."

A minute later a voice answered. "Copper Mountain, receiving from Mars Explorer, go ahead."

"Get Mason." Jack gritted his teeth while he waited.

"Sir, do you know what time it is here?"

"I don't give a rat's ass what time it is. Get Mason. No, wait. Get me Pie Traynor."

Jack waited as the minutes drifted by. Finally, he heard Pie's voice.

"Jack, how are you doing?"

"Just peachy. How the hell do you think I'm doing?"

Pause.

"I think you're having a rough time. I think you wished you'd never left Earth."

Jack felt his chin tremble and was shocked by the sudden rise of grief.

"Did you want to talk for a while?" Pie asked into the prolonged silence.

"No—actually I do have a question. Are you taking care of Roxy and Angie?"

Pause.

"Roxy takes care of herself. It wasn't until after her transmission to you that we were able to locate her at McGill and now she's gone again. She'll be found when she wants to be found and not a second sooner."

"You promised you'd take care of her."

Pause.

"And I will, as soon as she lets me."

"What about Mason?"

Pause.

"You don't have to worry about that. Rathburn has been exposed, but at least he did have the balls to admit that Roxy's been running the program. Mason needs her."

"I'm still worried."

Pause.

"Then you never should have left—hold that. I'm sure you think you're doing the right thing. Are you doing the right thing?"

"Yes, Pie, I'm doing the right thing. I'm going to fry my ass, but I'm doing the right thing."

Jack found the twenty-second delay to be increasingly irritating.

"Okay, Jack, I trust you."

"Then why do you have to say it? To convince yourself?"

Pause.

"You sound like you could use a little sleep."

"A little sleep? I could use a damn life! That's what I could use."

This time the delay was even longer.

"I know, Jack, I know."

"Do you really?"

Pause.

"Is there something I can do for you?"

"Yes, you can tell me how to activate a nuclear warhead and set a timer of some sort."

Pause.

"I thought Mason sent you that information."

"I didn't ask for a mathematical dissertation on electronics, or nuclear weapons. I want to talk with someone who knows what they're doing. You know, connect A to B sort of directions. Who sent this? One of Mason's prized council members?"

Pause.

"It came out of the Lawrence-Livermore bubble."

"Then let me talk with them. There must be someone there who actually works on these things, not just talks about them."

Pause.

"I'll do what I can."

"Okay, and I think I'll just sit out here and wait."

Pause.

"You can contact me anytime you want. I'll leave instructions with communications to find me any time, day or night."

Day or night. He pushed back in the chair and wondered how long it had been since he had slept. Time had so little meaning in space; one hour was like any other.

"Did you receive that last transmission?" Pie asked.

"Do you think I'm arrogant?"

There was silence. More than the usual time delay passed.

"Pie, are you still receiving?"

Pause.

"Yes, I'm receiving, and yes.

"You do?"

Pause.

"Doing a little soul searching?

"Not really. I was just wondering. Guess it's a little late to start working on things like that, isn't it?"

Pause.

"I wouldn't worry about it, Jack. I'm proud to call you my

friend."

"Thanks, Pie. I guess I won't be seeing you."

Pause.

"Guess not."

"Take care of her, Pie." *I know you want to anyway*, he almost added.

Pause.

"I will."

"Goodnight, Pie."

Pause.

"Goodnight, Jack."

CHAPTER 37

Jack opened the warhead. Parts he had scavenged from the command system of the Explorer were in webs around him; he wouldn't need a command system any longer, wouldn't need anything. He followed the detailed instructions that had been sent and then connected the power supply.

He floated above the floor of the radiation chamber. There was nothing more he could do; the rest was pure guesswork. He had to rendezvous with the alien ship and then he would either make Mason justified or pleased, depending on the results. But, for him, this was a one-way trip, always had been, from the moment he rode the rail.

He looked around the radiation cylinder, now cluttered with components, anything he thought he might need, but his thoughts were of Earth. He thought about Roxanne and Angie, about Pie and finally Jane. Good people. People he loved. He decided that they might actually love him; Roxanne had told him so and Roxanne wasn't one to say things she didn't believe. He grinned. *Soul mate*. He had found his soul mate. But now, circumstances dictated his actions. The best he could hope for is the complete destruction of the alien ship. He expected a sense of fulfillment, but there was only a cavity that swallowed every effort he made to make peace with his fate.

He slipped the warhead into the pyramid he had fashioned out of the tabletop-sized fragment of the alien ship's hull that Dodd had brought aboard so long ago. It had been a disappointment. He had expected the pieces of the ship's hull to heal, but he had to use a fuser to attach each piece. The last piece was cut and ready. A rainbow of refracted light reflected from the edge of the multi-layered creation.

He no longer believed in his idea. He took one last look at the warhead, nestled within, and placed the base on the upside down pyramid. He reached for the fuser, but when he turned back he pushed away from the pyramid and floated toward the overhead; it was changing, glowing with a golden light. It was molding itself, trying to form a spindle, but it had a bulge in the middle, like a snake that had swallowed a big rat.

He pushed off from the overhead and glided through the cylinder opening, twisting as he drifted into the command module so that he could slap the close-button. The cylinder rotated until the doorway was closed. The alien spindle was trapped inside.

He coasted toward the cannibalized command console. This is what he wanted, he told himself. He knew he must reenter the radiation chamber, but he didn't want to touch it, or hold it. It looked alive; he didn't want to be the one that was invaded.

The bomb that was sealed inside the creature was ticking toward detonation. He had set it for one hour...hadn't he? He wished he could take another peek at the timer. He glanced at the console. One of the few functioning systems was flashing.

He swam over to the command chair and pulled himself down to strap in.

"Open channel," he said, but nothing happened; there was no longer a voice recognition capability. He pushed a button.

"Mars Explorer, respond, urgent. Mars Explorer, respond, urgent." The message continued to repeat.

Jack pushed the send key. "This is Captain Nichols. You have a message for me?" *Were they sending a rescue ship?* The thought faded even as it formed. He waited for the message to reach Earth and for a response to travel back to Mars.

"Jack, this is Pie. The alien ship has left orbit."

The remainder of his energy drained from his body, only the straps of the chair kept him in place. He had an armed nuclear device in his ship. He could run and leave it behind. He had programmed the engines of the Explorer before disabling the command computer.

"Jack, are you receiving?"

"Yes, I'm receiving. It's all been for nothing. That's what you're telling me? That I threw my life away for nothing, just like Brinker and Patterson. Just big, stupid jerks."

Pause.

"Look out your port."

Jack saw a golden glow, nothing but golden light, no shape.

"Our surveillance scopes indicate that the alien ship is headed toward you. Can you see it?"

Jack continued to stare at the golden glow that filled the

forward window. "Yes, I can see it."
Pause.
"How far away is it?"
He unbuckled and pushed off. He hung in front of the window and tried to see as much as possible, trying to see shape, but there was only the glow. It seemed close enough to touch.
"How far away is it?" Pie repeated.
Jack glided back to the command chair and strapped in. He averted his gaze from the window, afraid that the golden light would find entrance to his ship and take over his mind: a superstitious fear that in the solitary silence of space seemed very real.
"Jack, are you reading us?"
"I would say it's about a meter away, give or take a meter."
Pause.
"Did you say a kilometer?"
"No, Pie. I said a *meter*."
There was a longer pause than usual.
Pie finally responded. "That's quite close."
"Think so?"
Pause.
"Tell us what you plan to do. After all—"
There was a break in the communication and Jack imagined the immense starship sucking his own little ship into it, but then the communication continued.
"—is hard, Jack. I don't want to lose you, but we need to know. So we don't repeat...well, you know what I mean."
"Thanks, Pie. That's real sweet of you. If I'd known you cared that much, I would've stayed home. Are you alone, or are there others with you?"
Pause.
"Mason and Clark are here. Tell us, Jack. If things don't work out, we'll still have to deal with it."
"I understand that, Pie. Ask Roxanne. She knows the answer."
Pause.
"Roxanne...but she's a molecular biologist."
"Correct." Jack looked up at the chronometer, one of the few functioning items aboard ship. How much longer should he wait? Until the last minute?
"Is that your answer?"

"I guess it is. My final words. Give my best to everyone. Thank you for your friendship. Goodbye my friend."

He punched the button as if to shove it into the console. He kicked the console with his metallic foot and then the anger was gone too. He thought about Spam fettuccini. He wanted Spam fettuccini. He wanted everything he could no longer have. His gaze drifted to the window and the golden glow. He shivered. It was alien magic: a technology from elsewhere, made by creatures without human thoughts.

The anger was back. "Damn it, you bastards! You're about to see what it means to mess with humans!"

Time passed. He was stalling, but knew it didn't make any difference because he was going to be toast, either way.

He struggled to put on his spacesuit for his last space walk; everything was the last, the last swallow, the last breath. When he was fully suited he pushed the button on the radiation chamber and it swiveled open. He almost expected the golden spindle to fly at him and grab him around the throat. He forced himself to pick it up. It was no longer brittle; it was supple, almost slippery. It tried to slither out of his grasp, but he held it tight with both arms and carried it to the lock. He wondered what would happen next. When would he die? What would it feel like?

He stood in the lock and punched the cycling button with his elbow.

"You're not going to get away," he told the golden spindle that squirmed in his embrace, triggering the memory of a fish he had caught as a boy, which had wriggled out of his hands and back into the lake.

The outer lock opened and the ship creature squirmed harder. He tried to hold on, but could not. He watched as the golden spindle undulated into space, using propulsion that wasn't even hinted at. The spindle disappeared from sight.

He closed the lock and wondered if the alien ship would kill him, turn him off, or whatever it did, but nothing happened. He cycled back into the ship.

He took off his suit and looked at the chronometer. There were three minutes until...maybe nothing. He drifted over to the command console and punched the button that activated the programming he had completed prior to cannibalizing the system. The engines kicked in and he grabbed onto the command chair so he could swing into it. Each second was an adventure in waiting. He waited for death to steal him away, but not knowing what form it would take. Catastrophic decompression? Blood bubbling in a froth out of his lungs? He really didn't like that possibility. He looked at the chronometer. One minute. He thought about hurrying to get into his spacesuit and then considered the radiation cylinder.

Thirty seconds. He unbuckled and was shoved aft. He barely managed to grab the edge of radiation cylinder door. He wondered if he still had time as he pulled himself in and punched the button.

Fifteen seconds. He was pressed against the curved wall by the acceleration of the Mars Explorer and felt a faint vibration as the room rotated to seal him in. He took one last deep breath and held it.

CHAPTER 38

Pie walked along the tiled hallway of the ancient monastery. He turned a corner and pushed the door open to step outside onto an earthen path. He paused to study the night sky. The solar storm had subsided. There were so many stars visible at this altitude. It was almost like being in space. He would get there, sometime. They couldn't keep him on Earth forever, just because he was too big.

He lowered his gaze. It was as if he had traveled back in time; clotheslines were strung across the path. White sheets fluttered in the nighttime breeze, and beyond were the light bulbs of the bazaar, strung along poles. He shook his head and wondered how his information could possibly be correct.

He walked past food bins, with real food. True, it had been nurtured under grow lights, but it had grown in the soil of the Earth. The bazaar wasn't busy. He stepped aside for a woman to pass; her basket was filled with potatoes, onions and carrots.

He wandered on until he saw the stand he was looking for. Beneath large Tibetan characters was an English translation: "Quon's Wild Rice". He studied the hand-lettered sign for a moment. The more time he spent here, the more certain he was that this was another dead end, but he had promised Jack and, besides, he wanted to find her. "For himself," he added in his mind and then swallowed the thought as deeply as he could. No one challenged him as he stepped around the bin of wild rice.

Light shown through the open doorway of a shanty that faced the stall. There was a baby crying within. He knocked on the doorframe and a woman looked up from where she sat in a crude wooden chair. It was a face he could never forget, a face that haunted his dreams.

"Hello, Roxanne." It seemed inadequate.

She brushed her hair back from her face. "Hello, Pie. Come to arrest me?"

He shook his head.

"Then you're welcome. Come in. Not much in the way of

seating." She pointed toward a rug on the dirt floor. "No shopping trips to Denver, or that sort of thing. What brings you out here?"

He settled cross-legged onto the rug before answering. "I promised Jack I would check up on you. See that you were taken care of."

"I don't need anybody to take care of me."

"That's what I told him." The crying was coming from the inner doorway, which was hidden behind a flowered curtain. He raised an eyebrow and looked back to Roxanne.

She smiled as few women were capable of and nodded. "He's four months old. Li, would you come in here?" she said in a louder voice.

A twelve-year old girl parted the curtain. She held a baby and behind her a little girl peeked around her legs. The girl screeched in her high-pitched voice and ran toward Pie, throwing herself at him, certain she would be caught.

Pie rocked back and grinned. "Angie my girl, I was afraid you had forgotten all about me." He looked to Roxanne. "She's the real reason I came, you know."

Roxanne laughed. "She's a joy."

Angie decided that Pie was a mountain to climb and planted her feet on his stomach on her way to his chest.

Pie nodded toward the baby. "What did you name...him?"

Roxanne nodded. "His name is Jackie." She looked with motherly eyes to her infant who began fussing again. "It's his nap time. Li, would you rock him to sleep, please?"

Li Quon nodded. Even in the dim light, her black hair glistened. Her dark eyes met Pie's. This was not the demur gaze of a preadolescent girl; it was defiant. It was this striking challenge that she left with Pie before disappearing behind the curtain with little Jackie.

"Doesn't she like men, or is it only me?" Pie asked.

"Li? You're mistaken." Roxanne lowered her voice. "She's a wonderful girl. I've been trying to get her interested in the sciences, but she's as strong willed as she is sweet. All she wants to do is study history. Her grandfather was a traditional healer and he expected her to take over for him, but...like most of us, she lost everyone. She talks about the starship all the time."

"The starship is an insane project. There's no chance of success. We're not ready to go the stars. It's nothing more than an expensive suicide mission."

"She wants to go. It's her risk to take, no one else's."

"Motherhood hasn't mellowed you much, has it?"

"It has changed me, but the truth is the truth," Roxanne said.

"If she really has her heart set on the starship, she'll need friends in high places and, the way things look, that creepy kid Geoffrey Slater is going to be designated as commander."

"Li can handle any male child and she does have friends in high places. Doesn't she, Pie?"

Pie nodded. "I guess she does. Her name is Li Quon?"

Roxanne nodded and smiled.

"I'll see what I can do. We've been talking about adding a humanity section to the crew. What have you been up to?"

"Lots of things, growing food the old fashioned way, being a mother, thinking about things. I'm learning Mandarin."

"I see. Sounds...." He looked up at the raw beams of the ceiling and then returned his gaze to meet her green eyes. "Well, to be perfectly frank, it sounds boring. When do you plan to come back? The pace of the cloning project has slowed considerably."

"I don't know. I don't know if I ever will. It would be odd being there without Jack."

"Yeah, it is strange not having him around, but I'm sure he'll be gratified to hear that you've named the boy after him."

"Believe in life after death, huh?"

"Not sure. But, as far as Jack goes, he's definitely not dead."

She sat forward and the chair creaked. Angie looked in Roxanne's direction and, when she saw the expression on her mother's face, stopped her climb toward Pie's head.

"Not dead?" Roxanne asked.

"No. I have a feeling the universe will come to an end and Jack will still be wandering around, complaining about Mason."

Roxanne scooted off her chair and sat with her knees pressed against Pie's leg, looking up at him. Pie smiled and didn't move away.

"That's not what I heard," she said. "I heard that when Brinker blew up the alien ship, both he and Jack died. Was that a lie? Is the alien ship still up there?" She looked to Angie who had finally settled into Pie's arms.

"Partly."

"What part?" She put her hand on Angie's back.

"The alien ship was destroyed, but it wasn't Brinker who did it. It was Jack. As you may recall, he had this secret plan. Said he got the idea from you."

"From me?"

"He said the ship seemed to be alive and then you showed him that invasive microbe, tricking its way inside a cell. He made a container out of part of the crashed ship's hull and hid a nuclear warhead inside it. The alien ship took it in and was obliterated from the universe. Pretty damn clever, wasn't it?"

"But...why haven't we heard?" She stood.

"The inner circle of the Federation knows but, so far, they've been remarkably loyal to Mason. Do you really expect Mason to admit to everyone that his plan was a flop and that a guy who stole a scramjet and hijacked the Mars Explorer, a man who Mason tried to kill with a nuclear missile of all things, managed to destroy the alien ship on his own?"

She paced in circles around the small room, her face lit by a broad smile. "No, I wouldn't expect Mason to do that. It would require integrity. So, where is Jack? In hiding too? I want to go to him."

"He's not in hiding. That's one thing about Jack, everyone underestimates him."

"Not me. Where is he? In custody at Copper Mountain?" She frowned and her lips pouted.

"Think about it. Does that make any sense?"

She stopped. "He's on Mars, isn't he."

"Bingo. He always said he was going to Mars. He managed to piece the lander back together from parts in the radiation cylinder that were protected from the electromagnetic pulse of the warhead. He landed at the Mars base and is living there."

"How long before he runs out of supplies?"

"Years."

"He doesn't like to be alone." She stopped pacing. "We need to get him back."

"Easier said than done. The Prime Cylinder of the space station has been completed. There are people living up there now. Mason has plans to add a second cylinder and the starship Pinnacle is still under construction, will be for years. A rescue trip to Mars would consume a considerable amount of our dwindling resources."

"You know what I think? I think the world is about to learn the truth. That we all owe Jack Nichols. Even Mason will jump aboard, once he sees the way sentiment is going. He has no real beliefs of his own, only projects and an addiction to power. Besides, no one knows when the next alien ship will arrive, or what it will bring. It may decide to bypass its fallen companion on Mars and head straight for Earth. We need to be prepared."

"If anyone can get him back, I'm sure it's you. By the way, he asked me to tell you something. He said that Mars is beautiful in a Frankensteinian sort of a way. A perfect place for a honeymoon."

"Do you think Angie and Jackie would be safe if we returned?" Roxanne asked.

"I personally guarantee it."

"Li will have to come with us. She doesn't have anyone besides me."

"That can be arranged."

Roxanne smiled. "I've got a few things to wind up here and then I'll message you. You're right. It *is* time to return to Copper Mountain."

She walked over and bent low to give Pie a kiss on his oversized nose, not what he would have preferred, but it would have to do, especially if Jack was coming home. And, with the two of them working together, well...Mason better head for high ground.

"When Jack gets back, we're going to have a party that's even better than his birthday party was."

"Better than his birthday party?" Pie chuckled. "Any message you'd like me to relay to him?"

"Yes. Tell him I can hardly wait for our next honeymoon. Tell him to take care of his beautiful ass until I can get my hands on it again."

"You want me to say that? You know security around the world will hear."

"Good. And I think I'll send a special video too. He's so susceptible to visual stimulation."

"If that's what you want."

She twirled and Angie climbed out of Pie's lap to dance with her.

"Mason's spin-machine is about to spin out of control. I love you, Pie."

"I love you, too," he mumbled and ducked his head. He

stood and handed her a communicator. "Message me when you're ready. See you at Copper Mountain."

She nodded and then ran her fingers through her red hair, brushing it back.

He felt himself being drawn toward her and knew he must not. It was time to leave. He stepped into the night air and looked up, searching until he found the red planet. "Jack Nichols, you're one lucky son of a bitch."

He walked away, toward the monastery and the aircraft beyond that awaited him. Things were going to get interesting again.

EPILOGUE

Roxanne glanced at the hands of the antique clock on the wall. It wouldn't be long now. The lander from the Mars Avenger was going to touch down at Copper Mountain in forty minutes. She felt a fluttering in her abdomen and pressed her hand against it. It had been four years since Jack had left on his quixotic quest to destroy the alien starship. Each time she thought about it, she was amazed anew. His status as hero was already firmly entrenched in the culture of those who had survived the Death. Oddly enough, the embellished stories of his feat were not far removed from actual fact.

She smiled. *Thank God he is so oblivious.* The only thing that worried her is that the adoration might feel more like a burden than a blessing. It might piss him off to such an extent that he'd do something equally extraordinary just to tarnish the legend. *Well, whatever will happen, will happen.* It wasn't her right to tell him what to do and that's the way it should be. She shook her head with admiration. He was such a contrarian.

She turned her attention to her children. She corrected herself, their children. Angie was playing with her computer pad. She had grown so much. Already six years old. Angie's black hair was a wild mass of curls, uncontrollable, as was she at times. Jackie stood next to Angie and watched her attentively. He adored his big sister.

Roxanne focused on her own pad to replay one of her favorite transmissions from Jack. He sat in one of the habitat domes wearing a t-shirt that did nothing but emphasize the muscles of his chest and shoulders. There were comforting signs of electronic activity in the colored lights on instrumental panels behind him. He was smiling.

"Hello, Roxanne. I miss you so much."

He rubbed the thick, black stubble of his beard as he thought. His appearance reminded her of that first time, so many years ago, when he had visited her office at the university.

He continued. "I've completed most of the original mission and I've spent time at the alien crash site but my most amazing discovery is that even though I'm alone, I don't feel alone. I have you and I have our children. I have a family. I still don't understand why I've survived but I don't even care to understand anymore. I'm just incredibly grateful. You can tell Pie I'm not a red marble anymore. He'll understand."

He leaned back as he thought and then returned his attention the screen. "Congratulations on your appointment as director of the Life Science section. It's about time. I am surprised that you've kept Rathburn on and that you've found him to be a competent assistant administrator. My thought is that with extensive training he might be able to develop the skills needed to clean toilets but, then again, maybe I'm expecting too much of him. On the other hand, I'm not surprised in the least that Mason has claimed credit for the destruction of the alien craft." He shrugged. "But to learn that he is characterizing the two of us as the best of friends...."

He laughed and the sound warmed Roxanne's heart, every time she played it.

Jackie wandered over to see what his mother was doing. "Daddy?" he asked, even though he knew the answer.

Roxanne paused the image and scooped the boy up to settle into her lap. She brushed his red hair out of his eyes and gave him a soft kiss on the forehead.

"Yes, daddy," she confirmed.

Jackie touched the screen with the tip of his index finger. "Daddy's coming home." He looked up at Roxanne.

"Yes, honey, daddy's coming home." She started the message playing again.

Jack wiped the tears of mirth from his eyes and again looked into the camera. "Haven't been able to learn much from the wreck. It's solid state and probably designed on a molecular scale. The research team aboard the Avenger will be better suited for that particular mission. I know you expected me to find a V-12 just like in your Austin Martin but no such luck, my dear." He smiled. "I guess they're not quite as advanced as we thought they were."

He was quiet for a few seconds before continuing. "It's been everything I expected, but I'm ready to come home. I want to be with you, and Angie, and Jackie." He paused again. "I hope they like me." He waved his hand dismissively. "I know. Right now you're probably saying I'm just being a dork. At least, I hope that's what you're saying. Anyway, I know you'll be there to help me if I stumble. I've thought about taking you to Mars for our second honeymoon but I like your idea of a campout, a bottle of wine, a crackling bonfire, and your body...." He smiled that roguish smile. "I guess I better leave it at that if you're planning on showing this to the kids. Well, I better cut this short. The Avenger will be arriving this week and I still need to do the dishes and sweep so they won't think I'm a slob. I'm sure you'll understand that." He winked and blew her a kiss. "I'll be home before you know it. Eight more months." He sighed. "I love you, dear. My love to the kids." The screen went dark.

There was a knock on the door of her apartment. She set Jackie down and walked over to open it. Pie stood there in all his bulky splendor.

"He'll be landing in thirty minutes," Pie said. "Ready?"

Roxanne ran her hands across her flat abdomen, smoothing the material as if there could be a wrinkle in the skin-tight top. "I chose emerald green, the color of the suit I wore on our first date. I look good but...." Her gaze shifted to the floor and then back to her friend's homely face, settling on his hazel eyes. "Do you think he still wants me?"

Pie raised his hands in surrender. "Half the time I spend reassuring Jack and the other half reassuring you. I can't wait for you two to get back together so I'll have time to get some actual work done."

She smiled that special smile and then turned to her children. "Let's go, kids. Time to bring daddy home."

Angie began jumping up and down. When Jackie saw this, he too began jumping.

Roxanne nodded. They were going to be just fine, more than fine, peachy fine. They were a family.

ABOUT THE AUTHOR

Gary Moreau grew up in a small town in Iowa called Estherville. He discovered science fiction in the fifth grade, beginning with a book by Alan E. Nourse entitled *Star Surgeon*.

He graduated from medical school at the University of Iowa and then completed a residency in emergency medicine at Los Angeles County/USC Medical Center. Following his training, he practiced emergency medicine at Long Beach Memorial Medical Center.

It is not likely that he became a physician because of Nourse's book, but it was the beginning of a lifelong love of science fiction. His plans for the future include a focus on his passion for storytelling. *Judas Gene* is a prequel to *Almost Human* (published in 2001 by Yard Dog Press).

He and his wife Gloria have two daughters, two sons-in-law, and five grandchildren. His greatest joys in life include family, friends, writing, art, and travel.

ABOUT THE COVER ARTIST

Artist **Mitchell Davidson Bentley** spent the last twenty years moving physically from place to place and artistically from traditional oils to cyber compositions. Trained in the traditional medium of oil by his mother, and inspired by his grandfather's love of science fiction, Bentley began his career as a full-time science fiction artist in 1989 from his home base in Tulsa.

While actively involved in the science fiction art world, Bentley also moved from Tulsa to Austin to Central Pennsylvania where his search for knowledge earned him bachelor's and master's degrees from Penn State University. Over the same period of time, Bentley shifted from the more traditional oil painting to airbrushed acrylics, and since 2004 has been working exclusively in electronic media.

As the Creative Consultant of Atomic Fly Studios, Bentley produces cover art, marketing materials and Web sites while he continues to produce quality 2D artwork marketed through the AFS Web site and at science fiction conventions across the United States.

Bentley has lectured at universities, worked in film (also as a part-time actor), edited publications and served as Artist Guest of Honor at more than a dozen science fiction conventions. He has also earned over 35 awards, and is a lifetime member of the Association of Science Fiction and Fantasy Artists.

He currently resides in Harrisburg, PA with his partner Cathie McCormick and their spoiled cats, Mr. Spike, Zöe and Drucilla.

Bentley's Web address is: www.atomicflystudios.com.

Yard Dog Press Titles As Of This Print Date

A Bubba in Time Saves None, Edited by Selina Rosen

A Man, A Plan, (yet lacking) A Canal, Panama, Linda Donahue

Adventures of the Irish Ninja, Selina Rosen

The Alamo and Zombies, Jean Stuntz

All the Marbles, Dusty Rainbolt

Almost Human, Gary Moreau

Ancient Enemy, Lee Killouth

The Anthology From Hell: Humorous Tales From WAY Down Under, Edited by Julia S. Mandala

Ard Magister, Laura J. Underwood

Assassins Inc., Phillip Drayer Duncan

Bad City, Selina Rosen & Laura J. Underwood

Bad Lands, Selina Rosen & Laura J. Underwood

Black Rage, Selina Rosen

Blackrose Avenue, Mark Shepherd

The Boat Man, Selina Rosen

Bobby's Troll, John Lance

Bride of Tranquility, Tracy S. Morris

Bruce and Roxanne from Start to Finnish, Rie Sheridan Rose

The Bubba Chronicles, Selina Rosen

Bubba Fables, Sue P. Sinor

Bubbas Of the Apocalypse, Edited by Selina Rosen

The Burden of the Crown, Selina Rosen

Chains of Redemption, Selina Rosen

Checking On Culture, Lee Killough

Chronicles of the Last War, Laura J. Underwood

Dadgum Martians Invade the Lucky Nickel Saloon, Ken Rand

Dark and Stormy Nights, Bradley H. Sinor

Deja Doo, Edited by Selina Rosen

Dracula's Lawyer, Julia S. Mandala

Dragon's Tongue, Laura J. Underwood

The Essence of Stone, Beverly A. Hale

Fairy BrewHaHa at the Lucky Nickel Saloon, Ken Rand

The Fantastikon: Tales of Wonder, Robin Wayne Bailey

Fire & Ice, Selina Rosen

Flush Fiction, Volume I: Stories To Be Read In One Sitting, Edited by Selina Rosen

Flush Fiction, Volume II: Twenty Years of Letting it Go!, Edited by Selina Rosen

The Four Bubbas of the Apocalypse: Flatulence, Halitosis, Incest, and... Ned, Edited by Selina Rosen

The Four Redheads: Apocalypse Now!, Linda L. Donahue, Rhonda Eudaly, Julia S. Mandala, & Dusty Rainbolt

The Four Redheads of the Apocalypse, Linda L. Donahue, Rhonda Eudaly, Julia S. Mandala, & Dusty Rainbolt

The Garden In Bloom, Jeffrey Turner

Through Wyoming Eyes, Ken Rand
Turn Left to Tomorrow, Robin Wayne Bailey
The Twins, Selina Rosen
Wandering Lark, Laura J. Underwood
Wings of Morning, Katharine Eliska Kimbriel
Zombies In Oz and Other Undead Musings, Robin Wayne Bailey

Fantasy Writers Asylum (A YDP Imprint):

Blood Songs
Julia Mandala

Tale of the Black Heart
Linda L. Donahue

Double Dog (A YDP Imprint):

#1:
Of Stars & Shadows,
Mark W. Tiedemann
This Instance Of Me,
Jeffrey Turner

#2:
Gods and Other Children,
Bill D. Allen
Tranquility, Tracy Morris

#3:
Home Is the Hunter,
James K. Burk
Farstep Station,
Lazette Gifford

#4:
Sabre Dance,
Melanie Fletcher
The Lunari Mask,
Laura J. Underwood

#5:
House of Doors,
Julia Mandala
Jaguar Moon,
Linda A. Donahue

Just Cause (A YDP Imprint):

The Bitter End
Selina Rosen

Death Under the Crescent Moon
Dusty Rainbolt

The Ghost Writer
Selina Rosen

It's Not Rocket Science: Spirituality for the Working-Class Soul
Selina Rosen

Meditations of a Hoarder
Melinda LaFevers

Not My Life
Selina Rosen

The Pit
Selina Rosen

Plots and Protagonists: A Reference Guide for Writers
Mel. White

Vanishing Fame
Selina Rosen

Non-YDP titles we distribute:

Chains of Freedom
Chains of Destruction
Jabone's Sword
Queen of Denial
Recycled
Strange Robby
Sword Masters
Selina Rosen

A Note to Our Readers

We at Yard Dog Press understand that many people buy used books because they simply can't afford new ones. That said, and understanding that not everyone is made of money, we'd like you to know something that you may not have realized. Writers only make money on new books that sell. At the big houses a writer's entire future can hinge on the number of books they sell. While this isn't the case at Yard Dog Press, the honest truth is that when you sell or trade your book or let many people read it, the writer and the publishing house aren't making any money.

As much as we'd all like to believe that we can exist on love and sweet potato pie, the truth is we all need money to buy the things essential to our daily lives. Writers and publishers are no different.

We realize that these "freebies" and cheap books often turn people on to new writers and books that they wouldn't otherwise read. However we hope that you will reconsider selling your copy, and that if you trade it or let your friends borrow it, you also pass on the information that if they really like the author's work they should consider buying one of their books at full price sometime so that the writer can afford to continue to write work that entertains you.

We appreciate all our readers and *depend* upon their support.

Thanks,
The Editorial Staff
Yard Dog Press

PS – Please note that "used" books without covers have, in most cases, been stolen. Neither the author nor the publisher has made any money on these books because they were supposed to be pulped for lack of sales.

Please do not purchase books without covers.

Made in the USA
Charleston, SC
01 December 2016